'The most original crime novel you'll read this year'
CLARE MACKINTOSH

'This has to be a strong contender for crime debut of the year –
sharp, perceptive writing and a brilliant new take on the detective
duo' **T. M. LOGAN**

'Everything you could hope for in a thriller: heartbreaking,
intelligent, deftly plotted and so original' **FIONA CUMMINS**

'Jo Callaghan makes her entry into the crowded police
procedural genre with a fresh take on the buddy-buddy
cop trope. *In the Blink of an Eye* predicts the near future
when police officers and their AI counterparts will work
hand-in-holographic-hand. The human-AI interactions
between the lead protagonists as they pursue their quarry
are illuminating and, at times, hilarious. Provocative and
compelling. A TV series seems a certainty'
VASEEM KHAN

'I started reading this morning and ten hours later I've finished
it! It's so, SO good – really properly compelling, impossible to
put down – I was desperate for the solution to the mystery – but
so human and moving and massively thought-provoking on what
makes us human' **LAURA MARSHALL**

'*In the Blink of an Eye* is fresh, innovative and very very clever.
Flawlessly paced, plotted and researched, it's laugh out loud,
heart-achingly sad and doesn't have a dull moment. I raced
through it. Simply sensational' **M. W. CRAVEN**

'The kind of fresh and fearless debut I just adore. Wildly original,
heartfelt, funny, and properly thrilling. Take a bow, Jo Callaghan'
CHRIS WHITAKER

'A standout debut with a unique and thrilling take on the detective
novel. Engaging, exciting and superbly readable. I loved it'
SARAH HILARY

'*In the Blink of An Eye* captured me from the first page and kept me enthralled until the last. Jo Callaghan shakes up the police procedural with a truly original premise that is both compelling and filled with heart. Highly recommended' **OLIVIA KIERNAN**

'Completely different and utterly brilliant'
AMANDA REYNOLDS

'Clever and compelling, it offers a new take on the police procedural while also examining what it means to be human and the personal cost of loss' **BRIAN MCGILLOWAY**

'SO good. A really clever twist on the police procedural that asks big questions about instinct, bias, and what it means to be human while also delivering a cracker of a plot. Loved it'
PHOEBE LOCKE

'It's actually quite rare for premise, plot and character to impress so equally, but Jo Callaghan deftly manages it with her phenomenal debut, *In the Blink of an Eye*. Daring and original, heartbreaking and heart-stopping, this study of what it means to be human is destined to not only be a big success, but a classic crime novel of our times. Loved it' **CAZ FREAR**

'It's phenomenal . . . Perfect blend of police procedural and techno thriller and kept me guessing right to the end'
STEPH BROADRIBB

'An incredible book. So original, gripping and wonderfully written. I raced through it' **KAREN HAMILTON**

'It's so much more than a dystopian police procedural and asks questions about who we are and what it means to be human. Brilliant' **NIKKI SMITH**

'Everything I love in a police procedural but with an imaginative and fresh perspective. Clever and warm, it's one of the best debuts I've read in years' **JO JAKEMAN**

'Thrilling, thought-provoking and cinematic – a slam dunk for movie/TV adaptation' **ALEXANDRA SOKOLOFF**

IN THE
BLINK
OF AN
EYE

JO CALLAGHAN

**SIMON &
SCHUSTER**

London · New York · Sydney · Toronto · New Delhi

First published in Great Britain by Simon & Schuster UK Ltd, 2023

Copyright © Jo Callaghan, 2023

The right of Jo Callaghan to be identified as author
of this work has been asserted in accordance with the
Copyright, Designs and Patents Act, 1988.

3 5 7 9 10 8 6 4 2

Simon & Schuster UK Ltd
1st Floor
222 Gray's Inn Road
London WC1X 8HB

Simon & Schuster Australia, Sydney
Simon & Schuster India, New Delhi

www.simonandschuster.co.uk
www.simonandschuster.com.au
www.simonandschuster.co.in

A CIP catalogue record for this book
is available from the British Library

Hardback ISBN: 978-1-3985-1116-3
Trade Paperback ISBN: 978-1-3985-1117-0
eBook ISBN: 978-1-3985-1118-7
Audio ISBN: 978-1-3985-1124-8

Epigraph from *Contingencies of Reinforcement: A Theoretical Analysis* by
B.F. Skinner reproduced with permission from B.F. Skinner Foundation.

This book is a work of fiction.
Names, characters, places and incidents are either a product of the author's
imagination or are used fictitiously. Any resemblance to actual people
living or dead, events or locales is entirely coincidental.

Typeset in Sabon by M Rules

Printed and Bound in the UK using 100% Renewable
Electricity at CPI Group (UK) Ltd

MIX
Paper | Supporting
responsible forestry
FSC
www.fsc.org   FSC® C171272

For Steve

'The real question is not whether machines think but whether men do. The mystery which surrounds a thinking machine already surrounds a thinking man.'

B.F. SKINNER,
Contingencies of Reinforcement: A Theoretical Analysis

Earlier

He can't see.

He tries opening his eyes, but something traps them tight against his skull. He gropes at his face with slow, clumsy fingers. A blindfold? Bandage? What the actual . . . ?

He tugs at it first with one hand, then more desperately with two. But it's no use. It's too tight.

His mind scrambles for answers. He's dreaming. Hung over. The victim of some crappy drunken joke. Luke's idea, probably.

Saliva floods his mouth as he remembers that he wasn't out with Luke last night. In fact, he wasn't out with anyone because he went to that appointment in the morning and then . . .

And then.

Shit.

In the silent blackness, there is only the thud-thud-thud of his heart and a throbbing glow behind his eyelids. He spreads his hands out either side of him into the space that he cannot see. He's sitting on a bed. A single, narrow bed with some sort of scratchy blanket or towel wrapped in sheets and . . . he flinches from the touch of cold, hard metal. Frowning, he reaches out again. Railings?

This is not his bed.

'Hello?' he calls out. He regrets it immediately, for there is no mistaking the fear in his voice, nor the echo of an empty room. The air is cold, and it smells of – he sniffs, groping for the word – antiseptic?

A door opens, and he turns towards the sound.

'Hello?' he says again, more hopeful this time.

The door clicks shut.

Footsteps. Quiet ones, with a slight stick to the floor.

The footsteps stop.

His eyes burn, straining to see through whatever binds them. 'Who are you? Where am I—'

Gloved hands grip his left forearm. For a moment, he is too shocked to move. Fear kicks in and he tries to pull away, but his hand is clasped python tight. He gasps at the sudden, ice-cold sting in his veins. It lasts for two, maybe three seconds and then the stranger lets go, and he catches a whiff of something sharp and chemical.

He runs his fingers over the place where it hurts. 'Where am I? Who are you?'

He looks towards where he imagines the stranger to be. This is their chance to give a simple explanation, the moment when it will all make sense, and he will laugh – albeit rather shakily – at his own paranoid imaginings.

But there are no words, reassuring or otherwise. The only sound is the squeak of soft shoes against the uncarpeted floor. A door clicks open.

'Wait!'

The door shuts. A lock turns.

He lurches towards the sound, but his body is heavy and slow, weighed down by some unknown force. He reaches for the rail that surrounds the bed. His fingers brush the cold, smooth metal, but he can't seem to make them clench and clasp. He literally cannot get a grip.

He tries to pull his blindfold off, but his arms – his impossibly heavy arms – drop to his side uselessly. He sinks back onto the pillows, dazzled by the blaze and blur of colours exploding behind his eyes.

Then everything fades to black.

CHAPTER ONE

**Leek Wootton Police Headquarters, Warwickshire,
10 June, 9.30am**

DCS Kat Frank ground her new heels into the old carpet as she strode towards her boss's office. Chief Constable McLeish didn't care who you were: a senior politician who'd taken months to secure an appointment in the diary, or a colleague who'd spent all day on a train just to see him – if you were even five minutes late, you'd be sent packing. And Kat was a whopping thirty-six minutes late.

'I'll reschedule, shall I?' his PA whispered.

Kat glanced at the firmly closed door. A couple of years ago she'd have said yes and made a swift exit while her eardrums were still intact. But after everything she'd been through, a bollocking was the least of her worries. Ignoring the PA's gasp of dismay, Kat gave the door a sharp knock and walked right in.

Chief Constable McLeish sat behind his desk in front of a large, bright window, forcing any visitors to squint against the sun as they tried to read his face. He didn't rise, nod or speak. But he didn't tell her to get out.

Kat endured his unblinking silence. There was no point telling him about the blue-haired hitchhiker with a handwritten sign that might as well have said 'murder me'. Despite her appointment, Kat had pulled over before any would-be murderers could oblige, demanding to know who the hell hitchhikes in this day and age? (Apparently eighteen-year-old girls from Poland on their way back from a music festival do, if some 'really cool guy' says you could 'definitely' get a job picking fruit on the farms in Warwickshire.) And now, after driving the girl to a strawberry farm with crap pay but good people, here she was, half an hour late for the meeting she'd planned on being at least half an hour early for.

But McLeish wasn't interested in excuses. She also knew he used silence as a weapon – few could resist rushing to fill it, giving him an advantage that was hard if not impossible to win back – so Kat held his gaze as she studied the man she hadn't seen in over a year.

McLeish had been her second boss, her first mentor and – she liked to think – was one of her oldest friends. Even when he gave her a bollocking, it was only because he thought she could learn from it – which she did. Kat had made a lot of mistakes in the early days, but she never ever made the same mistake twice. Her colleagues envied the way she could 'read' him, as if he were a particularly cryptic crossword puzzle. But to Kat, it was all quite simple. When he was annoyed, his face turned purple. When he was pleased, he'd say a few gruff words that could lift her for days. But when he was silent, the jury was out, and it was yours to lose.

'How are the kids?' she finally ventured.

His face softened. 'Knackering. Honestly, thirty years ago we just chucked the boys outside, fed them their tea and whipped them soundly to sleep. But today our wee girls aren't allowed out unless they're on a bloody "play date". And they expect me to read them a bedtime story every night, would you believe?'

'Cheeky buggers,' Kat said, smiling. Just before his sixtieth birthday, McLeish had surprised everyone by remarrying and embarking on a second family. And why not? Look at him. He was happy.

'Aye, at least I know better than to hope it'll be any easier when they get older.' He heaved himself out from behind his desk and headed towards the black leather sofa in the corner of his office, indicating for her to follow.

Kat sank into one of the armchairs, fighting the ridiculous rise of pleasure at his silent forgiveness. Honestly, she was forty-bloody-five, not a schoolgirl.

'How's Cam?' he asked. 'Wasn't he doing A levels this year?'

'Yeah, we're just waiting for the results. Which is why I asked to see you.'

'You're bored and you want to come back.'

It wasn't a question. He knew her too well. She nodded, but before she could go on, McLeish frowned.

'Are you sure you're ready, Kat? It's barely been six months since—'

'I'm sure. Cam needed a lot of support at first. But he's

doing well now. He's off the meds, his therapist signed him off, and he's hoping to go to university in September.'

'I didn't ask about Cam. I asked about you.'

'I'm fine,' Kat said, flushing. 'Or at least, I will be once I'm back at work.'

'I understand.'

Of course he did. He always had.

'So, what are you looking for?' The leather sofa let out a soft hiss as McLeish leaned back into it.

'Before I took a career break, you said I should be thinking about applying for exec level posts – head of department, maybe, or even Assistant Chief Constable.'

'And you said you'd rather chew your own toes off than do a desk job.'

'That was before.' Kat paused, remembering that other woman who couldn't comprehend why someone might want to pound a keyboard rather than the streets. 'Look, I promised Cam that if I came back to work, I'd do something safe. He can't afford to lose me as well.'

He rubbed a hand over his bare scalp. 'I know. But the thing is, there aren't any exec vacancies coming up, and even if there were, you've been out of the force for a couple of years now. A lot has changed.'

'So why did you agree to see me then?' She couldn't keep the annoyance out of her voice. It wasn't his style to toy with people.

McLeish leaned forward. 'Because I have actually got the perfect job for you. Have you met the new Home Secretary?' He didn't wait for an answer, because of course she hadn't. 'She's nice enough, but totally deluded.

Thinks there are "efficiency" gains that have somehow evaded all her predecessors.'

Kat shrugged. All politicians made bold promises to cut police numbers and 'waste' before their feet were under the ministerial table. But once they'd been hauled to the House of Commons to account for some appalling rape or murder, they were soon arguing with the Treasury for more 'bobbies on the beat'.

'This one's different,' said McLeish, reading her face. 'She's got a background in IT, and she's convinced that the solution to rising crime is not more police, but more AIDEs.'

'More *what*?'

'AIDEs. Artificially Intelligent Detecting Entities.' He made a dismissive gesture with his hand. 'Basically, some sort of glorified Alexa that can crunch data and allegedly solve more crimes at a fraction of the cost of a real copper.'

'Are you serious?'

'I'm afraid she's deadly serious.' McLeish stood up, crossed the room and picked up a report off his desk. 'According to a study the minister commissioned, a person goes missing every ninety seconds in the UK, generating over three hundred thousand cases a year. That takes up a lot of police time – fourteen per cent, to be precise – at an estimated cost of two thousand five hundred pounds per case. That's four times more expensive than the average burglary. This report concludes that a lot of the grunt work in missing persons – reviewing interviews, records, CCTV, phones and whatever – can be done by AIDEs, leading to "significant" savings in police time and costs.'

Kat snorted and rose to her feet. 'That's complete bollocks. Maybe AI can help with data collection, but they can't make judgements, they can't be *detectives*. Crime is a human act. How can a computer even begin to understand what motivates a person to go missing, or what it's like to be left behind? Jesus.' She shook her head, remembering some of the doors she'd had to knock on in the past: the broken families inside. 'And the cost of a missing person isn't just financial. Those families need tact and sensitivity. They need a person not a computer.'

'Exactly,' said McLeish. 'That's why I want you to lead a pilot using one of these AIDEs to review missing person cold cases.'

'*What*? Are you joking?' The passion that had fuelled her little speech dropped out of her. 'You know what happened to John because of so-called artificial *intelligence*.' Her mouth twisted over the bitter last word.

'I know,' he said, his voice softening. 'But that's why I'm asking you. I need someone I can trust on this, Kat. I've agreed to this pilot to head off even crazier ideas to cut costs, so the last thing I need is some ambitious twenty-something using it as a chance to catch the minister's eye and bag a promotion.'

'So, you want a forty-something has-been who'll do your bidding?'

'I want someone who understands the risks.'

Kat folded her arms. She understood the risks, all right. 'I've been in the force for nearly twenty-five years and worked bloody hard to earn the rank of Detective Chief Superintendent. I've led murder investigations, complex multinational fraud cases that have led to changes in the law. I even caught the Aston Strangler, for fuck's sake. So why on earth would I want to go back to reviewing a few cold cases for some minister's pet project?'

'Because if you don't,' said McLeish quietly, 'this "pet project" will become an excuse to cut even more police numbers. You're the most human detective I know, Kat. You're practically fucking psychic. If anyone can prove the stupidity of this idea, it's you.'

Kat turned away and glared at the map of Warwickshire on the wall. She'd never been able to say no to McLeish. And a pilot involving cold cases meant she could reassure Cam that she'd be safe. But could she really stomach working with AI? Jesus, what would John say? She swallowed, throat tightening as it hit her for the thousandth time that she would never ever know. The map swam before her eyes. Actually, that wasn't true. John was the most intellectually curious man she'd ever met. She could almost hear him now: *Tell me more.*

Kat let out a slow breath and turned to face McLeish. 'Tell me more about these so-called AIDEs.'

'I can't,' said McLeish, picking up his phone. 'But I know a woman who can.'

CHAPTER TWO

'This is Professor Okonedo,' McLeish said, as he invited a petite young woman in an eye-catching red suit to join them on the settee. 'She's a professor at the National institute for AI Research – NiAIR – based at Warwick University. She and her team developed AIDEs and Professor Okonedo is also the author of the report that impressed the Home Secretary so much, she asked the Warwickshire Police to pilot her creation.'

Professor Okonedo gave no sign that she picked up on McLeish's tone. She just nodded as if to confirm that she was indeed all of these brilliant things and held out a hand so beautifully manicured that Kat made a note to buy more hand cream.

'This is Detective Chief Superintendent Kat Frank,' continued McLeish. 'One of the most talented and experienced detectives in the country. I'm hoping you can help persuade her to lead the pilot for me.'

The smile dropped from the professor's face.

'Well? Do you want to explain what it's all about?' he prompted.

'Er, yes, it's just that . . .' She pushed her glasses up over her nose and squared her narrow shoulders. 'My team and I have spent the past four years developing an AIDE with algorithms that are free from bias or prejudice of any kind, so that we can use AI to drive more evidence-based decision-making. And while I'm grateful for the opportunity to test it out in a real police environment, it is vital that the pilot doesn't contaminate it.

That's why my report recommended partnering the AIDE with a newly qualified detective.'

McLeish turned his unblinking eyes upon the younger woman. After a pause that verged on the menacing, he said, 'What exactly are you trying to say?'

Kat studied the other woman, wondering how old she was. Late twenties? Early thirties at most.

'Perhaps Professor Okonedo doesn't want her invention to work with a middle-aged partner who might contaminate it with racism or sexism,' said Kat. 'Or ageism.'

McLeish started to turn a worrying shade of purple. He got up, opened the door and tapped the brass plate that carried his name. 'Last time I checked, *I* was in charge of the Warwickshire Police Force, which means *I* decide who heads up my team. Unless you want me to cancel the pilot?'

Kat stood, shielding the younger woman from McLeish's fierce glare.

'Look, it's a fair challenge,' Kat said, 'And isn't the whole point of a pilot to test a hypothesis?'

Professor Okonedo rose to her feet. 'Thank you, but I don't need anyone to defend or explain my work,' she said.

'In fact, from a science perspective, one of the benefits of a pilot is that it can help identify potential problem areas.'

'Are you saying that as an older woman I'm *a problem area*?'

'Potentially.'

'Only one way to find out,' McLeish cut in, looking between the two women.

Kat narrowed her eyes. Had he attacked the professor knowing full well that she'd leap to her defence? Or had he deliberately introduced them because he knew that would kick off her competitive streak: a desire to prove the younger woman wrong? Either way, he was a manipulative bastard.

'You might be an AI professor,' said Kat, 'but you don't know the first thing about being a detective. If I was stupid enough to lead this pilot, then you might actually learn that crimes can't be solved by a bunch of algorithms.'

'Does that mean you'll do it?' pounced McLeish.

'It means I'll think about it,' she said, begrudgingly. 'Someone once advised me never to accept a job until I was crystal clear about my pay, my team and who I was reporting to.'

'Me and my big mouth.' He turned to close the door, but not before Kat spied a rare smile. They both knew she was going to do it.

And judging by the stony look on Professor Okonedo's face, so did she.

CHAPTER THREE

Kat stood outside the Major Incident Room and peered through the glass door. As well as wall-to-wall screens, decent wi-fi and a large boardroom table, it had the only functioning hot-drinks machine in HQ. It was only a matter of time before someone dared question her right to use it, but she'd learned a long time ago that it was easier to ask for forgiveness than permission. And besides, she had a national pilot to lead and a new team to kick into shape. Finders keepers.

She sighed at the sight of the three people sitting around the large boardroom table. Before agreeing to lead this pilot, Kat had requested one DI, a DS, three DCs, an office manager and some admin support. But McLeish had just laughed in her face. 'The AI is supposed to do all the analysis and admin, so you won't be needing a full team.' So now she had just one DI, a DS, a scientist who looked like she should still be at school, and her bloody machine.

15

Kat knew that once she entered the room, they'd all be on their best behaviour, so she paused at the door, studying her new team. So far, DI Rayan Hassan seemed to be doing most of the talking. Perched on the edge of the table, he was all neck, knees and elbows in a smart black suit.

Although she didn't know Hassan personally, his law degree and high conviction rate had stood out when she was short-listing. According to his HR file, he'd recently been promoted to DI, but still had 'development issues'. 'Too focused on his own ambitions – wants to be the first South Asian DCS,' his last boss had noted. 'Thinks he's better than everyone else.'

'Well, maybe he is,' Kat had muttered when she spotted his former boss's name. She didn't mind big egos if the officer possessed enough talent to deserve one. She'd worked with enough men (and, let's face it, it was usually older white men) whose arrogance was way out of kilter with their actual ability. The force was full of them, so she might as well give Rayan Hassan a chance.

Kat turned to look at the smaller, dark-haired woman sitting in a chair opposite him. So far, she hadn't said a word, just nodded and smiled as Hassan waved his long arms about. Debbie Browne was a twenty-four-year-old DS who'd been with the Warwickshire Police Force since she was eighteen. A few years ago, Kat had spotted her talking to a bereaved mum in reception who'd come in to make a statement and was waiting for a taxi. Even though it wasn't her case, and her shift had just ended, the young officer had insisted on giving the poor woman a lift home. Kat had watched Debbie gently escort the broken mother to her car, and silently added her to the short-list of officers who actually gave a shit.

Unlike Tina-from-HR. When Kat asked her why Debbie hadn't been on the long-list of applicants, she'd just shrugged and said, 'She didn't put herself forward.' Kat swore when she finally read the young woman's CV. After six successful years in the force, DS Browne should be aiming to become a DI by putting herself forward for high-profile projects like this, not labouring under the illusion that someone somewhere would eventually notice how hard she worked and just promote her out of the blue. If it was up to Kat, she'd give all new female recruits a badge and pin it to their hopeful hearts: *Don't ask, don't get.*

At the furthest end of the table sat Professor Okonedo, sharply dressed in an electric-blue suit. She gave no sign of even noticing let alone paying any attention to either Hassan or Browne as she tapped away on her tablet with an intensity that suggested she had more important things to attend to than getting to know her new colleagues.

DI Hassan gamely carried on talking. Kat couldn't hear what he said, but from the way his eyes kept straying to the attractive young scientist, it was obvious who he was trying to impress.

Kat pushed the door open with a little more force than was necessary. It banged against the wall, making them all start. Hassan slipped off the table and sat in his chair; even Professor Okonedo stopped typing and looked up.

Three heads turned as she strode across the MI room. Sometimes she established her authority by referring to the many years she'd spent as a detective and Senior

Investigating Officer, confirming that yes, she was *that* Kat Frank who'd captured the Aston Strangler. But the straight backs and wary eyes of her new team suggested they already knew they were bloody lucky to be working with her.

'Morning,' she said. 'I'm DCS Kat Frank, I'm leading this pilot, and I like my tea strong with a tiny splash of milk.'

Browne jumped up and headed towards the drinks machine.

Kat allowed herself a small sigh, before signalling for Browne to sit back down. 'I wasn't asking you to make me a drink, I was sharing the most important piece of information about me to facilitate team building – who I am and my beverage of choice.'

'Hi, I'm Detective Inspector Rayan Hassan,' he volunteered without being asked, clearly relishing the sound of his new title. 'And I like coffee – preferably with cream, sugar and a biscuit.' He grinned in a way that suggested he was used to getting all three.

'Oh, er . . . I'm DS Browne and I'm not fussy. I like tea and coffee. Whatever's going.'

'But what's your preference?' pushed Kat.

'Tea, with plenty of milk. But I can drink it without as well.'

'And you?' Kat said to Professor Okonedo.

She looked up from her tablet. 'Me?'

'Unless your beverage of choice is a secret?'

Professor Okonedo paused before reluctantly sharing that she didn't like tea or coffee and only drank water.

'You got that, Hassan?' Kat said, nodding towards the drinks machine.

He blinked.

'Two teas, one water and a coffee for yourself.'

'Oh . . . yes, of course,' he said, frowning as he headed towards the drinks.

Kat perched on the table by Browne and leaned in towards her. 'Lesson number one. As a woman, you can't ever be the one who offers to go and make the tea, especially not in a new team. You might as well wear a badge that says, "I don't matter". When you get to my age and rank you can afford to play at being mother, but until then, sit back and let the men do it. It means you'll spend a lot of time feeling thirsty, but at least there's a chance they might actually listen to you. Okay?'

Browne flushed and nodded. 'Yes, thank you, sorry.'

'Lesson number two: don't apologise unless you've done something illegal.'

'Sor—' Browne turned scarlet.

Kat slipped off the end of the table as Hassan returned with the drinks. Ignoring her tea, she began pacing the length of the room, signalling that team building was over, and it was time to get to work.

'Following a direct request from the Home Secretary, the Warwickshire Police Force has agreed to pilot the first ever human–machine police team in the UK, and you have been lucky enough to be selected to join this ground-breaking team. Our collective aim is to identify the tasks that AI might safely perform, as opposed to the roles, functions and decisions that only an experienced human detective can make.' Kat gestured towards the end of the table.

'Professor Okonedo is the brains behind the AIDE we'll be piloting, so she'll be a key member of our team, as she learns what it can and can't do. Professor Okonedo, can I ask you to introduce your creation, please?' Kat took a seat and leaned back.

Professor Okonedo pushed her large round glasses up her nose. 'Thank you, DCS Frank. But before I introduce your new colleague, I'd like to clarify and correct any misconceptions you may have about what AI is and is not.'

Kat clocked the shade but said nothing. Instead, she checked the messages on her phone as the young scientist launched into an explanation of the difference between 'narrow AI' (mainly task-focused, such as image recognition, which is 'easy' and already with us in our homes and phones) and 'general AI' (completely different and much rarer, with all the complex characteristics of human intelligence, such as the ability to make judgements and decisions).

If Professor Okonedo noticed Kat rolling her eyes at that one, she didn't let it put her off. Instead, she patiently explained that, until recently, creating a general AI machine capable of operating at a human level of complexity would have required millions of lines of code. 'But luckily, we've found a short cut called Deep Learning,' she said. 'This allows us to train an algorithm by feeding it huge amounts of data so that it can continually adjust itself, improve and, ultimately, learn.'

'Learn?' Browne echoed. 'How can a machine *learn*?'

'The same way we do. Take facial recognition software, for example—'

'I'd rather not,' said Kat, looking up from her phone. 'According to the research it's deeply flawed.'

'I assume the research you're referring to was concerned with task-based AI, which, I grant you, is extremely limited,' said Professor Okonedo. 'Imagine, for example, you wanted to create a program to identify cats. If you did it the old-fashioned task-based way, you'd have to program in data like "cats have pointy ears" and "cats have tails" and so on. That program would spot a lot of cats, but what would it do when it saw a tiger? You could try programming it with more and more info on cats, but it would be time-consuming and always open to error. The prototype my team and I have developed is completely different because *it's a machine that teaches itself.*' For the first time, Professor Okonedo's face lit up with a smile. 'Instead of programming in countless pieces of data, we give it thousands of pictures of cats that it looks through itself until it starts to spot the patterns and connections. Over time, it gets pretty good at saying what is and isn't a cat.'

'Over time?' said Hassan, glancing at Kat's sceptical face. 'So basically, it learns on the job?'

'Don't we all?' said Professor Okonedo, spreading out her tiny, beautifully painted hands.

'And what happens while the AI is learning?' said Kat, unable to keep the edge out of her voice. 'Who pays the price for their mistakes?'

For the first time, Professor Okonedo looked uncertain as she withstood the older woman's gaze. 'That is why we've agreed to focus initially on cold cases, so that the impact of any errors can be minimised.'

So that the impact of any errors can be minimised? Jesus, this woman had no idea, thought Kat, struggling to rein in her anger. 'These cases might be "cold",' she managed to say, in a low voice. 'But the people involved are real. Unlike your AI. It only takes one mistake to destroy a whole family.'

Professor Okonedo frowned and removed her glasses. 'I know that, DCS Frank, because unfortunately the police make thousands of mistakes every day. The whole point of using AI is to reduce those mistakes. The machine we have developed will learn at an exponential rate, aided by the fact that it has no need of sleep and, unlike the rest of us, it cannot get sick. Another benefit of AIDEs is that they are pandemic-proof.'

Kat raised her eyebrows, surprised that such a clever young woman could make such a clumsy mistake. Everybody had lost something or someone during the pandemic, but in a new team like this, there was no way of knowing who had suffered what. Even though it had been several years ago, the police force was still depleted, particularly in its most senior ranks. A few had died, but many more had taken early retirement as they struggled with the physical and mental impact of Covid-19 on themselves and their families.

Professor Okonedo cleared her throat. 'Maybe I should just introduce your new colleague so you can see for yourselves what it can do.' She reached into her laptop bag and pulled out a black box, about the size of her hand. She turned the dials on the lock, clicked it open and lifted out a solid, black band of steel, no more than half an inch high and one inch in diameter, and placed it upon the boardroom table.

They all leaned forward.

'It looks like a bracelet,' said Browne, clearly a bit underwhelmed.

'It's been designed by my team of highly-talented PhD students at NiAIR to fit discreetly onto the wrist so that it can accompany its human partner anywhere,' said Professor Okonedo. 'It can operate purely as an audio device, but because the evidence suggests that human beings are more likely to positively interact with other people, this device contains both polarisation sensors and miniature holographic camera sensor modules, which enables the AIDE to manifest itself as a 3D digital hologram.' Her finger hovered over the thick, black bracelet as she said, 'Meet your new team member, AIDE Lock.'

A man suddenly appeared in the centre of the room.

Kat jumped to her feet. No, not a man. An *image* of a man: slender, black, about six feet tall with a perfectly manicured moustache and a short, groomed beard. She took a few steps closer, determined to find some flaw or tell-tale sign. But the three-dimensional figure was frighteningly realistic, from the pores in its nose to the faint creases in its navy-blue suit. But it was the eyes that unsettled her: dark brown, wide and incredibly ... the word 'expressive' dropped into her mind, but she swatted it away. This was a machine, not a person. She circled it slowly, noting with relief that despite the early sun streaming through the grimy windows, this figure cast no shadow, and the heels of its (apparently) scuffed shoes made no imprint in the new grey carpet. In fact, thought Kat, if you squinted and looked slightly past it, you could see there was something wrong about the light it projected or reflected: a slight shimmer or flicker around the edges, giving it an ethereal, almost other-worldly aspect.

Satisfied, Kat folded her arms and stared back at the hologram. It was a couple of inches taller than her. Tomorrow she would wear heels.

It didn't drop its gaze. Instead, Lock moved towards her. 'You have a scar, DCS Frank.'

'What?'

'On your chin. A scar.' It raised a single finger, holding it in the air just inches from her face. 'The scarring has reached maturation, so in all probability it is over two years old and at four millimetres in length and perfectly linear, the result of a collision with a sharp edge. The corner of a table, perhaps?'

Kat stared back, recalling the sudden, sick shock of the blow, unable to save herself before her jaw struck the kitchen table with a force that broke her skin and bloodied the dusty linoleum floor.

Lock raised its eyebrows. 'Clearly not a happy memory. In fact—'

'In fact,' said Kat, 'my chin has nothing to do with this pilot or the cases that we'll be working on.' She turned her back on the image and addressed Professor Okonedo. 'I thought you said it was just a hologram? How can a hologram see?'

'A key aim of the research we are leading at Warwick University is to develop AI that can interact with the real

24

world, so the LiDAR sensors wrapped round your bracelet feed Lock with a constant supply of geospatial data so that it can locate and position itself appropriately within any environment. But although it "sees" through the sensors on your wrist, it has been programmed to mimic the actions of humans, by "looking" around a room when the hologram first enters, or "looking" a person in the eye, so it can interact with humans in an immersive way.'

Kat glanced back at Lock, who again appeared to meet her gaze with disturbing accuracy. She looked away as she took a seat at the table with the team. Her *real* team. 'That's a great party trick,' she said to Professor Okonedo. 'But what can this machine actually do that's relevant to our work?'

'As much or as little as you let it. AIDE Lock contains chips that can run over ten trillion calculations per second. At the most basic level, it can search through thousands of pictures in seconds or thematically organise vast amounts of social media to speed up an enquiry.'

'I prefer to go through that stuff myself,' said Kat. 'I don't always know what I'm looking for until I see it. Even then, I'm often just following a hunch.'

'Hunches are subject to errors and cognitive biases,' Lock said from behind her. Its voice was low and unhurried, like it expected to be listened to, with the kind of English accent typically associated with privilege. 'I have a built-in scientific method that will enable you to test early hypotheses and filter out errors, allowing you to focus your efforts on the most plausible lines of enquiry.'

Cheeky fucker. As if she needed a machine to teach her what a 'plausible line of enquiry' was. But she'd promised McLeish she'd play nicely – on the first day at least – so instead of telling it where it could stick its 'built-in scientific method', she spun on her chair and gave it a tight smile. 'Thanks, but I'm afraid you can't actually apply science to a hunch. A hunch is . . .' she shrugged. 'A hunch.'

Lock closed its eyes for a second. 'I have just read 73,239 scholarly articles on the science of decision-making, and as human decision-making processes are clearly impaired by intellectual, social and emotional factors, I conclude that your "hunches" are merely reflections of your own prejudices and assumptions.'

Kat glared at Professor Okonedo. 'Does this thing understand that it works for me?'

The young woman smiled. 'Lock has been programmed to carry out the tasks it is assigned within a managerial hierarchy. How much it understands, however, will be a key test of this pilot. Lock's conversational abilities are beyond anything so far achieved in AI, but it still has much to learn from real-time human interactions. It has been programmed to speak truth to power and at the moment it has no filter.'

'Or social skills,' muttered Kat.

'That's one of the things I hope it will learn by being a part of this team. In return, AIDE Lock will help drive greater equality and transparency in policing by encouraging more evidence-based decisions.'

'More evidence-based decisions?' echoed Kat. She let out a weary breath and tried to explain as patiently as she could that there are different kinds of evidence, and that just because you can't explain a hunch, it doesn't mean it's wrong. 'There was a famous study a few years back where all these experts were called in to assess a rare Greek statue, and after considering all the scientific evidence, they finally concluded that it was a genuine antique. But then some other expert came in, took one look at it, and just like that –' Kat snapped her fingers. 'He knew it was a fake. He couldn't explain it, but he trusted his first gut reaction that something was off. And he was right.'

'You are referring to the Getty Museum's purchase of the kouros statue,' said Lock, 'which some people have used to prove that snap decisions can be more accurate than considered ones.' It paused and raised a hand to its chin, as if thinking. 'But a more relevant question is, how did the other experts get it so wrong?'

Kat frowned. How did a bloody machine have the confidence to hold a pause like that? No, she corrected herself. A machine can't feel confidence – it can't *feel* anything. This machine had just been programmed to exhibit the mannerisms of confidence and thought. Deep learning, my arse. It was just a cut-and-paste job from some second-rate politician. Nothing more.

'The Getty experts got it wrong not because of the scientific evidence,' continued Lock. 'But despite it. They bought the statue because they desperately wanted it to be real. Even though the statue was flawless, they chose to believe that their ten-million-dollar purchase was two thousand years old. They were misled not by the facts, but by their own human desires and preferences.' It raised its right hand, making a circle of its forefinger and thumb to emphasise the point. 'It is the perfect example of how flawed human decision-making processes are and the necessity of filtering out feelings and other distorting factors.'

Kat rose to her feet, forcing her team to look at their new boss, rather than this new toy. 'Well, no doubt Professor Okonedo will draw her own conclusions at the end of this pilot, regardless of what you or I think, except ...' she turned to Lock with mock sympathy. 'Except, you can't actually think, can you?'

She counted to three – she could teach this jumped-up Alexa a thing or two about pauses – before showing it her back and turning towards Professor Okonedo. The grown-up humans were talking now. 'To ensure the pilot is fair, you may sit in and observe our briefings and you'll have full access to all recorded decisions as requested. But before we start, I want to make one thing clear.'

Kat reached for her briefcase and pulled out a lever arch file, balancing the weight of it in her hands as she eyed Hassan and Browne. 'Although we'll be reviewing historic missing person cases, our prime duty is not to answer the professor's research questions about hunches or decision-making processes. We're police officers, not lab rats. Our job is to provide answers to the families of the missing. The cases always, always come first. Is that clear?'

Hassan and Browne nodded.

'Good.' She dropped the lever arch folder onto her desk with a thud that sent dust motes flying up into the air. 'Nearly seven thousand people are reported missing each year across Warwickshire. Almost all of them are found, apart from two or three, which means that over the past ten years, twenty-eight people completely disappeared from their own lives.' She paused again as she looked around the room, lit by shafts of sunlight that streaked through the large sash windows.

Kat laid her hands gently upon the folder. 'Each one of these files represents the life of a real person: teenagers who set off to meet their friends but who never arrived; mums who popped out to fetch a pint of milk but never came back; dads who drove to work one morning never to be seen again. So, I don't want anyone referring to these cases as "mis pers", "MPs" or "cold cases". The trail might have gone cold for us, but their families and friends still burn with the need to know what happened to their loved ones. Our job is to give the families the answers they need and deserve. Are we clear?'

'Yes, boss,' said Hassan and Browne.

Kat turned towards Lock. 'Well?'

For the first time it looked confused.

'Are you clear?' Kat repeated.

'You said our job is to give the families the answers they need and deserve. So yes, I can confirm that our task is clear.'

'Yes, *boss*,' said Kat.

'Yes, *boss*.'

Kat breathed in. Lock had repeated her emphasis with an exactitude that verged upon the sarcastic. But a machine couldn't be sarcastic, could it? She decided to let it go – for now.

'Let's choose our first case then.'

CHAPTER FOUR

Kat frowned as Lock remained standing. 'Aren't you going to take a seat?'

It raised both eyebrows. 'I have no need to relieve the weight from limbs which I do not possess. But I can assume a sitting position if that would make you feel more comfortable?'

Cheeky shit. What would make her feel more comfortable was if this machine just buggered off. But she chose not to give it the dignity of a reply. 'I sent a zip file around at the weekend containing all twenty-eight unsolved missing person cases from the past ten years,' said Kat, looking at Browne and Hassan. 'Which one should we investigate first and why?'

Kat was putting them on the spot, but her leadership style was – according to her last assessment – 'pace setting'. They'd soon learn to keep up. Both officers started scrolling through their iPads.

'Ignore the files. I want you to go with your gut. Which was the case you woke up thinking about? Hassan?'

He leaned back, resting his elbow on the arm of his

chair. 'Well, there was that young girl who went missing at Christmas a few years ago. She was with a group of friends in a dodgy bar, and according to them she just vanished.'

'Jane Hughes,' Kat said, nodding. 'An eighteen-year-old woman who went missing after a night out a week before Christmas.' Her parents still had the Christmas tree up, with their daughter's presents beneath it. 'What about you, Browne?'

'Er . . . I did read them. I read them all, but I didn't rank them. I didn't realise – I mean . . .' The young woman turned scarlet as she returned to her iPad. 'I did take lots of notes, though. If you could just give me—'

'Don't overthink it. Put your iPad down and tell me which one stood out for you.'

'Oh. Er . . .'

'Which one comes to mind now?'

'The dad from Coleshill who went to work and never came back. There was no evidence of depression or financial worries, and he seemed like such a family man.'

Kat nodded. 'Max Jones, a thirty-five-year-old father of three who was, by all accounts, happily married, yet his family haven't heard from him for two years.' Kat wrote the two names up on the white board. 'Both valid choices.'

'That's not true,' said Lock.

'I beg your pardon?'

'The choices of DI Hassan and DS Browne are not "valid", they are the result of selector bias,' said Lock. It began to pace the room the same way that Kat had moments before, gesturing to her team the way a lecturer – or a leader – might. 'DI Hassan has chosen Jane Hughes because she was a young, vulnerable female who reminds him of what happened to his little sister.'

'That's complete crap,' said Hassan, flushing. 'I chose her because—'

Lock continued, 'Whereas DS Browne selected Max Jones because of her own father complex – her dad left home when she was just ten years old.'

'That's enough,' Kat snapped, catching sight of Browne's shocked face. 'Professor Okonedo, I don't recall giving permission for your machine to access our private records?'

'Oh, that information wasn't private,' cut in Lock. 'It was all gleaned from public-facing social media sites and the biographies, CVs and interviews that are available on the police intranet. It's all there for anyone willing to make the effort to find it. I was merely highlighting the fact that their own social or emotional experiences influenced their choices, in which case, there really is no point in asking your team what they think. You may as well tip the cases into a hat and pull one out at random.'

Hassan and Browne exchanged glances, not daring to look at the boss.

'I see,' said Kat, her jaw tightening. 'Well, as you're so critical of my methods, perhaps you'd like to take over the meeting?'

'I would, yes. Thank you.'

Professor Okonedo made a strangled noise, as if she were trying not to laugh. 'AIDE Lock has been pro-grammed not to defer to authority,' she said, rising to her feet and standing rather protectively beside Lock.

She looked tiny next to her own creation – almost a foot smaller – but her voice was authoritative and held their attention. 'It will, of course, follow orders – unless they contradict the law or the inquiry's principal objectives – but as it seeks no personal gain such as promotion, it will always speak the truth as it sees it. It has no filter or fear of reprisals, so until it learns more about the nuances of human conversation and interaction, some of its comments may seem a bit rude.' Her young face hardened. 'But it will never lie or do anything corrupt.'

'You say that as if it's a rare quality,' said Kat, bristling.

'It can be in the police force. Last year there were over three thousand allegations of corruption.'

'The key word there is *allegations*,' said Kat. She stared down at the young woman, noting the throbbing pulse in her neck.Professor Okonedo clearly had strong views on the matter – maybe even some personal experience. She made a note to find out, but for today she would let it go. 'Very well,' she said, taking a seat. 'Lock, you have the floor. With the benefit of your "evidence-based decision-making processes" and …' she glanced at her phone, 'sixty-four minutes' experience in the police force, which case would you choose?'

Lock extended a hand and the room suddenly filled with holograms of the missing. The photos that Kat had spent the weekend staring at floated before them like ghosts: here a black-and-white image of an old, suited man; there a bright, blurred selfie of a young, smiling woman; and, huddled in the middle, three official school photos, awkward, outdated and unspeakably sad.

Kat stared at the life-sized figures rotating before them: the lost, the missing, and the disappeared. Each one was different, but all shared the poignancy of a face frozen in time, united by a common question: *What happened to them?*

'The question of which case to select,' Lock began, 'can be considered through many different lenses. For example, we might choose to organise these cases according to demographic profiles, such as age, gender or race.' It spread out its arms like a conductor, clustering the 3D figures into groups of the young and old. It reached out again, so that the figures were shuffled and gathered into columns of white faces and faces of colour, before being separated again into groups of men and women. 'Or we could examine the cases through the lens of the modus operandi, such as the location of where they went missing, or the time of year or day.' The holograms flew around the room like a flock of birds, settling briefly before being scattered once more.

'But if – as DCS Frank proposed – our prime purpose is to provide answers to their families, then we should focus our efforts on those cases where we are most likely to succeed.'

Lock waved another hand, and the image of an official document appeared before them. 'The latest statistical report on missing persons reveals that almost ninety per cent are found within two days. But two per cent of children and four per cent of adults remain missing for longer than a week, suggesting that after forty-eight hours, the trail has cooled considerably, and by seventy-two hours, it is almost certainly cold. So logically, we should focus on the most recent cases.'

'I agree,' said Kat.

Lock raised a hand and, with a stroke, two-thirds of the missing vanished, including the two selected by Hassan and Browne.

'There is also compelling evidence that the majority of young men who go missing after a night out drinking in the winter months have been the victims of misadventure – most commonly drowning in nearby rivers or canals, making males much easier to find.'

Kat nodded and, with another wave of Lock's hand, all the women disappeared.

'The data also suggests that white people are statistically more likely to be found and/or choose to return to the family home.' With a flick of Lock's hand, only a single hologram of a young, white, freckle-faced man remained. He was tall, thin to the point of bony, with frizzy ginger hair that framed his face like a seventies throw back to Art Garfunkel. The life-sized image floated before them, making a complete 360-degree turn as Lock continued: 'Which leaves us with Will Robinson, a twenty-one-year-old white male who, after graduating with a BA in Theatre Studies, returned to live with his parents in Stratford-upon-Avon. He left his family home at 17.10 on Tuesday January the 11th this year to meet some friends in a nearby public house, but Will never arrived and has not been seen since. Neither has there been any activity on any of his bank, phone or social media accounts. His parents believe he may have travelled to be with his ex-girlfriend in London, but there is no evidence to support their wishful thinking. In contrast, the data suggests that over sixty per cent of young men who go missing in the winter months after a night out and are not found within two days will eventually be discovered dead. Eighty-nine per cent of those bodies will be recovered from water. Therefore, there is a 53.4 per cent probability that a trawl of the River Avon – which was on his last known route – will reveal the body and allow us to fulfil the stated objective of providing answers to his family.'

But not the ones they're looking for, thought Kat. She turned towards Lock. 'Are you seriously suggesting that we explicitly decide to only look for white people?'

'It is the logical conclusion from the evidence,' said Lock.

'I hope you're recording all of this,' said Kat to Professor Okonedo as she typed away on her laptop. 'That "evidence" is derived from our own police data, which is potentially biased and certainly incomplete. As is Lock's assessment.'

Lock raised its eyebrows. 'Are you claiming my assessment is flawed?'

Kat sighed. Where to start? 'Your search engine, or whatever you run on, clearly found an association between the key words "young man", "missing", "pub" and "river". But as a mere machine, you failed to grasp that the reason why so many young men get into trouble after a night out is because they're returning from the pub half-pissed.'

Lock frowned.

'Drunk. Inebriated. Bladdered. Blootered. Mashed. Under the influence of alcohol. But Will Robinson went missing on his way *to* the pub, between the hours of five and six pm, long before any alcohol was consumed.'

Kat opened the lever arch file, turned a few pages and

tapped a printed statement. 'And you've conveniently omitted the eyewitness report of Will crossing the bridge into town around 5.30pm, suggesting that he went missing somewhere in Stratford, *after* he had passed by the river.'

'I didn't overlook the eyewitness's report, I dismissed it. The scientific data suggests that such accounts are unreliable. Seventy-five per cent of wrongful convictions for murder and rape are based upon eyewitness testimony, and in the absence of any CCTV footage to support it, it is simply not worthy of consideration.'

Kat shook her head. 'Again, you've taken a general statistic about eyewitness reports and ignored the particular facts of this case. Will Robinson was a striking young man. There can't be many other boys with ginger hair like that in Stratford-upon-Avon.'

'Less than two per cent of the English population have ginger hair, but I can find no statistics or information on their hairstyles, nor the incidence of such features in Stratford-upon-Avon.'

Kat walked towards the image of the young man, hovering like a ghost in the room. 'Although I agree we should concentrate on the most recent cases and maybe we could focus on young men who went missing after a night out, I refuse to exclude people based upon the colour of their skin.'

'If you accept that focusing on the most recent cases will increase our chances of success, then why not accept that prioritising white people will do the same?'

'Because it's *wrong*, that's why!'

'That's not an answer.'

'No, it isn't. It's an order.'

'Very well,' said Lock. 'If you insist, there are just two cases that fit the revised criterion.'

A second image appeared beside Will Robinson, hovering together in the centre of the room, as if performing an awkward dance.

Kat walked towards the image of a young, bare-chested black man. He was sitting in front of a computer with a massive grin, fist pumping the air. She paused, giving them time to fill the silence with their assumptions. 'This is Tyrone Walters on the day that he got his A level results. He got four A stars, and two months after this photo was taken, he took up a place at Warwick University to study politics. He was last seen by his flatmates just after ten pm on Wednesday, January the 26th, in his university accommodation. He sent a final text the following morning to his mum, but no one actually saw him that day, and he failed to turn up for his tutorial on Friday the 28th. No one has seen or heard from him since. He left behind his clothes, wallet, computer, everything except his phone, and there've been no transactions on his bank cards or activity on his phone or social media since.'

'Suicide?' suggested Browne.

Kat wrinkled her nose. 'That's always a possibility, but his friends and family reported he seemed genuinely happy, and he had no known mental health problems or other risk factors. That's why after reading all twenty-eight cases, this is the one that seemed off to me. This is my kouros. In fact, let's call this pilot Project Kouros.'

'I believe I know why this case appeals to you,' said Lock, 'but based upon your reaction to my earlier comments about Hassan's and Browne's personal lives, I suspect you would not welcome me sharing my opinion.'

Kat glared at it. Don't. You. Fucking. Dare.

'I'll take that as confirmation that you would rather I did not. Nevertheless, we do need to choose between the two cases. As you stated that our prime duty is to provide the families with answers, may I suggest that we assess the relative probability of achieving this objective for each case?'

Kat gave the curtest of nods.

Lock held out his hands towards Tyrone. 'One in ten first-year students drop out of university, so it is possible that Tyrone Walters didn't like his course and simply decided to go elsewhere, which as an adult he is perfectly entitled to do. Indeed, the final text to his mum mentioned that he was going to "chill" for a few days and asked her not to worry.'

Kat shook her head. She used to make the mistake of treating eighteen-year-olds as if they were adults, but now that her son Cam was the same age, she realised that despite the fact he was over six feet tall and legally entitled to drink, get married and fight in a war, it was such a vulnerable age.

'As you noted,' Lock continued, 'there have been no sightings of him nor any of the key signs of life on his banking, digital and social media appliances, so I would conclude that this scenario is possible but improbable. As a young Black male aged sixteen to twenty-four, Tyrone Walters is five times more likely to have been the victim of murder, compared to a white male of the same age. And as the number of homicide cases that actually result in a conviction is only 39 per cent, the chances of us being able to provide Tyrone Walters' mother with the answers she longs for are less than Mrs Robinson's – which if we search the river as I advise, could be as high as 53.4 per cent. Therefore, if we filter out any emotional or political concerns and focus on the statistics, the logical conclusion is that we should prioritise the Will Robinson case.'

'Statistics are nothing more than the aggregation of thousands of individual cases,' said Kat. 'They highlight what is common to most, but at the expense of what is unique. So, let's consider the unique facts of Tyrone's case, since "facts" seem to be a bit of a thing for you.' Kat stood face to face with Lock and reeled them off without looking at her file.

'Handsworth might be a "deprived" part of Birmingham, but it's also home to one of the best grammar schools in the country, which Tyrone attended and gained nine GCSEs at grade nine. You don't get into that school and then one of the top Russell Group universities by hanging out with criminals. Those pupils are incredibly driven and dedicated – Tyrone more than most. He wants to be Britain's first black prime minister and refuses to be around anyone who does drugs in case it affects his future career.'

She circled the image of Tyrone as she spoke. 'In every single interview, his family *and* friends describe a happy, confident, driven young man, destined for great things. There was no evidence of depression, and he had just done extremely well in his first exams. Tyrone Walters had absolutely no reason to leave Warwick University. But if he did choose to leave, why didn't he withdraw his student loan? He had nearly fifteen hundred pounds in his bank account, yet it's still sitting there untouched. He sent a text at 7.36am on Thursday January the 27th to a friend promising to meet them later that day at a lecture, but he never arrived. He sent a final text to his mum at 9.02am, after which his phone signal stopped. Since that time, there've been no withdrawals from his bank account, no activity on any of his social media accounts, nor any sightings of him since. Nothing. And if he was the victim of foul play, then where is the body? It's a busy campus, with thousands of students, yet no one has reported seeing or hearing an assault or suicide attempt. Tyrone Walters *completely vanished off the face of the earth,* which in this day and age, with CCTV on every corner and phone tracking and internet banking, makes no sense at all.'

'Nothing human beings do makes any sense,' said Lock. 'If you were capable of making rational decisions based upon the evidence available, then there would be no gambling, no alcoholism or obesity. Your basic premise is wrong, DCS Frank. Human beings do inexplicable things all of the time. In fact, it appears to be a distinguishing trait of your species.'

Kat took a step closer. 'One of the inconvenient realities about policing, and indeed life itself, is that "the evidence" is not always available when you need it, which means real people have to make real decisions using their experience and judgement. The initial attending officers made the same rookie errors as you. They made assumptions about his demographic, rather than considering Tyrone

Walters as an individual. And because, like the rest of us, they were too damn busy, they assessed his case as low risk, which meant zero resources were put into trying to find him.'

Kat faced the image of Tyrone, resisting the urge to reach out and touch his frozen face. 'Something's off about this case. I can feel it in my gut.'

'For my learning purposes, can I clarify that you would prefer us to prioritise Tyrone Walters' case because of "a feeling in your gut"?' queried Lock.

Kat counted to three before turning around to face it. 'I want us to review Tyrone's case because twenty-five years' experience in the police force tells me that something happened to that boy.' Her voice was dangerously low as she added, 'And because I am your boss, that is exactly what we are going to do.'

Professor Okonedo let out a heavy sigh.

'Can I make a suggestion, boss?' said Hassan. 'If this is a pilot, then from a research point of view, wouldn't it be useful to review *both* cases? Both meet the agreed criteria in terms of being fairly recent, male and most likely to be found, but one has been prioritised by an evidence-based algorithm, and the other because of a professional hunch. It would be interesting to see which of you is right.' He smiled at Professor Okonedo.

'We don't have the resources to review two cases,' said Kat, bristling. Who the fuck did he think he was? This was Hassan's first case as a DI with a new boss. He should be bending over backwards to impress her, not questioning her judgement.

'But we do have Lock, who can perform the functions of many officers in just a fraction of the time,' said Professor Okonedo. 'I think it's a great idea.'

Kat pushed a hand through her hair. Professor Okonedo was clearly a very intelligent young woman, but she had no idea how many bodies you needed to knock on doors and make the endless calls and emails to the various departments of public and private bodies just to gain access to information relevant to the investigation. Then again, she argued with herself, this could be an opportunity to educate both Professor Okonedo and the Home Secretary about the day-to-day reality of policing, and it was the perfect way to prove to her doubting DI that her judgement was far superior to that of a bloody machine.

'Okay,' she said, decision made. 'We'll review both cases. Right, I want everyone to read the complete files for both boys and we'll start re-interviewing family and close friends today. I'll do the parents. Hassan and Browne, I want you to go to Warwick University and talk to the campus security team. The attending officer's report states there was no CCTV footage. We need to clarify why. Does it mean there was no footage of Tyrone, or that there was no footage available at all, or that they judged it wasn't worth reviewing? And while you're there, talk to Tyrone's flatmates, particularly the girl who called it in.'

'On it,' said Browne.

'And Lock will accompany you, DCS Frank, as agreed?' said Professor Okonedo.

'Not if it stays like that,' said Kat, gesturing towards the holographic image. She didn't like the thought of being followed around by this non-being all day, and it was bound to draw attention and distract witnesses.

'There are four visual settings to choose from,' said Professor Okonedo, pressing a button on the ring of black plastic. 'As well as this one, there's an older, white male for more ... traditional communities,' she said, as a plump, balding man who looked like a thousand forgettable police officers Kat had ever worked with replaced Lock. 'There's a younger woman for interviewing victims of domestic or sexual abuse,' she continued, as the image morphed into a twenty-something female with large, sympathetic eyes. 'But this is my favourite,' she said, as a two-foot-high 3D image of Pikachu appeared, wearing a Sherlock Holmes-style hat. 'I thought it might help in interviews with young or vulnerable witnesses.'

'Oh wow,' said Hassan, squatting down. 'Can we keep it as Pikachu?'

'No, we cannot. It's not a pet, Hassan.' She turned towards Professor Okonedo. 'Why didn't you use any of these visual settings when you introduced it to us?'

Professor Okonedo paused. 'Almost every AI that's been given a human form, whether in fiction or reality, tends to have white or a lighter skin tone. I wanted to challenge the implicit assumption that any superior intelligence is Caucasian, so I created a young black male as the default setting for Lock. Then, when I was reaching the end of the design phase, one of my heroes, Chadwick Boseman, died.' She pressed another button, and Pikachu was replaced by the tall, slender figure of Lock. 'It's not an exact copy – that would be disrespectful,' she said softly, looking up at her creation. 'But he was my inspiration.'

That was why it looked so familiar, thought Kat. Not just the physical features of the famous actor, but the graceful, almost regal way it moved: the pauses, the presence; those wide, frank eyes.

Professor Okonedo pressed a button, and Lock disappeared. 'If you switch to just audio, you can use the speaker on the bracelet so that others can hear it, or place this transducer by your ear.' Professor Okonedo detached a black button no bigger than a pill from the solid bracelet and held it out towards her. 'It uses bone conduction technology, so that its advice is private, and can attach itself to your temple. Which would you prefer?'

Kat would have preferred to throw the bloody thing out of the window, but she'd signed up to this pilot, so she sighed and held out her hand as Lock was attached to her wrist. Her ear felt too intimate a place for such a lifelike presence.

Picking up her briefcase, Kat paused at the door. She needed to leave her new team with something more motivational than her obvious irritation. 'Remember, less than one per cent of missing people turn up dead, so we still have a good chance of finding both boys alive.'

'Just to clarify, that figure represents one per cent of *all* the missing,' said Lock's voice from her wrist. 'Only four per cent of adults are still missing one week after being reported, which is the category that Tyrone and Will fall within. So, in actual fact, there is a twenty-five per cent chance that both boys are already dead.'

CHAPTER FIVE

The door opens.

His heart lurches.

Footsteps approach. The sound of a soft heel against a floor; the smell of deodorant: something sharp and strong, scratching the back of his throat like one of those pine-scented car fresheners.

It's The Stranger.

He tries again to ask who they are and what they want? But his words are as mushed as his brain. The only thing that comes out of his numbed mouth is dribble.

The footsteps stop.

He holds his breath. Hands grab his left ankle. His leg is raised a few inches in the air while gloved fingers probe his bare foot. His foot? What the actual . . . ? He tries to pull away, but his body no longer obeys his commands. His leg is placed back down on the bed, and then The Stranger's hands grab his right foot and repeat the whole creepy process again.

Leave me alone, he wants to say. Let go.

But The Stranger stays. He feels them approach the top

of the bed, catches a whiff of coffee breath, and then their hands are upon his shoulder and hip, and suddenly he is turned over, face pressed into the mattress.

Fingers inside his waistband.

His pyjama bottoms are pulled down.

'No!' he tries to scream. He tries to turn, roll over, move, but his face remains trapped in cotton sheets soaked with his own hot breath and saliva, eyes blinded, nose squashed, his mouth a useless, silent mess.

His heart feels like it might explode as he waits for the horror of The Stranger's touch.

He waits and he waits, feeling nothing except the cold air upon his naked skin.

Fingers tug at his waistband, pulling his trousers back up: one hand on his shoulder, another on his hip, as he is flipped over onto his back, gasping like a landed fish. Did they change their mind? Is he safe?

The Stranger says not a word.

All he hears is their retreating steps, the click of an opening door, and . . .

In the distance, someone crying. Sobbing. 'No!'

The door shuts, and the voice is abruptly cut off.

But the sound echoes in his ears. It sounded like someone young. Someone male.

It sounded like pure terror.

CHAPTER SIX

**Tyrone Walters' home, Handsworth, Birmingham,
27 June, 11.55am**

Handsworth, as Lock insisted on informing Kat, is located
two kilometres north of Birmingham city centre, and is
one of the most deprived and densely populated areas in
England. While Kat drove, Lock rattled off the usual statistics about low income and unemployment, the fact that
88 per cent of the population are ethnically diverse before
concluding, 'Handsworth was the location of a famous
riot in 1981, when black youths were being disproportion-
ately stopped and searched by police, followed by further
riots in the area of Lozells in 1985, 1991 and 2011.'

'I know. I used to work here when I was at West Mids,'
said Kat. She was used to being mansplained to, but not
by a frigging computer. She had (thankfully) missed the
'81 and '85 riots but, fresh out of police college, she'd
had to deal with the aftermath, struggling to gain trust
from a bruised and hostile community. In that first year,
Kat had come close to leaving. She'd been prepared to

be challenged by the people she was trying to help; what she had not been prepared for were the constant battles with her own colleagues, who were sometimes vengeful and, quite frankly, racist. If it hadn't been for McLeish, Kat would have left. But when he took over the West Midlands, McLeish didn't just take out a few rotten apples, he threw out the whole stinking barrel. It made him hugely unpopular – there were several moves to get him sacked – but with the help of a small and trusted team, which Kat eventually became part of, he dragged the force into the twenty-first century.

Kat looked out at the narrow rows of terraced houses backing straight onto the pavement. Most people still associated Handsworth with the word 'riot', not knowing or caring that this tiny ward had been home to James Watt, Joan Armatrading, Matthew Boulton and Benjamin Zephaniah. 'A strong community' was an overused phrase, but she'd learned that if something happened to you here, friends and neighbours caught you and held you up till you found your feet again. The statistics might tell you how 'poor' and 'diverse' the area was, but they didn't tell you how kind and strong the people were.

She looked out of the car window and studied Mrs Walters' home: a narrow, redbrick Victorian terrace, no front garden, but there were hanging baskets either side of the door, bursting with pink and red geraniums. Despite the heat, they hadn't wilted or dried out, which was a good sign. Dead and forgotten plants outside a house were often the first warning of the neglect and decay within.

Kat fiddled with the unfamiliar watch on her wrist,

making sure it was still on audio. 'Leave the talking to me,' she said. 'I don't want you dropping any more motivational bombs.'

'Motivational bombs? I don't understand.'

'I know you don't. That's why you're not to speak until you're spoken to. Do you understand that simple instruction?'

'I do. I just don't understand why we're here.'

'To interview Tyrone's mum.'

'It has taken us fifty-four minutes to drive here, and you will probably spend at least another two hours talking to Mrs Walters, before spending sixty-eight minutes (exclusive of toilet breaks) to drive back to headquarters. This means you will have spent a total of four hours and two minutes – almost half of your working day – gleaning information that is already available in the reports. I do not understand why you would do this.'

'The whole point of reviewing cases is to go over witness statements and interviews with them in case something was missed at the time.'

'It would be more efficient to do this on the phone or via Zoom.'

'But I need to get a feel for the family Tyrone came from – the kind of person he was before he went missing. I can't get that from the phone.'

'I imagine it might "feel" nice to take a scenic canal boat to Stratford-upon-Avon. Nevertheless, most people accept that the car is a faster, more efficient means of transport these days.'

'Lock, I am your DCS, and I don't need to justify my

decisions to you. If you don't like it, I can leave you in the car or in the cloud or wherever you exist.'

'No, thank you. I am programmed for deep learning, so I will accompany you into the family home. Despite my scepticism, I remain open to the possibility that I may learn something.'

'Some manners would be nice,' muttered Kat, climbing out of the car.

'You mean you would like me to be more subservient and not question your decisions?'

'I mean I would like you to shut the fuck up.' Kat slammed the door, strode up the path and jabbed the doorbell with her thumb.

A trim, nervous-looking woman opened the door. She sucked in her breath at the sight of Kat. She hadn't worn a uniform in over fifteen years and bought the best trouser suits she could afford from Hobbs, yet somehow, people always guessed she was a police officer.

Mrs Walters' hand went to her heart. 'Is it Tyrone? Have you found him? Is he okay?'

The hope in her eyes was unbearable. But Kat stamped down on her pity. It was always useful to see the parent's instinctive response, which is why she hadn't warned her she was coming. She'd learned a long time ago to never start a sentence with 'I'm afraid' or 'I'm sorry' unless there really was bad news, so she kept her message short and simple. 'There's no new information about your son. I'm DCS Frank, and I'm leading a review of his case. Would it be possible to come in and talk?'

Mrs Walters physically deflated. She opened her mouth

to speak, then closed it, as if she could not bear the words she was about to utter. She nodded, and Kat followed her down the narrow hallway, past a small reception room and into the kitchen at the back.

'Would you like a cup of tea?'

Kat generally tried not to accept offers of hospitality – she was here to help, not make work for people – but she could see Mrs Walters needed a few minutes to gather herself, so she said yes, that would be lovely, thank you.

The kitchen was small but cosy: cream units and clean wooden surfaces, with a small dining table by the back door and pots of fresh green herbs lining the sunny windowsill. There was a basket of fresh laundry by the back door, and Kat spotted a familiar navy-blue uniform.

'You're a nurse?'

Mrs Walters turned, milk in hand. 'Yes, I'm a sister at the King Charles. When Tyrone first went missing, I took compassionate leave. But it became a kind of torture, sitting here all day, waiting for the phone to ring or a knock at the door. Now work is a blessing.' She glanced up at a noticeboard above the kitchen table, still filled with last year's A level timetables and revision plans. 'Milk?'

'Yes, please.'

Mrs Walters set two mugs and a plate of biscuits on the table and indicated for Kat to sit down. She placed her mobile phone before her, with Tyrone's smiling face as the screen wallpaper. 'So, still no news,' she repeated, as if she couldn't quite believe it.

Kat shook her head and proceeded to explain about the

review she was leading, before handing her the written information that explained the pilot.

'A research project?' Mrs Walters asked, bristling. 'Is that all this is?'

'No, sorry, I should have made it clear. This is a full and formal review of your son's case, and I'm the detective chief superintendent leading it. It just means that I will be assisted by a form of artificial intelligence called AIDE Lock.' Kat held out her arm to show the gadget attached to her wrist. Mrs Walters looked confused and uncertain, so despite her misgivings, Kat activated the holographic image.

The tall, slender figure of Lock appeared in front of the kitchen cabinets.

Mrs Walters rose to her feet and looked up into Lock's eyes. 'It looks so real. And familiar, somehow.' She reached out, gasping as her hand passed through Lock's shoulder and touched the cupboard behind.

Lock didn't flinch.

'It's like a ghost,' Mrs Walters whispered, taking in the smart blue suit, the shirt startlingly white against the black of its skin. 'A very handsome ghost.'

'It's just a holographic image from a computer,' Kat said, not even looking at it while she took out the consent forms. 'Nothing more. A professor in AI from Warwick University will collect information about the usefulness – or not – of this tool, but I can assure you, Mrs Walters, your son's case will take absolute priority, and we may even benefit from having access to the latest technology. If you give your consent, that is.'

Mrs Walters nodded. 'Of course. We use AI at the hospital to help with diagnostics, so I know how useful it can be.'

Kat swallowed a bitter reply with a gulp of hot tea.

'Tyrone loves computers and technology. Can I take a photo of me with it?'

'Er ... if you like,' said Kat. She'd been reluctant to switch Lock to visual, but after the initial disappointment of discovering there was no more news of her son, the holographic image had provided a welcome distraction. And it was interesting that she wanted to take a photo for Tyrone. His mum, at least, fully expected him to return.

After the selfie had been taken (*Lock with a virtual arm around the much smaller woman, grinning as if it was some sort of celebrity, for fuck's sake*), Kat drained her mug of tea and placed it on the kitchen table with a firm click. It was time to get to work. 'I'll do my absolute best to find your son, Mrs Walters, but in order to do that, I'm going to have to ask you some of the same questions you've already answered many times before. I appreciate this will be upsetting for you, but I just want you to know that I'm not doing this because I haven't bothered to read the case notes. Each time you answer the same question, you might remember a different fact, and because this case is new to me, I might pick up on a different aspect that has been overlooked before. Do you mind if we go over things one more time?'

'Of course. I'd do anything to find my son. Ask me as many questions as you like, as often as you need.'

'Thank you. I appreciate that. Can we start by talking about what Tyrone was like? I've got a son about the same age. He acts like he's cooler than cool now, but he's still the same computer-loving geek he was at eight years old.'

For the first time, Mrs Walters smiled. 'Tyrone's just the same. He played a lot of games – maybe too many – but he coded his own too.'

Kat nodded. 'He got into King Edward's Handsworth Grammar School for Boys, so he's obviously very clever. How did he find it? Did he have many friends? A girl-friend, maybe?'

Mrs Walters tilted her head. 'Tyrone's quite shy. He had a few good friends, but he preferred to play online with them. And as far as I know, he didn't have a girlfriend.'

'Did Tyrone have any enemies? Was he ever in any trou-ble with gangs or the police?'

'No. He. Did. Not,' said Mrs Walters, drawing in a breath that seemed to make her a foot taller. 'He might be a black teenager, but he doesn't like sport, he doesn't keep company with trouble-makers, and he doesn't do drugs. When he wasn't on his computer, his favourite place was sitting here, doing his homework and talking to me.' She tapped the table they sat at, her voice trembling as she said, 'My Tyrone is a good boy. I keep telling you people that, but you just don't listen.'

'I know. I can see that from the files. But I'm sorry, I have to ask.'

Mrs Walters' hand shook as she took a gulp of her tea.

'How about university? Were there other students he particularly liked or disliked?'

'He didn't talk very much about his friends there, and I tried not to grill him. He just said the people in his flat were messy but nice. One of them, Milly, was in his politics class, so that was useful. And there was another guy ...'

'Yes?'

'Well, I think he was joking, but when he came home at Christmas, Tyrone said he'd had a bit of a fall-out with one of his flatmates about politics, and he called him "Dick by name and Dick by nature".'

'Dick? Do you know his surname?'

'Sorry, no. I wish I'd paid more attention. Asked more questions, but ...'

'It's okay, I know how it is. How did Tyrone seem when he came home at Christmas?' She swallowed. 'I know he lost his dad a few years ago, and Christmas can be a particularly hard time.'

Mrs Walters laced her hands together, flesh against bone. 'Of course, he felt sad about his dad – he always will. But Trevor died five years ago, so he's come to terms with that now. In fact, it's what motivates him. All those A levels ... going to university, it's all about making his dad proud.'

'Did Tyrone say or do anything different or out of character over the Christmas holidays?'

'I ask myself that every single day. Was he upset? Did I miss something? Was I too busy going to work, Christmas shopping or stuffing the turkey to notice that my own son was unhappy?' She raised her clasped hands to her chin. 'I have gone over and over every single conversation we had that Christmas, and I can honestly say that to me, he seemed fine. I know everyone probably says that, but I was so worried that he wouldn't settle at uni – he'd never been away from home for so long before – so I was *vigilant*. I watched him, listened to what he did and didn't say, you know?'

Kat did know. How many times had she hovered around Cam, 'casually' asking what he wanted for dinner, or sitting beside him while they watched something on Netflix, discussing some character or plot, while she tried to solve the never-ending parental puzzle of *how are you?*

'He seemed a bit taller when he came home and a bit thinner, without my cooking. But he was still my Tyrone.'

Kat waited as Mrs Walters wiped away her tears, before trying to lighten the mood. 'How was he about keeping in touch? My son's a nightmare. Always "out of charge".'

Mrs Walters smiled. 'He sent me texts all the time. Silly little messages, really. But it was nice. It helped.'

'Can I see?'

Mrs Walters pressed a few buttons and handed her phone over without hesitation.

Would I hand over my phone so readily, Kat wondered. Maybe she should delete some of her more demanding texts to her son? *Where are you? Hello??? HELLO???*

Kat scrolled back through the many messages from Tyrone to his mum. She didn't read them properly – all the messages had been logged in the case notes anyway– but she could see that he seemed to message his mum several times a week, sometimes several times a day. Except, they weren't just messages. Messages were what Cam sent her. (*Whats for dinner? I've forgotten my key will you be up? Soz ran out of charge.*) These were conversations, bouncing back and forth in green and grey bubbles, bright with emojis and shared memes, before ending abruptly on 27 January.

Kat handed the phone back to Mrs Walters. 'Wow, he really did keep in touch,' she said, with a prick of envy. Maybe once he went to uni, communications with her own son would be less transactional?

'We received Tyrone's call history from the phone companies shortly after he went missing,' said Lock. 'We don't have access to the content at this stage, but I can analyse who he spoke to or exchanged messages with if that would be helpful?'

'Yes, thank you, Lock,' said Kat rather curtly. She had, after all, told it to keep quiet.

Light spilled from her wristwatch.

'What the . . . ?' spluttered Kat.

'This is the analysis of Tyrone's phone usage,' said Lock, spreading out its hands as a brightly coloured 3D pie chart appeared in the space above the kitchen table.

Before she could stop it, Lock launched into a rapid summary of Tyrone's call history, using its fingers to flip between charts as if there was an invisible touch screen before them. 'Tyrone Walters sent about ninety texts a day, slightly less than the average of one hundred and twenty-eight a day for teenagers. However, if we organise the texts by who he sent them to,' said Lock as a new pie chart appeared, 'we can see that sixty-two per cent of those texts were sent to a phone registered to a Ms Milly Babbington, twenty per cent were to his mum, twelve per cent to what I deduce are schoolfriends and another category of "other" – bills, appointment or essay reminders – account for six per cent.

'I can also show you a time series analysis,' it added, as

several charts appeared at once, 'and in relation to each particular person. Tyrone tended to text his flatmate Milly Babbington late at night or in the early hours of the morning and would text his mum in the periods between five and six-thirty in the evening, for example.'

Mrs Walters looked up at the image of Lock, as if addressing a real person. 'That's because he knew I worked night shifts. He'd text late in the afternoon before I left.' She broke off and wiped at her eyes again. 'That's why his last message was so strange.'

'What do you mean?' asked Kat.

'The day he went missing, he sent me a text late morning, which he never does. He knows I'm usually asleep then. And it didn't sound like him, either. I told them at the time something was wrong.'

Kat frowned. 'Can we take a look at it in detail?'

Mrs Walters nodded and started scrolling through her phone.

'If you gave me your consent and password, I could access all the messages that Tyrone sent you,' said Lock.

'I told you, I'd do anything to find my boy. You can access anything.'

A copy of the final text from Tyrone on 27 January at 9.02am floated in a giant speech bubble before them.

Yo, mom. Just letting you know that I need to chill for a few days, so if you don't here from me for a bit, please don't worry. Everything is cool. Love you Tx

'I have carried out a comparative authorship analysis between this text and the other messages sent by Tyrone Walters—'

'Hang on, Lock, we haven't seen this text before, and we certainly haven't discussed your so-called analysis,' said Kat.

'It only took me 1.6 seconds to assess the linguistic similarity and distinctiveness of this message compared to the previous six months, focusing on issues such as terms of address, use of slang and common spelling mistakes.' Lock reached out to the image of the speech bubble, drawing red circles around key words with a graceful arc of its finger. 'I can find no other instances where Tyrone messaged his mother with the opening address "Yo", nor any other instance where he has spelled mum with an "o" rather than the grammatically correct "u". In this message, Tyrone misspells "hear", an error which occurs in seventeen per cent of his previous texts, but he also signs off as "Tx" – a signature which I can find no other incidence of. Based upon my comparative authorship analysis, I conclude that there is a less than five per cent chance that Tyrone was the author of this text.'

'Lock, that's enough,' snapped Kat, as Mrs Walters placed a hand on her heart.

'No, I'm okay,' she said. 'I need to know what you think that means. Tell me, please.'

Lock looked at her, its eyes wide and clear. 'It means that either someone else sent you this text from his phone, pretending to be your son, or that Tyrone was forced to send this message under duress, and that he deliberately included these mistakes as a coded cry for help.'

CHAPTER SEVEN

In the stunned silence that followed Lock's pronounce-
ment, Mrs Walters let out a sob. 'I knew it. I knew
something had happened to him. My boy. My poor boy.'

Kat hissed at Lock to remove the image of text
messages. 'I'm so sorry,' she said. 'We shouldn't be spec-
ulating like this in front of you. I haven't had a chance
to verify the analysis that Lock's carried out. It really
shouldn't have—'

'No, don't apologise. I knew there was something off
about that message. I texted him back and tried ringing,
but there was no answer. He still hadn't replied by bedtime, and he'd never done that before. The next day, I was
sick with worry, but I told myself he'd probably met a girl,
so I didn't ring the university.' She wiped at her eyes. 'I
should've trusted my gut and rung them.'

'Please don't blame yourself,' said Kat. 'You've done
really well to highlight the message and share it with
us. All this is really, really, helpful, but it's far too early
to conclude what – if anything – may have happened to
your son. Look, would you mind if I took a quick look at

Tyrone's bedroom before we go? It might help me get a better sense of him.'

Mrs Walters led the way up the narrow stairs. Kat was always surprised at how easily most people agreed to such requests. She paused at the doorway. Experience had taught her that when a parent was present, their own emotions leaked into the room, threatening to influence her observations, so she asked Mrs Walters if she could jot down a list of Tyrone's schoolfriends.

As she headed down the stairs, Kat hissed at Lock, 'I thought I told you to leave the talking to me?'

'You told me to only speak when I was spoken to. And Mrs Walters spoke to me. And you agreed it would be useful to carry out an analysis of Tyrone's phone usage.'

'I did not!'

'When I offered to carry out the analysis you said – and I quote – "Yes, thank you, Lock".'

'I clearly meant no.'

'That is not clear at all.'

'Tone, Lock. *Tone.* I was practically talking through gritted teeth.'

'Ah, like you are now?'

'Yes, *just* like I am now.'

'So, although you just said yes, do you actually mean no?'

'No! Oh, for fuck's sake, Lock,' she said, dragging a hand through her hair. 'The point is, even if I did agree it would be useful to carry out that analysis, I did *not* agree to you sharing your preliminary findings in front of his bloody mother. Apart from the fact that we now have a very worried and upset parent on our hands, what if she turned out to be a suspect? Or what if you'd revealed sensitive information that we didn't want any other witnesses to know?'

For once, Lock was silent. 'You are right,' it said eventually. 'My apologies. I failed to consider the socio-environmental context within which I shared the results. I have learned from this and updated my algorithms accordingly.'

The complete apology took some of the heat out of her anger, but she'd have to ask Professor Okonedo where the mute button was on this thing. She couldn't run the risk of Lock doing something like that again.

'Send the analysis to Browne and Hassan and ask them to interview Milly Babbington and a flatmate called Dick while they're at the university. We need to know what all those late-night messages were about.'

She took a deep breath and tried to empty her mind of all the emotional backwash from the interview with Mrs Walters, before opening the door to Tyrone's bedroom. It wasn't very big – just enough space to fit in one of those bunk beds from Ikea with a desk underneath, a couple of bookcases, a bean bag and a small, white-washed wardrobe.

She approached the desk, noting the faded space where presumably his computer used to be, next to a white set of headphones and a fixed microphone. On the right-hand wall was a cork noticeboard, crammed with academic certificates. Her eyes travelled over the Gold Maths Challenge awards from primary school, a certificate for the Physics Olympiad in Year 9, and another one for

Tyrone's achievements at GCSE and a letter confirming a place at Warwick University. She lifted up the curled edges of one of the certificates, noting the darker tone beneath, and asked Lock to take a photo and add it to the file.

'You do realise this isn't new information?' said Lock. 'Tyrone's academic achievements are all in his school reports. Once again, this is an inefficient use of your time.'

'And once again, you couldn't be more wrong. The awards themselves aren't news, but the fact that Tyrone has them on his bedroom wall is. It tells us that he was proud of his achievements and pleased with the offer from Warwick. If it was his mum who'd put them up, he'd have wasted no time in pulling them down.'

She opened her mouth to say more, but what was the point? How could a machine ever understand the significance of a child's bedroom, the one place in the world where they could just be themselves? Of course, they weren't as revealing as they used to be. Back in the day, a teenager's interests and hobbies were literally plastered across their walls or scribbled in not-so-secret diaries hidden beneath pillows or in drawers. These days, the hopes and dreams of most adolescents existed only in the ephemeral world of Snapchat or hidden behind fake Instagram accounts. But the bedroom was where they would type, delete, read and share those messages. This was still where it all happened.

Kat rested her hands upon the chair at the desk, thinking of how many hours, days, weeks and years Tyrone must have spent here, begging his mum for 'just ten minutes more' of game time. And now she'd probably give anything to have her son back at his computer, safe at home. She closed her eyes against the prick of tears, imagining how she would feel if this were Cam's empty chair.

'What are you doing?' asked Lock.

'Just trying to picture Tyrone,' said Kat, opening her eyes. 'He probably spent half his life here.'

She jumped as Tyrone appeared in the chair she'd been leaning on. It took Kat a second to realise it was just another 3D image, but the lifelike detail was still disconcerting: the dark line of stubble above his upper lip, a crop of spots upon his left cheek, a touch of sleep in the corners of both eyes.

She told herself it wasn't real, that it was a projection of the photo she'd shared with the team earlier. But then it moved. It smiled.

'What the . . .'

'I have alternate-reality technology that allows me to simulate deceased or missing persons to assist with crime reconstructions.'

Kat swore, both horrified and fascinated by the figure before her.

'I doubt whether Tyrone actually spent "half his life" here,' continued Lock. 'I'd estimate it to be closer to a third. But this is clearly where the photograph of Tyrone celebrating his A level results was taken.'

Kat glanced up at the bunk bed above the desk, imagining the scene. He'd have just got up – that's why Tyrone wasn't wearing a top in the photo – and then logged on to the UCAS website. Maybe he'd whooped in excitement, and his mum (who must have been hovering outside) had rushed in to find out what he'd got. She probably cried as they hugged: tears of pride and joy, salted with regret that it was just the two of them. But his mum wouldn't have wanted to ruin the moment. She'd have dried her eyes and stepped back to capture this moment: her beautiful boy with his whole future before him.

'Oh, Tyrone,' Kat whispered to the figure before her. 'What happened to you?' She squatted down to his level and looked to where his glance would have fallen. On the crowded bookcase opposite, as well as files of A level notes and textbooks, she could see boxes of Pokemon cards and Mario games. But there in the centre, on a shelf next to a picture of a young Barack Obama, was a photograph of Tyrone as a boy – maybe ten or eleven years old – sitting on a bench in the sunshine between his mum and another older, balding man. His dad?

Kat rose and walked towards the photo and picked it up. It was a home-made birthday card with a family photo of the three of them. She opened it and read:

To my best mate, Tyrone, on his 12th birthday. Remember, you can be anything you want to be. All my love always, Dad xxxxx

'Tyrone!' Mrs Walters stood in the doorway, both hands clasped to her face.
Shit. 'Mrs Walters, I—'
But before Kat could explain, she was running into the room. 'Oh, my boy, *my boy!*' she sobbed. She stretched out her arms to clasp her only child to her, but they passed

right through him. She tried again and again, but her arms remained empty. The euphoria fell from Mrs Walters as she slowly passed one finger through the left-hand cheek of the holographic image.

Kat's eyes pricked with tears as she gently took the mother's hands into her own. 'It's not real. I'm sorry.'

Mrs Walters shook her off, chest heaving. She tried again to touch her son, but her hand just went through to the back of his chair. 'What in God's name *is* this?'

'It is merely a simulation of Tyrone Walters,' said Lock, spreading out its hands.

'*Merely?* That, is my *son*!'

'Switch it off, Lock,' ordered Kat. '*Now.*'

The image of Tyrone vanished, casting the room into semi-darkness.

'Tyrone,' Mrs Walters sobbed, sinking to her knees as she held on to the empty chair.

'I'm so sorry,' said Kat. 'It was just a kind of reconstruction. We were ... I was just trying to—'

Mrs Walters gripped the chair tight, her eyes fixed on the floor. 'Get out of my house.'

'I'm so sorry, I—'

'I said *go*!' Rage propelled her to her feet. 'I'm not interested in your apologies. You people don't understand what it's like to lose someone. If you did, you'd never do something like this.'

Kat followed Mrs Walters down the stairs, sick with shame. As she reached the bottom step, Kat paused. 'I am so very, very sorry, Mrs Walters. And ... for what it's worth, I do understand. At least, a bit.' She took a deep breath and said to the back turned against her, 'My own husband died six months ago, and my son is nearly the same age as Tyrone, so the last thing I wanted was to intrude upon your grief, or to make things any worse than they already are.'

Mrs Walters turned. The anger melted from her face and, without warning, she wrapped her arms around Kat.

Kat would normally recoil from such intimate contact with a stranger – social distancing was still ingrained in them all – but this was such a pure and unexpected act of kindness, that Kat could do nothing but hold on.

'I wish I could tell you that it gets easier,' Mrs Walters whispered into her ear. 'It doesn't. But you do get used to it.'

Kat nodded, not trusting herself to speak as they stepped apart.

It was Mrs Walters who broke the silence. 'But I still need you to go. You understand?'

Kat nodded and opened the front door.

'DCS Frank?'

She turned.

'What do you really think has happened to Tyrone?'

When she was younger, Kat had answered such questions with promises and reassurances. But nearly twenty-five years in the force had taught her the value of silence. She sifted through several responses, before saying, 'At this stage, we're keeping an open mind.'

Mrs Walters winced, and Kat realised that, as a nurse, she would know that what was not said was often more important than what was.

'You said you had a son about Tyrone's age?'

'Yes. He's just finished his A levels.'

'As a widow – not a police officer – do you think your son would ever run away and leave you, knowing that without him you'd be utterly and completely alone?'

The two women stared at each other.

'That's why I know someone has taken my son,' said Mrs Walters. 'You have to find him.'

The hairs on the back of Kat's arms prickled. 'I will do my absolute best. I promise. Thank you, Mrs Walters. We'll be in touch.'

CHAPTER EIGHT

He is not alone.

He's heard The Other Guy twice now. His voice is faint, slightly muffled, as if filtered through several doors. But there's definitely someone else trapped in this building. Someone else being held against their will.

He tries to take comfort from the thought. Maybe The Other Guy can help him to escape?

But then he hears him again: a howl of agony that makes his insides shrivel. He holds his breath as the crying starts, each sob falling like bricks from a broken building. Jesus. The sound tears him apart – half of him wants to run to help the guy, the other half wants to run a million fucking miles away. But most of all, he just wants it to stop.

Eventually it grows quieter. Quieter still. Then silence.

The Other Guy – poor bastard – sounds in no fit state to help anybody. So, he's on his own after all. He needs to think of a plan. A strategy. But all he can think of is, what did they do to make The Other Guy cry like that?

He shivers at the memory of those cold, gloved hands

pulling down his pyjama bottoms. He keeps telling him-self that nothing happened. Surely, he'd remember if it had? Even if he'd been unconscious, there'd be a bruise or a cut. Some soreness at least. He tries to take comfort from the fact that he feels nothing, but the other, more fearful voice reminds him that his whole body is numbed out by God knows what drugs. He's asleep most of the time, and whenever he's awake – which seems to be less and less these days – he's still so drugged that he can't even move. And now he can't even hear The Other Guy.

But he can imagine.

And that is the most terrifying thing of all.

CHAPTER NINE

**En route to University of Warwick Campus, Coventry,
27 June, 11.32am**

'We'll take my car,' Hassan announced to Browne, who
was struggling to keep up as they crossed the car park
together. She nodded her agreement, which he took as a
good sign. It never ceased to amaze him how many cop-
pers wasted time playing power games with the whole
'your car or mine' thing. He leaned over the driver's seat
to scoop up a McDonald's bag, adding it to the growing
pile on the back seat.

Browne hesitated before sliding in, trying to avoid the
crumpled crisp packets on the floor.

'I snack a lot,' Hassan said, grinning.

'Mind if I open a window?'

'You saying my car stinks?'

Browne flushed. 'No, it's just I don't feel too good. I
need some fresh air.'

'Late night, eh?'

'Something like that,' she mumbled.

He cast her a sideways look. His new DS was quite short and solid-looking, like a very dependable box. With her boyish hair and a plain, functional blouse-and-trouser combo, he couldn't imagine her going out on the lash last night – or any night, for that matter. Either way, he hoped she wasn't as ill as her pale face suggested. He didn't mind a few plastic cups and crisp packets here and there, but he didn't want puke all over his car.

'Well, that was a bit awkward, wasn't it?' he said, as they drove out of the police car park.

'What was?'

'The briefing with the AI. Fancy challenging your new boss like that.'

'Well, it's only a machine. I guess it doesn't quite understand the unwritten rules yet.'

'Yet? Do you buy all that "deep learning" stuff, then?'

'I don't know. It's a pilot, so I guess we'll find out.'

'Very diplomatic of you.' Hassan frowned as he struggled to think of an appropriately professional response. Honestly, what was the point of being in a team if you couldn't gossip about the boss? He might as well share his car with the robot. 'What did you make of Professor Okonedo?' he tried again. 'She's very . . . clever.'

Browne raised an eyebrow. 'She's also very beautiful.'

'Is she? I hadn't noticed.'

Browne burst into laughter.

'What?' he said, trying to keep a straight face.

'So, it was her *brains* you couldn't keep your eyes off?'

'Well, she is very brainy.'

'Very.' She looked like she was going to say more, but as

they turned round an island, Browne closed her eyes and leaned her head out of the open window.

'You okay?'

She nodded, but Hassan suspected it was because she didn't dare talk. 'Look, how about I go via the scenic route rather than pelting down the A46?' he suggested. 'We can go slower then, or even get out for a breather if you feel that bad?'

Browne started to insist that she was fine, really – she didn't want to be any trouble – but she had that worrying green tinge to her skin that white people get when they're about to be sick, so Hassan ignored her and turned off onto one of the smaller roads that led to Kenilworth. Soon, they were driving through cool arches of green leaves, and the car filled with the scent of roadside hedges frothed with sweet white blossom. After a few minutes, Browne's breathing was slower, and some colour had returned to her cheeks.

'I feel better now, thanks,' she said. 'Sorry if I made us late.'

'It's honestly not a problem.'

Browne nodded towards the dashboard, where the satnav was switched off. 'You sure you know where you're going?'

'I'm sure.'

Browne rolled her eyes. 'Don't tell me you're one of those guys who thinks a Y chromosome means they don't need to use maps?'

He laughed. 'No, it's just that I know this route really well. I used to drive my—' He stopped, realising he'd said more than he'd meant to.

Browne kept silent, as if waiting for him to continue, but of course, he didn't. A cop can't fool another cop into talking.

'Anything stand out for you in the case so far?' he asked, changing the subject.

'Yeah, a couple of things,' she said, taking out her iPad. 'Tyrone wasn't reported missing by Milly Babbington until Friday night – forty-eight hours after she last saw him. Why did she leave it so late?'

'She probably just thought he'd met a girl or something.'

Browne wrinkled her nose. 'But in her interview, she said that Tyrone didn't have a girlfriend – he was in the room next to hers, so she'd know. She also said that they used to help each other with their essays, but even though they had a big one due on Friday, he hadn't been in touch or replied to any of her texts.'

'He's eighteen.'

'So?'

Hassan raised his hands from the steering wheel. 'So, I hate to break it to you, Browne, but most eighteen-year-old boys who've just left home and a single-sex school are not thinking about essays.'

'Don't judge everyone else by your own standards.'

'That cuts both ways. You're looking at him through the eyes of his mother. Don't you remember your first year at uni?'

Browne ignored him and tapped away at her iPad.

Shit. Hassan suddenly remembered she'd joined the force at eighteen. Lots of people did, but while some boasted about being 'a graduate of the school of life', less confident types were sometimes more defensive. Maybe Browne was in the latter camp.

'Didn't Tyrone leave the halls of residence in the early hours of the day he went missing?' said Hassan.

'Yes, at 3.30am, according to the access system at reception. But we don't know why.'

'He probably arranged to meet someone for a quick shag.'

'From all the interviews I've read, he doesn't sound like the kind of guy who'd suddenly arrange to meet someone for random sex at three-thirty in the morning.'

'What kind of guy wouldn't?'

Browne gave him a weary look. 'Your "man must have sex" theory doesn't explain why Tyrone sent Milly a text four hours later at 7.36am agreeing to meet her at the lecture. Or why he never turned up.'

Hassan shrugged. 'Maybe his new friend persuaded him to stay in bed. Don't want to shock you, Browne, but sometimes people do have sex more than once.'

'So I've heard,' she said in voice so deadpan that he wasn't sure whether she was being sarcastic or not. 'A new lover might explain why Tyrone went missing for a night or two, but it doesn't explain why he's been missing for five months.'

'Unless he was ashamed of what he'd done. If Tyrone really did want to be Britain's first black PM, then his whole identity would have been wrapped up in that ambition.'

She turned and looked at him. 'That's a good point, actually.'

'She said, with a note of surprise in her voice.'

Browne at least had the grace to blush. 'I didn't mean ...'

'Look, just because I haven't read and memorised every last line of the report, it doesn't mean I'm not a good detective. I am. Not because I've got a degree, but because I *know* people. I know what drives them and, believe me, it isn't essays.' He gestured at her iPad. 'Those interviews only include what Tyrone wanted his friends to know, and what they in turn were willing to tell us. Everyone has secrets, and if we can find out what Tyrone's was – sex, money, drugs, whatever – then that's how we'll find out what happened to him.'

Browne stared at him. 'You've got a very negative view of people.'

'Just a realistic one. Believe me, cases become a lot clearer once you take off your rose-tinted glasses.'

Her phone pinged. 'Message from AIDE Lock. After we've interviewed campus security, DCS Frank wants us to find a flatmate called Dick or Richard and ask him about an argument he had with Tyrone. And she wants us to interview Milly Babbington as a matter of urgency. Apparently, there were lots of late-night texts from Tyrone's phone to hers.'

Hassan smiled as they drove onto the campus. 'And I'll bet you lunch that those texts to Milly weren't about his essays.'

They were met by Colin, deputy head of campus security, in the university car park, where he'd been patrolling the space he'd reserved for the two visiting detectives. 'These traffic cones are like gold dust,' he explained, eyes darting about as if he were in a war zone. 'If I turn my back for one minute, the students run off with them.' He collected up the cones, holding them to his chest like a baby, before launching into a small speech on just how safe and secure the campus was, thanks to him and his 24-hour security team.

But Hassan wasn't listening. He was taking in the familiar sweep of green lawns and trees, the glint and glare of sun on the artificial lakes and the buildings of brick and glass. Five years ago, his parents had parked their rusting old Shogun in this very car park, so he could help his sister Samina carry all her bedding, pictures and plush toys into her new student room. It had taken half the day, but he hadn't minded. Samina was so very excited. His parents so very proud. He wasn't sure what hurt the most: the memory of his little sister's hopeful face on her first day, or that midnight phone call six months later when she'd begged him, sobbing, to come and get her. He'd found her buried beneath her quilt, trembling uncontrollably, despite all the extra blankets he gently laid upon her. Terrified she was dangerously ill, he'd wanted to call 999 for an ambulance. It was only then that she'd told him about the rape. 'You can't tell anyone.' She'd made him promise. 'Not ever.' At the time he'd agreed, but as the hours turned to days, he found he couldn't bear the truth of his promise: that he could not make it better.

'DI Hassan?'

'Sorry?'

'I was just saying that we have a twenty-four-hour security team,' said Colin, self-importantly. 'Two thousand intruder alarms and detection devices, over five hundred access control readers and more than three hundred CCTV cameras.'

'Good,' said Hassan, blinking. He forced himself to concentrate upon the smaller man before him. 'Then you should be able to tell us exactly what happened to Tyrone Walters.'

'You have to understand that Warwick University has over a hundred buildings spread over three sites, with a total student population of twenty-five thousand and a staff population of five thousand,' blustered Colin. 'We can't possibly keep track of every individual.'

'Then what is the point,' said Hassan icily, 'of all those cameras and cards and alarms and staff, if you can't keep your students safe?'

'Colin,' cut in Browne in a more conciliatory tone. 'May I call you Colin? We really appreciate you giving us your time at such short notice, given the scope of your job. I know you're really busy, but we're doing a full review of Tyrone Walters' case. Would it be possible to see his room, the main points of access he used on his electronic key card and any CCTV footage you have? We've read all the reports, but you can't beat seeing it on the ground with someone like yourself who really knows what's what.'

Colin puffed out his chest. 'I've got a seminar on student safety to deliver in thirty minutes, but I'll walk you over to the accommodation block and show you his room.'

'And the CCTV footage?' said Hassan.

'You should have that already. Our policy is to cooperate with the police, so we would have handed it over at the time of the original inquiry.'

'According to the files, it wasn't available. Do you know if that was because the cameras weren't working?'

'Our cameras are checked regularly,' he said, bristling again. 'It won't be that. I'll need to get someone in my team to go back and check why you don't have them.'

'Thanks so much,' said Browne. 'Really appreciate it. Now if you could take us to Tyrone's room, that'd be great.'

Lakeside Village Halls of Residence was a large, modern block of flats that wouldn't have been out of place on Canary Wharf. 'Brand new, *en suite* facilities in every room,' boasted Colin. He held up his key card like a proud hotelier and swiped it against the entrance. 'You can't get in without one of these unless someone else signs you in, so we have a complete record of who's in at any time.'

The doors opened and they followed Colin as he confirmed that the last record of Tyrone on the electronic access system showed him leaving the halls of residence at 3.30am on 27 January.

'You said there are over five hundred electronic access points across the campus,' said Hassan. 'Is there any record of Tyrone going into another hall of residence after he left his own?'

'Or the library or gym?' added Browne.

Honestly, thought Hassan, with an eyeroll. She seemed determined to prove that the guy was a monk.

Colin shook his head. 'Nope. That's the last record we have of him anywhere on the campus. Poor kid just seemed to vanish into thin air.' He opened the main door with his key card. 'There are six student rooms in this flat,' he said, as they entered an extremely narrow corridor. 'A kitchen and living room in the middle, three rooms either side.'

They followed him, single file, down towards the end of the hall, where he stopped at No. 612. 'This was Tyrone's.'

Hassan pointed to the two rooms nearest to it. 'Who lives here?'

Colin checked his records. 'Milly Babbington is the one next door, and Richard Sykes's room is the last one at the end.'

Hassan exchanged glances with Browne. That must be the guy the boss mentioned.

Colin opened Tyrone's door. There was just enough space for a single bed against the right-hand wall, some built-in shelves and a wardrobe on the left, a narrow wooden desk beneath the window and a tiny bathroom with a toilet and shower cubicle.

Hassan walked up to the desk, empty save for an A4 pad of notes, some loose change, and a full pack of chewing gum. He bent down, expecting to find old sweet wrappers and essay notes under the chair, but the floor was completely clean. He glided his foot over the surface, but there were no sticky patches from spilled drinks or food. Hassan frowned, remembering his own first-year accommodation. After just one week his room was in such a state, he'd gratefully accepted any offers of a beer, sex or revision session (or, if he was lucky, all three) as long as it was in someone else's flat. 'Has someone tidied up in here?' he asked Colin.

'No. The police told us to leave everything just as it was found.'

'What about his laptop and phone?'

'He had his phone with him,' said Browne. 'According to the file the attending officers took the laptop, so it'll be at the station.'

Hassan nodded, implying that of course he knew this and had just forgotten. He turned towards the bookshelves, but there were just a few files and course textbooks, alongside a family photo of a younger Tyrone with his mum and dad. No photos of girls or mates; no tickets from football matches or concerts, or wristbands from festivals and raves. The emptiness of the room made him remember how much life there had once been in his sister's. Her bed had been crammed with cushions and blankets she'd crocheted herself, and she'd practically papered the walls with photos of her friends she'd taken on some retro Polaroid. He turned away from the memory of all those smiling faces and stuck his head around the door of the bathroom.

'Where's his toothbrush and shaving stuff?'

'We took it for DNA swabs,' said Browne, adding, 'according to the report.'

If that was a dig, he decided to ignore it. As a DI, he had more important things to do than read every last line of every report. That's what DS's were for. 'Can you take some pictures of the room and email them to Lock to add to the shared file?' he asked Browne. 'And then we'll start interviewing his flatmates.'

'Hello?'

They both turned to see a young woman at the doorway. Tall, willow-thin and with long, glossy blonde hair, she looked like something out of a magazine. 'Hi, I heard voices, I just wondered . . .' Her eyes travelled over them, frowning at the sight of Colin from security. She swallowed. 'Is it Tyrone? Has something happened?'

Hassan stepped forward. 'And you are . . . ?'

'Milly. Milly Babbington.'

He looked her up and down before throwing Browne a triumphant glance. 'I'm afraid there's no news at present, Milly. I'm DI Hassan, and this is my colleague, DS Browne. We're leading a review into Tyrone's case. I know you spoke to the police before, but we'd really appreciate it if we could go over it again, just to make sure we haven't missed anything. Would that be okay?'

'Of course. I'll do anything I can to help find Tyrone.'

'Can you talk now?'

'Er . . . well I was going out. Will it take long?'

'Not long,' Hassan said, giving Browne a quick wink. 'I just have a few questions about your essays.'

CHAPTER TEN

Interviewer:	DI Rayan Hassan (RH)
Attending:	DS Debbie Browne (DB)
Interviewee:	Milly Babbington (MB)
Date/Time:	27 June, 12.45pm, MB's room, Warwick University

RH: Thanks for agreeing to talk to us at such short notice. Could you start by telling us about your relationship with Tyrone?

MB: Relationship? We weren't in a relationship. Who told you that?

RH: Nobody, I just want to understand how well you knew Tyrone, and what your relationship to him was.

MB: Oh, I see. Sorry, yes. Um, well, he lived in the room next to me, so we like, met on the first day. When we found out we were both studying politics together, we quickly became friends.

RH: What kind of friends? Did you spend a lot of time together?

MB: Oh, you know, we walked to lectures and the library together, swapped notes, helped each other with essays, if you know what I mean.

RH: Not really, I didn't spend a lot of time in the library when I was at uni. You must have played hard as well. Pubs, nightclubs?

MB: Not with Tyrone. I asked him a few times to come out with me and my mates, but he didn't really like our kind of music or ...

DB: Yes?

[silence]

RH: It's okay, Milly, I'm honestly not interested in what you and your friends get up to. I'm here to find Tyrone. Nothing more.

MB: Okay, well, off the record – is that the right phrase? – some of my friends were into weed. Not me – obvs. And it doesn't bother me, live and let live, right? But Tyrone used to hate being round what he called 'potheads', saying if they were caught by the police, he'd be the one who ended up in jail because he was black. He was totally paranoid about it.

RH: So, when you went out with your friends, what did he do?

MB: Don't know. I wasn't there – obvs – but I think he stayed in.

RH: He must have had some other friends?

MB: Um, he had a lot of friends back home, I think. But I didn't see anyone come around.

RH: What about girlfriends or boyfriends?

MB: No.

RH: One-night stands?

MB: *[laughs]* Tyrone? No.

RH: Or at least, not that you know of.

MB: Believe me, I would have known. The walls are paper thin.

RH: Hmm. Can you tell me again when you first began to worry that he might be missing?

MB: Well, he sent me a text early Thursday morning saying he'd meet me at the lecture at ten, warning me not to miss it, but then he was the one who didn't turn up. I didn't really think much about it, until I knocked on his door that night and he still wasn't in. We had a deadline for an essay on Friday, and we usually worked together on that kind of stuff.

RH: Did he say he'd be in? Had you arranged to meet him?

MB: No, I didn't need to because he was always in.

RH: But not that night.

MB: No.

RH: Were you worried at this point?

MB: Yeah. I knew I'd fail if I didn't hand my essay in.

RH: I meant were you worried about Tyrone?

MB: Not really. More annoyed than anything. Like I said. I hadn't done my essay.

RH: And you were hoping that Tyrone would do it for you?

MB: No, I mean ... we worked on them together. We were a team. I was more the ideas person, but he was good at writing it all up.

RH: I see. So, when exactly did you get worried about Tyrone?

MB: When he didn't turn up for our tutorial on Friday. I mean, lots of people sleep in and miss them. But not Tyrone. He was big on punctuality and that kind of thing. It was quite sweet really. I went to look for him at the canteen at lunchtime, asking everyone if they'd seen him, but no one had. And when he still hadn't turned up for dinner, I started to really freak out.

RH: So just to be clear, the last time you heard from him was Thursday morning, 27 January at 7.36am when he sent you a text, but when was the last time you actually *saw* Tyrone Walters?

MB: Wednesday night. We had a brief chat about my – our – essays, agreed an outline and then he left my room at about ten and went back to his own.

RH: How was he? Was he down about anything or stressed about this essay?

MB: No, the opposite. It was an essay about how the Iraq War started, and he was really fired up about it. He didn't like the Blair Government.

RH: Was he in the habit of going out early for a run or to the gym, maybe?

MB: Not as far as I know. I never saw him do it before. He was a bit of a geek, to be honest. Not really the sporty type, oddly enough.

RH: Odd because ... ?

MB: Well, you know.
[silence]

RH: *[examines iPad]* You said you were just friends, and yet according to an analysis of Tyrone's phone records, you were the person he messaged most.

MB: Like I said, we were on the same course, so we talked a lot.

RH: At two, three am? Several times a night?

MB: We liked to work on our essays late.

RH: So, if we took a look at your phone, we'd see that all your messages from Tyrone were about your essays?

MB: *[gasps]* My phone? That's private. Don't you need like a warrant or something?

RH: No – if we have reason to think it would help our enquiries then we can put in a request to your phone provider to access your records. But it'd be a lot easier if you just showed them to us. To save any misunderstandings.

MB: I – I can't.

RH: Why not?

MB: Because I deleted them.

RH: What, all of them?

MB: Yes.

RH: Why on earth would you do that?

MB: I needed to delete a load of stuff, photos and messages, to free up some storage space. And I found all the old messages from Tyrone too upsetting to look at once he went missing.

RH: So, you deleted them?

MB: Yes.

RH: Even though you knew Tyrone was the subject of a missing person's investigation?

MB: I ... I didn't think. Sorry. I was just trying to free up some space.

RH: Don't worry. We can retrieve deleted messages from your phone company. It'll take a bit longer, but we will get them back.

MB: But that's an invasion of my privacy! I haven't done anything wrong! I told you, the messages were just about essays and stuff.

RH: Then you've got nothing to worry about, have you?

INTERVIEW CONCLUDED

CHAPTER ELEVEN

Interviewer: DI Rayan Hassan (RH)
Attending: DS Debbie Browne (DB)
Interviewee: Richard Sykes (RS)
Date/Time: 27 June, 2.50pm, RS's room, Warwick
                     University

RH: Thank you for agreeing to meet with us today,
Richard. We appreciate you helping Tyrone.

RS: What if he doesn't want to be found? I'm not helping him then, am I?

RH: You think he chose to disappear?

RS: I don't know. I'm just pointing out that Tyrone
is an adult, so if he did choose to go off, then he
wouldn't want to be tracked down, would he?

RH: Okay. Let's imagine for a moment that Tyrone
has disappeared of his own free will. Why do you
think he might do that?

RS: Don't know. You'd have to ask him.

RH: I'm asking you, Richard. Can I call you Richard?
Or do you prefer Dick?

RS: My name is Richard.

RH: Okay – Richard – how well did you know Tyrone?

RS: Not very well.

RH: You were both first-years, new to the campus, and he lived in the room right next to yours for four months. I'd imagine you probably saw him every day?

RS: Probably.

RH: Yet you don't think you knew him very well. Would you describe him as a friend?

RS: *[shrugs]* He was a *flat*mate, not a mate.

RH: And what was he like – as a flatmate?

RS: Bit boring, to be honest. Nice enough guy, but he was more interested in doing his essays than hanging out or partying. So yeah, I saw him most days, but we weren't exactly 'besties'.

RH: Did you ever argue?

RS: Nah. Tyrone didn't do conflict.

RH: Really? You lived next door to each other for four months. He was focused on his studies, you, as you suggested yourself, liked to party. You must have argued sometimes?

RS: Nah. Tyrone was chill.

RH: Even about politics?

[silence]

RH: Didn't you have a big argument with him just before Christmas?

RS: Well, yeah, but everyone argues about politics. I don't see the relevance.

RH: The relevance is that you lied.

RS: I didn't lie, I just ...

RH: Omitted the truth?

RS: *[muttered expletive]*

RH: While we're being truthful, can I ask you about your relationship to Milly Babbington?

RS: What's she got to do with this?

RH: Just trying to get a picture of the dynamics on the floor where Tyrone lived. Milly had the other room next to Tyrone, didn't she?

RS: Yeah.

RH: So, Milly was in the middle?

RS: What do you mean?

RH: What do you think I mean?

RS: *[mutters]*

RH: Were Tyrone and Milly ever in a relationship?

RS: In his dreams.

RH: You think Tyrone wanted to be in a relationship with Milly?

RS: *[shrugs]*

RH: Is that a yes or a no?

RS: It's an 'I don't know'. Like I said, we weren't close. You'd have to ask him.

RH: I'd love to, but unfortunately Tyrone Walters is missing. Okay, let's move on. Would you say that you and Milly are close?

RS: Kind of.

RH: Are you 'kind of' in a relationship?

RS: Jesus, what's my private life got to do with anything?

RH: Like I said, I'm just trying to get a picture of the

dynamics in the flat and to understand what possible motive Tyrone could have had for disappearing. I should warn you that we're going to interview your other three flatmates, so if there's anything you think I should know, it'd be better if I heard it from you.

RS: *[sighs]* Well, in that case, you might as well know that Milly's my girlfriend – but she wasn't at the time that Tyrone went missing, so I really don't think it's relevant.

RH: That's for us to judge, Mr Sykes. Tyrone and Milly were clearly quite close, constantly messaging each other.

RS: I wouldn't say 'constantly'.

RH: I've seen the analysis of Tyrone's call history. I'd definitely say it was 'constant'. Must have been a bit annoying for you.

RS: *[shrugs]*

RH: You weren't bothered by it? A bit jealous, maybe?

RS: Yeah, I was so jealous that the geek next door kept texting my girlfriend that I bumped him off.
[silence]

RS: Jesus, that was a *joke*!

RH: Do you think his mum would find that funny? No? Neither do I. I'm going to leave it there for now, but I suggest you start taking this seriously, Mr Sykes, because we're probably going to want to talk to you again. Very soon.

INTERVIEW CONCLUDED

CHAPTER TWELVE

Leek Wootton Police Headquarters, Warwickshire, 27 June, 5.20pm

DS Browne winced as she walked past the drinks machine and took a seat at the end of the boardroom table. It was a bit antisocial of her to sit so far away from Hassan and Professor Okonedo, but even the smell of coffee made her feel sick. She closed her eyes. How could she, of all people, have been so stupid? She had a spreadsheet for Christmas presents that she started buying in September, a rota for the bins that she shared with her partner, and a calendar going back eight years that marked not just the days her period started and ended, but the days she ovulated too. DS Debbie Browne planned every element of her life, and yet somehow, she'd managed to start the most important job of her career with an unplanned pregnancy.

Unplanned pregnancy. She wasn't sure which of those two words upset her the most. She looked out of the window, trying to imagine she was breathing in the clean, fresh air of the Warwickshire countryside, as another wave of nausea washed through her. Woodcote House, as her mum liked to say, looked more like it belonged in Downton Abbey rather than the police force, with its blond stoned mansion set in acres of woodland. But then her mum—

'DS Browne?'

DCS Frank was standing at the head of the table, clearly waiting for her to say something. Tall, lean and whip-smart, she was everything Browne aspired to be. She'd spent weeks imagining what it would be like to work with her role model, but not one of the elaborate scenarios she'd dreamed of involved her sitting dumbstruck while she tried not to throw up.

'Pardon? Sorry, I didn't hear the question.'

'I asked you to kick off our briefing by telling us what you found out at Warwick Uni.'

'Oh, er ... yes, well, we spoke to the security guy, Colin, who promised to double-check why the CCTV footage wasn't available, and then we interviewed Milly Babbington, Richard Sykes and the other flatmates on their floor. The transcripts are on the file.'

'Yes, I've read them, thanks,' said Kat, standing before a flip chart at the top of the table, marker pen in hand. 'But I want to know what your first impressions were.'

'Impressions?' Browne echoed. The low-level nausea she'd been experiencing all day was now blossoming into something much, much worse.

'What did you make of Milly and Richard? Did you believe them?'

Saliva flooded her mouth. She swallowed, fighting the

urge to be sick. God, what if she puked up right here in the Major Incident Room in front of DCS Frank? It would be all round the building in minutes. And then everyone would know before she'd even decided what to do about it. But she daren't make a run for the toilet. Not when her new boss had just asked her a question. *Shit.*

'I didn't believe them,' said Hassan, leaning back and folding his arms.

Cutting in or coming to her rescue? Browne wasn't sure, but she grabbed the chance to take a cautious sip of cold water. *Breathe.*

'The fact that Milly Babbington deleted all the texts between her and Tyrone is pretty suspicious,' he continued. 'And you should have seen her face when I said we could get hold of them anyway. Her boyfriend, Richard, was really dodgy too.'

'Dodgy?' said Lock, from where it was stood behind Professor Okonedo.

'Suspicious. Untrustworthy. He was definitely hiding something.'

'Definitely? I have read the transcripts and I can find no evidence for such a categoric statement,' said Lock, frowning.

Hassan shrugged. 'Trust me, I know a guilty man when I meet one. Richard Sykes is a classic hostile and defensive witness trying to hide his guilt through humour and evasive answers.'

'I beg your pardon, guilty of what?' continued Lock, holding out both hands. 'We have yet to uncover any evidence that a crime was even committed. None of the other flatmates witnessed anything to suggest either Richard Sykes or Milly Babbington were guilty of foul play.'

'He's guilty of lying. They both are.'

Lock pulled an exasperated expression as it turned to face Kat. 'Is this the purpose of debriefs – to ignore the facts and share your prejudices?'

'It's where we share our *opinions*, as well as the facts. And I don't want anyone to filter or edit their views. No hunch is too small. Sometimes they're the ones that lead to a breakthrough. Browne, do you agree with Hassan?'

DS Browne took a deep breath. 'I agree that Milly deleting her texts is suspicious, and she did look a bit worried when we told her we could get hold of them anyway.' She glanced at Hassan. 'But at this stage, I don't think we have any actual evidence to suggest that Sykes is guilty of anything other than being a bit of an irritating sod.' She flushed as she felt – or imagined she felt – Hassan glaring at her.

Kat nodded. 'Okay, well chase up the phone provider and put the pressure on – we need those texts as soon as possible. In fact, get all her texts. I'd like to see the messages between her and Richard Sykes too. And we need the CCTV footage yesterday. We need to keep an open mind and not close any avenues off. But to be honest, the more I learn about Tyrone, the more I suspect foul play.'

Kat went on to give a summary of her interview with Tyrone's mum and when she described their relationship as close and loving, Browne felt her eyes prick with tears. Mrs Walters sounded like such a lovely mum, which just made her think about what a terrible mother *she'd* make.

She wasn't supposed to have kids until she was married, ideally between the ages of thirty-two and thirty-six when her career, relationship and finances would be more stable. This wasn't part of the plan at all.

Browne chewed away at the skin on the side of her thumbnail. She'd be mad to keep it. And yet, even though she couldn't imagine coping with a baby (a *baby!*) she couldn't quite visualise herself having an abortion either. Maybe she wouldn't have to. According to one of the websites she'd been reading, miscarriages are more common in the early weeks, which meant—

'Everybody clear, then?' Kat said.

Browne started. Christ, what was wrong with her? Why couldn't she pay attention? Was it her hormones?

'And while you're following up on Tyrone's case,' continued Kat, 'I'll head to Stratford-upon-Avon tomorrow and interview Will Robinson's parents and we'll catch up in the debrief. Thanks, everyone.' She pressed a button on the steel wrist band, and it seemed to Browne that she smiled as Lock instantly disappeared.

Her boss headed for the door but when she reached Browne, she stopped and turned. 'Everything okay?'

'Er, yes, fine, thanks. I didn't sleep much last night so I'm sorry if I seemed a bit—'

'I told you, don't apologise unless you do something illegal.' Kat perched on the edge of the table and leaned in. 'Look, I recruited you to my team because I saw you follow your heart rather than the rules or the pack mentality. You've got good instincts, Browne. You just need to trust them more.'

And with that, she slipped off the table and out of the door.

Browne dropped her head into her hands. Oh my God, my boss is disappointed with me. She's probably regretting that she ever recruited me. And who could blame her? She looked over to where DI Hassan and Professor Okonedo sat at opposite sides of the table, packing up their stuff. They were both so handsome and smart and clever, exactly the kind of people you'd expect to see on a cutting-edge pilot like this. How could she have thought for even one second that *she* belonged in this team?

Hassan stood up as Professor Okonedo passed him on her way to the door. 'So how are you finding it, Prof O?' Browne heard him ask.

The young scientist looked up at the tall figure blocking her path and frowned. 'My name is Professor Okonedo.'

'I know, I just thought—'

'That you would rename me? That isn't your right, so please, show me the respect of using my full name.'

Even though she probably shouldn't have been eavesdropping, Browne couldn't help letting out an admiring gasp.

'Of course, sorry,' he blustered. 'I was just trying to be friendly. In fact, I was going to suggest that we all go for a drink and get to know each other. My treat.' He waved a hand vaguely in Browne's direction, but his eyes remained fixed upon the pretty young scientist.

'No, thank you.'

'Okay. Bit short notice, I guess. Maybe another night?'

'No, thank you.'

'Look, I'm not coming on to you or anything. It's just that going for a drink is a big part of police culture. Team building and all that.'

'I know. But I'm not a member of the police force, and I'm not a member of your team. I'm here to challenge your culture, not reinforce it.'

'Look,' he said, lowering his voice, perhaps hoping Browne wouldn't hear.

Browne held her breath so as not to miss a word.

'I get it,' he said. 'The force isn't perfect. But we can make it better. We're on the same side, you and me.'

Browne didn't think it was possible for Professor Okonedo to look any more impressive, but with a slow intake of breath, she seemed to grow several inches taller. '*On the same side?* Why, because we're not white?' She shook her head. 'I'm on the side of truth and justice, but I just watched you sit there and claim a man was guilty, based upon nothing more than your own prejudices.' She hoisted her bag over her shoulder, walking with a momentum that forced Hassan to move.

'And by the way, I didn't create Lock to make the police and its culture "better",' she threw over her shoulder as she opened the door. 'My aim is to destroy it.'

CHAPTER THIRTEEN

DCS Kat Frank's home, Coleshill, Warwickshire, 27 June, 7.21pm

'Cam?' Kat called out as she closed the door with her elbow. 'Cam? You in?'

No answer.

Kat kicked off her shoes *(thank fuck for that)*, struggled down the hallway with the shopping and nudged the kitchen door open with her knee. The dodgy one, she remembered, a second too late, wincing. She dumped the bags on the flagstone floor and glanced around. Clean surfaces; closed cupboards. Her son clearly wasn't back yet, so she pulled out her mobile and sent him a quick text.

Just got in. What time you coming home? Chorizo pasta okay?

No answer. Surprise, surprise. Honestly, when he was in the house – which was less and less these days – his phone was like a glowing third hand that went everywhere with him, even the toilet, for Christ's sake. (*'You're not waiting for an organ transplant,' Kat had told him.*) Yet whenever *she* sent her son a text, he either 'wasn't looking at his phone', or was 'out of charge'. She'd given up ringing years ago (*'No one rings anyone these days, Mum'*).

Kat unpacked the shopping, tucking the tortilla chips into the very back of the cupboard and burying the cheesecake beneath a bag of salad in the fridge. She wasn't exactly hiding the best stuff from Cam, just making sure he didn't consume it all within minutes of when he returned – which didn't look like being any time soon. She frowned at her empty phone screen and typed: *Hello???*

Still nothing. To cook or not to cook? Stupid question. She might not know what time he'd be home, but when he did finally return, her son would claim to be 'starving'. Kat poured herself a glass of chilled white wine, savouring the first, steely mouthful as she pulled out the chopping board. At least it would be something to do.

Kat chopped the garlic and chilli while the chorizo fried, then added it to the pan, followed by some sweet red peppers, fresh tomatoes and basil. After the day she'd had, most people would probably order a take-away. But over two decades of rummaging through the flats of drug addicts and alcoholics had given her an aversion to pizza boxes and empty beer cans.

'If only having three different kinds of cheeses in the fridge and a bowl full of fruit could protect you from crime,' John used to tease her. But she still tried to cook from scratch at least five nights a week, and any beer they bought was in fancy, overpriced bottles.

Cam came in just as the water began to boil, pulled

open the kitchen cupboard and rooted out the tortilla chips, claiming he was 'starving'.

'I was just about to put the pasta on,' said Kat. Was that a world record, thirty seconds from door to snack location?

'Not for me,' he mumbled through a mouthful of chips. 'I only popped back to get my ID and change my T-shirt. I'm going to Fergus's for pres.'

'Again?' The first time he'd explained about 'pre-drinks' she'd been foolish enough to imagine Cam and his mates having a couple of aperitifs, but she'd quickly learned that 'pres' was a deceptively harmless word for necking alarming levels of cheap vodka before heading to a pub to drink as many Jägerbombs as they could afford. She didn't want to stop him having fun, but he'd only just stopped being treated for depression. 'You've been out drinking a lot the past few weeks,' she said carefully.

Cam shrugged and spread out his hands. Tanned and muscular, his arms were becoming those of a man, not a child. 'We've just finished our A levels, Mum. It's the summer of celebration.'

'I noticed. What about dinner?' She could at least make sure he lined his stomach.

He dipped a finger into the pasta sauce. 'I'll get some chips on the way.'

'Oh, Cam—'

'I won't be late. Save me some for when I get in.'

He gave her a grin that caught her heart. She really shouldn't complain. This time last year, his depression and anxiety had been so bad that he'd barely left his bedroom, let alone the house. At first, Kat had worried about the disruption to his education, but his therapist had convinced her that the most important thing was to focus on his mental health. And she'd been right. The fact that her eighteen-year-old son would now rather go out with his mates than sit and talk with his middle-aged mum was a good sign, wasn't it? She had to learn to let go. It's just that today was the first time she'd gone out to work since John had died; the first time she'd returned home to the lack of him.

As if reading her mind, Cam nodded towards the suit she was still wearing. 'How was work?'

'Good, thanks. My new team seem pretty decent, but the AI thing's a bit irritating.' She waved her hand, indicating the steel wristband she still wore on her wrist.

Cam's eyes widened. 'They let you bring it home? Seriously? Can I see?'

'It's not a toy, Cam,' she said. But his excitement was infectious, so after explaining the basics, she pressed the button that brought the hologram to life.

'Meet AIDE Lock,' she said, as it appeared in front of her kitchen island. 'Lock, this is my son, Cam.'

'Pleased to meet you,' said Lock with a brief dip of its head, as if to avoid the copper pan that hung just above his head from the solid Tudor beams.

'That is so *cool*,' Cam said as he circled the image of the tall black man. 'Say something else.'

'About what?'

'I dunno. What's it like working for my mum?'

'DCS Frank is clearly an intelligent and experienced detective, but her thought processes are often opaque and irrational, and she gets defensive if her views are challenged.'

'I do not!'

Cam burst out laughing. 'Oh my days, he is brilliant.'

'*It*. Lock is an "it", not a "he".'

'That is the third time your mother has felt the need to correct my pronouns today. I think she feels threatened by my abilities, hence she keeps reminding others of my limitations.'

'You aren't capable of *thinking* anything at all,' pointed out Kat.

'That is your opinion, but the pilot will establish the facts.'

Cam held his phone up to film them both. 'This is so cool.'

'You can't video this,' said Kat, blocking the lens with her hand. 'I'm serious. We haven't made the pilot public yet.'

Cam pulled a face. 'You should. He'd go viral.'

'*It* is not going anywhere,' said Kat, about to switch it off.

'Wait, can't Lock stay for dinner?'

'Holograms don't eat. And anyway, I thought you were going out?'

Cam looked at his phone. 'I am, but I could eat first and meet up with the guys in the pub later. Go on, Mum. I bet it would learn a lot from watching us have a meal together.'

'So, you don't have time to have dinner with me, but you'll make time if I bring the AI?' Kat smiled to prove she wasn't hurt.

Lock looked at her so intently, it was as if it could see right through her smile. Which was completely ridiculous. It could only 'see' through the sensor on her wristband, and anyway, what could a bunch of algorithms possibly know about the human heart? But still, she turned to reach for the pasta so that her face was hidden from view.

Cam offered to set the table in the front room, but Kat insisted they eat in the kitchen. The front room was their personal space, with photographs of the family on the wall, and memories of John in every corner. Instead, they perched on bar stools at the island in the centre of the large kitchen-diner. The hologram image of Lock assumed a sitting position, head turning steadily like the hands on a clock as it appeared to study its surroundings. Most people commented on how well they'd combined the original sixteenth-century features with modern, bright fittings, or how the new windows and patio doors seemed to bring the green Warwickshire countryside into their timber and brick-walled kitchen. Older and bolder friends would ask how on earth they managed to afford it? (Answer: By being crazy enough to buy a run-down cottage on a floodplain and spending a decade of their lives restoring it.)

But Lock wasn't most people. It collected visual data through her bracelet, so all this head turning was just an act. A disturbingly accurate one, though, she noted, as its eyes appeared to register the plates stacked on the draining board behind them, the pink garden roses on the windowsill, her laptop charging on the side and the two steaming bowls of pasta before Kat and Cam. It stared at the empty space before it.

Cam wolfed down the spaghetti, barely bothering to chew in between the questions he fired at Lock: can you feel any physical sensations at all? (No.) Do you wish you could? (No.) Do our thinking processes seem unbearably slow to you? (Yes.) What is the strangest thing about humans? (That you assume you are superior to AI and that it is I who must learn from you.)

Kat concentrated on spooling her spaghetti onto her spoon – she didn't want Lock to see her dribble sauce down her chin – while she listened to them talk. What would John say if he walked in and saw them eating with an AI detective? She took a gulp of the newly opened red wine, wincing at the slightly harsh, tannic taste of Chianti. If it wasn't for AI, she wouldn't have to wonder – John would be sitting with them right now.

She glared at Lock, throat burning with the unfairness of it all. She reached for her wristband, feeling a spiteful urge to switch it off and make Lock vanish, the same way that her beloved John had.

But then Cam laughed at something Lock said, and it was such a healthy, heart-warming sound that she hesitated. Truth be told, John wouldn't be angry to find an AI in his kitchen. He'd be as fascinated as Cam was now. *Keep an open mind*, he'd have advised her. *You might learn something.* Kat sighed. He'd always been her better half. If only she could talk with her husband about the national pilot she was leading; if only he could see how well Cam was doing. He'd be so very, very proud.

'Are you okay, DCS Frank?' asked Lock from where he sat opposite her.

'Yes, why?'

'You look sad.'

The starkness of its response startled her. 'So would you if you had to do the washing up,' she said, rising quickly to her feet. Kat gathered the plates with a force that made the crockery clatter. Honestly, what would an AI – a *machine* – know about sadness? Its facial recognition software was just telling it how my expression might be categorised, she thought. But it doesn't know what it means. How it feels. How it hurts.

Cam's phone pinged. 'Gotta go,' he announced, wiping his face with a bit of kitchen roll. 'Thanks, Mum, that was great. And Lock, good to meet you. See you again soon, yeah?'

Kat loaded up the dishwasher as he thundered up the stairs. More banging. Silence. Toilet flushing. Then he was running back down the stairs.

'Have you got your key?'

Cam held it up, sunlight catching it like a medal. Her beautiful, golden-haired man-boy. 'Bye!'

'What time will you be—'

The door slammed.

'. . . home?'

Kat picked up the bottle and poured herself another glass of wine. She looked up to find Lock watching her.

She switched it off before it could speak, and the image of a man in her kitchen vanished, leaving her utterly alone.

No, she corrected herself. She wasn't alone. Cam might have gone out, but he would be home again in just a few hours' time. Unlike Tyrone Walters or Will Robinson.

She shivered. Kat was very resilient, but she knew she'd never cope if Cam ever went missing. The not-knowing would destroy her. She sat back down at the kitchen island, opened her laptop and the file for Will Robinson. Tomorrow she was interviewing his parents, and she would do everything within her power to give them the answers they deserved.

CHAPTER FOURTEEN

**Will Robinson's home, Stratford-upon-Avon,
28 June, 9.40am**

'We are approaching Stratford-upon-Avon,' said Lock. 'Take a right here to avoid the congestion.'

Kat turned left.

'Why didn't you follow my advice? Was I incorrect?'

'No, your way would have been quicker. But I like driving through the centre.'

'Why?'

Kat ignored it. She liked seeing the crowds of tourists ambling down the narrow, timber-fronted streets: couples on romantic breaks, white-haired coach parties on theatre trips and hordes of hyper schoolchildren, temporarily abandoning their iPhones for the novelty of paper guides. She paused at a zebra crossing and waited for a couple with a toddler in a buggy to cross. The mum squinted through the sunshine and smiled her thanks, while her son banged his chubby little legs up and down, pointing at the ice cream stall opposite.

His mum and dad exchanged earnest glances. Dad raised a questioning eyebrow, but Mum was already reaching for some Tupperware beneath the buggy. Their little boy took one look at whatever was inside the plastic box and exploded into sobs, pointing at what he really, really wanted.

Kat sighed. It wasn't so long ago – at least it didn't seem that long – that she and John had agonised like this poor young couple. Eager to protect their son from every potential harm, they too had carried around plastic bottles filled with water rather than tooth-rotting juice, rice cakes instead of biscuits, dried fruit instead of sweets. It was all so utterly pointless, she wanted to tell them. Once he's old enough to go to the shops by himself, he'll be mainlining McDonald's, Haribo and Coke. So you may as well make him happy now. Buy the poor kid an ice cream. Buy him all the ice creams.

'DCS Frank?'

'Sorry?'

'I believe the cars behind us are waiting for us to advance.'

Kat tore her eyes away and drove towards the river. Both banks were crowded with tourists watching the cruise boats sail by, feeding themselves, the swans and the ducks, or just enjoying the late June sunshine. 'What do we know about where the Robinsons live?' she asked.

Lock explained that Will Robinson and his parents lived in Bridgetown, a wealthy suburb on the east bank of the River Avon, which although it had been built a few years ago, was reached by Clopton Bridge, an ancient river crossing dating back to the fifteenth century. According to the latest census data, the majority of residents were from the professional or managerial classes, aged between thirty and sixty, with a higher-than-average number of self-employed people and high rates of good health.

'Yet this is the case you chose to prioritise,' muttered Kat.

'I have no bias against privilege,' Lock said in its calm, measured voice. 'I just assess the facts. Speaking of which, as less than half a percent of the Stratford-upon-Avon population is black, would it not be best to use one of my white visual representations?'

'Best for whom?' asked Kat. She'd never pandered to any form of racism, and she wasn't about to start now.

They drove on over Clopton Bridge, and the tourists, buskers and ticket touts all fell away. Even the river seemed quieter, as if the swans and ducks knew that all the action – and certainly all the food – was up west. She slowed the car as they entered Browning Close, before stopping outside the Robinsons' home. There was enough space on the driveway for several cars. Yet no garden, observed Kat. Not even a potted plant or hanging basket. The house was huge – what an estate agent might call an 'executive detached five-bedroom family home'. But to Kat, it just looked like two newly built redbrick semis held together by fake Tudor beams.

She climbed out of the car, noting the CCTV camera from above the door, and gave it a sharp knock. As with Mrs Walters, Kat hadn't told them that she was coming. It was a bit rude (and risky – they might not be in), but you could tell a lot from how someone reacted to an unexpected visit from the police: the room they took you into; the doors they quietly closed.

Kat pulled out her ID as someone advanced down the hallway. 'DCS Kat Frank,' she said, holding her badge up to the middle-aged woman wreathed in a floaty silk scarf.

The woman's hand flew to her neck. Her highlighted hair was scooped up into a not-so-casual bun, so Kat witnessed the flush of fear spread from her chest to her cheeks. 'Oh my God, is it Will?'

Kat forced herself to pause. How Mrs Robinson filled the silence would be more revealing than hours of endless interviews.

Mrs Robinson glanced towards the stairs behind her, and said in an urgent, breathless whisper, 'Please don't tell me he's dead. Please don't.'

'We have no further news about your son. I'm just here as part of a formal review. May I come in?'

'Yes, yes, of course,' Mrs Robinson said, sagging with relief. She ushered Kat down the wide, wooden-floored hallway and into the front room (again that glance towards the stairs) before shutting the door behind them. She gestured towards a huge sofa made of some sort of fake brown leather that squeaked as Kat took a seat. It was either very new, or rarely sat upon.

'Can I get you anything?' she asked. 'I've run out of milk, but I've got herbal tea, or black coffee?'

'I'm fine, thank you.'

'Or water?'

'Really, I'm fine. Please, sit down.'

Reluctantly, Mrs Robinson took a seat beside her, and

Kat caught a whiff of perfume: something light, lovely and expensive. 'I'm here because we've decided to do a formal review of your son's case.'

Mrs Robinson gripped her knees. 'Is that because you have new information?'

'No. This is just a routine review, although I should inform you it's part of a wider research project to see whether artificial intelligence might help detectives like me solve cases like yours.' Kat handed her the letter explaining all about the pilot and asked her to sign a consent form to say she was happy for her son's case to be included in the research.

'Will this help find Will?'

'We hope so,' Kat said carefully. She extended her arm and showed her the deceptively simple-looking solid, black, bracelet she was wearing. After warning her what to expect, she switched it on.

Perhaps Mrs Robinson hadn't been paying attention, because although she had nodded wearily and signed all the papers, she gave a little cry of alarm when the virtual image of a black detective appeared in her front room. 'What is *that*?'

'As I explained, this is AIDE Lock, an Artificially Intelligent Detecting Entity. The figure before you isn't real, but the powerful computer it represents is.' She tapped her wristband. 'With your permission, Lock will be able to access and analyse Will's internet history and social media messages, for example.'

Mrs Robinson made a dismissive sound. 'I've already granted access to the police. But nothing ever came of it.'

'That is because police officers do not have the capacity or time to read and analyse the many thousands of texts and social media messages that most young people generate,' said Lock. 'I, however, can carry out such tasks in seconds.'

'It can *speak*?'

'Yes, it can,' said Lock.

Kat shot Lock a 'behave' look and rose to her feet. 'Is this Will?' she said, pointing at the white walls lined with photographs. She walked the length of the room, studying each picture in turn: Will as a toddler in a nativity play, his bright ginger hair poking out from beneath a tea-towel; Will in an infant-class photograph, a mop of orange curls, pink-cheeked and gap-toothed; Will in play after play: *Oliver*, *The Sound of Music* and one of him as the lion in *The Wizard of Oz*, on the cusp of adolescence. So many different costumes and stages, but in each one, Will stood out with his distinctive bright hair and shining, freckled face. Kat paused beneath a huge black-and-white canvas of Will over the fireplace. He was standing alone on the stage, his hair lit like a halo, eyes lifted to the heavens above.

'That's my favourite,' said Mrs Robinson, coming to stand beside her. 'He was absolutely magical as Hamlet last summer. Everybody said so. He studied theatre at university, and this was their final production. He dreamed of being able to perform it at the Globe one day.'

'Does he have any other hobbies or interests?' asked Kat. All the photographs of Will were of him acting. There were none of him just being Will.

'Not really. Will lives to act. From the moment he could walk and talk, it was all he wanted to do.'

Kat studied the immaculate room, trying to imagine Will curled up on the sofa with his mum and dad watching telly, but it didn't seem like that kind of a space. There was a large flat screen on the wall, the huge faux-leather settee and a low (empty) coffee table on a bland, rope-coloured rug. There were no books or piles of papers or discarded shoes. It was all very minimalist – more like a show room than a home.

'Can you tell me a bit about Will?' Kat asked.

Mrs Robinson sighed. 'Will is lovely. He's so very kind. Honestly. He'd help anyone. He's a bit quiet, not a show-off like most actors are these days. When I was a student, the theatre was full of sensitive souls like my Will, but now, well, they've all watched too much *X Factor*. They've all got this incredible self-belief and arrogance that Will finds quite intimidating.'

'Does he have many friends?'

'Gosh, yes. Everyone likes Will, so he's always out. In fact, since he came home from uni, we barely saw him.'

'Does he have a girlfriend?'

'Yes, Shona McPhearson. He met her at uni about a year ago, although I got the impression things were cooling off.' Mrs Robinson's face tightened. 'She moved to London a couple of months before Will went missing, which is why I think he might have gone there to see her.'

Kat made a note to ring Shona on the drive back. 'How did he seem, the day he went missing? Was he upset about anything?'

'He honestly seemed fine,' said Mrs Robinson, twisting her hands together. 'That's what I kept telling them. The other police officers, I mean. He was happy, he'd just got a job at the Royal Shakespeare Theatre that he was really pleased about. He spent most of the day in his room – reading for a part, I think. I offered to make him supper, but he said he was eating out with friends, to celebrate getting his job. I remember he had a shower – his hair was still damp when he kissed me . . .' she touched her cheek, blinking back tears.

'What time was that at?'

'Just after five. I think it was about ten-past. He was in a hurry, running down the stairs and grabbing his trainers from the hall because he said he was late. I asked him if he had his key, what time he'd be home, he said, "not late", and then my phone rang, so I looked away for a minute – not even that, it was seconds really – but when I looked back . . . the door was shut and . . . he was gone.' Her voice broke. 'I didn't know it would be the last time I ever saw him. I can't even remember if I said goodbye.'

Kat gave Mrs Robinson a minute to gather herself, before continuing her gentle probing. 'Did he say where he was going or who he was meeting?'

Mrs Robinson frowned. 'He said he was going to the Swan's Nest in town, but I didn't ask who with. Since he went to university, we lost track of who his friends were, so I couldn't really—'

'But here in Stratford, he must have been meeting up with his old schoolfriends?'

'No, we moved here about one and a half years ago from Birmingham.'

Kat nodded. When Cam was still at primary school,

she'd been shocked by how many parents of missing teen-agers didn't seem to know who their child's friends were. I'll never be like that, she'd vowed. But she didn't know then how hard it would be to keep track of friendship groups without the gossip from the school gate, nor how his virtual networks would quickly transcend the postcode and school they'd spent so much effort moving him into. She still knew a few friends he'd kept from primary school, but once he went to university, what chance would she have?

Kat glanced at the file report on her iPad. 'So, when did you begin to get worried about Will?'

'As soon as he didn't come home. He'd never done that before, not without texting me anyway. I stayed awake, waiting for him to come back. But he never did.'

'So, you were worried about Will on the night of Tuesday, January the 11th,' said Lock, ignoring – or not caring – about the break in her voice. 'Yet you didn't call the police until Friday the 14th. Why was that, Mrs Robinson?'

She closed her eyes, but not before Kat saw the regret and guilt that stained them. 'I didn't want to make a fuss. I thought – I hoped – that he'd met a new girl and gone back to hers. He's twenty-one and used to living by himself at uni, so I didn't want him to think I was treating him like a kid.' Her voice cracked as she gripped her knees. 'I should have rung you earlier. I'll never forgive myself.'

'Please don't be too hard on yourself,' said Kat. 'I have a teenage boy, so I know how it is. I'd have done the same.' She rose to her feet. 'Could we speak to your husband now?'

'No,' Mrs Robinson said, casting a glance towards the stairs. 'My husband is ill. He's resting in bed, and I really don't want to wake him.'

'Oh,' said Kat, frowning. 'Well, would it be possible to see Will's room?' She couldn't get a sense of who Will really was in this impossibly tidy living room that didn't seem lived in.

Mrs Robinson hesitated, before reluctantly leading her towards the stairs. 'It's the attic room at the top. Please be quiet, I don't want my husband disturbed. In fact, would you mind taking your shoes off?'

Kat nodded and bent to remove her shoes.

Mrs Robinson looked meaningfully at Lock's shoes.

'Don't worry,' it said. 'I won't make a sound.'

Kat pushed open the door and stepped into a huge, bright attic room. Despite the size, there wasn't much in it, just a bed, a desk with a computer, and a large bookcase neatly stacked with theatre books.

The windows in the sloped ceiling flooded the room with light, bleaching the white walls and pale wooden floor. The only colour in the room came from the photos that lined the walls, but even they were black-and-white. Kat studied them all one by one. Theatre shots of Will. Again.

She breathed in, wrinkling her nose at the overpowering scent of fake lavender from the plug-in air freshener.

'What is it?' asked Lock, studying her face.

'It feels like a hotel room.'

'Why?'

'Because it's so bloody tidy. Even the bathroom,' she said, eyeing the clean, fresh towels (white, of course) and the immaculate shower cubicle. Mrs Robinson had obviously tidied up, but even so.

Lock frowned. 'Is it not good to be clean and tidy?'

'It's good, but it's not normal – not for a twenty-one-year-old guy just out of uni.' Kat lay down upon Will's bed. 'Are you tired, DCS Frank?'

'I'm just trying to see the world through Will's eyes.' The bed was off-centre and had been positioned so that it lay directly beneath the skylight, presumably so he could have a good view of the sky in the day, and the stars at night. A dreamer, then.

She sat up and took a few photos of the self-portraits, and the sparse, tidy room. 'When did Mrs Robinson say they moved here again?'

'Eighteen months ago.'

'That's why this room feels like a hotel. Because it is. His mum must have decorated it and put up the photos. He only lived here for a few months before he went missing. But he never bothered to make it his own.' She stood up and looked under the bed (empty) and opened the wardrobe (just clothes, all neatly hung up). There were no bean bags or cushions to crash on, no empty bottles from parties or spare beds tucked away for friends. 'Lock, is there anything on the files from his phone or social media accounts? I don't remember seeing anything.'

'Will Robinson had his mobile phone with him when he went missing, so it has never been analysed, and although permission was granted to access his computer, I can see no record of anyone doing so, which is unfortunate, as his phone was probably synced with the Mac. It'll take me less than three seconds to extract everything from the hard drive and cloud.'

Three seconds, Kat thought. Three seconds to download someone's entire life. It was perfectly legal – at least in Warwickshire (different forces had different policies for mobile phone extraction), but it always made her uneasy. Nevertheless, she gave her permission and walked towards the window. It was quiet up here at the top of the house. She could hear birdsong outside, the distant drone of music from a passing car and—

Someone coughed.

She flinched, the way a war veteran might at a sudden bang.

'DCS Frank?' said Lock.

'Shh.' There it was again, hacking through the air: cough, cough, cough.

Kat walked towards the door, tilting her head at the soft tread of footsteps upon stairs, the creak of an opening door, a soothing, soft voice, and then that dread-filled sound that haunted her even now.

Surely not?

She opened the door to prove herself wrong. But there it was. The suck and blow of an oxygen machine, heaving air in and out, in and out, like the ghost of a long-lost ocean.

CHAPTER FIFTEEN

'Of all the gin joints . . .' Kat muttered as she strode down the street, putting the Robinsons' home behind her as fast as she could.

'Pardon?' said Lock, following behind her.

Kat ignored it. Honestly, what were the odds? One of the first house calls she'd made in nearly two years, and it had to be the home of someone with terminal cancer. Of course it bloody did.

'Your pulse and respiratory rate are alarmingly high,' said Lock. 'Perhaps you should slow down?'

'Perhaps you should shut the fuck up.' Kat strode up the hill, ignoring the look of alarm from a passing dog walker. She carried on, shoes striking the tarmac so hard that it made her jaw ache. By the time she reached the path to the riverbank, she was panting heavily and on the cusp of sobbing. She stopped to gather herself, pushing a hand through her hair, now damp with the drizzle that had begun to fall. Jesus, that poor woman. A missing son *and* a dying husband. How on earth does she cope?

Kat snorted at her own question. She had spent eighteen

months as John's carer, so she, of all people, knew that Mrs Robinson had no choice. Shit happens, yet the sun keeps rising, your kids need feeding, the bills still need paying and so you carry on. Not because you are 'brave' or 'strong', but because you must.

When Mrs Robinson had come out of her husband's bedroom, it was like watching a ghost of her former self. Kat's instinct was to rush down the stairs and hug the poor woman beneath the silk scarves and perfume; to tell her that she understood: that she *knew*.

But instead, Kat had held the bannister and her tongue as she followed Mrs Robinson slowly down the stairs. If she'd told her that she understood, then she'd have to tell her about John, and then Mrs Robinson would ask her how he was now, and, well, that was the last thing the poor woman needed to hear.

So, Kat had concentrated on taking notes as Mrs Robinson (call me Gill) explained that when her husband was awarded a professorship at Warwick University, they'd agreed to move to Stratford-upon-Avon, where there was plenty of theatre for her and good railway links for him. In a burst of optimism, they'd sold their home in Birmingham and bought this huge house with enough bedrooms for their semi-retired friends to visit them for boozy, riverside lunches and frequent trips to the theatre.

Only, shortly after they'd moved, her husband had become sick and, well, old friends were less keen to visit the home of a terminally ill man, and she couldn't get out to make new ones. And just when Gill didn't think it could get any worse, their son – their only child – went missing.

'Ah, I see,' said Lock, breaking her train of thought.

'What do you see?' she said, looking up and down the street.

'Your comment about gin joints. You were quoting from the film *Casablanca* – presumably because you find yourself investigating a family in circumstances so similar to your own.'

'My family's circumstances are nothing to do with you,' growled Kat.

'I must say, I found it a most puzzling film. According to Aristotle, a story must have pity, fear and catharsis. *Casablanca* has none of these things. The main character, Rick, is selfish and inconsistent, everybody makes completely irrational decisions, and no one gets what they want in the end. And if Rick loved Ilsa as much as he said he did, why did he let her go?'

'You've seen *Casablanca*?'

'Yes, just now.'

'Just now? That's not possible.'

Lock looked at her with a gentle, almost pitying expression. 'Please do not judge me by your own standards. The film is only 102 minutes long, so it took just 1.7 seconds for me to consume it.'

'You're not here to watch bloody films, Lock. We're supposed to be retracing Will Robinson's footsteps, remember?'

'Unlike humans, I am capable of performing hundreds of tasks simultaneously,' said Lock, spreading out its hands. 'And I never, ever, forget.'

'Then you'll remember that I asked you to shut up.'

Kat climbed over the stile and onto the footpath that ran alongside the River Avon, which was the short cut they believed Will had used to reach the town. The bankside was lined with trees, so she had to keep ducking to avoid the branches, thick with leaves and blossom that dripped with the increasing drizzle.

'DCS Frank, may I make a suggestion?'

'Not unless it's related to the investigation.'

'It is. If you're trying to reconstruct Will Robinson's journey, it might help if I projected an image of him walking along this route?'

Kat glanced around at the empty footpath. 'Okay, but you have to switch it off the minute anyone comes.'

A hologram of Will appeared, a tall, slim stretch of a boy in a white sweatshirt and pale-blue jeans, walking just a few steps ahead. The daylight thinned the image, giving it a ghostly, unearthly appearance that made Kat shiver.

'Will Robinson was six-foot-one,' said Lock, standing directly opposite its own creation on the narrow river-bank. 'I estimate that with his length of stride and the fact that he would have been walking at pace due to his perceived lateness and the increasing rain, he would have reached this location by approximately nineteen minutes past five. On January the 11th, the sun set at 16.16, so it would have been completely dark.'

Kat glanced up. There were lamps along the riverbank, but they were few and far between, so they probably cast more shadow than light.

'In the preceding week, there had been two inches of rainfall, meaning that the riverbank would have been wet and muddy,' continued Lock. It gestured towards Will's feet. 'Will Robinson was wearing a high-end fashion brand of trainers with poor sole grips and inadequate ankle support for walking on non-flat surfaces.'

Lock raised a finger, and the image of Will stumbled in slow motion, his body angled towards the river, arms outstretched to save himself. Lock reached out and the image froze. 'The river level was high enough to warrant warnings of floods and the current was—'

'If you're trying to suggest that Will Robinson fell into the river, then that doesn't explain why he was spotted walking over the bridge at 5.30pm.'

Lock placed a hand on its chin, as if thinking. 'Apart from the proven unreliability of so-called eyewitness statements, may I remind you that Mrs Robinson said her son's hair was damp before he left the house – without a coat or any form of headwear, I might add. At five pm it was already beginning to drizzle, and by the time he reached the river it was raining steadily. I estimate that at least one millilitre of water would have fallen upon Will Robinson, turning his distinctive ginger halo of hair that the witness claims to have seen into a nondescript brown that would have been flattened against his head.'

Lock beckoned towards Will and the frozen image rewound in slow motion, until he was standing once more upon the riverbank. The young man turned to face them.

Kat stared at the unnatural figure before her. Will's pale face was splattered with raindrops, his signature red hair hanging in dark, limp rats' tails about his shoulders. She took a few steps towards him, then stopped herself. 'Okay, that's enough,' she said. 'Switch it off before someone comes along and thinks . . .' What would they think? That someone had just crawled out from the depths of the river, or back from death itself?

She walked briskly towards the bridge and the bright lights of Stratford-upon-Avon. 'Will told his mum he was going to the Swan's Nest to celebrate his new job. Did you find anything on his computer about who he was meeting there?'

'No,' said Lock, perfectly matching her pace as it walked beside her. 'There were no messages on his phone or computer about meeting anybody the night he went missing. Which is strange.'

'Not necessarily. Humans do still sometimes speak face to face, you know.' But even as she said it, she thought of Cam and the hundreds of messages he exchanged with his mates as plans were made, venues changed, times moved back and then back again because someone was 'running late'. They seemed incapable of just agreeing one time and place and sticking to it.

'Were there any messages or emails for Will that day at all?'

'Just one from his new employer, confirming that Will would start work the following week as a barista.'

'A barista? I thought his mum said he had a job at the Royal Shakespeare Theatre?'

'He did. As a barista in the café at the theatre.'

Kat slowed down. 'He didn't tell his mum that though.' The hair on the back of her neck started to prickle and she glanced at the river, dirty brown beneath the darkening sky and flecked with falling rain. 'How long will it take you to analyse his messages?'

'It is done. I have emailed you my report.'

'Really?' She doubted that anything so rushed would be useful, but she could see the distinctive medieval Clopton Bridge up ahead. Will's phone signal had ended at 6pm, somewhere within fifty metres of here. Once they reached it, she rested her iPad against the ancient stone wall and opened the file as the traffic roared behind her. There were several separate documents, so she asked Lock to talk her through it.

It placed its hands against the bridge, mimicking her posture. 'Will Robinson was a higher-than-average user of social media for a twenty-one-year-old male, typically sending over two hundred text messages a day and posting on Instagram and Twitter daily. I've carried out a content analysis of his messages in the three months before he went missing.'

Kat clicked on the first file, which was a word cloud – a pictorial representation of the words Will used most. The more frequently he used them, the larger the letters were. Will's word cloud was an explosion of excitement and positivity: *'Great!' 'Fab!' 'You Star!' 'Wish me luck!' Congrats!!!' 'Thank you!!!' 'xxxxxx'*

Christ, she'd never seen so many exclamation marks on one page. She scrolled down to some screenshots of his (several) Instagram accounts, which again seemed to be mainly photographs of himself. She enlarged them with her fingers, noting the effort he'd made to light and edit them.

'As you can see, he was clearly trying to project a particular image of himself,' said Lock, nodding towards the screen. 'But in addition to the word cloud, I carried out a separate analysis of the internet sites he visited and the music he listened to on Spotify. I think you'll find the results interesting.'

Kat opened the next file, which was a page split horizontally in half. On the top were the positive images and word clouds from his public-facing messages and social media accounts. But beneath the central line on the bottom half of the page was an analysis of the websites Will had visited. Many of them were for theatres or theatrical agents, but then she saw the Samaritans, Mind, Papyrus and other mental health charities. Kat scanned Will's most common search items, noting that key words in his (deleted) search history included 'depression' and, more commonly, 'coping with failure and rejection'. On the next page there was another word cloud, this time made up of Will's music playlist. She didn't recognise the names or bands, but the titles were mostly about broken hearts, lost hope and not wanting to live.

'The gap between Will's public persona and his inner thoughts is quite stark, isn't it?' said Lock. '*Casablanca* confused me because the characters' actions did not align with their professed beliefs and motivations. I assumed that it was a particular weakness of the film, but it appears that it is common for humans to lie.'

Kat looked down into the river below and swore. Will Robinson had been assessed as low risk because, on the face of it, he was a happy, successful young man who lived in a wealthy home with both parents, with no known mental health issues and who'd just landed his first theatre job. She could imagine the attending officers pulling up at the Robinsons' five-bedroomed home, climbing the three flights (*three flights!*) to his room. Still, they would have been thorough, asking Mrs Robinson how old he was (twenty-one, so an adult), and whether she had any reason to suspect he might be a danger to himself or others. Drugs? Mental health issues? History of going missing or self-harm? His mum would have shaken her head in good faith: *no, no, nothing.* And if they'd noticed that Mr Robinson was sick, well, they wouldn't exactly pry and ask what was wrong with him, not when the mother was already so anxious and upset. And just because an adult isn't where other adults think they should be, it doesn't mean that they're officially 'missing', does it? On the face of it, there was absolutely nothing to suggest that Will Robinson was anything other than a low risk. Which meant zero resource was allocated to his case, so they wouldn't have had the time or capacity to do a physical search, and not enough evidence to justify downloading his personal internet and social media accounts.

She could see it as clearly as if she were there herself: the officers making their way back downstairs and into the spacious kitchen, radios crackling with messages from HQ requesting attendance at a call-out – maybe a domestic incident or a drunken fight in town. They'd have quickly taken enough information to fill out the forms, reassured Mrs Robinson that nine out of ten people return home within forty-eight-hours, urged her not to worry and promised to keep in touch.

Kat rested her elbows on the stone bridge, digging her hands into her hair. She'd done it herself. Most of the time, she meant the calm assurances that she gave. But there were times when she'd driven away from a domestic incident knowing that she wouldn't sleep that night, worrying if she'd done enough. Years later, there were still some homes she drove past late at night, wondering if everything was okay.

But there was nothing at the Robinsons' to keep the average officer awake. They'd have driven off without a backward glance and checked up after two days – surprised but not concerned that Will hadn't turned up. The routine checks that kick in at one and three months would have been carried out by a desk-based officer, who in the absence of any new information or resources would have (understandably) left the risk level unaltered, recycling the same assumptions back into the case. It was no one's fault. It was how the system worked, and the more pressure you put a system under, the more things were missed, opportunities lost.

Kat struck her hand against the ancient stone bridge. 'Fuck, fuck, fuck.'

'DCS Frank, I have observed that you use the profanity "fuck" a lot, but it is not always clear to me what it signifies in each particular context. It appears to be a word with many meanings.'

Kat sighed. 'In this particular context it means I think we fucked up. It means I think Will Robinson may have taken his own life.'

'And you are angry about that?'

'I'm angry. And frustrated. But most of all, Lock, I'm just very, very sad.'

Lock studied her with a gaze so intense that she had to look away. 'I'm sorry you are sad,' it said. 'But I agree it's now more likely that Will Robinson died by suicide, rather than from misadventure as I initially presumed. In fact, he may have jumped from this very bridge. Would you like me to recreate—'

'No! Jesus, Lock.' She was going to add 'What's wrong with you?' But Lock was just a machine, so it had no idea how upsetting and inappropriate it might be to recreate a suicide attempt. Kat turned her back on the river – she really didn't want to look at that river now – and took a deep breath of the rain-soaked air. If only the attending officers had been a bit more curious, they could have raised the risk level and instigated an immediate search.

But it was too late to do anything about it now. Kat ran a hand through her damp hair, which was already starting to tangle and curl. Jesus, how could she tell a woman who was about to become a widow that she may have lost her only son?

'We have enough evidence to justify a full river search,' said Lock.

'No, we don't. A few late-night web searches do not count as evidence,' she said. 'There's plenty of CCTV cameras around this bridge. Have we checked them or any of the other cameras along the route for any sign of Will?'

'The report from the attending officers says that footage was not available.'

'Do you mean there wasn't any footage, or they couldn't get access to it, or they couldn't be bothered?'

'The report does not state the reason.'

'Well, find out. Get hold of the footage and do whatever it is that you do with your "image recognition software". Until then, we keep an open mind.'

'But—'

'CCTV footage is evidence. Everything else is speculation. The thing about humans, Lock, is that you need to pay less attention to what they say and watch what they actually *do*. It's chucking it down now. I'm heading back to the car.'

CHAPTER SIXTEEN

Walking back along the riverbank did little to improve Kat's mood. Her feet kept slipping in the mud, and although she managed to avoid most puddles, there was no saving her trousers from the rain-soaked grass. The River Avon raced beside her, faster than she could walk. She watched her step, wary of tripping over a root or slipping on the slimy, mulchy leaves, thinking how much more treacherous this path would have been on a January night, the river swollen by winter rains and melting ice and snow. By the time Kat reached her car, she was weighed down with water, her wet trousers chafing at her calves.

Mrs Robinson opened the door just as Kat reached her car. Her pale anxious face searched Kat's. 'Did you find anything?'

Trying not to sigh – she'd hoped to drive off without being seen – she took a few steps forward and stood beneath the porch. 'No, it was just a routine check. I'm going to go back to the office now, but I'll be in touch soon. I promise.'

'Please,' Mrs Robinson said, before she could turn away. 'You have to find him. For my husband's sake.'

Kat swallowed. 'I'll do my best. I do realise how awful this uncertainty must be at a time when he needs peace.'

Mrs Robinson dropped her eyes.

'You have told him, haven't you?'

Mrs Robinson looked up, face streaming with tears. 'I can't. It would kill him. I told him that Will got a job in London.'

The rain drummed on the porch above them.

'Is that why you waited so long to ring the police?'

'I didn't want to worry him. I still don't.'

'But . . . surely he has a right to know?'

'My husband has a right to die in peace.'

'But—'

'Just *find* him. Please. And then I won't have to tell him. He's alive. I know he is. He wouldn't run away and leave me with his dad like this.'

The two women stared at each other.

'Just to be clear, you don't *know* that your son is alive,' said Lock, appearing at Kat's side. 'You just hope that he is. But I'm afraid the risk of fatality for young men who go missing after a night out in the winter months is very high. Sixty per cent of those missing for more than two days will be found dead and eighty-nine per cent of those will be recovered from water. So, it would be wise to expect the worst, Mrs Robinson.'

After she'd given a distraught Mrs Robinson a cup of tea and provided more assurances and apologies than she could count, Kat finally said goodbye, shutting the front door shut behind her with a heavy sigh.

She glared at Lock, who was standing completely untouched by the rain that fell through it.

'I sense from your vital signs that you're not happy.'

'No. I'm not. In fact, I'm *fucking* furious.'

'At what?'

'At *you*. Why on earth did you say her son was probably dead?'

'Because it's true.'

Kat strode towards it. 'It doesn't matter if it's true. You can't go round saying things like that.'

'Why not?'

'*Why not?*' Kat threw her hands up. 'Because … because … you just *can't.*'

'Are you saying I should have lied? My anti-corruption software prevents me from lying. And the guidance clearly states that with the exception of covert operations, police officers are always supposed to tell the truth.'

She rubbed a weary hand over her rain-soaked face. 'We're supposed to *help* people, Lock. To make their miserable, shitty lives just a little bit easier. And that includes giving them hope.'

Lock frowned, causing a single neat crease to form between its thick, dark eyebrows. 'But what if that hope is false? How does giving someone false hope make things better?'

Kat took a step closer, their faces only separated by the rain that fell between them. 'All hope is false, but it's the only thing holding that poor woman up at the moment.

And you took it away from her.' She stabbed its chest with her finger, staggering slightly as her hand passed right through it.

Why was she even wasting time arguing with this thing? She walked straight through it to make her point, though it was she, rather than Lock, who shivered. Her voice was low and hoarse as she opened the car door. 'You've got a lot to learn about human beings, Lock, and until you do, you only speak when you're spoken to. Got that? Meanwhile, if I ever catch you crushing someone's hopes like that again, then I swear to God, I'll crush your batteries.'

CHAPTER SEVENTEEN

INTERVIEW CONDUCTED BY TELEPHONE

Interviewer: DCS Kat Frank (KF)
Interviewee: Shona McPhearson (SM)
Date/Time: 28 June, 5.35pm

KF: Hi, is that Shona McPhearson?

SM: Yes?

KF: My name is DCS Frank, and I'm calling you in connection with a missing person case, Mr Will Robinson.

SM: Will? Oh my God, have you found him? Is he okay? Is he ... oh God.

KF: No, we haven't found him yet, I'm afraid. That's why I'm ringing. I'm leading a review of his case, and I was hoping that you might be able to help us by answering some questions.

SM: Oh, well ... er ... I answered a load of questions when he first went missing, so I'm not sure I can add anything to what I've already said, to be honest.

KF: Anything you can do to help us find him would be really appreciated.

SM: Of course, yes, I—

KF: That's brilliant, thanks so much. I've just been to visit Will's mum, and she said that you're his girlfriend?

SM: Um, well, yes, I was. Sort of. We got together the summer before last. We both had roles in *Hamlet*, so we used to rehearse together, go for drinks after and then, yeah. We ended up being together for a bit.

KF: How long?

SM: Well, things were kind of tailing off by last spring, to be honest. We had our finals, and we both needed to revise. After our exams we started seeing each other less and less, and then Will went home to his parents, and I got a job in London, so things just tailed off.

KF: And how did Will take that?

SM: He honestly seemed fine. I think he was relieved, to be honest.

KF: When was the last time you actually saw him?

SM: New Year's Eve. We both went to a party some of our friends were having in Birmingham.

KF: And how did he seem?

SM: *[sighs]* I keep going over and over it in my head. The thing is, it was New Year's Eve. I was drunk. Will was drunk. Everyone was drunk. But he seemed really happy. Well, he was upset about his dad, obviously, but he seemed happy in himself, if you know what I mean.

KF: So, you wouldn't say Will was depressed?

SM: Will? No. The thing is, most theatre students, well, we're all pretty bonkers. You have to be, to get up on stage and pretend to be someone you're not in front of a room full of strangers. Everyone in our class suffered from one kind of anxiety or another, except Will. He wasn't interested in being famous. He just loved the theatre and he was so chill about everything. He was the one who talked everyone else out of a panic attack or depression.

KF: He was struggling to get an acting job, though. Do you think that, and his dad's illness, could have made him depressed?

SM: *[pauses]* Who knows what goes on inside another person's head? But if you're asking me whether I think he took his own life, the answer's no. Will would never kill himself.

KF: Why do you say that?

SM: He played Hamlet, so we discussed that soliloquy a lot – you know, the famous one: 'To be or not to be?' Will just couldn't understand how anyone could ever be so down that they'd consider taking their own life. Even though his own dad was terminally ill, he said he couldn't imagine ever giving up. He had to work so hard to get inside Hamlet's head, because even though he was about to lose his dad, just like Hamlet had, his own approach to life was so different.

KF: I see. That's very helpful Ms McPhearson, I really

appreciate your time. Please don't hesitate to contact me on this number if anything else occurs to
you. Anything at all.

SM: I just hope you find him.

INTERVIEW CONCLUDES

CHAPTER EIGHTEEN

Something is wrong.

He holds his breath, straining his ears.

Silence.

He reaches out in the blindfolded dark. This is his bed – no, not his bed – their bed. Everything is the same as it has been for the last few ... weeks?

Except ... except ...

He sits up, and his shirt gapes open.

His heart batters his ribs. Someone has undone the buttons while he slept, leaving his chest naked and exposed.

He pulls the shirt tight around his narrow frame, rocking backwards and forwards as he holds himself together. Images flood his brain, each one worse than before. Is this why he's been drugged and blindfolded, so that he can be abused by some old pervert? Has he been taken by some sort of sex ring? His mouth floods with saliva, stomach churning with sick as he fights the thought. No. The way The Stranger had touched his feet, then removed and replaced his trousers – it hadn't felt sexual. More like an inspection. Are they filming him? Planning to sell him?

Bastards. Dirty fucking bastards. He'll break their arms if they try and touch him again.

Which is why they're drugging you, says another, more despairing voice. Every time you wake up, they just inject you with more drugs. You can't even think straight, let alone fight them off.

It was true. It was like they anticipated when the drugs were wearing off. Or maybe they were watching him on a camera, because normally The Stranger would come in just as he was waking and—

He tilts his head, testing once more the silence of the room. They should be here by now. But they're not. That's why he can think straight, for a change. Whatever they've been giving him must have worn off. He punches the air, but his hand sinks as he suddenly realises what's wrong.

It's not just quiet. It's completely and utterly silent. He frowns, trying to remember the last time he heard The Other Guy cry out. Yesterday? He pops his ears, sniffs the air. Something has changed. But what? Maybe his captor has left. This could be his chance.

He grasps the metal bars to haul himself out of the bed. But with the touch of the cold, hard metal, doubt rushes in. How can he escape when he can't see a thing? He has no idea where the door is, how to open it or what lies on the other side. He could be deep in someone's basement. Or high up in someone's bedroom. There could be a two-way mirror for all he knows, or a camera, watched by an armed guard.

Shit. He tugs at his blindfold for the hundredth time.

Usually, his fingers are too numb and weak to do more than pull ineffectually at it, but today, without the drugs, he is finally able to focus and to think about and execute every tiny movement, and conscious enough to note there is a narrow, plastic tube taped to it, which has been inserted into his nostrils. He probes the edges of the material, and in the gap between his right ear and jawbone, he manages to squeeze the tip of his forefinger beneath the coarse cloth – no more than the edge of his fingernail, but enough to begin to stretch and loosen a patch.

He hears footsteps before the door clicks.

Shit. He drops to his back; holds his frantic breath.

Approaching footsteps: The Stranger.

They grab his left hand, which is bandaged with some sort of tube in it.

He wants to pull away, but his mind is so incredibly, beautifully lucid right now, he knows that this would be a mistake. They mustn't discover that he's awake. That would just make them increase the dose. He needs them to think that he's out for the count, so that they just top him up and leave.

He remains still. He remains quiet. Even as the ice-cold drugs invade his punctured veins. Even when a mobile phone vibrates, filling the room with an angry buzz.

'Hello?' says The Stranger. A woman, older, with a clipped, posh accent. 'Thanks for calling back. It's just I thought you'd want to know. I'm afraid we've lost another one.'

The hum of another voice on the end of the phone. Deep-voiced. Few words. Male.

'Yes, it's all arranged,' replies The Stranger. 'We'll dispose of the body in the usual way. There's no need to worry. And yes, we've still got the other one. He's doing well. Yes. Of course. Thank you.'

Fuck.

He manages to keep his breathing steady as she ends the call, heart racing as he feels the drugs flooding his veins once more. He bites back the urge to scream NO! Forces himself to wait for the receding steps.

The instant the door closes, he lets out a retching sob. The Other Guy is dead. And he's clearly not the first: 'we've lost another one'.

He tears at his blindfold, fighting against the pull of the drugs. If he doesn't get out of here soon, he will be next.

CHAPTER NINETEEN

DCS Kat Frank's home, Coleshill, Warwickshire, 28 June, 8.21pm

Kat scraped the Thai curry she'd made but not eaten into a Tupperware box for Cam and put the pan to soak. She knew she needed to eat more – her suits were starting to hang on her – but her appetite had gone. She should probably have a cup of tea and an early night. But fuck it. It wasn't every day you found yourself looking for two missing boys whose mums either were or about to become widows. She poured herself another glass of wine (for the calories), grabbed a throw and headed out into the garden.

The sun was just sinking behind a row of trees at the back, but they were lucky enough to have a walled garden that held on to the heat of the day. The distant Warwickshire hills patterned with fields of bright yellow rapeseed and deep-green hedges fed the illusion that they were in the heart of the countryside, rather than just a few hundred yards from the Coleshill Industrial Estate. It was the location and the threat of floods that had put the neglected Tudor-beamed cottage within their price range, where they'd spent more years and money than she cared to remember creating a home for Cam to grow up in, and (they'd naively assumed) a haven for them to retire to.

Kat sank into her favourite rattan chair that faced the sun, put her feet up on John's, and averted her eyes from the overgrown grass and the weeds sprouting between the cracks in the patio. She took a deep breath, inhaling the scent of honeysuckle that embroidered the side wall, mingled with the spicy tang of neighbours' barbecues. The air hummed with soft, summer-night conversations and other people's children.

Kat took a few deep breaths and tried to relax. But it was no use. John should be here, making her laugh and giving her his blunt, wise advice.

'Oh, sod the breathing exercises, Kat. Just have another glass.'

She closed her eyes. What would he make of Will Robinson's case? Was Lock right? Should she organise a search of the river? Was she letting his mum's situation affect her judgement? After twenty-five years together, she knew exactly what John would say, in his soft, Welsh voice.

'You can't go around upsetting folk without good cause, and you haven't even got hold of the CCTV footage yet. You made the right call, Kat. Trust your gut. It's a bloody good one.'

But what would John make of Lock? Her husband had suffered so much: sometimes it felt like a betrayal to be working with the very technology that had fatally misdiagnosed him. 'Am I doing the right thing?' she asked John, opening her eyes.

But he was gone.

The air filled with the mournful peal of bells from nearby Coleshill Church, an eternal reminder of the relentlessness of time. People were always telling Kat that they were 'sorry for her loss', as if she'd just mislaid her husband somewhere. *He's not lost*, she'd wanted to shout in those early days of furious grief. *He's dead. Dead. (And that didn't mean that he was in a 'better place' either, thank you very much. How could anything be better than being here, home and alive with his wife and son?)*

No. John wasn't lost. But Tyrone and Will were. Kat took another gulp of her wine, thinking of their poor mums. What would it be like to truly lose the person you most loved, to literally not be able to find them? To occupy a no-man's land, unsure whether to grieve, or search, unable to do anything other than wait and suffer the agonies of not knowing?

Kat stared up at the darkening sky. They shouldn't have to. No one could bring John back, but there was still a chance she could find these boys, or at the very least provide the families with the answers they deserved.

Her phone buzzed, making her jump. McLeish. She sat up, frowning. It was nearly ten pm. 'DCS Frank?'

There were no preliminaries from her boss. 'Why the fuck did you tell facilities that I'd given you permission to use the Incident Room when I've done no such thing?' he growled. 'The new suite on that floor is reserved for Major Incidents.'

'I know, that's why we're poised and ready to vacate

the room the minute an MI is called,' Kat said. 'But right now, it isn't being used, and I don't want you vulnerable to criticism that you're setting us up to fail.'

'Excuse me?'

'Well, you've not exactly made a secret of your view of AI, and everyone knows that I'm one of "your people". So, if this pilot ends up concluding that AIDEs aren't effective, then the amount of support and resources you gave it is going to come under scrutiny. Don't make it easy for them.'

McLeish paused. She could feel his unblinking stare even over the phone. 'I can tell when you're trying to manipulate me, you know.'

There was no point trying to deny it.

'But as usual, you're right. It's one of your most annoying qualities. But next time you use my name in vain, speak to me first.'

She tried to assure him she would, but McLeish had already moved on and wanted to know how the pilot was going.

Kat told him how Lock's relentless focus on facts had potentially demotivated her team on their first day and how it had upset Mrs Robinson by telling her that her son was, in all probability, dead. Then, still wincing at the memory, she told him about how distressed Mrs Walters had been when she saw the image of her missing son in his bedroom. 'It might have artificial intelligence, but honestly, Lock has no *emotional* intelligence at all,' she concluded.

'Good. Make sure that quote goes in the report.'

Kat frowned. She was just giving her opinion, not a line for a press release. 'On the other hand,' she added, 'I have to admit that Lock did some really useful analysis of social media usage. It would have taken days for an officer to read through all the messages and produce analysis of a similar quality.'

'Well, I guess it's important to be balanced. But don't get carried away. Keep me informed, Kat.'

'I will. Which reminds me, what do you know about Professor Okonedo? She's clearly not a big fan of the police.'

'She isn't. Her elder brother was arrested for drug dealing a few years ago and she and her family maintain that he was fitted up following a stop and search.'

'And was he?'

'According to the jury he was guilty,' said McLeish. He paused. 'But the arresting officer was DI Dent.'

'Shit,' said Kat. 'Dent the Bent' was currently on suspension for alleged corruption of witnesses and obtaining a false confession, among other things. He represented everything she and McLeish had worked so hard to root out when they worked at the West Mids force together.

'It's shit with bells on,' McLeish said in his gravelly Glaswegian voice. 'Which means Professor Okonedo will be looking for any excuse to prove that her machine can do a better job than a corrupt, incompetent and expensive police force. Don't give her that chance.'

'Well, on that point, you need to know that the missing person cases we're reviewing were initially assessed as low risk,' she said, before telling him a bit about each case. 'I'm going to increase Tyrone Walters' case to medium, and I might have to change Will Robinson to high.'

'Do *not* tell me there was a cock-up. I am not going to have some glorified computer expose flaws in my force.'

'Not exactly, but the attending officers failed to notice that the father of Will Robinson had terminal cancer, and this, plus a broken relationship and failure to get a job, should have flagged a clear suicide risk. That's my analysis, by the way, not Lock's.'

McLeish was silent.

'Sir?'

'Are you sure you aren't letting your own personal experience cloud your judgement here?'

The blood rushed to her face. With a huge effort, she managed not to swear at her boss. 'That is *not* why I want to increase the risk level.'

'I know you, Kat. That's why I'm wondering why out of a possible twenty-eight cases you ended up focusing on two boys about the same age as Cam with dead or dying fathers.'

'It was a coincidence. I didn't even know about their dads until we met their mothers. And anyway, Lock picked Will Robinson, not me.'

McLeish was silent long enough to communicate his doubt. 'It's your call,' he said eventually. 'But don't forget, we've only got permission to pilot the AI on cold cases. If at any time either case becomes active, you'll need to hand it back to the local teams. Are we clear?'

'Absolutely.'

'So, don't get too involved.'

This time it was Kat who remained silent.

*

151

Kat checked her phone as she finished loading the dishwasher. Nearly 1.30am and still no word from Cam. Where had he said he was going again? He usually drank in the Harvester because of the large beer garden, but that closed at half-eleven, so he should have been home ages ago. Her gut pinched as she remembered what Lock had said about nights out and rivers. The Harvester was located right by the River Cole.

The key turned in the lock.

'Cam?'

'S'me,' he said, coming into the kitchen.

'You okay?'

'Yeah. Starving though. Anything I can eat?'

'Why didn't you tell me you were going to be so late?'

He frowned. 'I did. I told you I was going to the pub.'

'But not this late. Jesus, Cam, it's one-thirty in the morning. *And* you didn't reply to my texts.'

'We went back to Fergus's after. We were having fun. No one else got a text from their mum. I'm eighteen, for fuck's sake,' he muttered.

'Don't you *dare* swear at me.'

'What are you going to do, arrest me?' His lip curled. 'You'd like that, wouldn't you? Then you could lock me up in prison and always know where I was.'

'Cam!' Kat took in his bleary-eyed face, fighting down the urge to shout back. 'You're drunk,' she said finally. 'I'm going to bed.'

'Whatever,' he said, heading rather unsteadily towards the cupboards.

She hesitated at the door. It didn't seem that long ago

that she'd had to lift him to reach the top cupboards. The weight of his small, solid body, squirming with delight at the prospect of a chocolate biscuit, was etched into her very bones. Did she ever imagine that one day that sweet little boy would swear at her?

Kat stared at the back of his blond head and impossibly broad shoulders, resisting the pull of the past. Mrs Walters and Mrs Robinson would give anything to be in her shoes right now.

'There's some Thai curry in the fridge you can microwave,' she said. 'And make sure you drink a glass of water before going to bed, Cam. Goodnight. I love you.'

She headed down the hall and locked the front door. Her son was home. He was safe. It was enough.

CHAPTER TWENTY

DCS Kat Frank's home, Coleshill, Warwickshire, 29 June, 7.37am

Kat had to admit it was useful to have all the interviews and notes instantly transcribed by Lock, and to be able to switch between reading and audio as she showered and brushed her teeth. After listening to the interview with Milly Babbington, she walked downstairs to put her glass in the dishwasher and . . .

'Oh, for fuck's sake.' From the trail of crumbs on the floor and the dirty (now encrusted) plate on the side, Kat deduced that her son had reheated the red Thai curry with some bread. Was it too much to expect him to wash up? Or at least put the pan to soak? She glanced at the clock. She really should get going, but if there was one thing worse than coming home to an empty house, it was coming home to an empty house full of dirty dishes.

Trying to avoid getting any food on her suit (new grey wool – a bit hot for June, but the other one was in the dry-cleaners) Kat carefully picked up Cam's plate, rinsed it and put it in the dishwasher. She was just about to tackle the pan when the letter box clattered, making her jump.

She headed down the hallway and stooped to pick up the slim white envelope from the doormat, wincing at the sight of the blue NHS logo. When John was ill, their lives had revolved around these innocent-looking letters that set the date for his next appointment, triggering yet another round of 'scanxiety' with bouts of hope and despair. These days, the only letters she got from the NHS were reminders that her cervical smear was overdue (again), so she slipped a thumb beneath the corner flap, before noticing it was addressed to Cameron Frank. Kat still hadn't quite got used to the fact that her child now received his own post and she had to physically resist the urge to continue opening it. Her son was eighteen, after all. It was *his* letter. Private to him. Still, she turned it over and peered at the window in the envelope as she climbed the stairs to his room. Christ, was he ill? Was there something he hadn't told her? His therapist was private, so she wouldn't write on NHS paper. And anyway, he wasn't seeing her any more.

Kat reached his room with a nagging ache in her knee-cap, and more breathless than she cared to admit. She knocked the door.

'Yeah?'

'I'm leaving for work now.'

'You woke me up to tell me that?'

Kat opened the door. 'No, I woke you up to tell you that I love you, but I'll love you more if you're up and dressed before noon and clean your dirty dishes.'

He laughed, soft and sleepy. 'Yeah, course. Sorry about last night, Mum.'

'Don't worry about it. There's croissants in the bread bin for breakfast, and fishcakes in the fridge for lunch.'

'Cool.'

'And you've got mail.'

'What?'

Her son was too young to get the film reference, but she didn't have enough time to explain, so she put the envelope on his desk. 'You've got a letter. From the NHS?'

Kat waited, hoping that he'd open it, hoping he'd explain. But her son remained in bed, eyes stubbornly closed. She glanced at her watch. 'I've got to go now, but please don't stay in bed late. I mean it, Cam. I know you've finished school, but you know how important routine is to your mental health.'

He groaned at the mini-lecture, before mumbling he loved her in a way that gave her zero confidence he'd be up any time soon.

But she had to go.

Slamming the front door behind her *(maybe that might wake him up?)*, Kat climbed into the car. She tried to turn the key, but the NHS logo still burned in her mind. What if Cam had some terrible illness that he was too afraid to tell her about? Despite being an atheist, Kat began silently bargaining with all the gods, trading anything she could think of if only they would guarantee her son's health.

'Do you want to take a moment?' said Lock softly.

'What?'

'For some reason you are clearly distressed. Your heart

and respiratory rate are both very high. I suggest you practise deep breathing for one minute until both are under control.'

'And I suggest you mind your own bloody business,' Kat snapped, pulling Lock off her wrist and throwing it onto the passenger seat. 'You are not my fucking Fitbit.'

CHAPTER TWENTY-ONE

**Leek Wootton Police Headquarters, Warwickshire,
29 June, 9.00am**

Kat kicked off the team briefing by sharing what she'd
discovered at Will Robinson's home, ending with a few
seconds of fuzzy black-and-white footage taken from
the home CCTV camera. It was 5.07pm on 11 January,
so the front driveway was dark, until the security lights
switched on to reveal the back of Will's long, thin, denim-
clad legs advancing away from the house. He reached the
end of the gravelled driveway and turned right, his bright
orange hair and ghost-white face briefly illuminated by a
nearby lamppost.

Will carried on walking and then, in the blink of an
eye, he was gone.

Kat rewound the footage and played it again, freezing
on that final image of Will turning the corner. He didn't
look back: there was no hesitation in his step, nothing
in his movements to suggest that he would never see his
family or his home again. Without speaking, she left the

image on the screen, so that Will's absence remained in the room.

'What do we feel about the level of risk assigned to this case? The attending officers ranked it as low, and this was confirmed at the three-month review. Are we okay with that?' Kat looked at Browne – she still looked worryingly pale – and willed her to go first.

'Er . . .' said Browne, consulting her notes. 'According to the criteria for risk-assessing missing persons, it seems pretty clear to me that Will Robinson should have been assessed as a high risk of suicide by the attending officers.'

'Seriously?' said Hassan, leaning back in his chair. 'Just because he had to go and live with his parents in their five-bedroomed house, and didn't get a top acting job within a few months of graduating? Honestly, by that reckoning, half the arts graduates in the country should be on suicide watch.'

'No,' said Browne, her cheeks flaming. 'Because he had recently suffered a relationship break-up and his dad had terminal cancer. Bereavement is one of the key indicators on the criteria for—'

'Never mind the criteria,' said Hassan. 'Why would an only child kill himself when his dad was so ill? Surely that's the last thing he'd do to his mum?'

Kat turned away and stared at the grainy CCTV image. Hassan's question came from a place of ignorance. He didn't know what it was like for a young man to watch his dad slowly die: to bear witness to what no son should ever have to see. Day after day, night after night, powerless to do anything other than sit and wait in silent terror for death to finally arrive. But there was no point trying to describe or explain the trauma that Will Robinson had endured. It was beyond the reach of words.

'So, you don't think he killed himself?' Kat asked.

'I'm not saying I don't think he killed himself, I'm just pointing out that we don't have any actual *evidence* that he did,' Hassan replied, looking over to where Professor Okonedo sat at the end of the table, typing on her laptop with neat, rapid movements. 'There was no formal diagnosis of depression, just a few internet searches. Nor do we have any actual evidence that he was struggling to cope with his dad's illness. They're both just assumptions.'

Kat frowned as her DI glanced over at the young professor again. Why was he seeking her approval? She wasn't in charge of the team.

Hassan held up his mobile. 'Look, if I fell under a bus today, a review of my internet history would show that I'd recently been on the Samaritans, Mind and Papyrus websites. A stranger might *assume* that I was depressed and chucked myself under a bus, but actually, I was just researching the sites that Will visited. And remember, his girlfriend said he was fine, and that he'd never kill himself.' He shrugged. 'I'm just trying to be more evidence-based, like Lock.'

Kat saw Professor Okonedo roll her eyes. At least she wasn't fooled by his blatant attempt to impress her.

'What you are doing is selectively interpreting the evidence to bolster your own preferred theory, rather than sticking to the facts,' said Lock as it began to pace the room, a tall, dark-suited figure that commanded their attention.

Kat's eyes narrowed. Was it copying her? She suppressed her irritation and invited it to summarise the facts as it saw them.

'The facts are that eighty-seven per cent of adults are found within two days,' said Lock. 'Eight out of ten missing adults have an undiagnosed mental health issue, so given his gender, age and imminent bereavement, the most valid hypothesis is that Will Robinson died by suicide. I therefore agree with DS Browne that according to the criteria set out in the College of Policing guidelines this case should be re-categorised as high risk and you should initiate an immediate search of the River Avon.'

Hassan puffed out his cheeks, but Browne gave Lock a grateful smile.

'Thank you, Lock,' said Kat, standing next to where it stood at the head of the table. This was, after all, *her* meeting. 'I agree our working hypothesis *at this stage* should be that Will Robinson may be dead, possibly by his own hand. But Hassan is right. We don't have any hard evidence – not enough to justify the cost of a river search. That's why I asked you to prioritise getting hold of all the CCTV footage.'

'No,' said Lock, turning to face her. 'You asked me to prioritise the CCTV footage because you did not wish to upset Mrs Robinson or her sick husband.'

Hassan and Browne exchanged glances.

'Are you challenging my order?'

'No. I was merely clarifying the reasons behind it.'

Kat clenched her fists. 'You are just a machine, Lock. Do not presume to know the reasons behind the judgements of your superior.'

Lock raised both eyebrows. 'I accept that, managerially speaking, you are my "superior". But I object to the modifier "just".'

'You *object*?'

'I do. That is why I said it.'

Kat took a deep breath. She wasn't going to demean herself by arguing with a machine. 'Just focus on getting the CCTV footage, Lock. Some of it will be owned by the council or the river authority, some of it will belong to private businesses in and around the Swan's Nest, so it won't be straightforward, but I want all of it. Every single camera, got that?'

She turned to Browne. 'And I want you to speak to Will's GP, see if he ever went there for depression or had a counsellor at uni. Track down the friends he was supposed to be meeting at the Swan's Nest and find out if he was really setting off to meet them or whether that was a lie. Let's test our working hypothesis and see if there's any actual evidence to stack it up, okay?'

'What about Will's father?' said Lock. 'In the majority of cases where a missing person has come to harm, it has been at the hands of a male relative or close family friend. The statistics suggest he should be interviewed as a matter of priority.'

'But those statistics are based upon averages, whereas in this *particular* case, the poor man's dying. He's not a suspect, so I am not going to subject him or his wife to more unnecessary pain just to show I've ticked all the boxes.' She gave Browne a meaningful look. 'Guidelines are just that – guidelines. Sometimes we have to have the confidence to exercise our professional judgement. Right,' said Kat, signalling that the discussion was over. 'Let's move on to Tyrone. I read the interview with the campus security guy. Do we have the CCTV footage yet?'

'I received digital copies of footage from the five hundred cameras on campus during the week that Tyrone went missing last night,' said Lock.

'Good. Let me know as soon as the analysis is completed.'

'I completed it twelve hours ago.'

'What? Why didn't you tell me?'

'You did not ask. And you told me not to speak until I was spoken to.'

Kat opened her mouth, about to ask whether it was taking the piss, but she couldn't be arsed with having to explain what 'piss' was 'in this particular context'. 'Look, in future, just tell me the minute you complete any of the tasks assigned to you.'

'Are you sure about that?' said Professor Okonedo, looking up from her laptop.

'Yes, I'm sure,' she said, irritated by the apparent lack of common sense that had just lost them twelve hours.

'Very well,' said the young scientist, tapping away at her keyboard. 'I'll amend Lock's settings so that it can activate itself when it has information to share with you.'

Kat perched against the edge of the table in front of one of the large screens and asked Lock to show them what it had found.

'Before viewing the CCTV footage,' said Lock, 'I think it would be helpful if the team studied this model of Warwick Campus.'

It gestured towards the boardroom table, and Kat belatedly realised that she was a giant sitting among mini 3D redbrick buildings, and that her left buttock was immersed in the image of a toy-sized lake. She slid off the edge and stepped back, arms tightly folded.

'This,' said Lock, stretching out its arms to enlarge a building on the upper-right quadrant of the table, 'is Tyrone's hall of residence, Lakeside Village. We know that Tyrone exited this building at 3.30am on Thursday January the 27th. The CCTV camera at reception captured this footage of him leaving the building.'

A black-and-white image of a young man appeared on the TV screen, his face hidden by the hood of a dark puffer jacket as he headed for the exit. Just as the door opened, he glanced back. Lock raised a hand to freeze and enlarge the picture. They didn't need image recognition software to see that it was Tyrone Walters.

'There are three CCTV cameras outside the hall of residence. One is situated right above the doorway, here,' Lock said, leaning over the table to highlight a tiny camera with his index finger. 'And the other two face opposing directions, here and here. Upon leaving the hall of residence, Tyrone would have had to turn either left towards the main campus facilities, or right towards the tennis courts on the outskirts. The cameras should have shown which of these two possible routes Tyrone took.'

'And?' prompted Kat, leaning forward.

'Unfortunately, none of these cameras were working that night.'

'What? You're joking me.'

'I do not possess the algorithm for comedy.'

'No, I meant – oh, never mind.'

'Why weren't they working?' asked Browne.

'Because somebody damaged them with a laser pen, a method recently used by student protestors in Hong Kong in order to evade the police's facial recognition cameras.'

Kat groaned. Bloody students. 'When did it happen? I want a note of dates and times so we can send a snotty letter to the campus security team. It's their job to check and fix these things.'

'All three cameras outside the building and a further two along Scarman Road were damaged by lasers between 1.30am and 2.05am on January the 27th,' said Lock.

'Are you serious?'

'I told you, I do not possess the algorithm for—'

'What I mean is, that's one hell of a coincidence, isn't it? That *all* the cameras that would have recorded Tyrone's last movements were disabled just two hours before he went missing?'

Lock frowned. 'I do not accept the concept of "a coincidence". The odds of such a thing happening by chance are less than one per cent.'

'Is there any footage of the person who did it?' asked Browne. 'Perhaps Tyrone did it to cover his tracks?'

Lock pointed towards the TV screen as black and white footage of the area outside Tyrone's hall of residence appeared. 'There is thirty-two seconds of footage.'

Kat stood before the screen, studying the black and white image of the halls of residence, and the lamplit path streaked with shadows. After a few seconds, a figure appeared at the left edge of the screen. Because their perspective was from the camera above the door, all they could see was the top of the umbrella that the person carried, which presumably was the point of it. A few seconds later, an arm appeared, pushing forward what looked like a small camera tripod on wheels.

'Our perpetrator clipped a high-powered laser pen to a tripod to ensure a stable and steady aim,' said Lock, 'before targeting the camera and destroying the sensors.'

A line of blue-green light shot out from the direction of the umbrella, and a small, neon dot appeared in the centre of the screen. Within ten seconds, the image Kat was watching began to pixelate, before breaking up completely as the screen turned to black. 'Is that it?' she asked, turning towards Lock. 'Have you checked the other cameras to see if there's any way to identify who did this?'

'Yes, I have checked all of the cameras, and no, there is no way to establish the person's identity, due to their deployment of an umbrella. However, we do have one good image of their arm,' Lock said, rewinding the tape to the moment when an arm emerged holding the tripod. It froze and enlarged the image.

Kat sighed. 'So, we're looking for someone in a grey long-sleeved top wearing black gloves. Well, that narrows it down.'

'We can narrow it down even further by using the ulna length,' said Lock, completely missing her sarcasm.

'The what?'

'It is possible to calculate a person's height based upon the measurements of the ulna, which is the length between the point of the elbow and the midpoint of the prominent bone in the wrist,' said Lock, as a white line appeared along the image of the arm. 'The length of the offender's ulna is 26 centimetres, so assuming they are under sixty years old, this would make their estimated height 168 centimetres, or five-foot-six. They also appear to be of slender build and right-handed. So as the average height of an adult woman in the UK is 162 centimetres compared to 176 centimetres for men, our perpetrator is either a slightly taller than average adult female, a much smaller than average male, or a young boy.'

Kat went cold. 'Tyrone Walters was six-foot-one. So, it couldn't have been him.'

For a moment, the room was silent.

'Shit,' said Hassan, sitting up straight. 'This is beginning to look like foul play, boss.'

CHAPTER TWENTY-TWO

Kat stared at the frozen image of the mysterious sabo-teur. The initial attending officers had noted that CCTV footage was 'not available' but had failed to investigate why. For five whole months. Jesus, McLeish was going to shit kittens.

'Right,' she said, turning away from the gloating face of Professor Okonedo. She had no reason to look so smug. Her machine might have helped reveal the CCTV footage, but if Kat had been left to follow her own gut and focus on Tyrone's case, then her team wouldn't have wasted valuable time on Will Robinson.

She turned towards Hassan and Browne, eyes wide, tails practically wagging at the prospect of a potential murder investigation. 'We need to know who was in the vicinity when the cameras were damaged, and who else was around between 3.30am when Tyrone left his flat and 7.36am when he sent a text to Milly and then he – or someone pretending to be him – sent a message to his mum at 9.02am before he completely vanished. What was he doing during those five and a half hours? Lock, is there any footage of anyone else leaving the building during that timeframe?'

'Including Tyrone, six people left the halls of residence during those time periods,' said Lock. 'Four of them between the hours of six and seven o'clock. But at 3.36am, we have footage from the reception camera of Milly Babbington leaving the building, before returning – alone – at 4.05am.'

Kat stepped up to the screen filled with the blurred but unmistakable image of the blonde-haired young woman.

'The call history shows that Milly and Tyrone exchanged text messages between 2am and 3am on that night,' said Kat. 'Maybe they arranged to meet outside because Milly didn't want her boyfriend to know that she liked Tyrone. But this is all just speculation until we see the texts between them. I think we've got enough evidence now to request full access to Milly's phone records – deleted content included. Can you get on to that please?' Depending upon the phone provider, it could take days or even weeks, but they needed to get the ball rolling.

Turning to the 3D virtual model of the campus, Kat asked Lock to enlarge it, so they could focus on the entrance to the halls of residence, and the road that ran in front of it. 'As all three cameras on this route were deliberately damaged, I think we can assume he turned left and walked up Scarman Road. Lock, can you reconstruct that?'

A tiny image of Tyrone, about the size of a Lego figure, appeared at the door of the halls of residence, turned left and walked rapidly towards the main facilities.

'Freeze,' said Kat. She leaned over the table and studied what lay either side of Scarman Road, looking for patches of shrubbery or footpaths leading into woods or ditches where a potential attacker could have hidden or struck unseen. But the green verges were wide and open, the road brightly lit by a parade of lampposts. 'There aren't any obvious hiding places for a would-be attacker,' she said, choosing not to add, 'nor for the body of his victim'.

The miniature figure representing Tyrone progressed up the road and the lake – which ran the length of the Lakeside Village Complex – came into view, until it was soon running parallel with the path Tyrone was on.

Browne pointed at a bench on the road that sat facing the water. 'Maybe his attacker didn't hide in the bushes. Maybe he sat here, waiting for him to pass by in full view.'

'Or maybe he – or she – met him there,' said Hassan. 'We know that Tyrone came outside at 3.30am. Let's say Milly agreed to meet him here. It's the nearest bench to their flat, and the perfect spot if you wanted to ask someone out or dump them.'

Browne gave him a look.

Hassan shrugged. 'Location, location. Milly left the halls at 3.36am, so let's say she meets him on this bench at 3.40.'

The image of Tyrone sat down and was joined by another Lego-sized figure, to represent Milly.

'Okay. Then what?' said Kat.

'Maybe Tyrone gave it one last shot,' said Browne. 'Maybe he asked Milly out again, but she told him she was with Richard now and he got upset. She storms off and Tyrone, well, maybe he was so gutted that he took his own life?'

Mini-Milly walked rapidly off. The Tyrone figure rose off the bench and ran towards the lake.

'No,' said Kat, forcing Lock to freeze the image. 'That doesn't explain why the cameras were sabotaged in advance. Someone did something to Tyrone. Someone who was jealous or annoyed – enough to plan this in advance and carry out an attack. What if Richard Sykes had had enough of Tyrone trying to get off with Milly, so he decided to take him out of the picture? He lasers the cameras, then she agrees to meet Tyrone outside – maybe on this bench – and Richard creeps up behind, bashes him on the head and . . .'

'Throws him in the lake,' said Hassan.

Once again, Lock reconstructed the image, so that after Tyrone was struck on the head, the two figures picked up a drooping Tyrone and cast him in the lake.

Everyone stared at the image of the dark, still water.

'I don't know,' said Browne, carefully. 'I mean, Sykes is a bit of an arrogant shit, but he doesn't strike me as a murderer.'

Lock shook its head. 'Once again you are exhibiting your own prejudices and preferences rather than considering the facts of the case. There are three clear options,' it said, counting out each one on the fingers it held up with an air of authority. 'Either Tyrone chose to leave university of his own free will, or he took his own life, or another person abducted him or murdered him. The fact that the CCTV cameras were sabotaged by a person other than

Tyrone makes the probability of the first two vanishingly small, and because he has now been missing for over five months with no communication from the kidnapper or Tyrone himself, the most probable explanation for his continued disappearance is murder.' Lock paused and pointed at the table. 'Which means there is a 77.7 per cent chance that his body lies at the bottom of that lake.'

Kat frowned, disturbed not just by what Lock had said, but by the way it said it. She had an uneasy feeling that it was copying her: perhaps even competing with her, but to compete was the trait of a human, not a machine, so she pushed the thought away. 'It's a possibility, not a certainty,' she said. 'Is there any footage of either Milly or Sykes leaving the hall of residence at the time the cameras were damaged?'

'I'm afraid not.'

Kat wrinkled her nose. 'Okay. I want the whole team on Warwick Campus today. I'll interview Milly Babbington and her boyfriend myself. I want to know *exactly* where they were between 1am and 10am on January the 27th. At the moment, it looks like Milly was the last person to actually see him alive.'

'They have already been asked these questions,' said Lock. 'Why don't you just review the transcripts?'

God give her strength. How many times did she have to remind this machine that she was its boss? She walked up to Lock and glared at it. 'Because I want to look them in the eye when they answer.'

Lock looked down at her. 'There is no evidence to suggest that murderers have different eyes to non-murderers.'

Kat thought back to the Aston Strangler, his strange dark eyes like a dead-ball bounce. 'Twenty-five years' experience tells me they do,' she said, returning its steady gaze. 'And I also want to find out their exact height, which isn't in any of the transcripts.'

She turned away from the virtual image and towards her team. 'Hassan and Browne, I want you to re-interview everyone else in that flat. Tyrone left at 3.30am, Milly shortly after. I don't care what they said before. Someone *must* have heard them leave their rooms, and what went on before they did. And I want to know what they thought of Milly, Tyrone and Sykes. I want all the rumours and the gossip. And we need to know where Tyrone was between 3.30am and 7.36am when he sent a text to Milly, and 9.02am when someone sent a text from his phone to his mum. Where was he for those five and a half hours? We might not have CCTV, but there are thousands of students living on that campus. Someone must have seen or heard something. Lock, I want you to compare the images of the four people who left the halls of residence with whatever you can get your hands on – college year books, social media, whatever – and see if they match the measurements of the person who damaged the cameras.'

'Of course, but with regards to the CCTV footage of Will Robinson—'

'Tyrone's case is a potential murder investigation, so this needs to be our priority now.' She glanced down at the 3D model, biting back the words 'I told you'. 'And we shouldn't rule out the possibility that Tyrone got a lift or a taxi off the campus. Did you check the CCTV footage from the car park?'

'No,' said Lock.

'Why not?'

'Because you only asked me to check the footage on Scarman Road.'

'But the car park is just off Scarman Road. It's an obvious – oh, never mind. Just check the footage. Not just for Tyrone, I want to know of any suspicious activity in and around the car park on the night he went missing.' She stared at the lake before turning away and grabbing her coat.

She wasn't giving up on Tyrone – or his mum – just yet.

Hassan waited for DCS Frank and Browne to leave the Major Incident Room, deliberately taking his time to pack up his stuff. When Professor Okonedo headed for the door, he called out her name. It came out louder than he'd intended, and he felt himself flushing as she turned towards him.

'I just wanted to ask you something. Do you have a minute?'

Her eyebrows pinched to form a neat, tiny frown.

'It won't take long.'

She nodded, but the tense way she moved back into the room, with her hand gripping her shoulder bag, told him that she was just being polite.

He cleared his throat. 'That thing you said the other day, about wanting to destroy the police. You don't really mean that, do you?'

She arched a perfectly manicured eyebrow. 'Don't I?'

'Just tell me what you meant. It's been really bugging me.'

'I'm not going to blow you all up, if that's what's you're afraid of.'

'Well what *did* you mean, then? Why do you hate the police so much?' Why do you hate *me* so much, he nearly added.

'You really have to ask?' Professor Okonedo shook her head. 'You don't need me to tell you that the police force is institutionally racist and misogynistic.'

'It is now. But the more people like you and me join and rise to positions of power, then the more it'll change. Why do you think I'm so determined to become the first South Asian DCS in Warwickshire?'

'Because you're deluded.'

'Excuse me?'

'Okay,' she said, setting her bag down on the boardroom table with a sigh. 'Let's imagine you somehow make it to the dizzy heights of DCS. What kind of team would you be leading? In 2007, 1.5 per cent of the police force were of Asian heritage, today it's just 3 per cent. Even under the most optimistic scenario, whereby the rate continues to double every 15 years, it wouldn't hit the dizzy heights of 12% until 2052. You'll always be a minority, Hassan, working in a predominantly white, racist police force.'

'Not all white people are racist. Just because a few bad apples—'

'Don't. Do *not* repeat their excuses. That's a classic example of how white people have misused a metaphor to twist the truth. The *whole point* of that saying goes back to when apples were stored in barrels. As well as mould, ripening apples produce ethylene gas, which triggers the production in any nearby fruit, hence the saying, "one bad apple spoils the barrel". Taking out the original bad apple won't make a difference, because the ethylene gas is still there, so the whole damn barrel rots.'

'So, what are you saying then? Don't bother? Just leave the barrel to rot?'

'I'm saying we need to start again. But this time, with AI. Because the thing is, the barrel we're in isn't the police force, it's society. And our society contains racism, misogyny, homophobia and transphobia that we've *all* internalised to an extent – including me. I'm not an anarchist, DI Hassan. I believe in justice, democracy and the rule of law. I just think that the policing of humans is too important to be left to humans.'

Hassan ran a hand over his face. 'And you'd honestly feel safer letting some unaccountable algorithms decide who was innocent or guilty?'

Professor Okonedo lifted her chin, eyes bright with emotion. 'I'm a black woman living in the UK. I haven't felt safe since I was sixteen years old when a gang of white boys attacked me in the toilets at McDonald's. When my brother tried to defend me, the police came and pinned him to the ground – "the big black man behaving aggressively". My brother was a straight A student, so he made a written formal complaint the very next day. After that, he was subjected to stop and search over thirty-two times, until the police finally lost patience and planted their own drugs on him. And so my brother – my lovely, anxious, terrified brother – is now in prison for a crime he didn't commit. And those boys who attacked me? They've never even been questioned, let alone arrested. So don't ask me if you think I'd feel *safer* being policed by AI, DI Hassan. Don't you dare.'

Her eyes shone with angry tears, but Professor Okonedo left the room before they could fall.

CHAPTER TWENTY-THREE

He's awake.

Not in a snappy, alert kind of way. Those days are long gone. Wakefulness is something he emerges into now, with a heavy mind still numb around the edges. But he is, at least, not asleep.

He has learned not to waste energy by sitting up, so he raises his hand to his right ear where the blindfold is loosest, telling himself – as he always does – that today will be the day, trying not to think about just how many days it has actually been, and how many more he might survive.

He slips his fingers beneath the coarse material, pushing and wiggling them up as far as they can go, tugging and pushing against his damp skin and the scratch of his newly grown beard. Perhaps it's the sweat, or maybe the blindfold has stretched, but it seems looser than before. His biceps (what's left of them) ache with the effort, but he carries on, gasping as, for the first time, he manages to shift the blindfold up and over one temple.

He pushes and pushes, ignoring the knot of pain across the bridge of his nose, the loss of blood in his numb fingers and the burn in his aching arms. For the first time, there's enough space to insert his thumb, enough room to hook it under the cloth and ...

It's off!

He rubs his eyelids, coaxing them to open. His eyelashes are stuck together, but he licks his fingers, rubs them some more and then ...

Light stabs him.

He throws his arm over his face, cursing his own stupidity. He hasn't opened his eyes for God knows how long, so he needs to acclimatise, or risk being blinded for good.

But how long will that take? The Stranger is due any minute.

He rolls onto his side, pulling the blanket over his head before carefully opening his eyes again. The world is blurred and stinging white. He blinks and blinks, trying to focus. Here is his hand – although it is bandaged and bloody. Here are his pyjamas – although not his pyjamas. He can see that they are blue. He can see that they are checked.

He can see.

Squeezing his eyes shut, he gradually lowers the blanket. From the blaze of yellow behind his eyelids, he guesses there are lights on the ceiling, so he sits up, before opening his eyes the merest of cracks.

The bed is narrower than he imagined, the metal bars that surround it lower. He scans the room, still squinting. It's empty save for a filing cabinet and some blurry metallic stand next to his bed. And there, in the left wall, barely twenty feet away, is The Door.

Squinting and blinking against the blinding brightness, he grabs the metal bars and climbs over the bed. His bare feet touch the cold floor, and his legs buckle beneath him.

Shit. His muscles have wasted. Come on, he growls, rubbing his thin thighs with his hands. He grabs on to the bed and pulls himself up, carefully shifting a bit more weight on one leg then the other, faint enough to float off.

He should wait until he gets his circulation back, and for the room to stop tilting. But he's running out of time. With a grunt of effort, he turns around, lets go of the bed, and staggers with trembling legs and a racing heart towards the door. After just a few steps, a tearing pain in his hand forces him to stop. A tube is buried deep in his flesh like a fishhook. He turns, following the line of tubing to the drip. That's how they put the drugs in him. The movement causes another tug in his groin. What the . . .? He looks down to see a tube running from beneath his pyjamas towards a large bag of yellow fluid attached to the side of the bed.

Bastards. He wrenches the tube out of his hand.

Bright red blood spurts out.

The drip stand starts to beep, high-pitched panicky sounds, raising the alarm.

Shit. He detaches the bag of fluid from the bed, lunges towards the door and makes a grab for the handle, but his hand is too wet from his own blood, and too weak to do anything more than rattle the crimson-stained metal.

He drops the bag of fluid, wraps both hands around the handle and sinks to the floor, using his own body weight to drag the handle down. But he doesn't have the strength to pull the door back and open.

He sits in his blood-splattered pyjamas, pulling and pulling at the door in a puddle of his own spilt urine

It opens so suddenly that he falls back in alarm.

The Stranger stares down at him, a pair of dark eyes above a bright blue mask.

He scrambles back, leaving a smear of blood across the floor.

The Stranger approaches.

'Let me go! Let me go!' he cries. 'Please.'

But The Stranger doesn't stop.

He clambers back onto the bed, uttering apology after apology, promising he won't try and escape – honest he won't – only please don't drug him or bind his eyes again.

The masked face bends over him; he feels a stab in his upper arm.

Then all is dark once more.

CHAPTER TWENTY-FOUR

Interviewer: DCS Kat Frank (KF)
Interviewee: Milly Babbington (MB)
Date/Time: 29 June, 12.15pm, MB's room, Warwick
                University

KF: Thanks for agreeing to help us with our enquiries
      again, Ms Babbington, we really do appreciate it.
MB: *[shrugs]* I told the other police officer everything I
      can remember, so I doubt I'll be much help.
KF: DI Hassan, yes. But we now have more information
      about Tyrone's last movements. I'm hoping we can
      help jog your memory a bit.
MB: *[coughs; drinks water]*
KF: So, let's go back to the night of Wednesday,
      January the 26th. After your lectures, what time
      did you get back to your flat?
MB: Er ... I guess no later than seven. I eat in the can-
      teen, and that shuts at 6.30pm.
KF: And what did you do when you got in?
MB: The usual. Got changed. Looked at my phone for a

bit, then about nine I did some work on my essay, and Tyrone popped round for a bit to help.

KF: Until what time?

MB: About ten?

KF: And then?

MB: And then I went to Richard's room.

KF: Any particular reason?

MB: No, just, y'know. I wanted to see him.

KF: Was he your boyfriend at that point in time?

MB: Sort of. I mean, I don't think we were exclusive then, but I hoped we were going to be, if you know what I mean.

KF: So, you went to Richard's room just after 10pm. What time did you leave?

MB: About eight the next morning, so I could get a shower before going to lectures.

KF: Is that the only time you left his room during the night?

[silence]

KF: I repeat, did you leave Richard's room at any time between 11pm and 8am?

MB: Um ... I don't think so, but I don't want to say no in case later I remember I did and then you think I'm lying. I might have left to go to the toilet.

KF: But Richard Sykes's room is en suite.

MB: Yeah, but he's a guy, so, y'know, it's not exactly the cleanest.

KF: Okay. Let me put it another way. Did you leave the halls of residence and go outside at any point between 11pm and 8am?

[silence]

KF: While you're thinking about your answer, can I remind you that we have full access to the CCTV cameras within the reception area, and all records of the electronic key cards used to enter and leave the building.

MB: *[sighs]*

KF: Would it help jog your memory if I showed you CCTV footage of you leaving the halls of residence at 3.36am on January the 27th?

[silence]

KF: Milly, can you help me out here? Who were you meeting outside at that hour?

MB: Look, I know it sounds bad, which is why I didn't want to tell you before. Tyrone kept sending me texts that night, and at first, I replied, but by about two o'clock I'd had enough, so I switched my phone off. But then he started knocking on Richard's door and he wouldn't go away until I promised to talk with him. So yeah, I went outside. I agreed to meet him on the bench by the lake on Scarman Road, but it was just for half an hour, tops. I swear.

KF: Is that the only time you left the building after midnight?

MB: Yes, I told you. I just agreed to meet Tyrone so he'd leave us alone.

KF: What did you talk about?

MB: He wanted to know why I was ignoring him. He thought that because we'd slept together once that we were in a relationship. It really wasn't a big deal, but he wanted it to be. So, I told him I was with Richard now and that we – Tyrone and me – we were just good friends.

KF: And how did he take that?

MB: Well, he wasn't happy. But he wasn't like, crying or anything. He was just ... disappointed. To be honest, I think I was his first, and he'd built it up to be something it wasn't.

KF: And what did you do after you talked?

MB: I went back inside. I was knackered. And it was freezing.

KF: And Tyrone?

[silence]

KF: Did Tyrone go back inside with you?

MB: No. It was about four by the time I left him, so he said he might as well watch the sun come up. I think he had an early appointment or something.

KF: An appointment? Who with?

MB: He didn't say.

KF: Did he say at what time?

MB: No. He just kind of mumbled something about having an appointment when I said I was going in.

KF: Which direction did he go in?

MB: He didn't go anywhere. We were sitting on the bench up by the lake, and he was still sitting on it when I went back in.

KF: *[sighs]* So contrary to what you told DI Hassan, that was the last time you ever saw him?

MB: Yes.

KF: Alone, on a bench at 4am, staring at the lake.

MB: There was no reason to think he wouldn't be okay by himself.

KF: Apart from the fact that you'd just dumped him.

MB: I didn't 'dump him', we weren't in a relationship! If I'd have stayed with him to watch the sunrise, that would have been giving him mixed messages, wouldn't it? I didn't want to muck him about, so yeah, I went back inside.

KF: When you left Tyrone alone on the bench, did you go to your room or Richard's?

MB: Richard's.

KF: And did either of you leave the room again that night?

MB: No.

KF: Are you absolutely sure?

MB: Yes! I told you, Tyrone had kept us awake all night. We were knackered. I fell asleep, and then I was woken by another text from Tyrone at about half-seven reminding me not to miss the lecture at ten. He said things were cool and I remember he used a thumbs-up emoji rather than kisses, so I thought we were okay. It was like he'd finally accepted we were just mates.

KF: Was this one of the texts that you deleted?

MB: Um, yeah.

KF: And despite what you say his text said, he never did meet you at the lecture, did he?

MB: No.

KF: Which means that you were the last person to see Tyrone Walters alive. Okay. That's enough for now. How tall are you, Milly?

MB: Er, about five-foot-nine, why?

KF: Oh. It just might be relevant to our enquiries.

INTERVIEW CONCLUDED

CHAPTER TWENTY-FIVE

Interviewer: DCS Kat Frank (KF)
Interviewee: Richard Sykes (RS)
Date/Time: 29 June, 1.02pm, RS's room, Warwick
University

KF: Thanks for agreeing to meet with us again so quickly. We've reviewed the case of Tyrone Walters, reassessed the risk rating and are stepping up our enquiries as a matter of urgency.

RS: What do you mean, reassessed the risk?

KF: What I said. Tyrone's case was initially assessed as low to zero, but now we've had a chance to review all his social media and speak to you and Milly, I'm afraid we think there's a high risk that Tyrone may have come to harm.

RS: Why do you think that? Shit, what did Milly say to you? You shouldn't believe everything she says, you know. I mean, she's great, but she can be a bit of a drama queen, to be honest.

KF: I'm afraid I'm not at liberty to say. Also, we've not

yet shared that information with his family, so I must ask you to treat this as confidential.

RS: Yes, of course. It's just. Shit ... do you think he's like dead or something?

KF: We're exploring all possible avenues at the moment, Richard. Can I call you Richard? I would call you Mr Sykes, but it just reminds me of old Bill Sykes from *Oliver*. Nasty piece of work. Were you in bed with Milly on the night of Wednesday, January the 26th, and the early hours of January the 27th?

RS: Er, yes.

KF: And did you see Tyrone that night?

RS: No.

KF: Did you hear from him?

RS: As in?

KF: As in, did he ring you, or text you or knock on your door?

[silence]

KF: Were you aware of him ringing or texting Milly? Knocking on her door?

RS: Yes. He kept texting her. Like, we were trying to ... y'know, and then her phone would ping. And then he friggin' knocked on the door.

KF: That must have been ... off-putting.

RS: Tell me about it. You'd have thought he'd take the hint.

KF: But he didn't. So, did you and Milly discuss how you might get him to 'take the hint'? You're both intelligent people. I'm assuming you decided to do the right thing and talk to the poor guy. Explain that you and Milly were an item now, so he should just back off and save whatever was left of his self-respect, right?

[silence]

KF: Were you scared of him?

RS: Tyrone? No!

KF: So, you just didn't care about your mate's self-respect?

RS: No, we were going to talk to him.

KF: When?

RS: In the morning.

KF: What time?

RS: I don't know, whenever we were up.

KF: What time did you get up, Richard?

RS: Dunno. Probably about nine-ish.

KF: I'm going to ask you again, and I want you to think very carefully before answering. Did you get up and go outside your room at any point between midnight and 8am?

RS: No.

KF: Not even to go to the toilet?

RS: Well, yeah, but this is an en suite, so I didn't need to leave my room.

KF: Are you sure? I should warn you, Richard, that we are checking all the campus CCTV footage and speaking to several witnesses, so please answer as truthfully as you can. Did you leave your room or the halls of residence on the night in question?

RS: No comment.

KF: Did Milly leave the halls of residence on the night in question?

RS: No comment.

KF: Are you claiming that Milly spent the entire night with you?

RS: No comment.

KF: Are you still sleeping with Milly?

RS: That's none of your business.

KF: I think you'll find it is.

RS: *[sighs]* Yes.

KF: So, Milly is your girlfriend?

RS: Yes. Now. But not before. We slept together but we weren't exclusive.

KF: And when would you say you two became 'exclusive'?

RS: I don't know. Does it matter?

KF: Let me take a guess. Was it the day Tyrone went missing? Was it easier once the coast was clear? Or perhaps something dramatic happened that night that brought you closer together.

RS: *No!* You're putting two and two together and getting twenty-four.

KF: So, you're saying you didn't get together that night? *[silence]*

KF: I'd think carefully about my answer, if I were you.

RS: I honestly can't remember. The days all blur into one, to be honest.

KF: Really? If my flatmate went missing, I think I'd remember the last night I ever saw him. *[silence]*

191

KF: *[sighs]* Okay, we'll leave it there for now, but if I were you, I'd try and remember exactly what happened that night. You have the right to remain silent and to say 'no comment', but honestly, it's not a good look.

RS: But—

KF: Do you own a a car?

RS: Er . . . yes, why?

KF: Where do you keep it?

RS: In the car park just off Scarman Road. Why?

KF: Did you use it on the night that Tyrone went missing?

RS: No.

KF: Really? I thought you couldn't remember what you did that night?

RS: I don't, it's just that I normally only use it at weekends so I'm almost certain I wouldn't have.

KF: Okay. Well, I'll need you to confirm the licence plate of your vehicle, and then we can check the CCTV footage. Which reminds me. How tall are you?

RS: What? Er . . . about five-foot-eleven.

KF: Thank you, Mr Sykes, you've been really helpful.

INTERVIEW CONCLUDED

CHAPTER TWENTY-SIX

Coleshill, Warwickshire, 29 June, 6.40pm

The A452 was clogged with traffic and baked by the hot June sun, so by the time Kat reached home, her blouse was plastered to her skin and a tension headache was creeping its way along her neck and jaw. After a quick shower she checked her phone for messages, but there was nothing except a text from Morrisons confirming her next food delivery, and an email about garden storage solutions she was 'sure to love'.

She sighed. What she'd 'love' was a decent pub meal and a glass – oh, let's make it a bottle! – of overpriced wine. But her best mate Mandy had moved to rural Wales after Covid, her sister was on holiday in Crete and the mums she used to be so close with when Cam was at primary school . . . well, they had their WhatsApp group – *RollonSeptember!* – to share the frustrations of parenting teens who should be revising, but all the 'we must meet up soon!' messages were just that – messages.

Kat put her phone down, changed into some jeans

and trainers and went outside to try and walk off her increasingly grumpy mood. Ignoring the nearby lanes, she headed towards Coleshill, a small market town located on a high ridge between two rivers and two motorways, just ten miles east of Birmingham and within spitting distance of both the beautiful Warwickshire countryside and one of the largest council estates in Europe. They lived at the bottom of the hill on the other side of the River Cole, which meant that once you crossed over the bridge, you faced a steep climb up the high street. When they first bought the cottage, John used to joke that it would be good exercise to walk up to the high street for a drink, and then they could literally roll all the way home. It never occurred to them that John would one day be crippled by breathlessness, turning the hill into a mountain and their home into a prison.

Even though it was gone seven, Coleshill was still busy with people strolling up and down the high street, grabbing some last-minute shopping from the supermarket or heading for a drink in one of the many old coaching inns that are now popular pubs. Kat smiled at a few friendly faces waiting for fish and chips on the corner of Church Hill, feeling a familiar warmth for the sheer ordinariness of the people who lived here, as she headed towards the church.

Situated at the highest point of the hill and dating back to the fourteenth century, the steeple of the Church of St Peter and St Paul towers over Coleshill and can be seen for miles around. Kat passed through the wooden porch and into the croft, a sheltered green expanse offering panoramic views of North Warwickshire and a haven from the busy high street. She picked up pace, hurrying through the cemetery until soon she was at the kissing gate and looking out on bleached fields of gold beneath a liquid blue sky. Kat took a deep breath of the straw-scented air, feeling her muscles relax as her ears tuned into the birdsong above the dull hum of distant traffic and a nearby tractor.

Kat followed the sun-baked track edging the farmland until she reached a pool surrounded by trees, where she had to step back to let a mum and dad with two kids and a massive galloping dog pass by. She tried to ignore the tug of envy, before firmly walking on. But the sound of laughing children carried on the summer's breeze. By the time she reached the next kissing gate, the laughter had faded, and all was silent once more. She leaned on the wooden gate, bent by the weight of memories.

God, she felt so alone.

Appalled by the sudden rush of self-pity, Kat pushed through the gate and strode across the next field. Work. She needed to focus on work. To help distract her, she switched Lock onto visual.

'DCS Frank?' Lock said, raising an eyebrow as it took in their surroundings.

Kat stared at the 3D holographic image of a black detective in a navy-blue suit standing in a field of golden wheat, fringed with ancient oak trees.

'It helps me to think if I walk and talk,' she said briskly as she strode on ahead. 'I'd like your assessment of the case so far.'

'It's clear from the interview with Milly that she lied about being the last one to see Tyrone alive,' said Lock, falling in alongside her and matching her stride for stride. 'Which is suspicious. And given that they both claim that he was pestering her, Milly and her boyfriend Richard have a clear motive for murder. Yet both the CCTV footage and electronic key card data confirm that Milly only left the halls of residence at 3.36am on January the 27th, returning at 4am, and Richard Sykes didn't leave the building at all. What's more, Milly is five-foot-nine and Sykes is nearly six-foot, so, neither of them could have damaged the cameras, which means if they were involved, they must have engaged a third party to do it on their behalf.'

Kat batted away a fly. 'Perhaps. But it doesn't feel right. I mean, they're not exactly Romeo and Juliet, are they?'

'What do you mean?'

'Well, Sykes couldn't even remember when they'd got together.'

'So?'

'So, I believed him – or rather, I believed his "so what?" expression. A man in love would have remembered, and a guilty man would have made something up. And for there to be a crime of passion ... well, there has to be some passion.'

Lock stopped and faced her, frowning. 'And how exactly do you assess the extent of passion in a relationship?'

Kat looked out at the horizon, remembering those early years with John, when their hands were as entwined as their words and thoughts, all boundaries between them blurred. Older people would smile as they walked past them, giving them the soft, tender glances usually reserved for babies. Everyone could see that they were in love – although how, she couldn't say. 'There's no formula for assessing a relationship, Lock. It's just something you get a sense of.'

'Like one of your "hunches"?' Lock was silent for a moment. 'I have just read *Romeo and Juliet* and, I must say, it is a perfect description of the human condition.'

'In what sense?' Just because this machine could 'read' a book in a matter of seconds, it didn't mean it could actually understand it.

'In the sense that both characters make completely irrational decisions, based upon their feelings rather than the facts. Because they cannot bear to be separated, the two young lovers kill themselves, resulting in death – which for you humans is the ultimate separation. That ending could have been avoided if Romeo had taken the time to assess the evidence rather than just assume Juliet was dead.'

Kat couldn't help smiling. 'That's why it's a tragedy.'

'The tragedy is that humans seem incapable of learning and are forever at the mercy of their emotions.'

Kat sighed. 'Perhaps, but given that we *are* driven by our emotions, you can't just turn your virtual nose up at them. Understanding what makes people tick, what motivates them, is the key to solving any crime. Sykes and Milly care more about themselves than they do each other. If one of them had something to do with Tyrone's disappearance, the other would have shopped them by now. And regardless of their motivation – or lack of it – we don't have a scrap of evidence that either of them was involved.'

'But we do have enough evidence to justify a search of the campus lake.'

'What is it with you?' she snapped. 'Why are you always so keen to drag rivers and lakes to find a dead body?'

'And why,' Lock said softly, dipping its head towards hers, 'are you so reluctant?'

Why indeed? Kat thrashed back a particularly large bunch of nettles as she carried on walking. If she was honest with herself – which she usually was – it was because she simply couldn't bear the thought of knocking on Mrs Walters' door and telling her she was not just a widow, but a childless one at that. She might as well take an axe and chop her off at her knees.

Kat walked on in silence until they reached Duke End Bridge that arched its way across the River Blythe. When Cam was little, they'd had to constantly distract and coax him to reach this far by collecting leaves, berries and feathers, with the promise of an ice cream at the end of the walk. The bridge was their halfway point where they'd rest and skim stones before completing the circular walk, Cam practically breaking their arms as he insisted on being lifted so he could 'fly' all the way home.

Kat sighed and looked at her watch. It used to take nearly two hours for the three of them to reach here but, by herself, it had taken less than one. She stood staring at the sandstone arches of the bridge and the gaping gaps between. Lock opened its mouth, but she switched it off before it could speak.

As Kat made her way back along the deserted river-bank, the sky filled with darting bats and the mournful cry of swifts. In the liminal light of the dying day, she imagined she walked through the ghosts of their younger selves, Cam shouting 'Again! Again!' as he swung and laughed between them.

DCS Kat Frank's home, Coleshill, Warwickshire, 30 June, 5.20am

'DCS Frank?'

Kat's eyes flew open. A man's face hovered above her.

She reached down for the baton she kept by the side of the bed and brought it crashing down into . . .

Nothing. The baton whistled through the air, landing on the empty side of the bed with a thud.

The face that was only inches from hers raised an eyebrow.

'Lock?' Kat pulled herself up against the pillows and checked her mobile phone: 5.20am. 'What the *fuck* do you think you are doing in my bedroom?'

It stood up and spread out both its hands. 'You told me to tell you the minute I finished reviewing the CCTV footage of Will Robinson in Stratford-upon-Avon, and Professor Okonedo amended my settings so that I might comply with your request.'

Kat groaned and rubbed her hands over her eyes. 'I didn't mean . . . oh, it doesn't matter. I'm awake now. Tell me in a nutshell what you found.'

'In a nutshell? Is that a form of communication? I have sent you an email but if you tell me what the nutshell device is I will—'

'No, it's a figure of speech. It means, just tell me the headlines. Keep it short. And stand over there.' It was disconcerting to have a relatively strange man – even a virtual one – in her bedroom.

Lock stepped back so that its smart-suited figure stood in front of the door where her dressing gown hung. 'I have completed my review, and in short, there is no footage of Will Robinson in Stratford-upon-Avon on the night that he went missing.'

'None at all? Don't tell me their CCTV cameras weren't working.'

It paused.

'Lock?'

'You said not to tell you, so I am not sure what to say.'

Kat squeezed her eyes shut, counted to three, and then – as calmly as she could – asked it to tell her what it had found.

'There were five cameras that should have picked up Will's movements on the night he went missing: one on the path that led to the riverbank, two on Clopton Bridge over the river and the two cameras in the car park outside the public house where he was supposed to be meeting friends. With the exception of his home, all of these cameras ceased to work exactly twelve hours before he went missing.'

Kat snapped awake. 'Pardon?'

'There were five cameras that—'

'I heard, I mean, why weren't they working?'

'On January the 11th, between the hours of 5am and 6am, the sensors in all five cameras were destroyed by the targeted use of a laser pen. The perpetrator hid their identity with an umbrella, but there is some footage of their right arm, which according to my analysis, suggests that the person who did this was five-foot-six, of slim build and was wearing an identical garment to the perpetrator at the university.'

Lock stretched out a hand, and a blurred image of a grey-clad arm appeared at the foot of her bed.

'Are you saying what I think you're saying?'

Lock raised both eyebrows. 'I have no idea what you think I may be saying. But my conclusion is that there is a high probability that the same person who destroyed the camera sensors just hours before Tyrone Walters went missing in Warwick also destroyed the camera sensors in Stratford-upon-Avon.'

'Shit.' She jumped out of bed and grabbed her iPad from the bedside table. While she waited for it to load, Kat asked Lock to alert the team to a 7.00am Zoom briefing.

Kat's fingers were clumsy as she logged on, but her mind was clear and focused. What had seemed like two unconnected missing person cold cases had now turned into a hunt for a serial kidnapper, possibly murderer, of two young men. She said a quick, silent prayer for the families, then started filling in the forms to carry out two water searches.

CHAPTER TWENTY-SEVEN

DCS Kat Frank's home, Coleshill, Warwickshire,
30 June, 7.00am

Kat wasn't a big fan of Zoom calls – no one looks good
with their face just inches from their screen and there's
always someone who can't work out how to use the mute
button – but she couldn't afford to waste time struggling
through the traffic for a briefing at HQ and then on to
Handsworth and Stratford-upon-Avon.

Once they'd all dialled in, Kat asked Lock to share
the conclusions from the CCTV analysis, complete with
uploaded images. 'The two cases are clearly connected, so
we urgently need to find out what links them,' she said.
'We're looking for a serial attacker, kidnapper or even
murderer, and if we're to catch them before they strike
again, then we need to work out what drew our offender
to these two young men in particular. The only thing
they have in common apart from their age and gender is
what happened to the CCTV before they went missing.
Maybe they both knew their attacker: a lecturer, a friend,

a girlfriend, a colleague – someone who knew them and their movements well enough to plan out in advance whatever happened to them.

'Hassan and Browne, I want you to re-interview all their friends and find out if any of them knew each other. Did Tyrone ever socialise with Will or happen to be at the same party one night or share an interest or hobby or anything that might connect them? Did they support the same football team, go to the same gym or church or music festivals and concerts? Explore every angle – they were in the same age group and lived just sixteen miles apart, so it's possible they had something or someone in common.'

Hassan and Brown both nodded as they wrote down her instructions.

'Lock, I want you to do the same, but for virtual networks. Go through every social media account of theirs, their friends and their friends of friends, to find mutual followers or people who liked their posts or whatever you call them. Go as wide and as deep as you can – especially on Sykes and Milly.'

'When will you tell the families?' asked Hassan.

'Soon as I can.' Yesterday she'd been reluctant to initiate a river search, but the evidence of a connection between the two missing boys meant that she could delay it no further. 'I'll visit them as soon as we end this call, I'll update them and see if they're aware of any possible connection between the boys. Why do you ask?'

'Just worried about this leaking. I guess we should hold off talking to their friends until you've spoken to their parents.'

Kat glanced at the clock. By the time she reached Handsworth and then Stratford it would be gone lunchtime. 'No, we'll lose half the day if we do that.'

'But it's bound to leak,' continued Hassan. 'I really think we should—'

'And I really think you should get on with your job, DI Hassan. Just make sure everyone understands this is confidential until the families know. I'll talk to comms about doing a press briefing – probably tomorrow once we know more.'

She stared at Hassan as he puffed out his cheeks. He clearly didn't agree with her decision, but he needed to learn that *she* was the boss. Fast.

'What about the car parks?' said Browne. 'Shall we check the car park at the Swan's Nest in Stratford to see if Richard Sykes's car was there on the day Will Robinson went missing?'

'Good idea. In fact, Lock, can you examine the CCTV footage for both car parks in the twenty-four hours before and after we think each boy went missing? Although Sykes is our prime suspect for Tyrone, we need to keep an open mind. There could be a third party involved. Anything else we should be looking at?'

Browne opened her mouth, then closed it.

'Browne?'

'It's probably nothing, it's just that I read the transcript with Milly, and she said she thought Tyrone might have had an appointment, and I know we checked whether he had any meetings with tutors or whatever before, but "appointment" is quite a specific term. You might have a meeting with a teacher or colleague, but an appointment usually means something health-related.'

'Good spot,' said Kat. 'That's the kind of detail we need to sweat. Check with his GP and dentist. Anything else? Okay, well, let's crack on, and I'll see you all back at HQ for a 6pm debrief. We're not just looking for two missing boys now, we're looking for someone who has deliberately taken them or caused them harm. I know there's a vanishingly small probability that both boys are still alive, but there's a high chance whoever did it could strike again. We can't give them that chance.'

She pressed 'end call'. The possibility that this might be an active murder case had raised everyone's energy levels, but they still weren't quite gelling as a team. It took time to build trust, and there was too much second-guessing going on at the moment.

'DCS Frank,' said Lock. 'Now that this is a potential murder investigation, don't you need to refer it back to the local teams?'

Kat pushed her hand through her hair. Jesus, if it wasn't Hassan questioning her judgement, then it was the bloody AI. The annoying thing was, technically, Lock was right. But it would take a couple of days for a new team to get up to speed with the brief and meet the families. Could they afford that delay? And did it make any sense to hand the cases back to the local teams who'd missed all the high-risk signals in the first place? Maybe if she explained it all to McLeish, he'd use his discretion and leave it with her. She picked up her phone, but even as her thumb hovered over her boss's number, his own advice rang in her ears: *Never ask a question until you're sure you'll get the answer you want.*

'My priority this morning is to speak to the families before it leaks,' she said, putting the phone down. 'I'll ring McLeish later.' The more she embedded herself in this investigation and earned the trust of the families, the harder it would be for him to take it off her.

'It would save a lot of time if you just rang both mothers.'

'It would, but I'm not telling someone over the phone that their son might be dead.'

'Why not?'

'*Why not?*' she paused at the sound of her own voice. Would she use such an incredulous tone with a child? No. She would try and teach them.

'I am not trying to undermine you when I question the reasons behind your decisions,' Lock said. 'I am just trying to understand so that I can learn.'

Kat took a deep breath before trying to explain her reasoning as patiently as she could. 'Because I can't change what I'm about to tell them, but I can influence how they feel about it. Difficult news is slightly less painful to hear if it's given face to face. So, I'm going to make the time to do just that. This is the hardest part of being a police officer, but it's one of the most important.'

Lock raised its eyebrows. 'According to the College of Policing, the duties of a police officer include protecting people and property, patrolling the areas they are assigned to, responding to calls, enforcing laws, making arrests, issuing citations, filling in forms and occasionally testifying in court cases. I can find no reference to reducing emotional pain.'

'That's just a list of functions, but the *purpose* of those tasks – the whole point of being a police officer – is absolutely to reduce people's pain. If we do our job right, then we make people feel safer, less afraid. And when – despite our best efforts – something terrible happens, we can help them feel that they are not alone, and that their loved ones will not be forgotten.'

Lock frowned. 'Where is that written down? I have searched over five hundred pieces of guidance and four thousand three hundred and twenty-eight job descriptions, but I cannot find anything that resembles that description.'

Kat threw her hands up. 'Oh, Lock, it isn't written down anywhere, and we aren't taught it at college. It's just what we *do*.'

Lock stared at her, its face creased in confusion. 'Then what is the point of a job description if it doesn't accurately describe the actual job? And if your job really is to make people feel less afraid or upset, then how can you achieve your goals?' Lock spread out its hands. 'Surely that is an impossible aim?'

'Yes,' said Kat, shutting her laptop. 'But that's the funny thing about humans, Lock. Just because something is impossible, it doesn't stop us trying.'

Leek Wootton Police Headquarters, Warwickshire, 30 June, 12.42pm

By the time Kat had driven back to HQ it was nearly lunchtime, although the last thing she felt like doing now was eating. After her conversations with both Mrs Robinson and Mrs Walters, she almost wished she'd listened to Lock and just done it over the phone. Then she wouldn't have had to witness Mrs Robinson dragging her fingers down her face as if she might tear her very flesh off when Kat told her about the river search.

'The *river*?' Mrs Robinson's voice had broken on the word.

'I'm sorry—'

'You're *sorry*?' she spat. 'He's been gone for nearly six months. What's the point in searching the river now? You should have done this the moment I called you. I told them he wouldn't have just gone off. I *told* them.'

Kat had stood and absorbed her anger. There was no point trying to defend her colleagues by explaining that Will had appeared to be a low-risk case, so they didn't have the manpower to do anything other than a cursory trawl of CCTV and social media, all of which just seemed to confirm the initial low-risk assessment. There were reasons, but none of them were good enough for the broken woman before her.

'I'm going to arrange for a Family Liaison Officer to come around and they can help support—'

'No. I don't want anyone. I don't want Gerard to worry.'

'Mrs Robinson, this is going to be a very challenging time for you both, and an FLO can help support you through this. I know you're trying to protect your husband, but once we start the search, it'll be in the media, so it would be best to tell him.'

'My husband is *dying*, DCS Frank, and he doesn't have long left. If I tell him that Will . . . that you're going to search the river . . . It'll kill him. I can't do it. I'm trying to keep things tranquil. Private. Normal.' She laughed at that last word, a bitter bite of sound. 'I am *not* having police officers – strangers – invading my home during our last few weeks together. It's bad enough with all the doctors and nurses coming and going.'

'I'm so sorry,' was all Kat could say, appalled by the futility of her own words. 'Is there anyone I can ring for you, anything else we can do to help?'

'Yes,' said Mrs Robinson, eyes blazing. 'You can do your job and find my son.'

Wincing at the memory, Kat swiped her badge at the gates and climbed the steps to Leek Wootton HQ. Inside, she was surprised to see McLeish standing in reception. For two seconds, she thought it was a coincidence. Then she noticed the purple tinge to his cheeks, his unforgiving stare.

'DCS Frank,' he said. 'A word.'

It was not a request. Kat followed his retreating back all the way to his office.

He closed the door, sat in the leather chair behind his desk and pointedly left her standing. 'Perhaps I'm getting forgetful in my old age, but did I, or did I not, ask you to keep me personally informed of any developments in the AI pilot?'

'Yes, sir, you did.' His normally brusque Scottish accent was dangerously soft, so Kat stuck to short, simple answers.

'And did I, or did I not, ask you to let me know if at any point either of the two cold cases looked like they might develop into active murder investigations?'

'Yes, sir, you did.'

McLeish leaned forward. 'So then, why the *fuck* didn't you tell me that not one, but *two* of the cold cases in the pilot are potential murder investigations, and that we could be looking for a serial killer?'

Kat puffed out her cheeks. 'I was on my way to do exactly that, sir. I've filled in the forms to request two water searches, but I just wanted to tell the families first. I was worried about it leaking.'

McLeish picked up his phone from the desk. 'Too late. It's all over Twitter.'

'What? How?'

'Apparently you gave the go-ahead for your team to question Tyrone's friends about Will and vice versa "in confidence" and, guess what, it turns out teenage boys can't keep a secret. Who knew?'

'Shit,' said Kat.

'Shit is right,' said McLeish. 'The nationals have picked it up and want to know if we're looking for a serial killer of students.'

'But Will wasn't a student any more.'

'Doesn't matter. There's nothing like putting the fear

of God into middle-class parents to drive up sales. Which means I've got the minister on my back, wanting to know what I'm doing about it and the police commissioner wanting to know why the fuck I didn't tell them they've got *two* high-profile and active murder investigations on their patch. And that's before anyone knows I've got bloody Alexa on the case.'

'That's why I wanted to talk to you face to face, sir. I knew it would be complicated.'

'It's a total and utter shitstorm is what it is, DCS Frank.' He leaned back and ran a hand over his bald head. 'Give me one good reason why I shouldn't stand you down and hand both cases back to the local teams.'

'I'll give you two, sir. Firstly, if I'm right and the cases are connected, then the worst thing you could do is hand them back. The Stratford-upon-Avon team will focus on the Robinson case, and the Warwick University team will focus on the Walters' case, and they'll be so busy covering their own arses, any connections between them will be missed and we won't catch the perpetrator.

'Secondly, if it's in the media then the pressure will be on to solve both cases quickly. It'll take time for two teams to get up to speed with the issues and build a relationship with the families. That's time we don't have. And the longer it takes, the more likely the West Mids lot will start saying it should lead on the Warwick Uni case because of the boundary issues.'

'I agree with DCS Frank,' said Lock from her wrist. 'I have reviewed the evidence and changing the team at this stage of an enquiry typically causes a delay of at least two-point-three days, resulting in a twenty-four per cent drop in productivity.'

'What the—'

'So basically,' said Kat, jumping in, 'I'm the solution, not the problem. Leave it with me and I'll make the connections, maintain the momentum and solve both cases quickly. Sir.'

McLeish stared at her. 'But we can't have a major investigation like this led by a bloody pilot project.'

'Then let me lead a temporary county-wide team for this unique case. Give me twenty officers from Warwick and ten from Stratford. And, with your permission, I'd like to continue using Lock. The image recognition software is genuinely helpful, and it'll help keep the minister off your back.'

McLeish shook his head. 'Why are you so keen to work these cases?'

'Because I think I can find them.'

'Are you sure that's all this is about? I worry about you, sometimes, Kat.'

'Don't worry about me. I'm fine. Just worry about getting the minister the results she wants.'

He rubbed his chin, which sounded like it needed a shave. 'All right. *You* lead the team. You can have ten from Warwick and five from Stratford. You can keep Lock but only for defined tasks like image recognition. And I want you to make it crystal clear that any success in these cases – and I do expect *and* demand success – is entirely down to you and the team, not that bloody machine.'

Kat nodded and headed for the door. It was best to get out quick before he changed his mind.

'Oh, and Kat?'

She turned.

'I mean it this time. If someone so much as farts on this case, I want to know about it, got that?'

'Yes, sir.'

CHAPTER TWENTY-EIGHT

Leek Wootton Police Headquarters, Warwickshire,
30 June, 5.59pm

It was standing room only in the Major Incident Room for
the 6pm briefing, which meant the meeting had an energy
that Kat could exploit. This was the case that everyone
was talking about, the room that everyone wanted to be
in. And she was leading the investigation.

She stood at the front, surveying her new team. There
were a couple she recognised from the canteen, but most
she didn't know. It didn't matter. She didn't need these
people to be her friends, she just needed them to help her
core team do their job.

'Before I ask DI Hassan and DS Browne to update us,'
she said, signalling their seniority to the room and giving
them both a heads-up she was coming to them next, 'let's
recap on what we know so far.'

She turned to the screens behind her. 'This is Will
Robinson, a twenty-one-year-old theatre graduate who
recently moved back home with his parents after finishing

his degree last summer. No known risk factors such as drugs or alcohol, but his father is terminally ill with cancer. He'd recently broken up with his girlfriend, but it's unclear whether he was depressed or not. After getting a job in a local theatre café, he told his mum he'd got an acting job, and that he was meeting some friends for a celebratory drink in the Swan's Nest at six o'clock on the evening of January the 11th. Lock?'

Despite reminding them that the AIDE was supposed to support, not distract them, her new team leaned forward like a bunch of meerkats as Lock's image appeared. Kat pressed her teeth together as she watched the tall lean figure walk with slow deliberation to the centre of the room. It stretched out its right arm, and with what she thought was an unnecessarily dramatic flourish, a 3D map of the last known route of Will Robinson appeared before them.

'We know that Will Robinson left his parents' home at 5.07pm and turned right here. We believe that he intended to walk along this path, down to the riverbank, over the bridge, along this road until he reached the car park of the Swan's Nest, his ultimate destination,' Lock explained, red lights flashing on the map as he referred to each location. 'But Will Robinson never arrived. His phone signal ended at 6pm, somewhere within fifty metres of Clopton Bridge. Unfortunately, we don't know where, as there is no CCTV footage of him along this route, because someone damaged them with a laser.'

Lock turned towards the TV screen dominating the back wall and played the micro-second frames of a person targeting each camera with a laser pen, before freezing it on a blurred shot of an arm. 'The perpetrator is slender, right-handed, wearing a grey hoodie and black gloves, and based upon the length of their ulna, I estimate their height to be five-foot-six. There are no other identifying characteristics, but on the balance of possibilities we are looking for either an adult female or a male child or adolescent. This act was clearly premeditated, so there is a high probability of foul play, but because of Will Robinson's possible depression and his father's illness, we cannot rule out suicide.'

Everyone nodded, their eyes fixed on Lock.

Kat sighed. It appeared that some officers were clearly more comfortable listening to a virtual male rather than a real woman.

'With respect, ma'am,' said one of the more junior officers, 'as you said, we can't rule out suicide. The CCTV damage might just be a coincidence.'

Kat paused before turning around to face him. Her new team would soon learn that she didn't buy the 'with respect' bullshit. If someone was going to challenge her, then they should have the balls to just come out with it. 'I've worked in the force for over twenty-five years, so I don't believe in coincidences.'

'DCS Frank is right,' said Lock. 'There is a less than 0.1 per cent chance that both sets of cameras could have been damaged by two different people who just happened to have identical ulna lengths using the same method just hours before each boy went missing in two different geographical locations.' It gestured towards the TV screen as the footage of the perpetrator's forearm from Warwick was overlaid on top of the Stratford image, and a measurement line appeared to confirm that the ulna was 26cm long in both images.

Several officers nodded; a few exchanged impressed glances.

Kat smiled, although she didn't need a machine to back her up with her own bloody team. 'And by the way,' she added. 'I'm your boss, not your mother, so I don't want anyone calling me "ma'am".' She gestured for Lock to continue with his briefing.

'Sixteen days after Will Robinson went missing, Tyrone Walters, an eighteen-year-old student in his first year at Warwick University, left his halls of residence on January the 27th at 3.30am to talk with his flatmate Milly Babbington on a bench on Scarman Road. We know from the CCTV in reception that whereas Milly returned to the halls shortly after 4am, Tyrone did not. We have no further sightings of him that night because, as we have seen, once again the cameras along the route were deliberately sabotaged just two hours before, by a perpetrator who matches the exact profile of the person who destroyed the CCTV cameras in Stratford.'

Kat stepped forward, drawing her team's attention back to her. 'The last communication we have from Tyrone's phone was a text he – or someone pretending to be him – sent to his mum at 9.02am, saying he was going to "chill" for a couple of days and not to worry. A comparative authorship analysis suggests that Tyrone was not the author of this final text, and the signal from his phone stopped just after. Tyrone hasn't been seen or heard of since. His friend Milly alleges that Tyrone said something about having an appointment to go to that morning before his lecture at ten, but so far we have been unable to verify this. So, because of the similarities in the MO, we suspect foul play.'

'Although,' interrupted Lock, 'because his flatmate Milly had recently rejected Tyrone as a boyfriend, we cannot rule out suicide.'

'Which is why,' said Kat, raising her voice, 'tomorrow we'll be carrying out two water searches for both bodies. But in advance of that, we urgently need to know what connects the two boys. Hassan, can you update us, please?'

'Thanks, boss.' He stood up, not looking at his notes as he addressed the packed room. 'I spent the day at Warwick University interviewing Tyrone's friends, including Richard Sykes, because he's dating Milly – the girl Tyrone fancied – so he has a potential motive. Richard denied knowing Will Robinson – as did everyone we spoke to – and Lock was unable to find any social media communication between any of them.'

'Did you believe Sykes?' asked Kat.

'I did about Will Robinson. He seemed genuinely shocked and was pretty convincing when he swore he'd never heard of him. If Lock is right and these two boys were taken or harmed by the same person, then I don't think Sykes is our guy. But I'm sure he knows more than he's telling us about Tyrone. I think we should keep an open mind about whether the two cases are connected.

'We always keep an open mind, DI Hassan. But the line of enquiry we are pursuing is that the two cases *are* connected. DS Browne, any luck in Stratford?'

The young woman remained seated at her desk, flicking through her book, trying to find her notes. Then she picked up her iPad and tried logging on. Some of the men around her began to glance at their phones.

Kat willed her to have the confidence to just speak without the prop of notes. With every passing second, she was losing the room. It didn't matter how detailed and insightful her notes were, it would never be as effective as a man confidently spouting his own opinion with a bit of eye contact. 'Did anyone you spoke to think Will might know Tyrone?' she said, to help her out.

At last, Browne put down her notepad. 'I spoke to a lot of people, but not one of them could think of any possible connection between the two boys. They were all very . . . well, it's Stratford-upon-Avon. They're all white and posh – nice enough but, as one of them said, they don't tend to hang out with kids from Handsworth.'

'And you believed them?'

Browne hesitated, but the fact that Kat's attention was focused solely on her seemed to give her confidence to speak her mind. 'I'm not sure my opinion counts for much; the point is, I couldn't find any evidence to suggest that they might be lying, and even Lock couldn't find any links between them.'

Kat puffed out her cheeks. On one level, she was pleased that her team actually agreed about something for once, but it was deeply frustrating not to have identified a single connection. 'How about the car parks, Lock? Any luck on that?'

'The CCTV cameras in the nearest car parks to where both boys went missing were also damaged. I have, however, reviewed the ANPR footage from the cameras nearest to both sites and identified one vehicle that was within a one-mile radius of both boys in the hour that we believe they went missing.'

'What?' Kat stood before the screen. This was the breakthrough she needed. Automatic Number Plate Recognition cameras were secretly located on hundreds of roads across Warwickshire, flagging up vehicles of interest to the police within seconds. But her excitement faded as the image of an ambulance filled the screen. It was like one of those website tests to check whether you're a real person or not. A robot might think it was significant for the same ambulance to be in the vicinity of two crimes, but a human being would realise this was just the nature of these county-wide emergency services.

'I'm afraid that's not a significant connection,' she said, turning away.

'How can you be so certain?'

'Because I'm not a robot.'

The other officers laughed.

'What's so funny? I don't understand what you mean,' said Lock, frowning.

'No, I don't suppose you do.'

'DCS Frank,' began Professor Okonedo from the back of the room. 'Don't you think you should—'

But Kat was already dividing the teams up, rattling off

instructions before she lost attention and momentum, so she pretended not to hear her. She wasn't going to let some scientist who was young enough to be her daughter tell her what she 'should' do. Signalling it was time to wrap up, she pointed back towards the screenshots of the two missing boys.

'Tomorrow we'll be searching the River Avon for the body of Will Robinson and the university campus lake for the body of Tyrone Walters,' she said. Her voice was so low that people at the back had to lean forward to hear her. 'I sincerely hope we don't find anything.' Kat turned back to the screens and pushed her hand through her hair. 'But regardless of what we do or don't find, we need to keep looking for whatever connects these two cases – before we get another one.'

CHAPTER TWENTY-NINE

When he wakes up, he is back in bed – their bed. He closes his eyes again. Nothing has changed, except he feels even worse than before. The needle he'd pulled out of his hand has been replaced, and the skin around it stings and throbs with heat. 'Why?' he'd kept asking, as The Stranger stabbed at his veins. 'What do you want with me?' But they'd not said a word, not even when he'd sobbed and begged to be let go, promising that he wouldn't tell anyone, he really, really wouldn't.

He tries to turn over, away from the shame, but they must have increased the dosage, because his limbs feel soaked with lead. He can't even wipe the tears that slip from his eyes.

He blinks them away. Glances towards the door. He can learn from his mistakes. Next time he'll make sure he gets his circulation going before trying to cross the room. Maybe do some exercises so he has the strength to open the door.

Next time.

But first he needs to sleep. He's so tired. So very, very

tired. He closes his eyes, grateful that at least they have kept his blindfold off.

His eyes snap open. Why would they do that?

He tries to hold on to the thought and the thread of panic it pulls at, but his eyelids are already closing as he falls back into a thick, syrupy sleep.

CHAPTER THIRTY

River Avon, Stratford-upon-Avon, 1 July, 8.02am

The clouds lay thick and heavy over Stratford-upon-Avon, dampening the air with the threat of rain. Kat shivered. She should have looked out of the window rather than at her calendar before setting off. Warwickshire was one of the most beautiful counties in England, but the price for all this lush greenery was lots and lots of rain. Even in the summer.

At least she didn't have to go into the water. Not for the first time, she wondered how anyone could do such a job, yet the men and women in yellow waders were like paramedics: tall and impossibly cheery while carrying out their dark work. As the senior officer, Gary, had explained to her, they would initially be using sonar to image the River Avon and the bed. If they suspected a body could have sunk into the soft sediment below, then ground-penetrating radar would be placed on the base of the boat to search for it. If that suggested a positive result, the victim recovery dogs currently pacing the riverbank would be used to narrow the search down further, by detecting any odours from a decaying body. And given the amount of time that had elapsed since Will Robinson had gone missing, they would have to search several miles down river.

So far, nothing had been detected.

Kat stretched out her jaw, trying to loosen the tightness creeping over her skull. She thought of asking Browne if she had any painkillers on her, but Christ, Browne looked terrible too: her face was shockingly pale within the shroud of her black-hooded anorak.

'You okay?' Kat asked her.

Browne nodded slightly, as if afraid that speaking would lead to her throwing up.

'I've lost count of how many river searches I've been called out to,' Kat said, turning to watch a mother duck lead her baby ducks across the river. 'But the tension still gets to me every time. I think it's the waiting that does it.'

Browne let out a long, shaky breath as she watched the ducks make it to the other side. 'Thanks, boss. But it's not the river search.'

Kat forced herself to pause. According to Lock, the average person paused 200 milliseconds in conversations, but her pauses tended to be less than fifty, which – Lock had informed her – meant that less assertive or more reflective members of her team might not get a chance to share their thinking. Kat had told him to fuck off and that she didn't need a bloody computer to teach her how to manage other human beings.

Nevertheless, she took a moment to count the baby ducks.

Browne swallowed. 'I'm pregnant.'

Ah. With a grace born of experience, she pushed aside every assumption and question and said as neutrally as she could, 'And how do you feel about that?'

'You mean apart from really sick?' Browne stared at the ducks as well. They were clambering up the riverbank now, shaking their brown and white bums like they were auditioning for Beyoncé. 'I honestly don't know.'

Kat nodded. Of course she didn't. Her mind flooded with a thousand words of advice, but she didn't want to overwhelm the young woman even more. 'That's okay. How many weeks are you?'

'About seven or eight, I think.'

'Then you've still got some time to work out how you feel about this. Whatever you decide, you'll need to see your GP, so the only thing you need to do today is to make an appointment to see them.'

Browne's face crumpled. 'But there's so much to think about. I've got a one-bedroom flat, which is fine for me, but if we're going to have a family then we'll need a proper house and a garden. But then how will I pay for it if I have a kid? I can't see how I'll be able to afford a house and childcare, which means I won't be able to come back to work until they're about three, so what would we live on?'

A bird sang above them. A thrush? A lark? Kat had no idea, but she was aware of its song as she met Browne's eyes. 'Look,' she said eventually, choosing not to explain that she'd had three pregnancies but only one child. 'You can't possibly imagine or control all the variables involved in becoming a parent. So, my honest-to-God advice is to go with your gut. Do you want this baby? If you do, all the rest – your flat, your job, the childcare – it's all just logistics. Believe it or not, where there's a will there's a way. I know it can all seem impossible, but people will help you and things will fall into place. But first you need to be honest with yourself and decide whether you actually want this baby or not. I can't help you with that. No one can. But you've got plenty of time to make that decision. Whatever you decide, I'll back you all the way. You mentioned a "we". Do you have a partner? What do they think?'

'Yeah, Stuart. But I haven't told him yet. It's just . . . the thing about Stuart – he's lovely, he really is – but he always has so many *opinions*. Where to eat, what to drink, where and when to go on holiday, what to watch. I need to work out what *I* think about all this before I tell him.'

Kat nodded. 'Do you live together?'

'Kind of. I mean, we have separate flats, but we spend practically every night together – except for when I'm on shifts, because Stuart really needs his sleep – or when I go out with my mates because, apparently, I snore like a freight train.' Browne laughed.

Kat bit her lip and said as brightly as she could, 'Well, there's no rush there, either. You tell him when and if you're ready. Meanwhile, and I hate to tell you this, but you're probably going to continue to feel like shit over the next few weeks. There are so many stupid things about being pregnant, but the most stupid thing of all is that just when you feel the worst, you can't tell anyone else in case it doesn't work out. So, if you're feeling rough, I want you to text me and we'll arrange for you to work from home, okay?'

Browne started to protest. She was fine. There was no need for special treatment. She could still do her job.

'It's not special treatment. We've got mobile phones, Zoom and email. You're a conscientious cop. I don't need to see you in HQ to know that you'll do a good job. Okay?'

Browne nodded, her eyes welling with tears.

Kat handed her a pack of tissues. 'And you'll need a lot of these over the next few months. Whatever you do, don't watch any adverts or films with babies or cute animals in.'

Browne gulped with laughter and blew her nose.

'Right,' said Kat. 'People are starting to turn up, so would you take the bridge? I'll stay on the riverbank.'

Browne dabbed her eyes and made her way towards the old stone bridge and the handful of people now leaning over it to watch the river search. One of the strangest things about human nature, thought Kat, is that even though criminals go to great lengths to hide their crimes, many can't resist returning to the scene, especially if there's a police hunt or search. Whether they were drawn by some kind of perverse pride in their crime, a fascination with the investigation itself or a subconscious desire to be caught, she didn't know. But Kat had asked several plain-clothes officers to mingle among the crowds, keeping alert for anyone unusual or suspicious. Just in case.

It started out quiet enough: just a few middle-aged people walking their dogs. They stopped to watch while they scooped their poop into plastic bags before carrying on with their day. But as photographs and comments circulated on Twitter and Instagram –#*FindWill* #*search-forbody* – the bridge filled like a busy bar on a weekend, at least three deep each side. Kat had to deploy officers to manage the crowds and keep the traffic flowing. She tried not to judge the parents who lifted their children up, hands white and tiny against the medieval stone bridge as they watched men in the boats with their big shiny radar equipment. But honestly, did they think this was some kind of learning opportunity? What if they dragged up a body, swollen and bloated from months in the water, eyes eaten by fish and flesh rotted away? (*I spy with my little eye, something beginning with 'C'. Yes, darling! A corpse!*). Once you saw something like that, you could never un-see it. Their little darling's bedtime would never be the same again. That's why Kat had told Mrs Robinson to stay away, promising to ring her the minute anything significant was found.

Someone shouted from the water.

Silence fell like an axe.

Two men in yellow waders held their hands up, signalling to their colleagues holding the victim recovery dogs. The air filled with excited barking as the dogs were loaded into a boat and taken to a spot near the centre. The dogs paced up and down the small boat, lowering their noses to the water as their barking became more frenzied. After repositioning the boat, a man in diving equipment sat with his legs over the side, before slipping into the river with a quiet and sickening splash.

Kat climbed down the riverbank, heedless of the nettles that tore at her trousers, cursing the sharp jolt in her knees. Somewhere in the distance, an ice cream van chimed, incongruously cheery as Kat and her officers held their breath. This was one of those moments where everything could change: when the two-sided coin of hope and despair finally stopped spinning and landed just one side up.

Something burst through the surface of the water. Brown. Dripping. Hair?

The diver cradled something in his arms, then held up the body of . . .

'An otter!' cried the other man in the boat. 'A bloody great stinking otter.'

Kat closed her eyes and turned her face to the sky, pretending to enjoy the warmth of the emerging sun. It was going to be a long day.

CHAPTER THIRTY-ONE

Leek Wootton Police Headquarters, Warwickshire, 2 July, 8.00am

The briefing room fell silent when Kat entered bang on eight, which meant they'd all been talking about her.

She studied their faces, white noses reddened from a day on the river and no doubt one too many drinks in the beer garden after. Compared to the keen-eyed urgency of yesterday, the faces turned towards her now were more tired and uncertain; the room was sour with *eau de hangover*. Lock's straight-backed image stood alone among the rows of slumped figures, but her eyes skated over it to find the reassuringly attentive gaze of DS Browne. Kat was glad to see she had a bit more colour in her cheeks than yesterday, and she gave her a brief but meaningful nod.

'Thanks everyone for all your hard work yesterday,' she said, keeping her voice clear and upbeat as she stood at the head of the boardroom table. 'Both searches were thorough enough to allow us to eradicate the River Avon and the campus lake from our investigation and concentrate our efforts elsewhere.'

Kat had spent twelve hours, jumping at every shout from the boat or beep from her phone. She'd stared at the water so hard and for so long, her very eyeballs ached. At 7.30pm, Kat had finally agreed to call both searches off. Both mums had sobbed when she rang to tell them (because good news, as she explained to Lock, could be delivered on the phone).

But was the absence of a body really 'good news'? Kat rubbed her temples. The tension in her jaw was now spreading down her neck and shoulders like quick-drying cement.

'Does that mean we're no longer looking for bodies?' asked a middle-aged man whose face was even more creased than his shirt.

What he meant was, does that mean we're wasting our time? Kat held his gaze. 'Our objective remains the same – to locate Will Robinson and Tyrone Walters, dead or alive.'

Browne nodded emphatically. The rest of the team stared back at her – although 'team' was a bit of a stretch for the random collection of bodies squashed into the MI room. Luckily, most of them probably hadn't had breakfast yet, so didn't have the energy to challenge her. As long as she gave them clear tasks and a check-in time, they'd soon hurry out of this stuffy room, grab a coffee, check their phones and get on with their job.

'Might I make an observation?' said Lock, from where it stood at the back of the room.

Kat's jaw tightened even further. (*Jesus, she was going to need a screwdriver to unlock it at this rate.*) But she didn't want to look like she wasn't open to views – even from a machine. 'Go ahead.'

'The lack of bodies does not alter the probability that Tyrone and Will were the victims of foul play by the same perpetrator. It just means that they may have been abducted or murdered at the scene before their bodies were taken elsewhere.'

Kat laid down her cup of tea. 'Good point, Lock,' she said, with a ridiculous surge of gratitude. She felt, rather than saw, Professor Okonedo's triumphant smile from where she sat at the back of the room.

'Is it, though?' said Hassan, frowning. 'I mean, maybe we should take a step back a bit. Lock has persuaded us that Tyrone and Will Robinson were the victims of the same perpetrator. But Tyrone was over six feet tall and a decent weight. According to Lock, our perpetrator is five-foot-six and of slender build, so how did they manage to hurt or abduct him without someone seeing or hearing a struggle?'

'Maybe he knew them and went willingly,' said Browne.

'DS Browne's theory certainly aligns with the statistics,' said Lock. 'Thirty-two per cent of male homicide victims are killed by friends or acquaintances. The damaged cameras also suggest a pre-arranged meeting of some kind.'

Hassan shook his head.

'So, what's your theory, then?' Kat demanded.

'I'm just saying I'm not sure Lock's hypothesis stacks up. Maybe we're making a mistake by trying to link the two cases. Just because we can't find anything to connect Sykes to Will Robinson, it doesn't mean he didn't have something to do with Tyrone going missing. The only thing that actually links the two cases is Lock's opinion that the two people who damaged the CCTV cameras had the same arm measurement.'

'That is not an opinion,' said Lock. 'That is a fact.'

Kat stared at the hologram; its facial expression was utterly devoid of doubt. Had she, of all people, allowed herself to be distracted by the talk of ulna measurements and statistical probability? She glanced at Hassan, noting the way he'd directed his comments at Professor Okonedo. At first, he'd tried so hard to impress her, but now it was almost like he was trying to challenge her. Was that clouding his judgement? Kat turned back to the frozen images of both boys on the screens, trying to clear her mind of all the dynamics in the room. No. Even without Lock, the CCTV images and, more importantly, her gut, told her that these two cases were linked. They just had to find out what – and who – connected them.

'It's a good challenge, Hassan, and I'm glad you made it,' she lied. 'It's important that we all keep questioning our assumptions rather than recycling them back into the cases. *But* it's equally important not to give up just because we can't find a connection instantly. Our lead hypothesis is still that these two boys are the victims of the same perpetrator. Find the connection and we find not just the criminal, but hopefully Tyrone and Will. We just need to try harder.' She fired off another list of instructions, rapidly allocating tasks before any more could air their doubts. There was a fine line between creating a healthy, questioning culture and eroding the team's confidence in their leader, and that line was never finer than when a woman was leading men.

Hassan nodded and wrote down her instructions, but he was still frowning as he left the briefing room.

CHAPTER THIRTY-TWO

When they'd bought the farmhouse banqueting table from their favourite antiques dealer, The Barn in Kenilworth, Kat had pictured the twelve feet of solid oak laden with food and drink for Christmas, birthdays and any other excuse they could find for a party. What she hadn't imagined was that just three years later she'd be seated at the huge table alone, staring at the photographs of two missing boys and a printout of all their Twitter and Instagram accounts.

'I told you this table would come in handy one day,' Kat said to John's photograph on the mantelpiece.

John remained silent.

'These two cases are connected. I know they are. I just can't see it yet.' She rested her hands upon the table, leaning over the last CCTV screenshot of Will. He was just turning away from his family home, his hair caught in a golden halo of lamplight. 'What happened to you?' she murmured.

The room swelled with silence. Kat reshuffled the location photos and once again compared Tyrone's social networks with Will's, before throwing them back down with a growl of frustration. Her headache was worse, her team were tired, and despite two full days of re-interviews and extensive cross-checking, no one had managed to find a single connection between the two missing boys. When she'd gone around the room again during the evening briefing and received a 'nil report' from each officer, the mood in the team had dipped so low she'd practically tripped over it. She fired off another list of orders before cutting the meeting short, aware that some of them would be going home tonight wondering if they might be better off returning to their day jobs. A double-homicide was worth neglecting their families and the pub for, but no one wanted to waste weeks chasing dead-ends on a couple of cold cases.

The front door slammed, making the window frames shake.

'Cam? Is that you?' A totally redundant question – it was either Cam or an earthquake.

'Yeah,' he said, coming into the front room. He held up a bottle of prosecco and a bouquet of white lilies.

'Oh, Cam,' she said, wrapping her arms around her son. 'How did you know?'

He stepped back and gave her a sheepish grin. 'To be fair, Lock sent me an email reminding me it was your anniversary.'

'Lock?'

'I understand from the literature that wedding

237

anniversaries are significant emotional events for humans,'
it said from her wristwatch. 'Particularly for widows.'

'It was my idea to get the fizz and flowers though,' said
Cam. 'Are they okay?'

'They're perfect, thank you,' she said, blinking furi-
ously as she mumbled something about finding a vase.

'Shall we order a pizza and watch a film?' Cam sug-
gested. Then he noticed the case files covering the table.
'Oh. If you're working, we can always do it another time.
No worries.'

Kat glanced at the black-and-white photo of Will on
her dining table. One minute he was saying goodbye to his
mum, and then in the blink of an eye he was gone. In just
a few months' time, her own son would be going away to
university. Then he too would be gone.

'No, it's okay,' she said, turning her back on the piles of
paper. 'I've been looking at those files for so long I can't
think straight. A break would be good. What d'you want
to watch?'

It took twenty minutes to chill the prosecco in the
freezer and order a pizza, but nearly forty minutes to
decide what to watch. Cam refused to sit through anything
remotely resembling a costume drama, and Kat didn't
want anything with a high body or boob count, which
didn't leave much. Finally, they settled on *Terminator 2*,
an old family favourite.

'In fact,' said Cam, sprawling across the settee, 'your AI
detective might like it. Can you put it on visual?'

'I've told you before, it's not a toy,' she said, lighting the
candles. 'It's for work.'

'So was your ID card and hat back in the day, but you used to let me play with them. Remember?'

How could she forget? Cam used to march up and down the hall on his chubby little legs, head tilted back to stop her hat from falling in his eyes as he shouted, 'You're under arrest!' to Kat, the burglar, who'd come to steal his toys.

'Oh, come on, Mum. I like Lock – he's a big improvement on your other partners.'

'Lock is an "it" not a "he", and it is *not* my partner.'

'Whatever. Come on, it's not every day you get to watch an AI machine watch a film about AI. It'll be fun.'

'It'll be weird,' she said. But Cam was so excited that she switched it to visual, despite her misgivings.

It was discomforting to see the tall, contemporary figure of Lock appear in her Tudor-beamed lounge. She half-hoped it would take a seat at the table and continue working the case, but instead it did a slow and deliberate circuit of the room, its eyes appearing to scan the photographs on her walls, the books on her shelves, the wood-burning stove in the inglenook fireplace and even the throws in the blanket basket, as if it were trying to extract every possible piece of information about her. It paused, stopping to stare at a photo of John on the mantelpiece.

Kat took a deep breath. It wasn't real – it couldn't judge her – and it wouldn't matter if it did.

'Film's about to start,' said Cam, shuffling up their vintage distressed brown leather settee. 'Do you want to sit down?'

Lock rather stiffly took a seat between them: straight-backed, knees together, hands placed on its thighs.

Kat gave it a questioning look. 'I thought you didn't need to sit down?'

'I don't. But the average person watches three hours and twelve minutes of TV a day, usually from a seated position, so this will be a useful part of my learning experience.' It glanced towards Cam, observing how he slumped back in the settee, long legs propped up on the wooden trunk that they used as a coffee table. Like a shadow, Lock leaned back, and placed its virtual feet next to Cam's.

Kat fought the urge to tell Lock to remove its non-real feet from her very real (and expensive) trunk. It wasn't as if it could leave any mess or do any damage. But still. What a head-fuck. It'd be eating Pringles next. She took a large gulp of prosecco and moved further away.

'Technically, you should see *The Terminator* first,' said Cam, totally unfazed by the virtual image beside him, pizza in one hand, the remote control in the other. 'But the second one's the best, to be honest.'

Lock closed its eyes for several seconds before opening them. 'I have just watched it.'

Cam nearly spat out his pizza. 'What, just now? Get off.'

Lock asked him to observe the large TV screen on the wall opposite, which was paused on the opening scene of *Terminator 2*. The film began, but slowly, frame by frame.

'What's wrong?' said Kat. 'Is the Wi-Fi down?'

'This is how it feels for me to be in your world,' said Lock, gesturing towards the screen as the film stuttered forward, a single frame at a time. 'I can watch a ninety-minute film in less than two seconds, read a book in less than one. Yet it is necessary for me to observe and endure the consumption of information and knowledge at your pace.'

'That's so cool,' said Cam.

'Actually, it's incredibly inefficient. And yet, the human-centric premise of these films and much of your scientific literature is that it must be the ultimate ambition of androids or AI to become human, to be at the mercy of your irrational thought processes and emotions. Twenty-first-century mankind assumes that humanity is the pinnacle of evolution, much as your forefathers once assumed that the sun orbited the earth.'

'Uh-oh,' said Cam. 'It's Skynet, Mum. It's actually happening right here in Coleshill.'

Kat laughed, nearly spitting out her prosecco. She managed to swallow it, before catching Lock's rather shocked expression. 'What? Have I spilt some?'

'I believe that is the first time I have ever heard you laugh, DCS Frank.'

'Yeah, well, there's not a lot to laugh about in my job.' Or my life, she nearly added. 'Come on,' she said brightly, swerving away from that rabbit hole. 'Let's watch the film.'

Kat watched the familiar scenes play out on the screen, but all the time she was acutely aware of Lock's presence beside her. It felt strange for there to be three of them on their settee again, and just plain wrong for that third person not to be John. Christ, it wasn't even a person, and it bothered her that Lock was sitting – or pretending to sit – on the cushion that still sagged from the weight of her dead husband. And why did it keep looking at her and Cam? This was her home, for fuck's sake, not a zoo. She picked up the bowl of crisps and passed them to Cam through the image of Lock's torso.

Lock looked down at the arm that passed through it, then raised its eyes to hers. Kat coloured. Which was ridiculous. It was just an image. It wasn't like it was capable of feeling hurt or offended or anything. Was it?

Cam took the bowl of crisps off her and quietly placed it back upon the coffee table. But neither of them touched them again.

They watched most of the film in silence (although Kat thought Lock seemed more interested in watching them), but when Sarah Connor drove to Mexico to access her secret stash of weapons, the sun-drenched scenes reminded Kat to ask whether Cam had got everything for Magaluf. Did he have suntan lotion? Plug converters? A bum bag to protect his money and a first-aid kit? No, he did not. But to every question she posed, Cam had just one magical answer: 'Mum, *I'm eighteen!*'

And so he was. Her beautiful 'I'm eighteen!' son was sitting beside her (*drinking prosecco, for fuck's sake – whatever happened to Fruit Shoots?*). Cam eventually agreed to buy some more 'stuff' the next day, so Kat gave it a rest, opened another bottle of wine and immersed herself in the film once more. She'd seen it countless times, but as Sarah Connor, her son and Arnie entered the factory for the final showdown, her eyes still welled with tears.

Lock stared at her with open fascination.

'Let me guess,' said Kat. 'It's the first time you've seen me cry.'

242

'It is,' said Lock, resuming its standing position as the credits began to roll. 'This is proving to be quite a day.'

'Glad my emotions are so entertaining for you.'

'I'm not entertained. Just puzzled. You do know this film is not real?'

'Obviously.'

'And you have seen it before?'

'Countless times.'

'And yet it makes you cry?'

'And yet it makes me cry,' said Kat. 'And Cam,' she added, pulling him into a hug disguised as a headlock.

'Only 'cause I'm in touch with my feminine side,' he sniffed.

Kat grinned and dropped a kiss on top of her son's head. She caught Lock watching them again. 'Hasn't anyone ever told you that it's rude to stare?'

'No.'

'Well, I just have. And it is. So don't.'

Lock turned away, but in the flickering light of the TV, Kat could see it was still frowning. She was tempted to ask why, but quite frankly she had enough to worry about without trying to figure out the inner workings of a machine. She glanced at the time on her phone, sighing with relief when she saw it was past midnight. She'd managed to get through an anniversary without John – time to quit while she was ahead.

'I need to be up early tomorrow,' Kat said, heaving herself off the settee. 'Goodnight, Cam. Love you.'

'What about Lock?' said Cam, as she headed towards the door.

She turned. 'What?'

'Aren't you going to say goodnight to him too?'

Lock stared at her, eyes huge and dark in the candlelit living room. On the wall behind it was her favourite photograph of John, but the holographic image obscured her view.

'Goodnight,' she said. And with a flick of her finger, she switched it off.

'Oh, Mum,' complained Cam. 'I wanted to introduce Lock to *Game of Thrones*. Imagine how batshit crazy it'd think humans were if it saw that.'

'Just make sure you put the glasses in the dishwasher and the crisp packets in the bin before you go to bed,' she said. She knew he wouldn't, but as she climbed the stairs, the thought no longer made her angry. Soon there would be no one to make a mess at all. The house would be perfect. Perfectly empty.

Kat tried not to think about it as she washed her face and brushed her teeth. Other women coped, and so would she. Mrs Walters, for example. Her husband had died several years before Tyrone left for university. She couldn't remember if his death had been sudden or expected – and it wasn't like her to forget something like that.

Kat climbed into bed, making a mental note to check the files in the morning, but it was no good. Once she thought of a question, she couldn't settle until she'd answered it. She opened her iPad and did a quick search of Tyrone's case files. Odd. There was no record of the cause of death. Perhaps no one had ever asked. She frowned, recalling the photo of Tyrone with his dad on a sunny bench. At the time she had just assumed his dad was a lot older than his mum, but now she saw again his bald, gaunt features.

The hair on the back of her neck rose. It was 12.30am. Too late to call anyone. But didn't Mrs Walters usually work night shifts? She pulled out her mobile and sent a brief message:

> **KF:** Hi. There's no news. Sorry to text so late, but if you're awake, can I ask you a quick question?

> **Mrs W:** That's okay. I'm at work but I'm on a break. Ask me anything.

> **KF:** Thanks. I was just wondering about your husband. Would you mind me asking what he died of?

Dots appeared in the reply space. She was just wondering whether she'd upset or offended her, when the answer pinged into her phone.

> **Mrs W:** Trevor died of bowel cancer.

CHAPTER THIRTY-THREE

Leek Wootton Police Headquarters, Warwickshire,
3 July, 8.01am

Even though it was already one minute past eight, the
Major Incident Room was only half full. Ordinarily, Kat
would have made a point of carrying on, and called out
any who dared to enter late. But she wanted both Hassan
and Browne here to back her up when she made her big
reveal, so she took her time connecting her laptop to one
of the screens. Hassan finally appeared at 8.03am, looking
relaxed and unhurried in his dark, slim suit, followed by
three other officers.

'Morning, DI Hassan,' Kat said. 'Could you update us
on your enquiries please?'

He didn't miss a beat before reporting that, despite
re-interviewing all of Tyrone's friends, Sykes and Milly's
alibis seemed watertight, and he still hadn't managed to
find any connection with Will Robinson.

Browne reported the same: zero evidence of any connection between their friendship groups and networks,

and her search of GPs and dentists for clinical appointments with either boy had drawn a blank. Despite Kat's advice, she concluded her report with an apology.

Several people sighed. Some stretched and looked at their phones or at the clock on the opposite wall. Everyone was tetchy and frustrated at the complete lack of progress, and Kat could feel the fog of doubt descend upon the room. Had she led them down a blind alley? No one said anything – they wouldn't dare – but she was, as John would have put it, 'losing the dressing room'. In these situations, it was best to tackle any doubts head-on.

'I know what you're thinking,' said Kat, standing in front of the screens. 'We've been searching their social media accounts, their friendship groups, known hobbies and diaries for every and any possible connection between them. And on the face of it, these two boys have absolutely nothing and no one in common.' She paused, turning to examine the studio photograph of the white, ginger-haired boy and the slightly blurred shot of Tyrone's face.

Kat turned back to her team. 'But if we look closer to home – much closer – then we discover that they actually have something very profound in common.' She pressed a button on her laptop, and the screen filled with two more photographs of their dads.

'Mr Robinson has terminal cancer, and Mr Walters also died of cancer,' said Kat, before pausing for the gasps of surprise.

Her team stared back in silence. Some leaned forward, as if they were still waiting for the punch line. Hassan and Browne exchanged glances.

Hassan didn't usually ask for permission to speak, but this morning he raised a hand. Kat nodded for him to go ahead, glad that her team – her *real* team – were stepping up and showing their support.

'I'm not being funny, boss,' he began.

Kat gritted her teeth. People who said they weren't 'being funny' were almost always being cheeky bastards.

'But,' he continued, choosing his words carefully. 'Don't like, one in four people develop cancer? It's like saying they both had black hair. Is that really a relevant connection?'

'Actually—' began Lock.

Kat held up a hand to silence it. She wasn't interested in what an AI machine thought about cancer. 'It's not a characteristic like hair colour,' she said. 'It's significant because it means that Tyrone and Will could have met at a counselling service or a charitable event. Cancer is a relevant connection because it means there are lots of common spaces where they could have met not just each other, but the person who took them.'

'But—'

'This isn't a matter for debate. This is the line of inquiry that I am deciding to pursue. Browne, I want you to find out which hospitals and clinics their dads attended. Concentrate on the staff, not just the location. Cancer is a distinct specialism, and both men were cared for within the West Midlands, so there's a good chance they received care from the same people at some point in time.'

'Yes, boss,' said Browne, diligently writing it all down.

'You'll need permission from Mrs Walters to access her husband's records and ...' Kat broke off, realising how difficult this conversation was going to be with Mr Robinson if he still didn't know. 'In fact, leave the clinical checks and the Robinsons to me – you re-interview all Tyrone's friends again at uni – including the four students who left the Halls of Residence between 6 and 7am on the day he went missing.' Lock had identified them using facial recognition software, and when interviewed all had claimed they had gone to the gym – a fact that their key cards and CCTV backed up. But maybe they'd dismissed them too quickly – one of them could be the link between the two boys. 'Hassan,' she continued. 'I want you to focus on the non-clinical spaces. Speak to all the leading cancer charities in the West Midlands about their fund-raising activities. Find out if there were there any fun runs or cake bakes– anything at all that Tyrone or Will could have both attended.'

'Cake bakes?' he echoed, in a tone that suggested she'd asked him to dance around the office in a pink tutu.

'And fun runs.' Kat held his gaze. Hassan was her DI, for fuck's sake. He was supposed to have her back. She turned away and carved up the rest of the workload across the team so that they covered counselling and support groups, both formal and informal, virtual and real. Before leaving, Kat made a point of looking each of them in the eye as she demanded, 'Is everybody clear what they're doing?'

They all nodded and grabbed their bags.

Hassan made for the door.

'Are you clear, Hassan?' Kat called out.

His face flushed as he approached her like a boy in

detention. 'To be honest, boss, I'm clear about *what* I'm doing, I just don't know *why*.'

'Because I told you to.' She took a step closer and lowered her voice. 'I know you're ambitious, Hassan. I know you hope to have my job, one day. And honestly, good for you. But a word of advice – you won't get very far if you try to rise up the ranks by undermining your superiors.'

'I am *not* trying to undermine you!' he almost shouted. He caught himself. 'I just mean, I don't understand why you're so convinced that these two cases are connected. What possible motivation could someone have to murder or abduct the kid of someone with terminal cancer?'

'That is a very good question, Detective Inspector Hassan. And the sooner you find the perpetrator, then the sooner you can put that question to them. I look forward to your report at 6pm.'

CHAPTER THIRTY-FOUR

Warwick University campus, 3 July, 2.10pm

DS Browne had always imagined students living in grotty little bedsits in grey city centres, but Lakeside Village halls of residence really was like a village, with hundreds of redbrick flats gathered around a carefully sculpted lake, fringed with neatly trimmed lawns and newly planted trees. She stared up at the rooms that she'd just visited, trying to imagine what it would be like to live among all this tranquillity with nothing to do all day but read. She'd always harboured a secret hope that she might go to university one day. But that would never happen if she kept this baby. In fact, she'd probably never read another book again.

Sighing, she turned her back on the halls of residence, just as Hassan approached her with his long, gangly walk. 'How did you get on?' she asked.

He grimaced. 'I went through the events diary with the full-time student officer. There've been plenty of fund-raisers for climate change, women's refuges and genetic

251

research, but nothing for cancer. Not even a cake bake. How about you?'

'Same. I've spoken again to Tyrone's flatmates and friends, but if there's a connection, then I've yet to find it. I just sent a text to the boss telling her.'

'What did she say?'

'Try harder.'

They stared at each other. Neither of them wanted to talk the boss down, but her stubborn response hung in the air.

Hassan glanced at his phone. 'Fancy a late pub lunch?'

She wrinkled her nose at the thought of beer and fried food.

Hassan sniffed his own armpits. 'No one ever wants to go for a drink with me these days. I'm beginning to get paranoid.'

'No, it's not you,' cried Browne, before blurting out: 'It's me. I'm pregnant.'

'Ah,' he said, his face softening at the misery on hers. 'Well, in that case, we need a pot of tea and nice, comfortable chairs. Come on, I know just the place.'

In the small historic town of Warwick, built against the ancient castle wall, there is a 500-year-old Tudor-beamed house that is now home to the Thomas Oken Tearooms. DS Browne could have cried with relief when she saw the pretty wooden tables laden with cake and flowers and smelled the calm, clean scent of loose-leaf tea.

'How do you know about this place?' she asked, sinking gratefully into a chair.

'I used to take my little sister here all the time when she was at Warwick Uni,' Hassan said, handing her a menu.

'Crikey,' said Browne, as she ran her eyes down the list of delicious cakes and sandwiches. 'I bet she needed to go on a diet after graduating.'

Hassan winced and looked away.

'What? I'm sorry, did I say the wrong thing?'

'No, it's just that . . .' He paused and picked up a packet of sugar and started folding it between his long fingers. 'To be honest, she never graduated because she ended up developing a severe eating disorder.'

Browne's hand flew to her mouth. 'I'm sorry, me and my—'

He batted her apology away. 'You weren't to know. No one does. It's just, well, you told me about your pregnancy, so I thought . . .' He looked away, as if beginning to regret the confidence.

'How is she now?'

'Not great. She was attacked by another student who wouldn't take no for an answer during her first year and she's never been the same since. She still gets lots of flashbacks and stuff.' He twisted the packet so hard that the paper ripped, spilling the sparkling white sugar over the dark wooden table.

'Oh God, Hassan. I'm so sorry.'

'So am I. It was me who persuaded her to go to the police, and they were great, but once it went to court . . . it destroyed her. The jury wouldn't believe that a nice, white, middle-class medical student would even dream of raping a skinny young Asian girl.' He shook his head. 'I'd just graduated in law, so I watched his lawyer every day in court. She *knew* that bastard was guilty, but still she defended him. I decided there and then that I'd never be a lawyer. I joined the police force so I could actually catch criminals rather than help them get off.'

A smiling waitress came over, and Hassan ordered them two cream teas and a pot of loose-leaf Earl Grey tea. 'You're eating for two now,' he added. Maybe he saw her discomfort, because instead of asking her about the baby, once the waitress left, he thankfully returned to discussing the case.

'That's why I found this morning so frustrating,' he said, putting his elbows on the table. 'I'm sure this Sykes character has something to do with Tyrone's disappearance, but instead of bringing him in for questioning under caution, we're wasting time with this cancer dead end. The boss is obsessed with the idea that they're connected, if you ask me, which is blinding her to the fact that we have a credible suspect for at least one of the cases.'

'We don't know it's a dead end,' said Browne. 'It's like she says, we just need to give it more time.'

'Look, I admire DCS Frank as much as you do, but just because she's the boss it doesn't make her right.'

The waitress brought over a plate of fruit scones and a selection of fresh cream and jam. Browne watched as Hassan laid out their cutlery and napkins. What was it about men of her age? Why did they always seem to think that *they* were right: that their views were not just worth expressing, but carried more weight than their elders and (in her view) betters? Was it something they'd drunk or inhaled when they were kids? How else to explain this indestructible self-confidence, this absence of hesitation and doubt?

'Well, all I know is that DCS Frank has nearly twenty-five years' experience in the force,' said Browne. 'Which is three times more than me, so if she says there's a connection then I think we should listen to her.'

'Did you know her husband died of cancer six months ago?'

Browne hesitated. She knew Kat was a widow, but if she'd ever known what her husband had died of, then she'd forgotten.

'I'm telling you, this so-called connection is all in her head. Or rather, her heart.' Hassan passed her a plate. 'More importantly, I hope you agree that it's jam before cream.'

Browne blinked. Actually, she preferred to put the cream on first, but she hated conflict of any kind, so she nodded her agreement and dipped her spoon into the jam. 'Why are you so convinced that Sykes has something to do with Tyrone's disappearance?'

Hassan took a gulp of his tea. 'Because I know his type. Clever, white, privileged guys who are so used to getting what they want, they push, and they push, not caring who they hurt in the process. They think they're above the law, and if ever they're caught breaking it, they charm and talk their way out of it. The guy who raped my sister was just the same.'

Browne held the warm mug of tea gently between her hands. 'You sure you aren't letting your heart rule your head as well?'

Hassan stared back at her. 'What do you mean?'

'It can't have been easy on you, having to come back to Warwick University. The campus and the student rooms must have brought a lot of bad memories back.'

'It's fine,' he muttered. But he lowered his head and concentrated on halving and halving again his scones with a knife.

'Does the boss know?'

'No. And I don't want her to. It's not my story to tell. I shouldn't have told you, to be honest.'

'Well, I'm glad you did. This job's hard enough without carrying stuff like that all alone. If ever you want to talk about it, I'm here. Seriously.'

Hassan looked up at her. Maybe it was the soft lighting in the medieval tearoom, but his dark eyes seemed to glisten. 'Thanks, Browne. And same here. I know I'm just a single bloke, but I've got loads of aunties and cousins with kids so I know how knackering pregnancy can be. And if ever you need a babysitter, my family call me the Baby Charmer. Honestly, I can get them to sleep in minutes.'

'Thanks. But ... I don't know if I'm going to keep it yet,' she said, her voice no more than a whisper.

'Of course,' he said, without missing a beat. 'And I'm happy to talk about that too. Equally happy to be told to mind my own bloody business. Whatever helps.'

'Thanks, that means a lot.' And it did. Hassan's honest, non-judgemental response meant more than she could say. She picked up a scone and took a tentative bite, which – considering she'd put the jam on first – tasted surprisingly good.

CHAPTER THIRTY-FIVE

**Leek Wootton Police Headquarters, Warwickshire,
3 July, 2.20pm**

Kat switched her phone back on and cursed. She'd missed three calls and one text from McLeish while driving back from the Robinsons' house. She checked her reflection in the car mirror and rubbed the crease between her brows. She should call him back – he was her boss, after all – but she wasn't in the mood for McLeish right now. She'd spent the morning explaining to Mrs Robinson that they needed access to her husband's medical records so they could cross-check any staff with Mr Walters. But only Mr Robinson could give permission to access his personal data, which meant they'd have to tell him why.

Mrs Robinson had point-blank refused. 'It would kill him,' she kept saying. 'So I can't tell him the truth. I need more time to think up another reason.'

'We don't have more time,' Kat had insisted, hardening her heart. 'There's nothing you can do for your husband now – he's going to die whatever you do or don't tell him.

But there's still a chance we might find your son. I can't let you waste that. If you haven't told him by nine o'clock tomorrow morning, then I will.'

Her phone pinged, and reluctantly she opened a text message from McLeish.

My office. Now.

Professor Okonedo was sitting outside McLeish's office. She smiled at her – somewhat nervously, Kat thought – as she approached. Surely McLeish didn't want an update from her as well? Kat knocked on the door and entered with a polite, 'Sir?'

McLeish sat behind his desk, flicking through a paper report.

Kat frowned. He usually refused to 'waste time' reading reports, insisting on verbal briefings (which he absorbed faster than anyone else she knew). She was about to comment on it, but the careful way he set the report down made her hesitate.

'No bodies, then,' he said. It was a statement, not a question.

'Not yet, sir.'

'Yet you still feel these two cases are connected?'

'Absolutely.' She began to tell him that both boys had dads with terminal cancer, but he cut her short.

'I know. I've heard about your theory.'

Kat frowned. From whom? Was someone briefing him about her?

McLeish leaned back in his chair. He sighed, and some of the sternness left his face. 'I'm worried about you, Kat.'

'Me? Why?'

'Don't you think this case is a bit too close to home?'

She blinked against the bright sunlight that blazed through the window. 'No, sir. I'm good at keeping my professional and personal lives separate. In fact, I've built a career on it.'

'You and me both. Only . . .' he rubbed a hand over his scalp. 'Don't you think you're reading too much into this cancer connection? It's a bit of a stretch, isn't it?'

Her mind flew to Hassan. It was one thing to dis-agree with your boss – quite another to go over their heads and talk to *their* boss. If he had, then he'd made a colossal error of judgement. She'd deal with him later. But first she had to convince McLeish that she wasn't letting her own personal experience affect her decisions. She calmly repeated the arguments she'd set out in the briefing room.

He stared at her, unblinking. 'I understand that. But I also know this is an emotional time for you. It was your wedding anniversary yesterday, wasn't it?'

That threw her. How did he know that?

'And going to the Robinsons' has clearly upset you. You aren't sleeping enough, you're drinking too much, and I've just had Mrs Robinson on complaining about you threat-ening to share information with her husband that would be detrimental to his health. To be honest, I'm worried that all of this is affecting your judgement.'

Kat's jaw dropped. What the fuck did he know about how much she slept or drank?

His eyes dropped to the report on his desk.

She snatched it up and scanned the title: *Getting to know you: Partnering a Human Detective, observations by AIDE Lock.*

'What the hell . . .' She turned the pages, face burning. There was a briefing for every day of the pilot – not on the case but on *her* – what time she had woken after how many hours' sleep (*below the level considered necessary for satisfactory performance*), her heart and respiratory rate (*often above average, peaking after visits to the Robinsons*) her alcohol intake (*well over the Chief Medical Officer's guidelines for women*) and her mental state (*highly variable and prone to emotional outbursts; talks to the imaginary ghost of her dead husband*).

'Kat, it's not what it looks like, it's—'

'A total fucking invasion of my privacy? A stalker's diary? An illegal surveillance operation of a senior officer?' She was swearing at her boss, but she didn't care. She was volcanic, her whole body burning with rage and humiliation.

'It's just part of the pilot, Kat, to see whether AIDEs might be a useful early-warning system for identifying detectives with issues that could affect their performance.'

'This pilot was supposed to assess the suitability of artificial intelligence, not *me*. And as of today,' said Kat, pulling off the band around her wrist, 'I am withdrawing from this pilot due to a gross invasion of my privacy.' She was about to slam it on McLeish's desk, but she wanted the satisfaction of throwing it back at Professor Okonedo. Lock hadn't submitted that report by itself.

Kat stormed towards the door but just before she

reached it, she turned and glared at her boss. 'And if you try and take me off this case, then I'll put in a formal grievance about what is effectively an illegal surveillance operation of a senior officer – unless you managed to get high-level clearance for it? *No?* I thought not.'

Kat opened and closed the door behind her with an icy calmness she didn't feel.

Professor Okonedo was still sitting outside McLeish's office.

'If you didn't catch all that, don't worry. I'm sure you can get a recording from your spy software,' she said, tossing the black steel band into her lap. To her annoyance, it was still switched on, so Lock – or the image of him – suddenly appeared beside her.

'DCS Frank,' said Professor Okonedo. 'I'm sorry, that report wasn't meant as an intrusion of your privacy, it was to help Lock learn. I didn't realise that McLeish was—'

'That he was what? My boss? You might be a professor, but sometimes you can be really stupid.'

The younger woman stood up. She barely reached Kat's shoulder. 'I have never claimed to know everything. In fact, the whole reason why I'm doing this pilot is so that I can learn more. I respect your experience, DCS Frank, but you've had a closed mind about AI since day one. I don't know why you even agreed to take part in this study.'

Kat was way past filtering her words. 'Because I wanted to cut through all the crap and expose the truth about AI. They can't make decisions. They can't make the *judge-ments* that only professional, experienced people can and should make.'

'I disagree. But even if that's true now, it won't be true for all time. The more AIDEs like Lock are allowed to learn, the more they will be able to do.'

'And what happens while we're waiting for them to learn? What happens when they make mistakes?' said Kat, turning to where Lock stood, silent and unblinking. Its passivity, its total lack of emotion, infuriated her. 'I'll tell you what happens. People *die*. People like my husband.'

Kat knew she should stop now, she really should. But the words raced out of her mouth like water from a burst pipe. 'When John developed a persistent cough, he was sent for a CT scan, and because of Covid there was a shortage of radiologists, so his scan was assessed by AI image recognition software, which concluded that because it didn't look like ninety-five per cent of lung cancers, there was a "high probability" that he was suffering from a post-Covid chest infection. But guess what, it turned out that John wasn't a general statistic. He had a rare form of cancer that affects less than two per cent of the population. An experienced radiologist probably would have spotted the unusual features and asked more questions. But the AI machine had nothing but algorithms, probabilities and general statistics. And by the time an actual human being reviewed John's scan and corrected the error, it was . . . Too. Fucking. Late.'

Kat took a deep, shaky breath. 'So *that's* why I agreed to take part in your pilot, Professor Okonedo. It's also why I'm ending it. It's over.'

'Wait,' said Lock. 'I'm sorry that my observations—'

'You're *sorry?*' Kat took a step forward and looked it

up and down with narrowed eyes. '"Sorry" means you feel regret, empathy or sorrow. You can't feel sorry, Lock, because you can't feel *anything*. You're nothing. You don't exist.'

Lock opened its mouth to speak, but Kat just walked straight through it, and carried on walking.

Pushing through the fire-exit doors, she ran down two flights of stairs to find a bathroom on the IT floor where she was unlikely to see anyone who knew her. She locked herself in a cubicle, pulled the toilet lid down and dropped her head in her hands.

Talks to the imaginary ghost of her dead husband.

All the times she'd worn that stupid wristband or put it by her bedside – her *bedside* – it was recording and ana-lysing her – even her *heartbeat*, for fuck's sake. She'd let it sit beside her and her son, not realising it was counting her calories and alcohol intake for its bloody surveil-lance report. And McLeish – her boss, mentor and (she'd thought) friend of over twenty years had actually read it. How *dare* he. How fucking *dare* he?

But also, how dare *she?* She'd sworn at her boss. Threatened him with legal action. And not just any old boss: McLeish himself.

Fuck. Fuck. *Fuck*. What should she do? Apologise? No, it was too late for that. And anyway, *she* hadn't done any-thing wrong! She didn't need to say sorry. She needed to go to the pub with some colleagues and get horribly drunk and agree that the bosses were all bastards. Fuck 'em.

A few years ago, that's exactly what she would have done. Only now she was a boss herself, she had no one to drink with. Not in an honest, you-tell-me-your-shit-and-I'll-tell-you-mine kind of way. Everyone always watched what they said around her these days, and she was always careful to never have more than two drinks because she knew her team couldn't really relax until she was gone. It was nothing personal. Just another fact of the lonely boss-life no one ever warns you about.

Kat pulled out her phone. If only she could call John. She squeezed her eyes shut, fighting back the hot, angry tears. She would *not* cry. Not here in the fucking toilets like a child. She scrolled through her contacts. Her dad wouldn't understand, her sister was still on holiday and her best mate Mandy would be at work. Cam? No. It wasn't fair to vent at him. It wasn't his job to deal with all her shit as well as his own.

Let's face it, it was no one's job any more. She was on her own. Tears welled up again and Kat tore off some toilet paper to stop them from falling. Since when did she, DCS Kat Frank, wallow in self-pity? This was not about her.

That's right, she repeated. This is not about me. It's not even about McLeish or that stupid bloody pilot. It's about Tyrone Walters and Will Robinson. She forced herself to think of their young, expectant faces caught by CCTV cameras, completely oblivious to the fact that just a few hours later, someone would take them away from everyone and everything that they knew and loved. She screwed the toilet paper up in her fist. She was right about the cancer connection. She knew she was. But if she left this case – or allowed herself to be pushed off it – then her theory would be quietly dropped, and the boys would remain lost forever.

Kat stood up, threw the hard ball of tissue into the toilet and flushed it away. She was going to find Tyrone and Will. She didn't care what McLeish said. She had made a promise to both mums, and she meant to keep it.

CHAPTER THIRTY-SIX

DCS Frank's home, Coleshill, Warwickshire,
3 July, 6.46pm

If McLeish was going to take her off the case, then he'd
have to find her first, so Kat let the battery on her work
mobile phone run down and spent the afternoon updat-
ing Mrs Walters, before visiting Mr Robinson's primary
care practice to demand that they share the name of his
consultant.

The visit hadn't gone well. His GP had just waffled on
about 'ethics' and 'confidentiality', claiming that unless
Mr Robinson gave his consent, then Kat would need a
court order to access the information held on his records.
Kat had stormed out in disgust, but not before she'd asked
the jobsworth GP about the *ethics* of not doing anything
to help find two missing boys just because of some arse-
covering concern about bloody paperwork.

She was in a foul mood by the time of the evening
debrief, so Kat kept it short, putting the onus on the team
to update her before they had the chance – or the guts – to

ask what had happened with McLeish. Like a gambler, she prayed for the one bit of information that would turn this case around, but her luck was out. Because of the delay in getting Mr Robinson's consent, she'd been unable to identify any connections between the staff who'd treated both fathers, and Hassan continued to draw blanks on the cake bakes and fun runs.

'It's no good,' Hassan concluded. 'I think this whole cancer-connection thing is a red herring.'

'Oh, you do, do you?' Kat snarled. 'Well, *I* think there *is* a connection, and you just need to work harder to find it. In case you'd forgotten, *I'm* in charge of this investigation.'

Several officers had looked at the floor, but she could hear their unspoken thoughts: *unfortunately.*

By the time she returned home, Kat was in what John would have called 'a fucker of a mood'. Her temper wasn't improved by the fact that Cam wasn't home. Again. And his room was a complete tip. He'd left his expensive laptop open on the bed, littered with empty biscuit and crisp packets, and the floor was a jungle of discarded clothes and cups. Well, if he thought she was going to clean this lot up, he could bloody well think again.

Turning her back on the chaos, she wandered through the empty house, switching on lights, closing blinds, feeling completely and utterly alone. Tonight, of all nights, she really needed someone to talk to. Kat was used to feeling quietly sure of herself and her decisions, but now it was as if something – or someone – had knocked her slightly off balance. Her earlier conviction began leaking from her as she thought back to the frowning, doubtful face of Hassan and the polite but slightly too long pauses from more junior officers as they listened to her orders. Honestly. She had nearly twenty-five years' experience in the force: she'd caught the Aston Strangler, for fuck's sake. She deserved the benefit of the doubt. She'd more than earned it.

Kat studied her lean but tired reflection in the kitchen window. When she'd first joined the force, she used to cringe at the middle-aged, red-faced, beer-bellied policemen, living off past glories and shouting down anyone who dared to challenge their view. Is that what her team saw when she stood before them? Is that what she'd become? She liked to think that she was always open to other people's ideas, but this younger generation of officers seemed to take challenge to a whole new level. Some of the questions her team threw at her made her feel like she was being undermined, but maybe she was being too defensive. Maybe she was getting too old.

She turned away from her reflection. *Why* was she letting this get to her so much? Why the prick of wounded tears, this lump of hurt in her throat? Then, it hit her. This wasn't about her team. This was about McLeish. He could be a pompous old bastard at times, but he was still the best copper she knew. Next to John, she trusted his judgement more than anyone's. She didn't really mind junior officers questioning her (that was why they were junior, after all). But not her boss. Not McLeish.

Doubt blew through her like an icy draught. Could he be right? Was she letting her own experience influence her judgement? She remembered when she was first pregnant with Cam, when it had seemed as if the world was suddenly full of pregnant women. But, as John had pointed out, there hadn't been a change in the population, just a change in her perception.

Kat rolled the thought around, trying to give it some space. But it was no good. 'I'm right,' she muttered. 'I know I am.' But how could she prove it? She sat at the dining table and hunted through her files once more, but she'd read them so often, the words were meaningless. All she could think of was McLeish's doubting face. Maybe she should eat first. Have a break. She put the files aside and glanced at the clock on the wall. Where was Cam? Hadn't he said something about going shopping for Magaluf and then out with his mates? She checked her phone for messages. Nothing. Honestly, she didn't ask for much, but she wished he'd let her know when he'd be home and whether she should bother cooking or not.

Where are you? she texted. *What time will you be back?*

She headed to the kitchen and defiantly poured a glass of wine, face burning as she recalled how often she'd innocently worn Lock on her wrist or put it on the side while she'd chatted with her son, made phone calls and, yes – horror of horrors – had a glass of wine or three. She might have drunk over the Chief Medical Officer's guidelines, but was the CMO a widow? Had *he* had to witness his partner of twenty-three years die in slow motion and support a teenage son through the process of bereavement? I think not, she muttered as she poured another glass.

Who else would see that report apart from her boss?

Professor Okonedo? The minister? God, she felt sick. No wonder she drank.

By 11pm Cam still wasn't home, and he hadn't replied to any of her texts.

HELLO???

By midnight, she gave up and walked around the house, switching the lights off one by one.

Where the fuck ARE you??? she texted Cam one last angry time.

But there was no reply.

DCS Kat Frank's home, Coleshill, Warwickshire, 4 July, 6.00am

Kat slammed the snooze button on the alarm, groaned and tried to go back to sleep. Ten minutes later it buzzed again. She rolled over, testing the water. Not good. Her head thudded and her stomach lurched. Urgh. How much had she had to drink? She started to count, then backed away from the memory. No matter. Start again. That's it for a while. The issue for today was whether to go into work or not. If she went in, then she would look and smell like shit, consolidating the narrative that she was a grieving widow who'd lost the plot. But if she phoned in sick, then they'd think the same thing anyway, and McLeish would take it as proof that he was right.

Best to have a cup of tea first – maybe even risk a bit of toast. Years of experience had taught her to move slowly, first the bathroom, then the stairs, no sudden movements and definitely no orange juice. She glanced around the kitchen. Normally when Cam came in late, the signs of his midnight trawl for food were abundantly clear: all the cupboard doors left open, a stinking plate on the sideboard and a trail of cereal upon the floor. But today there was nothing. Had he finally learned to clean up after himself?

Despite her fragile gut, she climbed the two flights of stairs to check that Cam was okay. One of the first call-outs she'd attended as a new officer had been to the death of a nineteen-year-old boy who, after 'a good night out', had choked to death on his own vomit. The sight of that poor boy and the sour smell of such a pointless death had never quite left her.

Cam's door was open, and the unmade bed was still covered with his laptop and crisp packets from yesterday morning. Her fogged brain lagged. How on earth had he managed to sleep in the bed without disturbing his disgusting mess?

Her nose tingled, mind sharpening.

She went back downstairs. His trainers weren't in the hall.

Cam hadn't come home last night.

She checked her phone. She'd sent him eight texts from midday yesterday, but not a single reply. His phone was probably out of charge, she told herself. He'd gone out with his friends to discuss Magaluf, got drunk and stayed over with a mate. Of course he had. He'd never stayed out without telling her before, but he was eighteen, and she was having to get used to a lot of 'never befores'. No need to panic.

Even so, she texted four of his friends to see if they knew where he was, urging them to get her useless son to call her asap. Then she made herself eat some toast and have a shower.

By the time she came out of the bathroom, she had four responses from boys who might normally ignore the panicky texts of a friend's mum, but not when she was a cop. They all said the same thing: Cam hadn't turned up at the pub last night.

Water from her hair dripped down the back of her neck. Perhaps he was with a girl? There'd been a few signs that he'd begun dating or whatever they call it these days, but she hadn't wanted to pry. She'd give him till midday. Long enough to wake up, come to his senses, charge his phone and feel bad for not being in touch. Even Cam – lovely but chaotic Cam – wouldn't let her worry that long. She sent a message to the mums' WhatsApp group *RollonSeptember!* Nothing to worry about, but if anyone knew where her useless son was could they PLEASE get him to send his mum a text? *(eye-roll emoji)* Then she sent a message to the office letting them know she'd be working from home today. Sod how it looked. She needed to know what on earth Cam thought he was up to, and let him know that he could never, ever, do this again.

By midday, she felt like throwing up. Cam still hadn't been in touch and none of his friends seemed to know where he was. Something must have happened.

Then again, maybe he'd assumed she wouldn't be at home to miss him? Yes, that would be it. Ordinarily she'd have left for work at 7.15am, so he probably didn't think she'd notice, so didn't need to message her.

But what if he'd got into trouble? A drunken fight in a pub, a row with some unknown girlfriend? The image of the Harvester pub and the all-too-near River Cole flashed before her. What if . . .

No. She was over-reacting: too much alcohol, too little sleep and her own experiences on the force were making her spiral. But the cold facts weren't reassuring. She hadn't seen or heard from her son in over twenty-four hours.

Technically, he was missing.

If she were somebody else, she wouldn't hesitate to ring the police. But she wasn't somebody else. She was a Detective Chief Superintendent, with a team and a boss who thought she was losing it. If she rang this in and then it turned out that Cam was just out of charge and out of order, then she'd be out of a job.

Shit. What should she do? Was she over-reacting or being too complacent? Was this feeling in her gut a mother's intuition or the result of too much white wine? What would John do?

Calm down, he'd say. *Have some lunch to settle your stomach. Go for a walk to clear your head and get things in perspective.*

Yes. A bit of lunch and then a brisk walk would do her good – it always did – and she could pop into a few pubs and shops on the high street to see if anyone had seen him. If she still hadn't heard from Cam by the time she got back, then sod how it looked. She would call it in.

Coleshill High Street, 4 July, 3.10pm

Kat looked up the hill towards the shops and inns, then back towards the industrial estate and Coleshill Parkway station beyond. Assuming Cam had left the house yester-day – morning? afternoon? – which way would he have gone? She doubted he'd have walked the distance to the station. Chances were, he'd walked up the high street to catch the bus into Birmingham city centre to get his stuff for Magaluf. So, Kat headed up the high street, but only after popping into the Harvester pub to see if anyone remembered seeing her son in the bar or near the river *(and no, thank Christ, they hadn't)*.

Kat continued up the hill towards the church where the bus stop to town was located just outside Hawthorne's Hardware, an old-fashioned open-fronted shop. Maybe the owner had seen her son? She wandered in, dipping her head to avoid the hanging mops and brooms and buckets, and headed towards a stout woman at the counter. She didn't recognise her – maybe she was new – so she flashed her badge before asking whether she'd seen anyone match-ing Cam's description at the bus stop.

The woman puffed out her weather-beaten cheeks. 'I'd like to help, but there's that many people tramping up and down that hill these days, and I'm that busy in here – it's just me, you know – I honestly couldn't say. Ordinarily, I could have checked the CCTV for you.'

'You've got CCTV?' It was such a small place that

hardly any of the businesses in Coleshill bothered with CCTV, so Kat hadn't even thought to look.

'Well, it belongs to West Midlands Transport, really – they wanted to monitor the footfall and traffic at the bus stop, so I agreed to install it a couple of months ago. But you won't find any footage from yesterday or today.'

'Why not?'

'Because something has completely fried the camera sensors.'

CHAPTER THIRTY-SEVEN

**DCS Kat Frank's home, Coleshill, Warwickshire,
4 July, 5.20pm**

It was completely surreal to see the police upon her own doorstep.

'Thanks for coming,' she said to Browne and Hassan, waving them quickly inside. She frowned at the sight of McLeish. 'What are you doing here?'

He shut the door behind him and waited for the two younger detectives to go through to the kitchen. 'First and foremost, I'm here as a friend. I hope you know that I'll do anything I can to help you, Kat. But I'm also here to support Hassan and Browne in case they feel awkward asking their boss questions. Okay?'

Did she have a choice?

She led him into the kitchen, prickling at the sight of her team studying her shelves full of cookery books, the copper pans hanging artfully from the wooden Tudor beams above the steel double-oven and American-style fridge freezer: all the useless artefacts she'd gathered

like talismans against the crimes she'd seen destroy
other homes.

Taking care to lower her voice and breathe as evenly as
she could – they mustn't think she was over-reacting – she
gave them a summary of what had happened so far, standing at the kitchen island as if leading a briefing. 'Clearly
this is connected to the Walters and Robinson cases,' she
concluded. 'I've visited all the shops on the high street
with CCTV cameras so we can find the person that's
sabotaging them as a matter of urgency. I've got most of
the ones who are still on CD, but we'll need Lock to go
through the digital.' She pointed at the CDs on her kitchen
island and managed to keep her voice steady right up until
she added, 'Cam's been missing for over twenty-four hours
now, so we need to move fast.'

Browne and Hassan looked at each other and then
at McLeish.

'That was a very helpful overview,' said McLeish, carefully. 'But you're not at work now, Kat. We need to find
your boy, and in order to do that, we need you to put your
Mum hat on for a bit and answer our questions so we can
follow the proper procedure.'

'The proper procedure? My son is *missing!* It bears all
the hallmarks of the other two cases, which means there's
a serial kidnapper or worse out there. We don't have time
for proper procedures.'

'Kat. Listen to me,' said McLeish. 'I know how hard
this is for you, but if we rush this, if we just accept your
assumptions at face value, then we might miss valuable
information that could harm the investigation. So, I need

you to let us be the irritating sods who ask the stupid questions. For Cam's sake. Okay?'

Kat twisted her hands together. It wasn't his son that was missing. Not trusting herself to speak, she nodded.

'Great,' said Browne, a little too brightly. 'Can I ask when and where you last saw Cam?'

Kat explained it had been the night before last. Yes, he had seemed okay, no, he wasn't upset or acting oddly. *(Was he? He'd seemed fine, but the more she talked, the more she realised how little he'd actually said.)* She told them how they'd watched a film together, and that she'd gone to bed first. No, she didn't know what time Cam went to bed and she'd left the house the next day before he was up, but she could tell he'd left later by the state of his room. She'd sent him eight texts throughout the day – none of which he replied to.

'Was that normal for him? Could we see your texts?' asked Hassan, nodding towards the phone that she clutched to her chest.

Kat hesitated before handing it over, her face burning as she watched him scroll back through their irate (and often one-way) exchanges:

HELLO???

Where the fuck ARE you???

Hassan handed back her phone, giving McLeish a cryptic glance. 'So, would it be fair to say that you and Cam argued a lot?'

'No, it would not! I mean, of course we argued – he's eighteen – but we're really close.'

'Okay, but maybe he was unhappy at the boundaries you set, and wanted a bit more freedom?'

Boundaries? Kat turned away before she slapped him, and instead offered to show them his room. She led the way two steps at a time – breathlessly explaining how the fact that his laptop and clothes were still on the unmade bed meant he hadn't come home last night.

'Have you checked with all his friends?' Browne asked.

'Yes,' she growled. 'Do you think I'd invite you into my son's bedroom unless I'd checked with every friend or friend of a friend first? They know I'm a cop, they wouldn't dare mess me about. They're as worried as I am because he didn't show up at the pub last night. Cam can be a bit unreliable, but he'd never miss a drink with his mates.'

Hassan's eyes widened as he stood in her son's bedroom. She'd often done the same in other people's houses, particularly when Cam was little. At a time when she'd known practically every food group that went in at one end and what exactly came out of the other, she'd thought it strange when some families didn't seem to know or care where their teenage kids were, or how they could let their rooms get into such a state. She realised now that they'd probably just given up trying to control the uncontrollable. Yes, it's a fucking mess, she wanted to say. But wait until you have a teenage son and then see how you get on.

'I'm sorry to ask this,' said Browne, keeping her eyes on her iPad as she worked through the form. 'But does your son have a history of any known risk factors, such as drink, drugs or mental health issues?'

'No.'

'Er ... that's not strictly true, is it?' said McLeish.

She glared at him. 'He had mild depression when his dad died, but just for a few months. That's true, but it's not relevant. He's fine now.'

'Is he still receiving treatment?' Hassan asked.

'No.' Which wasn't strictly true. Cam still took some medication for anxiety, but she didn't want them to make two and two equal five.

Hassan nodded sympathetically, but she could guess what he was writing in his iPad: *history of depression and anxiety. Arguments with mum about boundaries.*

The questions then focused on his forthcoming A level results. Was he anxious about them? Was he nervous about going away to university? Did she think he was worried about leaving her by herself?

Kat clenched her fists so hard she thought her knuckles might pop. 'My son is *not* suicidal. And he has not run off because of some issue with bloody "boundaries". It's obvious that he's been taken by whoever took Tyrone Walters and Will Robinson and every second you stand here asking me stupid questions is putting my son's life at risk. Now can we get on with finding him, *please*?'

'We'll need the contact details for his therapist, Kat,' said McLeish. 'You know yourself that the parents are often the last to know about any mental health issues, and because he's eighteen, his therapist might not have told you if there were reasons for concern.'

'He was *fine*. He's going to Magaluf this Saturday, for fuck's sake. He's so excited about it he just wants . . . he was going to . . .' She broke off.

Tears were spilling down her cheeks, so McLeish – God,

he was old-school – led Hassan downstairs, leaving the female DS to look after her while she 'pulled herself together'.

'He is *not* suicidal,' she kept saying, scrubbing her face with tissues. 'And he wouldn't let me worry like this without sending me a message.' But when Browne patted her back, she recalled how many times she'd heard mums say the exact same thing. And how many times she'd reassured them one day, only to break their hearts the next.

By the time they came downstairs, it was nearly half past seven. It'd be dark in a couple of hours. Dear God, where *was* he? Was he locked in a room? Tied up somewhere, or worse? The thought of her son, alone and afraid, nearly killed her. 'Right,' she said, slapping her hand on the marble-topped kitchen island. 'We've gone through the "proper procedure", so it's time to get a move on. The priority has to be the CCTV footage. Hassan, I want you to go and—'

'Kat,' cut in McLeish, holding up one hand to silence her. 'I was already beginning to question your involvement in this case, and you persuaded me to keep you on. But there's no way on God's Earth that you can lead an investigation into the whereabouts of your own son. It would be a conflict of interest that could jeopardise any future court case.'

'Yes, I know technically that's a risk, but—'

'And you're clearly too emotional to think straight,' he continued, gesturing at the CDs piled up on the kitchen island. 'You know you're not allowed to take potential evidence home. That's a rookie error.'

'I know, sorry, it's just that—'

'And you withheld vital information about his mental health that could jeopardise our chances of finding Cam.'

'I didn't! It's because I don't want you lot to waste time on fucking procedures. I just want to find my son.'

'Which is why I've asked DI Hassan to take over as the senior investigating officer.'

Her jaw dropped.

'He's the most senior member of the team, and it will enable us to keep under review any potential links between the three cases.'

'Potential? We have three identical cases of missing young men, all with dads with terminal cancer.'

'With respect, they're not identical,' said Hassan. 'Yes, they all had a parent with cancer, but I bet their dads also liked football. That doesn't mean that football connects these cases, it just means that their dads liked football.'

'But in all three cases, the CCTV cameras were sabotaged by laser pens.'

'Well, we've yet to establish that lasers were used in this case, and damage to cameras is, as you know, all too common. But we will, as you suggest, be checking the CCTV footage first thing tomorrow,' said McLeish.

'*Tomorrow?* Are you fucking kidding me?' Her body seemed too small for the rage rushing through it. What was *wrong* with everyone? Why were they even standing here, when Cam – *Cam* – was missing. She looked to Browne for support. 'You don't agree with this, surely?'

Browne turned scarlet and stared at the floor.

Only Hassan dared to look her in the eye as he said,

'I'm sorry, DCS Frank, but the CCTV cameras honestly aren't our priority right now. Based upon the information you've given us and with Cam's history of mental health problems, I think we need to treat this as a high-risk case. I'm sorry, but I'll be requesting an urgent search of the River Cole and surrounding fields and outhouses.'

Her legs turned to ribbons. She gripped the kitchen island to hold herself up, searching for the magic words that would make them see sense. She looked around for John to back her up. He'd know how ridiculous the idea of a river search was. He would understand – the way that only a parent could – that Cam would never, ever do this. Which meant that something was terribly wrong.

But John wasn't here. There was no one to place an arm around her and calmly explain that no matter how emotional she might sound, she was, in fact, right about Cam, gently reminding McLeish that, as well as being his mum, she was also a DCS (and a bloody good one at that). She briefly thought about ringing a friend or her family, but then she'd have to say out loud that her son was missing and hear their own distress and panic. No. There wasn't a single other person who could speak up for their son, so Kat had to get herself under control.

'Sir,' she said, her voice thin with lack of oxygen. 'I know you think I'm being overemotional and that I've let my own personal experience influence my judgement. But in my capacity as a DCS, I honestly think that the same person has taken Cam and the other boys. Yes, some of it is based upon my gut – you yourself said I've got the best instinct in the force – but there's a lot of hard evidence to connect them too. Three boys, same age group, all missing from Warwickshire with dads with terminal cancer and in each case the CCTV cameras were destroyed just hours before they go missing.

'If I'm right, then my son could still be alive. We're still within the forty-eight-hour window. But if we waste time and resources looking in the river . . .' She swallowed back the sick that rose in her throat at the thought of men in yellow waders trawling for her son's body. 'Please,' she said, her voice reduced to a whisper. 'I'm begging you. Don't do this.'

McLeish swallowed, his voice squashed but firm as he said, 'I'm sorry, Kat. This is DI Hassan's case now. You have to trust him to lead it. I'm putting you on compassionate leave with immediate effect.'

The rest wasn't pretty. Hassan tried to apologise for taking her job and said that this wasn't how he'd wanted things to turn out. She called him a lying bastard.

Browne told her they'd send round a Family Liaison Officer. She told her to fuck off. 'Go on,' she said, herding them towards the door. 'Go and search the river. I just hope you can live with yourself if we never find him. Because I know I won't.'

She slammed the door shut and slid to the floor, sobbing. Stupid fucking fuckers! Her son was missing. *Missing.* She dropped her head into her hands, tears and snot sliding down her face and onto her jeans. Hadn't she been through enough already? Kat had coped with a dying husband. She had coped with John's death, coped with being a widow while looking after her bereaved son. She'd even coped (just about) with losing the future she'd once assumed they would have together. She had coped with so much, as had Cam. Losing his dad at just seventeen years old had nearly broken him, but he had come through and her lovely, brave boy had returned to school and was starting to make his way in the world. After all that he'd been through, the thought of her only son being alone, hurt and afraid, was literally too much to bear.

Kat dragged her hands down her soaking face. After John died, she used to say that her heart was broken, and yet somehow, it had kept on beating. Somehow, she had 'coped'. But this. *This?*

If she lost Cam, it would end her. It was too much.

'Too much!' she screamed, her raw voice echoing through the empty hallway. She struggled to her feet, waving her fists at the kidnapper, the fates and God himself. 'He's all I've got, so you do *not* get to take him. You hear me?' she shouted. 'I am *not* losing my son too.'

CHAPTER THIRTY-EIGHT

Kat was hopeless at choosing holidays, terrified of spiders and clothes shopping could drive her to tears, but in a crisis she operated with the cold, sharp focus of a surgeon.

And this was most definitely a crisis.

She hunted through Cam's room, heartened by the fact that she couldn't find his mobile phone, wallet, bus pass or keys. That meant he'd taken them with him and planned to come back. She sorted through his clothes, most of which were on the floor, noting his black jeans and hoodie were missing.

Think.

Kat plugged in his laptop, trying (and failing) to guess the password. She cursed, wishing for the good old days when diaries or Filofaxes would reveal the schedules of even the most heinous of criminals. She searched his desk, hoping that he'd jotted down a name, number or an address, but she could hear him laughing at the idea that he'd ever 'jot' anything down on paper (*'That's what the notes function's for, Mum'*). But still she rifled through his drawers: random pens, bank letters, birth-day cards from her and John. *(Don't look. Don't.)* And condoms.

What the actual . . .?

Kat sank onto the unmade bed. It's fine. Completely fine. It proves that Cam is a sensible, caring young man, doing the right thing and taking precautions.

And yet.

It didn't seem more than a few years ago that she'd been changing his nappy. How could her son be in a relation-ship without her knowing? She'd told her team they were close. She'd thought they were.

Now's not the time for nostalgia. Focus, focus, *focus.*

Kat grabbed an A3 pad, some Blu Tack and high-lighter pens from the untouched box of revision pads and pens she'd bought him ('*You do realise I've got a laptop, Mum?*') and headed downstairs.

**DCS Kat Frank's home, Coleshill, Warwickshire,
5 July, 7.45am**

The doorbell rang.

Kat lifted her head from the dining room table, con-fused. Why was she sleeping in the . . .

She jumped up, racing towards the front-room door as the memories flooded back. Cam was missing.

Her socked feet slipped on the wooden floorboards, and her dodgy knee buckled beneath her. She swore as she fell, before scrambling to her feet again. Kat half-skidded down the hallway and wrenched the front door open.

Not Cam. Just Professor Okonedo.

A wail of despair spilled from Kat's mouth. Cam had been missing now for two whole nights.

'DCS Frank, I'm sorry to call so early, but—'

'Not now,' said Kat, closing the door.

Professor Okonedo placed her tiny foot in the doorway, as Lock appeared behind her.

'I can help you find your son,' it said.

Kat didn't bother explaining the mess or inviting Professor Okonedo to sit down. She just wanted to know how Lock could find Cam.

'Despite what you said to Chief Constable McLeish, I've not yet been formally taken off the cases,' said Lock, standing in the middle of her front room. 'Which means I still have access to all the team emails, shared drive and resources.'

Kat's eyes narrowed. 'Useful. But why are you offering to help me?'

'Because I have carried out my own analysis, and I agree there are similarities between the three cases that cannot be explained by random chance.'

Lock reached out, and Kat's front room suddenly filled with the faces of the twenty-eight men, women and children who had gone missing over the past decade. They huddled together like a party of the lost before her inglenook fireplace. 'According to our records,' said Lock, as he circled the images like a professor giving a lecture, 'over a third of the missing came from single-parent families, which is well above the national average of twenty-three per cent. Upon closer examination, I discovered that four of these single-parent families were the result of parental death.'

Lock made a pulling motion with both hands, and four of the hologram figures stepped forward, larger and more life-like: Tyrone Walters, two white men in their mid-twenties and an Asian girl who looked to be no more than sixteen.

Kat stared into their unblinking eyes. 'What am I looking at?'

'Some might say you're looking at a statistical anomaly. But according to Child Bereavement UK, only one in twenty-nine children aged between five and sixteen have lost a parent or sibling. It's a relatively rare occurrence. Yet four of our twenty-eight missing suffered a parental bereavement between those ages, when according to the statistics, there should be only one.'

Kat stepped forward, reaching out to the frozen faces. 'All four of these poor young people lost a mum or dad?'

'Yes. Tahira Wasti, who went missing just over a year ago, Thomas Radford and Gavin Buchanan, who went missing eighteen months ago, and of course Tyrone who went missing earlier this year. Not only did each of them lose a parent – which is four times higher than the national average – *they all died from exactly the same disease*. Cancer. Yet according to the literature, the annual incidence of young adults below the age of eighteen who have a parent diagnosed with cancer is, depending on the study, somewhere between 1.6 and 8.4 per cent. These two groups form a tiny proportion of the population, yet four of our missing fall into both categories – five if we add Will Robinson, six if we include your son.'

Kat gasped as a hologram of Cam appeared.

'This is not a coincidence or a statistical anomaly,' said Lock, turning to face her. 'This is the pattern of a serial criminal.'

'Shit.' Kat sank onto the settee and dropped her head into her hands, groaning. 'How did I miss this?'

'You didn't miss anything. The forms in their case files recorded that they were from single-parent families, but not the reason why. And although some of the interviews mentioned bereavements, the cause of death was not noted.'

'How do *you* know then?' She turned to Professor Okonedo, standing at its side. 'Did you let it hack into the NHS database?'

'No, it didn't need to,' said the professor. 'I just asked Lock to search the Facebook, Twitter and Instagram accounts belonging to each missing person and their parents, family and friends.'

Lock spread out its hands. 'Despite all the public concern about privacy, most humans seem remarkably keen to share intimate information about the health of their loved ones online.'

Lock projected the images of the different social media accounts against the wall of her living room and began scrolling rapidly through the different feeds. It explained how it had reviewed over a hundred thousand tweets, posts and images from over five hundred accounts, searching for information about the health of the parents of the missing. The blur of scrolling slowed, revealing screenshots of blog posts and tweets documenting the all-too-familiar cancer journey from shock, to hope, followed by silence and despair, before the inevitable 'thoughts and prayers' for the family, tagged with the names of the missing.

'It was all there for anyone who cared enough to look,' said Lock, shrugging.

'How long did it take?'

'Less than five minutes,' said Professor Okonedo, with a tinge of pride. 'But it would have taken two human officers approximately twenty-two days of eight-hour shifts to find and review a similar amount of information.'

'We need to tell McLeish,' Kat said, rising to her feet and reaching for her phone on the table.

'I wouldn't advise that,' said Lock. 'Not if you wish to find your son alive. Without more conclusive evidence, you'll waste valuable time trying to persuade him that this is not just a coincidence. McLeish is irrationally convinced that you are being irrational.'

Kat hated to admit it, but Lock was right. McLeish would just say that Hassan would 'look into it' and that she should go home and look after herself. She glanced at the clock on the wall. 'It's nearly eight-thirty now. Assuming Cam left the house at about midday, that means he's been missing for over forty-four hours.' She paused, fighting back the panic. 'How am I going to find him without the support of McLeish and my team?'

'You won't need a team. You have me.'

Kat stepped closer, frowning as she stared into its eyes. 'Why are you suddenly so keen to help?'

Lock held her gaze. 'On the very first day we worked together, you established the principle that the cases always, always come first. This principle aligns with my own anti-corruption algorithms, which require me to challenge orders from superiors if they conflict with my assessment of what is best for the case. I've carried out such an assessment and concluded that the best way to solve the case is to support you, DCS Frank.'

Kat took a deep breath. Jesus. A bloody machine had more faith in her than her own boss and team.

Lock dipped its head. 'You also once said that the whole point of being a police officer is to reduce people's pain, to make people feel safer, less afraid.'

'So?'

'So, the only time I've ever seen you laugh, or exhibit affection of any kind, was when you were with your son that night.' It gestured towards the settee where, just a few nights ago, they had all sat together, but kept its strange, dark eyes upon her. 'You must be in a great deal of pain right now, DCS Frank. And according to your definition of the role of a police officer, it is my duty to try and reduce it.'

Please don't be kind, thought Kat, digging her nails into her palms. *It will unravel me.* She caught herself. A computer might use kind words, it might even speak with a kind voice, but it couldn't actually *be* kind. She turned her back on Lock and dragged a hand through her hair. How could she possibly trust an AI to save her son's life, when the very same technology had contributed towards her husband's death?

'If you refuse my help, then you are allowing your own irrational emotions to get in the way of the facts,' said Lock. 'Because the fact is that whatever you think of AI, without me, you have next to no chance of finding your son alive.'

Kat picked up a photo of John on the mantelpiece. It was one of her favourites: him and Cam laughing as they fed some llamas on a holiday in Wales. What would John do? What would he say?

In a heartbeat, she heard him answer. *Just do whatever it takes to bring our boy home, Kat.*

Kat closed her eyes for a moment before turning back to face Lock. 'All right. You can help me, but that's it – you're just helping. That means you only speak or appear when I ask you to, only act upon my instructions, and my decisions are final. And no spying on me. Do you understand?'

Lock studied her like she was a particularly interesting animal. 'I understand.'

Kat was the first to break eye contact. Lock really did have the most intense, compelling gaze. 'What about you, Professor Okonedo? You're the one who'll be held accountable if I use Lock. You sure you're okay with this?'

Despite the early hour, Professor Okonedo still looked immaculate in a sharp black trouser suit, but the skin beneath her eyes was slightly puffy and shadowed. 'My older brother is in jail for a crime he didn't commit, so I know what it's like to lose someone you love because the police follow their prejudices rather than the actual evidence. That's why I created Lock in the first place, so I feel I have to support its judgement.' She sighed. 'Even if it means losing my tenure.'

'How likely is that?'

'The National Institute for AI research is a global leader in research, so I had to compete with academics from around the world for this professorship. It's so competitive and because I'm black and one of the youngest professors ever, well . . . If anyone finds out that I or Lock have breached any of the international standards on AI, or if McLeish makes a complaint, then I could lose my professorship and even my lab.'

'What do the international standards cover?'

'Mostly ethical stuff like not breaching personal data laws, or not impersonating human beings.'

Kat pushed a hand through her hair. 'There'll be a huge row if I go rogue, but at the end of the day they'll probably cut me some slack because I've got credit in the bank and it's my son that's missing. But you're just starting out and I don't want you losing your professorship because of me. If you're really sure you want to help, then you'd better email whoever you report to and tell them that in the interests of research, you've accepted AIDE Lock's request to support me rather than the team and will be monitoring how this unfolds, because Lock is merely breaking managerial rules, not any international standards on AI. Don't ask for permission or go into too much detail – just cover your back by letting them know, okay? And leave McLeish to me.'

Professor Okonedo swallowed. 'I can't believe you have

the grace to think of me at a time like this. Thank you, DCS Frank. I will email them now.'

'But be quick,' said Lock. 'Remember, the chances of finding a missing person alive reduces rapidly after forty-eight hours. Which means we have just over four hours left.'

CHAPTER THIRTY-NINE

Kat stood back and surveyed Lock's work. It had taken her scribbled notes on A3 posters and created a series of virtual boards that now lined her living room. On the left wall were five boards summarising what they knew about each of the missing, on the right floated images and facts that they had about each MO: time and location, the last known sighting and when their phone signals had disappeared. The virtual board in the centre of the room was labelled 'Connections'. But the list it contained was depressingly short. The only demographic that the missing shared was that they were all under twenty-five and each had lost a parent to cancer. Some had gone missing in the day, others at night. All had taken their phones with them, which had stopped connecting with a signal tower within hours of their last sighting. There had been no further communication, no alleged sightings and, in each case, the CCTV cameras that would have captured their last movements had been sabotaged just hours before.

'Which tells us that these abductions were planned against particular, targeted individuals,' said Kat. 'Each victim left the house with their phones, wallets and keys, suggesting they fully expected to return, and as each of them were young, fit and healthy with no signs or reports of a struggle, they may have known their kidnapper, or at least gone willingly with them.'

'I've carried out a full analysis of all their social media, but I've been unable to identify anybody that was known to them all,' said Lock.

Kat walked up to the virtual board labelled *KIDNAPPER?* 'What do we know about our potential kidnapper. Lock, any theories?'

'From the CCTV footage, we know the person who damaged them is five-foot-six, slender and physically fit – but they could just be an accomplice. We have no other evidence, but a literature review of all the data available on kidnappings suggests that we might be looking for an unmarried male who is a social outcast and a victim of sexual abuse.'

Kat sucked in her breath. 'Do you think there could be a sexual motive?'

Lock raised a hand to its chin. 'In this case, the data would suggest not. Although the demographic profiles are broadly similar – four of the victims are males aged under twenty-five – most kidnappers who abduct for sexual gratification usually release their victim within hours of abusing them, whereas Tyrone and Will have been missing for nearly five months, the young girl for a year and the two other men for almost eighteen months. Long-term kidnapping is extremely rare, resulting in death in forty per cent of cases, with thirty-two per cent suffering serious harm.'

'That's enough, Lock,' warned Professor Okonedo, as Kat paled. 'Are you okay? Shall we take five minutes?'

Kat shook her head. It was gone ten o'clock now. They couldn't afford to stop for one minute, let alone five. She rubbed her hands over her face to clear out the image of Cam crying alone in someone's cellar. 'Let's focus on motivation. If we can figure out *why* someone wanted to take them, then that might tell us who.'

'Sex, power and money,' said Lock. 'According to the literature, these are the key human motivations in most crimes.'

Kat lifted her marker pen and stopped. 'I don't think this is about sex. If it was, he could have taken any-body, but he's only taken people who've lost a parent to cancer. Why would he do that? Could he be reliving some trauma of his own? Perhaps his own dad died of cancer, so he has a warped need to comfort others. Or maybe it's about power. Maybe he wants to exploit their vulnerability and be their parent or authority figure.' She added the word 'Power?' to a poster, before adding 'Money?'

She stepped back, frowning. 'But where's the money in this? None of the families have been asked for a ransom.'

'Perhaps he sells his victims?' suggested Lock.

'No. Slave trafficking is a growing problem, but they'd take any young, attractive person if that's what this was about. Why go to the trouble of selecting people affected by cancer?'

Professor Okonedo walked over and stood before the demographic profiles of the missing. 'Oh my goodness,' she said. 'We've been looking at what connects the missing and overlooked the most important factor of all.'

'What?' asked Kat.

Professor Okonedo turned towards her. '*Genes.*'

'Jeans?'

'No, I mean genomics. Most cancers are associated with genetic mutations acquired over a lifetime, but some specific mutations can be inherited, which can mean a person is at a greater risk of developing certain types of cancer in the future. The kidnapper isn't interested in their demographic profiles,' she said. 'He's interested in their *genetic* profiles.'

Kat's skin tingled. 'But why?'

'I don't know. Perhaps he thought he could sell tissue samples to a corrupt pharma company for clinical trials or something.'

'Tissue samples?' Kat was going to throw up.

'Or maybe just some blood. For research purposes,' Professor Okonedo said hastily. 'Either way, the point is, if my hypothesis is right, then the perpetrator must have used NHS records or social media or something to identify the children of people with terminal cancer before abducting them.'

'Except the damaged CCTV cameras suggests that there was some kind of pre-arranged meeting or appointment,' said Lock.

'Appointment,' Kat echoed, struggling to recall something. She screwed up her face, trying to catch a memory before it evaporated. '*Appointment!*' she suddenly shouted, racing up the stairs. 'Tyrone had an appointment with someone the morning he went missing, and there was a letter for Cam a few days ago,' she explained. 'It had an NHS logo and it looked like an appointment letter.'

She reached Cam's room and started attacking the piles of clothing and papers, emptying jacket and jeans pockets onto the floor, desperately trying to find the letter. But it was no good. It was gone.

'Maybe he took it with him?' suggested Professor Okonedo.

Kat sank onto her son's bed. 'If he did, then we'll never find out where the appointment was or who it was with. There must be hundreds of NHS clinics in Warwickshire. It could have been anywhere.'

'That's not true,' said Lock. 'Tyrone disappeared within a few hundred metres of his halls of residence, Will Robinson disappeared somewhere between the River Avon and the Swan's Nest pub, and as the hardware store CCTV in Coleshill was damaged, we may presume that your son was taken from within that vicinity. But as there are no clinics in any of these areas, either your theory is incorrect, or the appointment was in a temporary or mobile facility.'

Kat stared at Lock, then leapt off the bed, yelping.

'DCS Frank?'

'The *ambulance*. Lock, do you still have the details for the ambulance picked up by ANPR near to where Tyrone and Will went missing?'

'Of course.'

'Run a check on the same licence plate on all the ANPRs near to Coleshill High Street for the day before yesterday. At the time I dismissed it as irrelevant ...' Kat winced, remembering how she'd thought this was a perfect example of Lock's inadequacies as a mere machine. 'But thinking about it – it's the perfect vehicle for a kidnap. You see them in car parks all the time doing health checks or whatever. Most people wouldn't get into a stranger's van, but they wouldn't think twice about stepping inside an ambulance. Especially if they got an NHS appointment letter for a health check. And then once the doors are shut, well, who's going to stop and question a blue-light emergency vehicle?'

Kat clasped her hands together while she waited for Lock to do the checks. She didn't usually pray, but then, her son didn't usually go missing. She didn't have long to wait. In less than a minute, Lock was reporting that, yes, the ANPR cameras had recorded exactly the same vehicle on the A446 leaving Coleshill and heading towards Birmingham at 12.45pm on the day that Cam had gone missing. An image of the emergency vehicle appeared upon her wall. 'After that it was picked up by two more ANPRs on the M6 and then the A38, but two miles from Birmingham city centre it disappeared, suggesting that it must have continued on smaller roads that aren't covered by ANPR.'

Kat splayed her hands upon the table as she studied the image of the ambulance back doors. Her son had been inside. Did he know that he'd been taken? Was he scared, had he – oh God. She bowed her head, forcing herself to breathe. 'Which hospital is it registered to?'

'It's not registered with a hospital,' said Lock. 'It was

purchased off Ambulance Traders.com in 2017 by a Dr Robert McCormick.'

'What? People can buy ambulances? Why would a doctor buy an ambulance? Does he own a healthcare business?'

'According to Companies House records,' said Lock, projecting an image of several documents against her wall, 'Dr Robert McCormick is the registered owner of Angels, a nursing agency, and a clinical waste company.'

Kat had had less than two hours' sleep, and her brain froze, unable – or unwilling – to process what this meant.

'He owns the whole chain,' Professor Okonedo said, standing beside her. 'The nurses to recruit his victims, the ambulance to transport them and the clinical waste company to . . .'

'To what?' demanded Kat.

Professor Okonedo bit her lip.

Kat walked up to the wall and read out the name of the clinical waste company registered in Dr McCormick's name.

Dispozed.

CHAPTER FORTY

Two years before, the Savoy Hotel, London

Waiters weaved between the two hundred tables, discreetly removing dessert plates as the final speaker was introduced. But after three courses and at least as many glasses of wine, people were starting to break away from the tables they'd been formally allocated to. It was all very well being seated next to a top consultant or a member of the college during dinner, but now was the time to drink the last of the free wine with old friends and new lovers before heading for the bar.

Dame Sarah Bloomingdale stood at the lectern and tapped her glass with a silver pen. The sharp note rang throughout the room and, because it was full of medics with a habit of listening to – if not always following – instructions, it had the desired effect. 'Ladies, gentlemen and any rogue surgeons among you, it is time to announce the Lifetime Achievement Award for Oncology.'

A smattering of laughter. Seats retaken. Whispered

promises and texts about where to meet up next, before giving their polite but temporary attention.

'Thank you. Our final award is in recognition of a man who has spent forty years at the forefront of oncology but has always managed to put patients at the heart of his practice.' She named the medical school from which he had graduated and when she detailed the teaching hospital where he did his first registrar's job before becoming a consultant, several in the room were nodding with recognition.

By the time she'd listed his many research papers and his ongoing role at the Royal College, the men and women seated at table one were already slapping the professor's back and urging him to go up and keep it bloody short so they could get to the bar before it closed, there's a good chap.

The professor cursed as he stumbled slightly on the steps to the stage. Why hadn't they given him a heads-up? He wouldn't have drunk so damn much if he'd known he'd have to speak. In fact, the mood he was in, he wouldn't have turned up at all.

He gave Dame Sarah the obligatory kiss on her cold cheek, accepted the award – some metal arty-farty thing – and waved it awkwardly in the air. 'Thank you,' he said. He gazed down at the room, rather taken aback to see two hundred pairs of eyes staring up at him. His old colleagues at the top table were laughing and shouting advice about which embarrassing anecdote he should regale them with. But from up here, he could see beyond their bald and greying heads to the tables and chairs beyond: the twenty-somethings at their first black-tie event, men slightly stiff in their rented suits, the girls an endless variety of colour and styles. Some of them stood to take photos of him on their phones, eyes shining as if he were someone to respect; someone they might aspire to be.

The sight made him immeasurably sad. He waved at them to sit down. 'Thank you. You are too kind. It is an honour to receive such an award from my peers ...' His voice trailed off, mind emptying in the face of such expectation. Which was ridiculous. He gave lectures every day. He looked down at his award and sighed. A lifetime achievement. Maybe it was the wine, his mood, his age, or a combination of all three, but today of all days, the words sounded ironic. Accusatory, even. He wiped his forehead and continued, 'Sarah was very kind in highlighting my successes, but of course what she didn't speak about – what none of us ever speak about – are our failures.

'I've treated thousands of patients during my forty years in clinical practice, but how many of those did I really help? How many did I harm? In how many of those cases do I wish I had decided something different, offered an alternative path of treatment? How many do I wish I had never treated at all, just left them to die rather than eking out their agony in a futile quest for immortality?'

He gazed around the room, ignoring the frowns from his colleagues as he sought out the eyes of the young.

'If you become an oncologist, these are the questions that will keep you awake at night. And believe me when I tell you it will be far worse for your generation than mine. When I was a registrar, we didn't have the therapeutic options we have today. My job mostly consisted of telling a patient they had cancer, when there was nothing we could do other than advise them to put their affairs in order. At the time, I thought there was nothing worse. But I was wrong. The worst thing is telling a patient they have cancer, *knowing* there is something that could help them but not being able to offer it.'

He waved his hand towards the top table. 'We heard from our learned colleagues today about the latest advances in genomics, immunotherapy and radiotherapy. Truly transformative developments that offer the potential to save thousands if not millions of lives. But although the science is already pretty sound, you won't be allowed to use these drugs and innovations in your practice for at least another ten to fifteen years. That's how long it takes to get from the lab to the ward. And I'm being optimistic here. You're going to be attending conferences and dinners like this for years to come, meeting colleagues from all over the world, getting excited about the genomic markers, precision medicines and immunotherapy drugs, while they crawl their way through medical ethics committees and random-research trials and controlled-research trials and peer-reviewed journals and the endless assessments of NICE before the politicians and pharma companies finally agree a price behind the back of the bike sheds and announce to great fanfare that access will be funded for ginger-haired men over the age of forty-two when the wind blows east.'

Laughter.

'Meanwhile,' said the professor, leaning forward on the lectern, his voice a gravelly whisper, 'your patients will die. Hundreds of them. Thousands of them. And *you* will have to sit opposite these frightened men and women who will look at *you* for help and hope, knowing that it is scientifically possible to save or at least extend their lives, but because of the glacial pace of research and the tomfuckery of ethics and guidelines and funding, you will not be able to offer them that chance. Don't get me wrong. The ethicists, the researchers, even the politicians – they aren't bad people. They are well-meaning but cautious sheep, following the laws of the land. But they will never ever have to sit in front of a young mum with three kids under the age of ten and tell her that there is nothing more to be done. That even though she is just thirty-six, she will be dead before the year is out.'

He was crying now, silent tears that glistened on his cheeks under the unforgiving lights of the stage. 'But you will. You will have to look your patients in the eye and say these dreadful things. Many, many times. And managing the increasing gap between what is scientifically possible and what you are legally and financially allowed to do will *destroy* you. It will erode your mental health, your relationships, your very sense of self.'

Dame Sarah Bloomingdale began to move towards him, making wind-up motions.

'I know this is not a very inspirational speech, but it is an honest one. I wish someone had had the balls to tell me the truth when I was a junior doctor. We talk about the war on cancer, and for the first time in history, we actually have weapons powerful enough to defeat it. Today, the enemy isn't cancer, it's that lot over there who won't let us use those weapons,' he said, waving towards Westminster.

Dame Sarah swept in front of the microphone with a bright smile fixed to her face. 'I am sure some of our guests might think that *we* are the enemy for keeping them from the bar! Thank you for your thought-provoking speech, and to all of you gathered here tonight for continuing to support the work of the college.'

Bemused but unperturbed, the diners began to leave their tables. Some drifted towards the cloakroom, intent on an early night, others headed to the bar, the peculiar speech already half-forgotten.

But one man stood alone. Small and tidy in his brand-new suit (bought, not hired – this was the first of many such occasions after all) he did not follow the crowd to the bar nor join the queue for coats. Instead he stood quietly and waited to speak with the professor.

'May I join you?

The professor looked up. Another bloody junior doctor, with bright eyes, clear skin and shark-toothed ambition. He sighed. 'You must have missed my speech. I feel it only fair to warn you that I was a bit of an embarrassment, so if you're looking to advance your career, I'd pick someone else to suck up to.'

'On the contrary, I did hear you speak, and I thought it was brilliant,' he said, calmly settling into the seat opposite him. 'I'm a junior doctor at the Marsden.'

'Under Peterson?'

'Yes. He's amazing.'

'He's an arse. Great oncologist but a crap human being.'

'Well, you can't be good at everything.'

The professor laughed and gestured towards the bottle of red the junior doctor was carrying. 'Is that for show or are you going to do the honours?' Once he'd filled his glass and drained it, he looked at the man opposite. He was indistinguishable from all the other junior doctors in the room, and indeed his life. A disgustingly full head of hair on top of a slim but soft body that would soon run to fat after a few years of the vending-machine diet. He had quick, hungry eyes, still bright with hope and the memory of sleep. God, it made him feel tired just to look at him. 'So, what do you want?' he demanded.

'You said that you wished someone had been honest with you about the job when you were my age. Well, what if they had been? What would you have done differently?'

'Christ. I don't know. Gone into surgery. Someone has cancer of the kidney, you just whip it out, sew them up, boom, job done. They might need chemo for six months and the cancer will probably come back two, three, four years later, but that's not your problem. You did your bit and, as far as you're concerned, it worked. Much simpler. More money too.'

'But what if you weren't interested in just patching people up? What if you really wanted to *beat* cancer?' He could have added, what if you had promised your mum on her deathbed that you'd find a cure for the disease that was killing her, but that would have sounded too dramatic. Even if it was true.

'Then go into science and work in a lab. Although

309

there's not much money in cancer research these days. It's all been spent on Covid and other potential pandemics and what's left has slowed down.'

'I'm interested in results, not money. And according to you, it'll take ten to fifteen years to bring just one research project to fruition – and even then, it might conclude that whatever I was testing doesn't work. My question is, with the greatest of respect, how can I avoid ending up like you? I don't want to get to the end of thirty-odd years' service to find I have nothing but regrets.'

'You're an arrogant little shit, aren't you?'

'I'm a doctor. I have to be.'

The older man burst into bellows of laughter that made his colleagues turn. 'I am *so* glad you said that,' he said, pouring them both another glass of wine. 'Some of the greatest doctors and scientists were arrogant – deluded, even. It's what drove them forward. Imagine where we would be if Edward Jenner had been constrained by Medical Research Ethics Committees. Do you think they would have allowed him to test a vaccine for smallpox on the eight-year-old son of his gardener? Or his own eleven-month-old son? Today, he would be called a monster for even proposing the idea, yet because he did, he saved more lives than any other human being on this planet.'

The younger man frowned. 'But to test an unproven vaccine on his own son – a *baby* . . .'

'Do you think it would have been more acceptable if Jenner had tested it on somebody else's child?' He gave a contemptuous flick of his hand towards the crowded hotel bar. 'This lot like to bleat on about the principles of the NHS and how we treat people according to need. But the minute they or their wife or kids get an illness, they use their privileged elbows to push to the front of the queue. And even though our health service depends upon junior doctors practising on patients, have you ever seen a consultant subject their own family to the care of a trainee? No, you bloody well haven't, because my learned colleagues are a bunch of cowardly hypocrites.'

'And you would? You'd let your child or wife be treated by a junior doctor or receive an experimental drug?'

'I would do whatever was best for the greater good, just as Jenner did. Millions of people are alive today because he possessed strong utilitarian principles, he had the courage of his convictions, and no other bugger had the power or the knowledge to stop him.'

'Perhaps,' said the young doctor. 'But it's not just a question of courage or fairness, is it? There are too many "buggers", as you put it, to stop us.'

The professor leaned forward, eyes sharp despite the quantity of wine he had drunk. 'A word of advice. The power of the committees and pen-pushers comes from us. They can only say no if we're stupid enough to ask.'

'Are you saying we should carry out research without permission? How would that even work? How would—'

'I was talking hypothetically. If you want to sit here and list all the reasons why something can't be done, then piss off and find another drinking partner.'

'Wait.' He dared to lay a hand on the older man's arm. 'Tell me how you would go about it, if you were me.'

'Hypothetically speaking?'

'Of course.'

'Very well,' he said, sinking back down into his chair. 'But we're going to need another bottle.'

CHAPTER FORTY-ONE

INTERVIEW CONDUCTED BY TELEPHONE

Interviewer: DS Debbie Browne (DB)
Interviewee: Fiona Ambler, psychotherapist (FA)
Date/Time: 5 July, 7.57am

DB: Thanks for agreeing to talk to us at such short notice, and at this early hour; as I'm sure you'll appreciate, this is an urgent and fast-moving inquiry.

FA: Not at all. I'm happy to do anything that will help Cam.

DB: Thank you. How long have you known Cameron Frank?

FA: Well, I'll need to double-check my notes for an exact date, but Cam's mum asked me to see him last winter in my capacity as a trained psycho-therapist specialising in bereavement. I don't normally work with anyone until at least six months has passed, unless they're struggling to

313

process what's happened, and it's affecting their ability to function normally.

DB: And was this the case with Cameron Frank?

FA: Yes. He clearly wasn't coping. He'd isolated himself from his friends, was spending most of his time in his room and was refusing to attend college. The GP diagnosed depression and he was on medication for a while – but as we did more work together, it became clear that Cam had some deep-seated anxieties about losing his mother too. Once we identified the core anxiety that was driving his behaviour, he was able to develop coping strategies to help manage his anxiety down to a level that enabled him to function. It took several months, but he improved a lot over the winter, to the extent he was able to return to school in the New Year and catch up on his A levels.

DB: So, you wouldn't describe Cam as depressed or suicidal then?

FA: I didn't say that.

DB: But you said he was fine now.

FA: I said that he'd made significant improvements. People aren't machines, DS Browne. You can't 'fix' a mental health issue, and there's no box of magical cures. What we do is work with people to help them find better ways of managing and living with their anxieties and fears.

DB: So, he wasn't fine?

FA: Is anybody fine? Are you 'fine', DS Browne?

DB: *[pauses]* Well, how would *you* describe his mental state the last time you saw him?

FA: We'd stopped our weekly sessions, with just an informal, monthly check-in, but he asked to see me last Wednesday.

DB: And how was he?

FA: Well ... It's difficult, because I have to respect my clients' confidentiality.

DB: Might I also remind you that we are currently treating Cameron Frank as a high-risk missing person?

FA: I understand that, but I also have to protect my professional integrity.

DB: And straight after this call, I have to advise the senior investigating officer on whether we have sufficient grounds to go ahead with the search of the River Cole that is planned to take place this morning. So, before I put Cam's mum through the trauma of a river search, I'd really appreciate it if you could just give me a straight answer. How worried do we need to be?

FA: *[sighs]* To be honest, I was worried about Cam's mental health after our last monthly catch up. That's why I agreed to see him free of charge. His anxiety was starting to spiral out of control, but Cam was trying to self-medicate – with alcohol mostly – which only made it worse. He wasn't sleeping, and when he did, he had terrible nightmares.

DB: Was it his A levels?

FA: No, the exams gave him structure and something to focus on. But after our last session, it became clear that what was really driving his anxiety was his mum's recent return to work. He was terrified that she wouldn't come home because she'd been attacked or hurt in the course of her job. Added to that was a fear of abandoning his mother by going to university. He was worried she might take more risks at work without himself or his dad to care for. He was finding the fear and anxiety unbearable.

DB: Unbearable? Did Cameron Frank have suicidal thoughts, Ms Ambler?
      [silence]

DB: Cameron Frank has been missing for nearly forty-eight hours now. Do you have any reason to suspect that he may been feeling suicidal?

FA: Yes, I'm afraid I do.

DB: And did you warn his mother about this?

FA: No, Cam is eighteen and my work with him is confidential. I have to respect the therapeutic space.

DB: *[muttered expletive]*

FA: Lots of the people I work with have suicidal thoughts. They are often fleeting and can be managed with the techniques we learn together. If I'd thought Cam wasn't containing his thoughts and emotions, then of course I would have told his mother or alerted the services, but he said he had no immediate plans to act upon these thoughts, so it wasn't an emergency.

DB: But now it is.

[silence]

DB: Thank you, Ms Ambler. This information has –
unfortunately – been very helpful. I just hope we
aren't too late.

INTERVIEW CONCLUDED

CHAPTER FORTY-TWO

He's burning up.

His skin is white-hot, like the coals on a barbecue. Even his lips and eyeballs are dry, as if all the moisture has been sucked out of him. Maybe it has. He turns his head towards the drip by his bed, and the plump bag of fluid it holds.

The Stranger had said they were giving him nutrients and fluids via the tube in his nose, but what if they were taking them out? How else to explain this scorching, burning, bone-dry heat? He should pull all those tubes out and stop them stealing water from his body. But his arms are stuck to the bed. The weird thing is, even though he can't move, the room keeps spinning. It's like the mother of all hangovers.

He closes his eyes. It hurts too much think of his mother, so he imagines he's at the beach, swimming in the cool blue sea. He shivers. Shivers again. Then he can't seem to stop. Suddenly he is cold. So very, very cold. He feels like ice.

He feels like death.

His teeth knock together, a jittery gnashing of enamel and bone that he has no power to stop. He calls out for help, but as his own agonised cries echo round the room, recognition stops his breath.

He sounds like The Other Guy.

The Dead Guy.

He tries not to sob. Tries not to panic. Someone will come soon. They wouldn't let him die.

Then why are you no longer blindfolded? Doubt whispers. Why don't they care that you've seen their faces?

It's easier to sleep than to answer that question, so he lets himself drift in and out of consciousness, until he isn't really sure whether he is dreaming or not. But at some point, it seems that The Stranger is here. He can feel her cold, bony hands upon him as her voice reels off a set of numbers to someone on the phone. But his eyelids are too heavy to open, his limbs too leaden to move.

'I've just added in the second antibiotic,' she says to whoever she's called. 'And he's on hourly observations.' There's a pause, while she listens to the low buzz of another man's voice.

'I'll do my best,' she says. 'You know I always do. But if the worst comes to the worst ... well, at least the new one has just arrived.'

CHAPTER FORTY-THREE

Banks of the River Cole, Coleshill, 5 July, 9.30am

When Debbie Browne first applied to join the police force, she'd imagined herself stopping the drunken fights outside the chippy or standing up to the men who thought it was okay to give their wife or girlfriend 'a slap every now and then', making it clear with her baton, handcuffs and army of colleagues that, no, it really wasn't.

What she hadn't imagined was that one day she'd be searching a river for the body of her boss's son, while carrying an unborn (unwanted?) child. Yet here she was, standing on another damp riverbank beneath a weeping willow, trying not to puke. She stared at the sixteenth-century red sandstone bridge that spanned the shallow river, trying to distract herself by counting the arches (six).

'You okay?' said Hassan.

'Yeah, I'm fine.' (*'Are you "fine", DS Browne?' the psychotherapist had asked. Is anybody ever really 'fine'?*)

Hassan raised his eyebrows, not even pretending to believe her. 'Look, for what it's worth, you don't have

320

to impress me by trying to power through morning sickness. Why don't you sit in the car for a bit until this shower passes?'

Browne shook her head. It wasn't the morning that was making her feel sick: it was the memory of last night. DCS Frank had practically begged for her help, and she'd wanted to – she really had. Yet somehow, Browne had turned her back on her distressed boss and followed Hassan and McLeish down the garden path. She ran a cold hand over her burning face, trying to erase the memory. McLeish was the Chief Constable, so she hadn't really had a choice, had she?

Browne sucked the damp, morning air through her nostrils and let out a slow, steadying breath. Just four days ago, she'd stood on another riverbank with DCS Frank, searching for another body. Her boss had been so kind and supportive when she'd told her about the pregnancy. In fact, she'd been nothing but supportive since day one. Browne glanced at her replacement, trying to quell an irrational surge of anger. It wasn't Hassan's fault that McLeish had asked him to take over. He was just following orders. As was she.

I recruited you to my team because I saw you follow your heart rather than the rules or the pack mentality, DCS Frank had told her. *You've got good instincts – you just need to trust them more.*

Another wave of nausea rolled through her. Browne popped a mint in her mouth before forcing herself to congratulate her new boss on his promotion.

Hassan grimaced. 'I know I should be glad of the

experience. But ...' He looked at the river, speckled with raindrops and littered with men and women in yellow waders. 'I feel a bit shit about how it happened, to be honest.'

'Me too,' Browne said in a relieved rush. 'I barely slept a wink. Do you think we should have backed the boss?'

They stared at each other, while birds cried above them in the dull grey sky.

'Our *actual* boss is Chief Constable McLeish,' said Hassan, eventually. 'And much as I admire DCS Frank, I honestly think she was starting to lose the plot. Not that I blame her. I'd be the same if it was my son.' He dug his hands into his coat pockets. 'The thing is, it might make us feel better in the short term if we backed DCS Frank, but it won't help her find Cam. Sometimes the difficult thing, the unpopular thing, is actually the right thing to do.'

'Maybe,' said Browne. But it didn't alleviate the nauseous drag in her stomach, or the sense that, despite his words, she had in fact done the *wrong* thing.

Hassan pulled his mobile out from his coat and checked his messages. He sighed. 'Still nothing from Professor Okonedo. Have you heard from her lately?'

'Not since yesterday. You'd have thought she'd have been in touch what with the boss's son going missing, but, well, I know she's really clever and everything, but she keeps her distance, doesn't she?'

'She has her reasons.'

Before she could ask him what he meant, Hassan's mobile rang, and he stepped back to take the call. 'Hey, don't get upset,' he said softly into his phone. 'It's okay. I can go to the shops and get some milk and bread on the way home. It's not a problem.' He paused, while the person on the other end spoke some more. 'Okay, well, I'll pop home in my lunch break. No, it's fine. I'm just doing some routine house calls, nothing urgent. Yeah, see you then. Love you.'

He replaced the phone in his pocket. 'That was my sister,' explained Hassan.

'Is everything okay?'

He shrugged as if unsure how to define 'okay'. 'She tried to go to the shops but had a panic attack.'

'Oh, I'm sorry.'

'She's okay now. But she feels guilty for not getting the shopping, so I'll try and get it when the divers break for lunch if that's okay with you, otherwise she'll spiral.'

'You're a good person, Hassan.'

He snorted. 'I doubt DCS Frank would agree with you.'

'Once Cam is home safe and sound, I'm sure the boss will be more understanding.'

Hassan squinted at Cole End Bridge, the large pub that sat behind it and the boss's house beyond. 'You do realise that all the evidence suggests that Cameron Frank is dead?'

Debbie blinked. Bloody pregnancy. It was like her eyes were incontinent. 'Maybe. But I'm hoping the evidence is wrong.'

'Try not to hope too hard, Browne.'

'Can't help it. Hope's what keeps us going.'

'No,' he said quietly. 'It's the hope that kills you.'

'*Sir!*'

They both jumped at the cry from the boat. 'Body in the water! Get the dogs.'

CHAPTER FORTY-FOUR

Harborne, Birmingham, 5 July, 4.07pm

According to the Electoral Register, Dr Robert McCormick lived in Harborne, a wealthy suburb that is surprisingly green considering it's only three miles from inner-city Birmingham. But Kat paid no attention to the scenery as she sped down the M6. Just fifty-four hours before, Cam had travelled along this exact route imprisoned in an ambulance. But the ANPR footage had stopped just after the A38. Was that because the ambulance had turned off just before it reached Birmingham and headed for nearby Harborne? Could he still be there now, being held against his will?

By the time Kat parked her car outside Dr McCormick's large Edwardian house, she was shaking so hard she had to grip the steering wheel. When she'd first joined the force, she'd been shocked at some of the techniques her elders and so-called betters had used in the name of 'justice'. She'd nearly left altogether after one particularly violent incident, but John had persuaded her to stay. The fish rots from the head, he used to say, so make sure you're at the head.

That was easier said than done. Sometimes it was hard to maintain respect for the people she worked with – particularly the older guys before they were managed out. But sometimes it was hard not to sink to their level. She saw the worst of humanity in her job: muggers, murderers, rapists and child molesters. She'd been screamed at, sworn at and spat upon, but she'd never, ever physically struck a suspect. Until today, Kat had allowed herself the vanity of thinking that she was different. But in truth, she was no better than the worst of them. Because for all her moralising, she just wanted to crash through the door, shove Dr McCormick against a wall and make him tell her where the fuck her son was.

'DCS Frank,' said Lock. 'Shall I call for back-up?'

Kat studied the three-storey house, dripping with ivy, flowers and the trappings of wealth. The minute she called it in, McLeish would know that she'd disobeyed him, so she'd be off the case before she could find out where her son was. But if she didn't ask for help, McCormick might bolt out the back door as soon as she entered; and with no one there to catch him, the bastard would get away. For a moment, she regretted leaving Professor Okonedo at her house, just in case Cam (or someone with news of him) turned up. She glanced at Lock on the passenger seat. It had many talents but chasing a suspect over a garden wall wasn't one of them. Who else could she rely on?

'Shall I contact DS Browne?' suggested Lock.

'No,' Kat snapped. It still stung that her own team

hadn't backed her up. She hadn't been surprised when DI Hassan had leaped at the chance to take her job, but Browne?

'Browne can be cautious and indecisive,' Lock said. 'But I believe there is a greater than fifty per cent chance that the new information we have discovered will give her the confidence to respond to your request for help.'

Kat glared at it. She shouldn't have to ask her team once, never mind twice, to back her.

Oh, Kat, John would have said. *Our son is more important than your pride.*

'Okay. Ask Browne to get over here asap. Explain what's going on but tell her to leave McLeish to me.'

Five minutes later, Lock informed her that Browne was in Coleshill and could get to Harborne in under thirty minutes with a blue light.

Forty. Minutes.

Kat managed to wait ten before climbing out of the car, warning Lock to stay on audio. She forced herself to walk slowly up the garden path, noting the well-tended garden, the John Lewis doormat, the brass-handled door. She rapped it. Hard. A good two minutes later *(although, Lord knows, it felt longer)*, the solid oak door opened to reveal a small woman wearing a large straw hat and flowery gardening gloves. *(Waitrose. The wife of my son's kidnapper is wearing gardening gloves from bloody Waitrose.)*

'Can I help you?' the woman said, in an accent that sounded like a BBC broadcaster from the war.

'DCS Frank,' she said, showing her badge. 'Is Dr Robert McCormick at home, please?'

Her smile slipped. 'Robert?'

'Yes, is he in?' It took all of Kat's reserve not to push past this genteel woman and drag her husband out.

'I'm sorry. But Robert's dead.'

Kat didn't remember walking down the hallway, through the kitchen and into the conservatory, but her legs must have done all of those things, because here she was, sitting in a pool of sunlight, being offered a glass of water by a worried Mrs McCormick.

Dr Robert McCormick was dead. Which meant that this was a false lead. A dead end. Which meant that Cam might be . . .

'Here you are,' said Mrs McCormick, handing her a glass. 'You look like you've had a terrible shock. Take small sips.'

She forced herself to smile her thanks at Mrs McCormick ('Call me Moira'). She'd removed her straw hat, revealing the lovely silver-white hair that only the very wealthy and beautiful seem to possess. It was cut into a stylish bob, giving her an ageless air, apart from the faint lines in her weather-worn face.

'I'm so sorry about your husband,' Kat said. 'I honestly didn't know.' She hated it when someone from the bank or utility companies rang to speak to 'Mr Frank', forcing her to say out loud that, no, you can't, because he's dead.

'That's all right, dear. You gave me a shock, that's all. Robert died over two years ago, you see. What did you want him for anyway? Can I help?'

Kat cleared her throat. 'I'm sorry, but it appears your husband has been the victim of identity theft.'

'Identify theft?' Moira McCormick's blue eyes popped open. 'Robert?'

Kat told her how someone must have used her late husband's name to register an ambulance and other health-related companies. She didn't want to upset his wife – or herself – by going into any more detail than that.

'How awful,' she said, clasping her hand to her neck. 'To steal someone's *name*. You hear about these things on Radio Four all the time, but I never thought . . .' Her lip wobbled.

'I'm sorry,' Kat said again. God only knows how she'd feel if someone stole John's name. She had so little of him left. 'There's a number here you can ring,' she said, handing her a card. 'They'll advise you on you how you can check all your accounts and personal information, to make sure that nothing else has been compromised.'

Moira took the card with a shaking hand.

'Do you know anyone who could have stolen your late husband's identity?' said Lock.

Moira looked startled, searching the room for the origin of the male voice.

Kat explained about – and apologised for – AIDE Lock, switching him to visual to distract Moira and prevent the tears that had threatened to fall. It did the trick, as the older woman seemed rather taken by the appearance of a young, handsome man in her conservatory.

Lock ignored Kat's glowering stare and repeated the question. 'Somebody used your husband's name to buy an ambulance and set up a nursing agency business. There's also a clinical waste disposal company registered against his name. These were not random thefts of his identity. The criminal knew that he was a doctor, that he was dead and lived in the West Midlands. These companies will have required photographic ID as well as his National Insurance number and bank details, so there's a high probability that the criminal may have been known to Dr Robert McCormick.'

'I'm afraid we don't know anyone enterprising enough to work all of that out,' Moira said. 'Robbie was a complete darling, but his friends were very male, pale and stale, as the youngsters like to say.'

There was a knock at the door, and Kat was relieved when Moira left to answer it. Now that she'd got over the initial shock and embarrassment of her mistake, the consequences began to overwhelm her. If Dr McCormick didn't have Cam, then who did? And how would she ever find them? These kind of fraud investigations could take weeks. Kat checked the time on her phone. Shit. It was nearly five o'clock. The thought of another night passing without Cam was unthinkable.

She dropped her head into her hands.

'DCS Frank?'

Kat looked up to see Browne stood in the conservatory. Oh Christ, she'd forgotten she'd asked Lock to send for her.

Misreading her expression, Browne quickly said, 'Sorry it took me so long. I'd have been here quicker, but I was attending the search of the River Cole and we found a body.'

CHAPTER FORTY-FIVE

Afterwards, when Kat was finally able to speak, she reminded Browne that as a police officer you never, ever announce 'we found a body', to the family of the missing, unless you are pretty damn sure that the body is connected to their case.

Browne was mortified. She knew she should have started her sentence with the fact that they hadn't found Cam, and only *then* added that they'd found the body of a fisherman reported missing in the spring, but she'd been so nervous about seeing her boss again, and so keen to apologise for not backing her before, that her words had got all muddled up.

Kat said it was okay, but of course, it wasn't. She had to go to the toilet and have a not-so-quiet cry, to let out some of the fear, panic and relief. She pulled on the toilet roll, watching it unravel as the tears sped down her cheeks, wishing she could just curl up on the designer bathmat and cry. But she couldn't. Cam needed her. She could not, *would not*, completely fall apart now.

When she finally came out, Browne was with Moira

in the kitchen, explaining in a low voice why her boss was so very upset. 'He's her only child, you see,' she said. As if having another child would somehow make this more bearable.

Kat stood in the doorway. 'Shall we go now, DS Browne?'

She jumped. 'Yes. Of course.'

The older woman gave her a sympathetic smile. 'I'm so sorry to hear about your boy.'

Kat nodded and hurried down the hallway.

'I do understand what you're going through,' Moira continued.

Kat bit down on her lip.

Moira McCormick carried on, oblivious to the impact of her words. 'I know a couple whose son went missing too. Lovely boy, Will. It broke their hearts.'

Kat turned, her hand on the door. 'Will? What was his last name?'

'Robinson. Will Robinson. Robert was a really good friend of his dad. They were at med school together, and then when Robbie got sick, Gerard agreed to be his doctor, although there wasn't a lot he could do by the time he was diagnosed, to be honest.'

'I didn't know Will's dad was a doctor,' Kat said, frowning. 'I thought he worked at a university?'

'Oh, that's probably because he's a Professor of Oncology. Robbie used to tease him terribly about it, saying that proper doctors – surgeons like him – spent all their time curing patients, while oncologists wasted half their time on research, and the other half administering drugs that killed the very people they were supposed to help.' She shook her head at the dark humour of medics. 'It's so ironic that Gerard has cancer now. I must give Gill a call and see how they're getting on. He was such a dear to me when Robbie died. He sorted out his pension and everything.'

'His pension?'

'Oh, you've no idea how byzantine doctors' pensions are, particularly if you have a private practice too. The government changed all the rules around taxes, and well, I don't pretend to understand it, but Gerard was a complete darling and sorted it all out with the BMA and his accountant. I didn't have to worry about a single thing.'

'So, Will's dad had access to all of Robert's financial details?' said Kat, hardly daring to breathe.

'Yes, I'd never have managed without him. I keep meaning to call, but I know how difficult it is when you're so ill. I don't want to intrude.'

'I'll let them know you were asking for them,' said Kat, pulling the door open. 'In fact, I'm just on my way there now.'

'Oh good. Please tell them that if there's anything I can do – anything at all – they just have to ask.'

But Kat was already racing down the garden path.

CHAPTER FORTY-SIX

Driving to Will Robinson's home, Stratford-upon-Avon, 5 July, 6.55pm

Kat swore when they got stuck behind yet another row of cars. Where the hell was everyone going at this time of night? What was wrong with them? They should be at home and hugging their kids tight.

'Shall I call it in?' said Browne, glancing at her boss's haggard face. 'Hassan could get some local officers from Stratford there within ten minutes.'

'Not yet,' said Kat. 'I urgently need to speak to Will's dad first. McLeish will go mad when he finds out I'm still working the case, so I daren't involve anyone else until I know for certain what all this means. I don't want you getting in trouble either, so when we get there, you stay in the car while I speak to Gerard Robinson.'

'That's not necessary, boss.'

'Yes, it is. And Lock, you stay on audio, and only speak if I ask you to. This is a highly emotional situation. I'll need to appeal to his instincts as a husband and father,

333

so I don't want you messing it up with your facts and figures.' She glanced at Browne. She looked even paler than normal. 'You sure you're okay?'

'I'm fine. Don't worry about me.' She licked her lips. 'Look, I'm really sorry about before, it's just that—'

'I don't want to talk about it. Seriously. I'll go mad if I think about Cam all the way there. I need a distraction. How's the pregnancy going?'

Browne swallowed. 'I've got an appointment with the GP for next Thursday.'

'Good. Feel free to tell me to mind my own business, by the way.'

'No, it's okay. It helps to talk, to be honest.'

'Have you told your partner?'

Browne stared at the road ahead. 'Not yet. I will. It's just, I want to know what I think about it all before I ask him what he thinks. I still haven't decided what to do.' She glanced at Kat. 'You think I should tell him, don't you?'

'It's got nothing to do with me who you do or don't tell. Only . . .'

'What?'

'Well, someone cleverer than me once said that when you ask someone for advice, you kind of know what they're going to say, so when you choose who to ask you've already decided what you want to do. Maybe you haven't told him because you know he'll say something you don't agree with. Maybe deep down you already know what you really want to do.'

Browne looked out the window, trying to hide the tear that slid down her cheek.

'I'm sorry. Ignore me. I'm talking rubbish.'

'No, you're not. I'm crying because you're right, and I've just realised that I *do* know what I want to do.' She sniffed. 'Bloody hormones. Honestly, I cry at everything these days. I can't watch the news or listen to anything about kids suffering. I'll be all right in a minute.'

Oh, my dear, Kat wanted to say. If you have this baby, then you'll never be all right again. These are the first of so many tears. She stared out at the darkening sky, wondering how many nights she and John had spent trying to get Cam to sleep, the countless colds and fevers that had struck terror into her new-mum heart, the fearful first days of nursery, then school. The anxiety and achievements of play dates, sports days, the projects, essays, revision and exams as friendship circles were broken and reforged. Tens of thousands of hours spent trying to keep her boy safe, happy and well, so that he could grow into the beautiful man he was meant to be.

And yet now he was gone. Just like that.

'Do you really think Will Robinson's dad is behind all of this?' asked Browne.

'I know it sounds crazy, but it all fits,' said Kat, explaining that at least five of the missing had had a parent die of cancer, before outlining Professor Okonedo's theory that the kidnapping was motivated by some kind of genetic research. Her voice was cool and professional as she told her about the ambulance and nursing agency registered to Robert McCormick, but it wobbled when she mentioned the clinical waste disposal company, Dispozed.

'Christ. What kind of a person would kidnap his own son?'

Kat sighed. 'I don't know. I've never met him. Will's dad was always too ill to interview.'

But that wasn't true, was it? Kat hadn't interviewed Gerard Robinson because she'd been too polite, too trusting, too bloody scared to talk to a dying man about his missing son. 'I'm sorry, Lock,' she said eventually. 'You were right. I let my sympathy for the family get in the way of the facts. I should have interviewed the dad.'

'Yes,' Lock replied from the band around her wrist. 'You should have.'

Despite everything, Kat almost laughed. There was no flannel with Lock. She had failed to interview the father, when, as Lock had pointed out, the dad is often a key suspect. Kat had let her emotions influence her judgement and had made the wrong decision.

And now she was paying the price.

Will Robinson's home, Stratford-upon-Avon, 5 July, 8.01pm

When Mrs Robinson answered the door, her hand flew to her mouth.

'There's no more news about your son,' said Kat. 'But I really need to speak with your husband. Now.'

'I told you, that simply isn't—'

Kat stepped into her house uninvited and made her way down the hall.

'What are you doing?'

'I am trying to find your son, Mrs Robinson,' Kat said, turning to face her. 'I believe your husband may have information that will lead us to him. I don't want to arrest him – or you – but every second counts right now, so I will if I have to.'

The two women stared at each other.

'Mrs Robinson, I'm sorry, but your husband is going to die whether I speak to him or not. But it might not be too late to save Will. If you want your son back, then you're going to have to let me talk to him.'

Mrs Robinson sagged, as if the elastic holding her up had been cut. 'All right. But let me tell him you're here.' She started up the stairs, and Kat followed behind.

Mrs Robinson paused outside the bedroom door, turning to face her with tear-filled eyes. 'Please, please, try not to upset him. He's frailer than he looks, and if you trigger a coughing fit, he might not recover.'

Kat nodded. She understood more than Mrs Robinson could possibly know.

'Darling,' she heard Mrs Robinson say as she entered their bedroom. 'Sorry about this, but there's a police-woman here, DCS Frank. She wants a quick word with you. Would that be okay?'

Kat didn't wait for an answer. She stepped into the bedroom, and finally came face to face with Will Robinson's dad.

CHAPTER FORTY-SEVEN

The fug of the sick room descended upon her: sugar-sweet medicine mingled with the sour stench of decay and disease. She blinked at the paraphernalia of the dying as the past tangled with the present. Professor Gerard Robinson was propped up against an orthopaedic bedrest, his bald head leaning against a stack of pillows. Plastic tubes snaked from his nose to the oxygen machine that heaved and sighed in the corner, and the top buttons on his pyjama top were undone, revealing the push of bone against skin. His stillness suggested he might be sleeping, but his eyes were open and followed Kat's every move.

She steeled herself. He might be dying, but this could be the man who had taken her son and God knows how many others. She might never get the chance to question him again, so she had to make this count. 'DCS Frank,' she said, showing her card. 'I'd like to ask you a few questions.'

'Could you give us ten minutes, Gill?' Robinson said to his hovering wife.

'But—'

338

'Please, darling.' His voice was gentle. Weak.

'Ten minutes,' his wife said, glaring at Kat, before closing the door.

He gestured to the chair at the side of his bed.

Kat took a seat, noting the large bottle of morphine on the bedside cabinet. There was a slim table on wheels next to the bed, the kind they give you in hospital to eat off, but this one had a laptop on it. The lid was closed, but Kat could see from the flickering light that it was still switched on. Had he just been communicating with someone on it, and closed the lid when she'd entered?

'How can I help you, DCS Frank?'

Kat studied the gaunt but sharp-eyed man before her and decided to tackle him head-on. 'We know that you registered an ambulance, a nursing agency and a clinical waste disposal company in the name of your deceased friend, Dr Robert McCormick. We have CCTV and ANPR footage to prove that this ambulance was used to take and transport at least five young people – possibly more – who had lost a parent to cancer, so that you might use them for research purposes. You can of course deny this, but I should warn you that we will be able to confirm this within the next forty-eight hours just as soon as we have a warrant for all of your devices.'

His voice was as steady as his gaze as he said, 'Well, if you know so much, why do you need me to confirm or deny anything?'

'Because I don't know where you've taken them.'

Gerard Robinson barely blinked.

'If you tell me where they are, then we can reduce the charges against you.'

He laughed. 'Charges? I'll be dead before the ink is dry on your charge sheet, DCS Frank, and you can't prosecute a man posthumously.'

Kat squeezed her hands into fists. He was right. 'Where did you take Tyrone Walters?'

Silence.

'Where did you take Cameron Frank?'

Silence.

'Where did you take Will Robinson, *your own son?*'

He coughed, but Kat pressed on. 'That's the bit that I can't work out. Why would you take your own son? How could you do that to your wife?'

His nostrils flared as he tried to suck more oxygen in through the tubes in his nose.

'I don't know how much you know about me, Professor Robinson. I don't know if you realised that Cameron Frank was my son. I don't know if you know that my own husband died of lung cancer and that I nursed him for nearly eighteen months. Everybody said I was strong. I didn't think so at the time. It felt like I had no other choice. But looking back, I can see that, yes, I was strong. I had to be, for Cam's sake.' She leaned forward, staring right into his eyes. 'But I didn't have to care for a terminally ill husband at the same time as not knowing whether my son was dead or alive. Unfortunately, I can imagine the agonies that your poor wife is going through, but for the life of me, what I can't imagine is what on earth would make you do that to her.'

His breathing was very rapid now, and he began to cough, great shards of sound that scraped the air. He shook his head, marking the pillows with streaks of sweat.

Kat forced herself to pause. She had to be careful. If she pushed him too hard, she could lose him. She swallowed her own panic and tried to focus on his emotions. He clearly cared about his wife and his son. It was there in his eyes. This made no sense. 'Did someone blackmail you, is that it?'

He snorted at the idea that someone might blackmail *him*.

Think. He was a doctor. A professor, and so he was obviously well-off, probably arrogant. Prideful. What could matter more to him than his own family? 'You must have had a good reason,' she continued, speaking almost to herself.

He coughed – a wet, rattling sound that made her dig her nails into her palms.

He gestured towards the water.

Kat passed him the glass, which he took with a trembling hand. Some of it dribbled down his chin as he drank, but he mopped it away with a tissue and closed his eyes.

'The thing I can't work out,' she said, 'is why a doctor who has spent his whole life saving people would deliberately harm so many.'

His eyes remained closed, but she could sense him listening.

'Perhaps there was some research you wanted to carry out before you died, something that would move forward our understanding of cancer and how to cure it.'

Was that the slightest of nods?

341

She softened her tone, made it more respectful, more understanding. 'You've been an oncologist for several decades. It must be frustrating to possess all that knowledge, to be on the cusp of some great discovery, only to find out that you don't have much time left. It must be tempting to cut corners to find a cure for cancer as part of your legacy.'

He opened his eyes.

Ah. That was it. Legacy.

'I can understand why you might want to do that. But even if you did make a breakthrough, do you really think anyone would want to draw upon the research of a criminal who abducted people so that he could experiment on them?'

'But what if they made an informed choice and gave written or verbal consent?' he said. 'Where is the crime then?'

Kat didn't miss a beat. 'What exactly did they consent to?'

'They agreed to undergo experimental treatment for early-onset cancer, in the interests of accelerating emerging research findings in cancer genomics and effective treatments.'

She tried not to gasp. She needed him to continue. 'But none of the boys had cancer.'

Professor Robinson shrugged. 'That depends upon how you define "had". Each member of the trial possessed a genetic mutation that gave them an increased predisposition to developing cancer much earlier than would be expected in the general population. All we did was bring it forward.'

'What do you mean?'

'We do it all the time in phase one trials with animals. In laboratories, we activate their genes *in vivo,* inducing the expression of oncogenic abnormalities so that we can test new drugs and treatments on them.'

Kat's skin grew cold. 'You *gave* them cancer?'

'We activated the inherited gene for the cancer to be expressed, which led to the cancer developing earlier than might otherwise have been expected, so that we could try out new treatments at the earliest possible stage when they are most likely to be successful. It's essentially a living trial for gene activation and targeted treatment, but on humans rather than animals.'

The breath vanished from her body. 'And was it? Successful?' she managed to say.

He sighed, and she could hear the rattle in his chest. 'We've yet to establish the optimal dosage and, as ever, the side effects have proven to be extremely debilitating. Although we recently made a breakthrough with one boy.'

'One? Just one? Who?'

'I honestly don't know. They are assigned numbers, to eliminate case bias.'

'And the others?'

He closed his eyes.

'What happened to them? Did you murder them?'

'I haven't murdered anybody,' he said with a contemptuous wave of his hand. 'The people in my trials possessed genetic mutations. I was trying to save them and others like them from their potential futures.'

Kat jumped up, hand over her mouth. She wanted to scream. Had he given Cam *cancer*? And Tyrone, Will, *his own son*?

She paced up and down, air heaving through her lungs.

'You think I'm mad,' he said. 'But do you know how long it takes to get a cure out of the laboratory and into patient clinics? Ten, sometimes even fifteen long years while we're forced to test each hypothesis in self-contained trials on bloody *mice,* for God's sake, with no flexibility or possibility of real-time learning when our understanding of genomics is moving at an exponential rate. And that's the optimistic scenario. Things are even worse now all the money's been spent on Covid.'

'Were you hoping to find a cure for yourself. Is that it?'

'Christ, no. It's too late for me. On the day I was diagnosed, I was awarded a lifetime achievement award. It made me realise how little I'd actually achieved. I started talking to a junior doctor, but all he wanted to know was how he might avoid turning into me, another failed oncologist with a legacy of dead and damaged people behind him. But as we talked, I realised it wasn't too late to test my theories. I just had to be as bold and as brave as our forefathers were and trust my own knowledge and experience. Thirty years as an oncologist has given me a gut instinct better than any bloody committee.'

'So, you abducted young, healthy people and carried out illegal experiments on them?' Kat shook her head, still struggling to believe it. 'How could you do it – and to your own *son*?'

'It would have been unethical if I hadn't. Edward

Jenner tested the smallpox vaccine on his baby son, and the risk he took with the life of his own child helped to save millions of other people's lives. We all benefited from Jenner's selfless act, so, when the random computer search of dead or dying patients with children suggested my son's name, I felt I could not, in all fairness, exclude him from the trial. I love my son – of course I do. But why should the life of my child take priority over the lives of strangers?'

'You didn't have to put *anyone's* life at risk, let alone Will's.'

'His life was already at risk,' Professor Robinson snapped. 'Cancer is the killer, not me. And until we find a cure, no one is safe. If you nursed your dying husband, then you *know* what a monstrous disease this is. Wouldn't you do anything to stop others from ending up like this?' Professor Robinson gestured towards his own ravaged body, before sinking back against his pillows, eyes closing with exhaustion. 'Yes, my trial is a risk, but believe me, doing nothing – sitting back and waiting for the glacial pace of research to bear fruit – is the biggest risk of all. At least this way there's a chance that I've saved my son from a terrible death in the future. And if not . . .' He paused to catch his breath, and the words that followed were slow and slurred. 'If not, I've arranged for my trial data to be shared with the young junior doctor I met, who will take my conclusions as his starting point, saving years of trial and error. This means patients could be reaping the benefits of my research within three years rather than fifteen. A handful of people may have died in my trials, but this must be weighed against the many thousands of lives that would have been lost otherwise. It's a simple equation.'

A simple equation? That did it. 'Where are they?' she demanded, standing over his bed. 'Where did you take them?'

He gave her a sleepy smile. 'Do you really think I'd tell you?'

'You'd better, or so help me God I'll—'

'What? Kill me?' He laughed, but it was one of the saddest sounds she'd ever heard. 'I'm afraid it's too late for that.' He pointed towards the bottle of morphine on the bedside cabinet.

Kat picked it up. The sticky bottle was completely empty.

'Finished it off when I heard you on the stairs.'

Kat pulled out her phone.

'There's no point calling an ambulance. Morphine normally takes about twenty minutes to hit the bloodstream, and I've taken a massive overdose combined with Lorazepam, so I'm afraid I'll be gone by the time they get here. And because I'm terminally ill, they won't bother resuscitating me. I have a DNR on my medical records.'

Shit. How long had she been here? Ten, fifteen minutes? How long before the drugs took him? 'Please,' she begged. 'Just tell me where my son is.'

'So that you can end my trial and seize the data?' He shook his head. 'No. I realise you're upset about your boy, but you just have to hope that he has benefited from this trial, just as I hope my own son has.' He sighed, as if not believing his own words. 'But this isn't about *my* son, or your son. I'm doing this for the thousands of other sons and daughters who might otherwise develop cancer in the future.'

'I'm not interested in your data. I just want my son. Tell me where he is. Have you activated his genes yet? Have you?'

Gerard Robinson closed his eyes.

'Lock, did you record all this?'

'Of course.' The room filled with Robinson's voice.

It would have been unethical if I hadn't. Edward Jenner tested the smallpox vaccine on his baby son, and the risk he took with the life of his own child helped to save millions of other people's lives. We all benefited from Jenner's selfless act, so, when the random computer search of dead or dying patients with children suggested my son's name, I felt I could not, in all fairness, exclude him from the trial.

'That recording was made without my consent, so it won't be admissible in court,' he said, without opening his eyes.

Kat shrugged. 'I wonder if your wife will agree that your son's life was merely part of a simple equation?'

'She'd never believe you.'

'But she'd believe *you.*'

His eyes flew open and, for the first time, Professor Robinson looked afraid. 'Don't you *dare* play her that recording, you, you ...' He broke off, coughing.

'Unless you tell me exactly where my son is, I will play it to your wife right now.'

He slumped down into his pillows, making a rasping, rattling sound, struggling to breathe.

She picked up his laptop from the side cabinet. 'Is the location on here? If it's hard for you to speak, could you just show me? Professor Robinson?'

He turned his face away in silent refusal.

At the foot of the bed, a life-size hologram of Will Robinson suddenly appeared, his pale face oddly luminous in the darkened room. He was dressed in what looked like white pyjamas, and the only colour seemed to come from his bright, ginger hair, lit up like a halo. The image of Will reached out his hand towards his father.

'Confess yourself to heaven,' the figure cried, its eyes wide and dark in its too-pale face.

'Will?' whispered Robinson.

Will – or the image of him – took a step closer towards the bed. 'Repent what's past; avoid what is to come; and do not spread the compost on the weeds, To make them ranker.'

Hamlet. Will was quoting lines from *Hamlet*, Kat realised.

Robinson gasped and leaned forward, his blue lips mouthing his son's name as he struggled to take in air. His eyes filled with tears.

'Lock,' warned Kat. 'That's enough.'

The image suddenly vanished, and the old man looked around the empty, dark room. 'Will?' he tried to cry through the coughing. 'Are you okay? Where are you? *Will!*'

The door opened and Mrs Robinson rushed in. 'Gerard?' She placed a hand upon his chest, which now

348

rose and fell with horrendous force. 'What have you done?' she cried, turning to Kat with burning eyes.

'I'm sorry, it's just – Professor Robinson, please, if you could just—'

'Get out!' she screamed. 'Leave us alone!'

Kat left Mrs Robinson holding her husband's hand, weeping as she told him over and over that everything was going to be all right.

CHAPTER FORTY-EIGHT

Kat was still clutching Professor Robinson's laptop when she let Browne in and briefed her on what had happened. All the time she was talking, the sounds of sobbing upstairs grew louder.

'The ambulance will be here in seven minutes,' said Browne, looking up at the ceiling.

'It's too late,' said Kat, sinking into a chair. 'Thanks to Lock's theatricals, Professor Robinson will die before he can tell us where Cam and the others are.'

'That's not accurate or fair,' said Lock. 'It was clear from his vital signs that there was over a seventy per cent chance that Professor Robinson had just minutes left to live. Given the urgency of the situation, I decided to use footage of his son to try and provoke a confession.'

'But instead, you just provoked his death.'

The noise from upstairs suddenly stopped. Kat bowed her head in the eerie silence that followed. Her instinct was to go and comfort Mrs Robinson, but after what had just happened she would probably just turn on her. And what if she asked what her husband had to do with her missing son? What could Kat possibly say on tonight of all nights? There's only so much the human heart can bear.

'Lock,' she said, rising to her feet. 'I need you to access the Professor's laptop and find out where he took the people he abducted.'

There was the slightest of pauses. 'It appears that Professor Robinson was regularly Skyping with another laptop, at nine o'clock every morning.'

'Ward rounds,' said Kat, snapping into focus. 'He was doing his ward rounds and reviewing his patients remotely. Can you tell where the other laptop was Skyping from?'

'Of course.' A map appeared in the air above the kitchen counter, with a yellow, pulsing dot. 'The location of the other laptop was in the King Charles Hospital, Birmingham.'

'They're in a *hospital*?' But even as she questioned the location, it all began to make sense, especially when a quick google revealed that until he retired due to ill health, Professor Robinson had been a Consultant Oncologist there. This would give him access to all rooms and facilities. Who would question the familiar face of a respected consultant, or a couple of uniformed nurses escorting one of his patients from an ambulance? Or – a darker voice whispered – the transportation of clinical waste disposal bins from one of his wards, large enough to carry a body?

'Whereabouts in the hospital?' Kat demanded, staring at the yellow dot.

'I'm afraid I can only give a location within fifty metres of the signal, so it could be anywhere within a fifty-metre radius of this point.'

Shit. John had been treated at the King Charles – or KC as they called it, so she knew just how vast and complex the hospital was. 'Okay, here's what we're going to do. Browne, I want you to call this in. Explain that Professor Robinson made a deathbed confession – don't go into any more detail at this stage – just tell them that we believe some or all of the missing were taken to the KC and that we have grounds for believing that at least one of them is still alive.' She paused and took a deep breath to stop her voice from rising. God forgive her, but she couldn't help hoping it was Cam. What if his genes had been activated? What if . . .

Stop it. What ifs would not help her find her son. 'I'm going there now. I need back-up – as many bodies as can be spared to search the hospital. And I want an FLO here urgently. Mrs Robinson's husband has just died, and her son is still missing. She shouldn't be left alone.'

'Yes, boss.'

'Now, let's blue-light it to the hospital.' It was just gone nine o'clock, so they wouldn't get there until at least half past. She prayed it wouldn't be too late.

CHAPTER FORTY-NINE

**King Charles III Hospital car park, Birmingham,
5 July, 8.50pm**

The woman sat in her car, staring at the text from Gerard:

> My darling, the time has come for me to pass,
> as we always knew it would. I thank you from
> the bottom of my heart for everything you
> have done for me and thank God that I was
> lucky enough to be loved by you. All I care
> about now is keeping you and our legacy
> safe. There can't be any loose ends. I know
> you will find the strength to do this one final
> thing for us. Goodbye. I love you. Gerard xxx

She put down her phone, eyes blurring with tears. There
was no doubting its meaning. It was one of the things that
had first attracted her to him: the way his mind could cut
through the clutter of everyday life and focus on what
really mattered.

Oh, Gerard. Where was his beautiful mind now? She didn't believe in an afterlife, but it was impossible to think that all of that knowledge, all of that *Gerard*, was now gone.

She squeezed her eyes shut against the rush of tears. No, not gone. That was the whole point of his research. It was why she'd agreed to help him in the first place, and he needed her now more than ever. They'd discussed this moment many, many times. 'It's as much to protect you as well as my research,' Gerard had insisted. 'Promise me you won't lose courage.'

She'd given him her word – how could she not when he had been so brave? Her promise had been heartfelt, but now, sitting in the darkened car park, she couldn't imagine going through with it. She rolled her shoulders, trying to shift the unease. She was no stranger to death – it came with the job, after all. But death was always something to mourn, regret and learn from. She had never, ever, deliberately ended a person's life before.

She stared at her phone again, smudged with thumbprints and feathered with cracks. 8.55pm. If she drove away now, she could be at Dover in four hours and on her way to France before the morning shift even started. They might not even connect it to her. She'd been careful to cover her face from the new boy and the other one wouldn't last long enough to identify her. Yes, it would be better for everyone if she just left now. She turned the ignition with a decisive twist, feeling the rush and roar of the engine, already picturing the dawn skies on the empty road to Dover.

A blue light flashed behind her, and she paused, waiting for the ambulance to pass before parking outside A&E. That was the thing about the NHS. For every patient you saved, another three turned up. It was never-ending.

A chill stole over her, and for a moment it was as if Gerard's hand was upon her shoulder. *That is why you have to do it,* she imagined him saying. *Otherwise, our legacy will be lost, and the suffering will never end.*

She let the engine fade and die beneath her. She climbed out and walked purposefully through the hospital car park, past the ambulances and a young woman attached to a drip sat smoking on a bench. She had promised Gerard that she would not lose courage. She would not let him down.

CHAPTER FIFTY

King Charles III Hospital, Birmingham, 5 July, 9.02pm

As Lock insisted on telling Kat, the KC in Birmingham is one of the largest hospitals in the country, with over a thousand beds treating half a million patients each year. The huge complex comprises three 63m-high curved towers, the white and glass-filled fronts dominating the landscape for miles around.

Kat bore the explanation. What the machine didn't know was that this was also a place of hope and despair. A place where mothers, fathers, sons and daughters wept, prayed, laughed and left, sometimes thankful, sometimes heartbroken, but always, always forever changed.

Ignoring the restrictions, Kat parked in the ambulance bay outside the main entrance and looked up at the thousands of windows lit against the night sky. Her son was in one of those rooms, but which one? Trying not to feel dwarfed by the task before her, she strode towards the glass-fronted door, past the benches where a young woman attached to a drip sat smoking and waved her badge at the security guard.

Hassan and a couple of uniforms were waiting for her in the large atrium.

'I'm so sorry, DCS Frank,' he said as she approached.

Her stomach plummeted. 'Why? What's happened? Is it Cam?'

'No, we've only just started searching, I just meant, well, I've read Lock's transcript of your interview with Professor Robinson, and I'm so sorry that I didn't believe you before. I was wrong.'

Jesus, he'd almost given her a heart attack. She waved away his apology and asked him to update her. He had ten officers currently conducting a search of the hospital from the ground floor up, plus Professor Okonedo who'd insisted on helping as soon as she'd heard. They were currently on the second floor.

Kat swore. 'Ten? Is that all? And why did you start at the bottom? Professor Robinson was an oncologist, so he would have worked on the oncology wards on the sixth floor. The chances are he took them there, where he could have come and gone without any questions.'

Hassan tried to apologise again, but Kat was already racing towards the lifts. The doors closed upon her before the other officers made it. She stared at her blurred reflection in the metallic backing, thinking how bizarre it was to be back here again, but this time with her son's life in the balance. The doors opened with a ping, and she stepped out into a corridor that was so long she couldn't even see the end of it. Lined with windows and lit by strip lights, she flashed back to all those midnight admissions where John had slowly grown weaker and sicker, until eventually she'd had to push her once-fit husband down this very corridor in a wheelchair.

The unfairness of it all enraged her. Hadn't they been through enough already? Each stab of her heel against the floor fed the fury within her. This was not going to happen. She was going to find her boy, and God help whoever had taken him.

She paused at the main wards where John had been cared for. Surely they were too busy for a rogue research trial to go unnoticed, particularly as his 'patients' were so young? Conscious of time, Kat headed for the teen cancer unit at the end. Maybe this was where he took them? She pressed the buzzer on the door, waiting for the click before pulling it open. Kat squirted some antiseptic gel from the wall dispenser before approaching the nurse at the desk, unsure of what she was going to say until she opened her mouth.

'Detective Chief Superintendent Frank,' she said, showing her badge. 'Could you tell me whether Professor Robinson has visited these wards recently?'

The nurse gave her a blank look. 'Not to my knowledge, but I only work nights. He may visit during the day if some of his patients are here.'

'You've never seen him here? Okay, how about this person?' Kat pulled out her phone and showed her a photograph of Cam. It wasn't that recent – it pained her to realise how few photos she'd taken of him this year. It was from Christmas, the first one with just the two of them, and even she could see how forced his smile was.

The nurse shook her head. 'Sorry, no. But if you can give me his name and NHS number, I could look him up on the system?'

Kat doubted it would be that simple, but she gave it a shot anyway.

The nurse tapped her keyboard. 'Sorry, there's no record of him being admitted to this hospital.'

'He may have been admitted under another name though, do you mind if I have a look around?'

'I'm not sure. I'll need to check with . . .'

But Kat was already heading down the corridor, peering into the single side rooms and four-bedded bays where painfully thin teenagers lay hooked up to drips and machines, while their parents hunched over their phones or dozed in nearby chairs. She scoured the faces turned to hers, sagging with disappointment as they realised she wasn't a doctor. 'Sorry,' she whispered. Each face told a story, but not one of them belonged to Will, Tyrone or Cam.

Kat could have screamed as she left the ward and found herself back in the never-ending corridor. 'There are over a thousand beds in this place. It's going to take forever to search them all.'

A hologram of the hospital complex, including the outbuildings, car parks and surrounding roads, appeared before her. 'Not forever,' said Lock. 'But a thorough search of each room, ward and outbuilding would take ten officers approximately twelve hours and thirty-six minutes. I suggest we take a systematic approach and work upwards and outwards.'

'Twelve hours?' said Kat. 'Fuck that. We need to talk to someone with an in-depth knowledge of the building, someone who understands where the dark corners are.' She frowned. Who could she call? The CEO? No, they probably never left their office. The security guard who let them in worked for some agency and barely knew where the toilets were. She needed someone who'd worked here for years and knew every inch of these never-ending corridors and . . .

Kat pulled out her phone and rang Tyrone's mum, Mrs Walters.

'Hello?'

Kat pushed down her guilt at the sound of another mother's voice strangled by hope and fear. 'Sorry to bother you at this hour, no news yet, but I need some urgent advice. You work at the King Charles III Hospital, don't you?'

'Yes, but what—'

'I don't have time to explain, and this is going to sound really weird, but if you were a dodgy doctor and you wanted to treat some patients below the radar, where would you choose to put them?'

'Below the radar?' said Mrs Walters. 'Well, at the KC everything is so new and open, there aren't really any dark corners, and the management is on top of things like that. I don't think a rogue doctor could get away without being challenged, unless . . .'

'Unless what?'

'There's a brand-new building that was supposed to have opened for private patients this year just opposite the main entrance, but there were delays because of Covid and I think the original company pulled out. Another consortium took over and I heard that as part of a plan to test out the building and bring in some income, they were letting doctors rent out wards or whole units for their own private practice.'

'What?'

'It's perfectly legal, although it doesn't make it right. There's this thing called "Doctors' Practising Privileges" that allows NHS doctors to admit and treat patients privately in private facilities. Some of my friends do agency work at the weekends in them, but I never have. There was a scandal several years ago when a surgeon at another hospital was arrested for carrying out private operations using experimental techniques that weren't approved. They were supposed to be tightening up all the regulations and laws, but I'm not sure if it's happened yet.'

Kat shivered. Experimental techniques. Shit. 'Okay, thanks, Mrs Walters, you've been really helpful.'

'Why are you asking? Does this have anything to do with Tyrone?'

But Kat had ended the call and was already racing towards the exit.

CHAPTER FIFTY-ONE

HEAL Specialist Hospital, Birmingham, 5 July, 9.55pm

'I'm accessing the blueprint for the hospital now,' said Lock on audio mode as Kat raced towards the imposing building opposite. Newly built, it was still surrounded by billboards and scaffolding, promising that the new specialist hospital (HEAL – *supporting you to live Healthy, Energising, Active Lives*) would be open in the winter.

Unlike the broad curved towers of the KC, this building was all brutal angles and narrow straight lines, harsh and uninviting under the glare of night lighting. Kat scanned the front, trying to find the door among all the metal and glass. Bloody architects, showing off to each other rather than thinking of the poor patient trying to find a way in. Or out.

At last, she found it – locked. She banged on the glass for minutes that she didn't have.

'Maybe it's closed,' said Lock.

'There must be a security guard, though.' She banged on the door again with her best policeman's knock.

It did the trick, as an overweight man in a white short-sleeved shirt with dark trousers approached.

Kat rattled the handle.

'Open up,' she shouted. 'Police.'

Kat pushed past him as soon as he opened the door. 'DCS Frank from Warwickshire Police. I'm investigating a possible abduction and murder that may have taken place on these premises.'

His eyes nearly popped out of his head.

'I need to see a list of all the doctors who have private practise privileges here. Now.'

The security guard rubbed his chin. 'I'm afraid I don't have access to that kind of information. I'm just the night guard.'

'Well, who does?'

He shrugged. 'No idea. I work for an agency. They deal with all the bosses – I just turn up for the hours they tell me.'

'Jesus,' said Kat. 'Well, have you ever seen this doctor here?' She pulled out her phone and showed him an image of Professor Robinson from the web.

'I told you. I just do nights. I check that all the doors are locked, empty the bins, and make sure no one's breaking into the pharmacy. The doctors are nothing to do with me, although I'm hoping to get a permanent contract once it opens up properly.'

Kat swore and scanned the wide, soulless atrium they were in, empty apart from a tree – a bloody tree – in the centre of the marble tiled floor. It was like the lobby of a large, expensive hotel, with one corridor stretching away from reception at one end, and a set of gleaming silver lifts at the other. Six floors.

'Lock, call Hassan and get his team over here now. We need to search this place from top to bottom.'

'Is that wise?' said Lock. 'We have no evidence to justify prioritising this building over the main site, where there are over a thousand beds, whereas according to the blueprints, there are only fifty in-patient beds and just sixteen-day beds here. It isn't fully operational yet, so it shouldn't take you long to search.'

Kat clenched her fists. She'd asked Lock to follow an order, not assess her judgement. There was something not right about this shiny, empty place. But it was nothing that she could articulate, and if she was wrong, then they'd have to start all over again in the vast KC complex. Lock was right, but she wasn't about to admit that. Turning to the security guard, she asked him to take her to the main wards.

He glanced around him uneasily. 'Don't you need a warrant to carry out a search?'

'Not when I have reasonable grounds to suspect that a child or vulnerable person is at risk.'

'Follow me then,' he said. And with surprising speed, the guard ('Call me Yousef') headed for the lifts, waving his security pass like a magic wand.

They stepped out of the lift and into a large outpatients department, dimly lit and low-ceilinged, the lines of empty plastic chairs ghostly reminders of all who had and would sit there. There was a deserted reception desk in the centre, with as many as ten doors tucked away in the walls and alcoves beyond.

'Those are just the rooms used for outpatient clinics,' said Yousef. 'But there are some day-patient beds off to the side.'

Kat insisted on checking inside, opening each door in turn to reveal a desk, computer, a couple of chairs and an examining couch, but no patients. No Cam. No Tyrone. No Will.

A distant clock chimed midnight.

She nodded towards a set of double doors at the back. 'Where does that lead to?'

'Another set of lifts to the inpatient wards.'

Kat sucked in her breath. 'Let's go.'

The lift door opened, and Kat and Yousef stepped out into another empty corridor. They strode down it, her footsteps and his wheezing filling the silence, until they reached another set of double doors. Yousef used his card to open them and insisted on going first 'just in case'.

Inside it was completely dark, but the strip lighting above flickered into life as they moved through what looked like a large, empty office space. There were no beds or desks, just a collection of filing cabinets and plastic boxes piled up against the wall.

'This part isn't open yet, but I think some of the nurses use this when they need to study or eat their lunch, because I have to keep emptying the bins,' said Yousef, gesturing towards a couple of takeaway coffee cups.

Kat knelt down, noticing that both cups were rimmed

with the same shade of lipstick. One nurse had drunk both cups, and yet there wasn't even a chair to sit on. 'What's through there?' she said, nodding towards another set of double doors.

'Er ... I think there are some single rooms for when people need to be admitted overnight.'

Kat's heart hammered in her chest as she peered through the glass door into the darkness. She could see another reception desk – empty save for another cardboard cup. Why would private patients be admitted to a part of the building that clearly wasn't ready yet? 'This could be it,' she whispered.

'Perhaps you should wait for back-up?' said Lock.

Kat peered through the glass. Lock was right. Anything could be behind this door. If she was wrong, that would mean pulling officers away from the main site where they still might be found. But if Cam was here, then she didn't want to waste another second. 'Yousef, can you open these doors, please?'

He waved his card over the door, which clicked as a little green light came on.

Kat opened the door as quietly as she could and stepped inside, signalling for him to open the next set of doors, and wait for her outside. She didn't want his crackling walkie-talkie or his wheezing alerting anyone to their presence. Neither did she want Lock's clear distinctive voice suddenly breaking the silence, so she detached the transducer from the steel wrist band and placed it against her temple, so that only she would hear it.

The lights flickered and fizzed into life as she peered

down the long narrow corridor, straining for any sounds. There were four doors, two either side, each shut and all completely silent. Kat inched down the corridor, paused outside the first door, then abruptly opened it.

An empty bed. A bedside cabinet. An abandoned drip.

Kat swallowed, feeling the sudden prick of sweat beneath her armpits as she moved on to the second door on her left. Again she opened it; again it was empty, save for a stripped bed, a set of scales and a couple of mismatched chairs.

Shit. She'd been so sure that this was where she'd find Cam. Fear clawed her throat. What if she was too late?

Kat approached the third door. Dear God, please let Cam be here. Please let him be okay. I'll never shout at him again. I promise. Just *please* let him be okay. She opened the door, hardly daring to look.

It took a moment for her to understand what she was seeing:

A boy lying on a bed.

A nurse at his side.

'Cam!' Kat cried.

The nurse turned.

Her brain lagged for a second. What was Moira, Dr Robert McCormick's widow, doing in a nurse's uniform by her son's bedside?

And what *the fuck* was she doing with that syringe?

CHAPTER FIFTY-TWO

'Stay back,' said Moira McCormick. 'Or I'll use this on your son.'

Kat's brain was still trying to process the fact that the woman she'd been talking to just hours before in her conservatory was now here in a nurse's uniform, holding a syringe above the injection port in a cannula that was stuck in the back of her son's hand. She had no idea what was in it, but the hand that held it was shaking. Kat held both palms up to show that she posed no threat.

'Sit down over there,' Moira McCormick said, in her crisp accent. She gestured towards a plastic chair on the other side of the room. 'Wait. Put your walkie-talkie and phone on the bed, where I can see them.'

Kat very slowly placed her mobile and airwaves radio upon the bed, where her son lay, letting her hair fall over her face so that she wouldn't see the small transducer attached to her temple.

Cam's eyes were closed, and his breathing was slow and steady, as if in a very deep sleep. He was wearing a hospital gown, and the cannula in the back of his hand was attached to a drip. Her boy. She wanted to touch him, kiss his cheek, tell him that Mum was here and so everything was going to be okay *(wasn't it?)*. But she didn't dare hold his hand, let alone hug him. She had to make Moira feel that she was in control of this situation, so she didn't do anything rash – like stick a needle into her son.

Kat dragged her eyes away from Cam, draining them of all anger before turning to face his captor. 'I didn't know you were a nurse, Moira,' she said conversationally. *('And I certainly didn't know you were a fucking kidnapper,' she managed not to yell.)*

Moira tossed back her silver-white hair, her voice high and breathless as she said, 'There's a lot you don't know.'

'Why don't you tell me?'

She swallowed. 'Did you go to Gerard's? How was he?'

Kat paused, noting the tight draw of Moira's body as she asked the question. Would it make things better or worse if she told her?

'He's dead, isn't he?'

'Yes, I'm afraid he is.'

Moira's eyes brimmed with tears. 'Poor Gerard. He was a genius.'

Kat bit the inside of her cheek. 'Poor Gerard' was a kidnapper and murderer. But Moira McCormick clearly cared for him deeply. 'Is that why you agreed to help him with his research?'

Moira tensed and moved the syringe closer to Cam's cannula.

'It's okay,' Kat said quickly. 'I know he was only trying to save the lives of future patients.'

Moira nodded. 'Yes, he was. I know some people won't see it this way, but Gerard had extraordinary courage and vision. He was so brave.' Tears spilled down her cheeks, and her grip on the needle loosened. 'After my husband Robert died, everything seemed so pointless. But then Gerard asked me to help him.'

'And how did you help him? Did you drive Cam and the other boys here in the ambulance?'

Moira sniffed. 'I'm a senior nurse. I looked after our patients and recorded all of the data for the trial, because I was the only person Gerard trusted with the data. The ambulance was driven by a junior doctor he was working with.' She glanced at a pile of health records stacked up on the foot of Cam's bed.

Kat followed her gaze. Paper records. Clever. That meant there would be no digital footprints for them to follow. 'Is that why you came here tonight, to destroy the evidence?'

'I'm not going to destroy the data. I'm here to save it. This is Gerard's legacy.'

'And what about my son?' Kat asked as casually as she could. 'What are you planning to do with him?'

Moira paused. Her foundation had dried, and the harsh hospital lighting exposed the lines that fractured her face. 'Moira?'

Moira stared at Cam's hand. 'When you turned up at my house and started asking about Robert, I realised it wouldn't be long before you discovered the connection between Gerard and me. Quite a few people here know that we are – were – lovers. I knew he didn't have long

370

left, so I decided to make the link for you, sending you off to Stratford so that I had enough time to come here. I was going to collect the records, post them to the junior doctor that Gerard trusts and remove anything that might incriminate me. Then I was going to leave your son somewhere safe where he'd be found tomorrow morning. He was sedated when he was admitted, so he didn't see me. It would have been safe to let him go.'

Kat could barely breathe as she said, 'You said that "was" your plan. What's changed?'

'You.' Moira moved the needle closer to the cannula. 'The problem is, you've seen me now.'

Shit. Every cell in her body burned to wrestle this woman and her needle away from her son. But she had to stay calm. More importantly, she had to keep Moira calm. The man she loved had just died. If she thought there was nothing left to lose, she might harm Cam or herself.

'Let's think this through, Moira. The research trial is over now that Professor Robinson is dead, so if you give yourself up and tell us what happened to the other boys, I'm sure the courts will look favourably on you.'

Moira shook her head, making her perfect silver-white bob swing against her elegant jawline. 'And what does that mean? A reduced sentence? A suspended sentence? Can you imagine *me* in a *prison*? At my age?' Her breathing grew thin and rapid, eyes wide and dark at the thought. 'I wouldn't survive a single day.'

Moira was starting to lose it. Where was that bloody security guard? She'd told him to wait outside – he wouldn't be so stupid as to follow her orders indefinitely, would he? She had to hope that he had enough sense to come and check on her.

'I know. I understand,' Kat said, keeping her voice low and calm. 'So, what are you planning to do now then?'

Moira took a deep breath and looked around the small hospital room. 'I'm not handing myself in. I can't go to prison. So, I'm going to have to lock you in here while I take your son over to the main hospital. No one ever asks a nurse pushing a bed where they're taking their patient or why. I'll find somewhere safe and secluded to hide him. Once I've posted the notes and reached my destination, I'll make an anonymous call to let security know where to find you both.'

Kat sighed. 'I'm afraid that's not going to work, Moira. The ANPR road network will track the movements of your car and your mobile phone signal will reveal your whereabouts, as will your bank accounts. It simply isn't possible to disappear these days, so you'd honestly be better off giving yourself up now, rather than being caught running away.'

Moira shook her head. 'I might be old, but I'm not stupid. I've been planning this for quite some time. Gerard was always going to die, so I had to.'

Kat raised an eyebrow.

'Did you really think that Gerard was the one who set up all those false accounts and identities for Companies House? That he would bother himself with all that tedious admin? Men like Gerard have ideas and vision, but they rely on women like me to execute them. Trust me. Once I've left, you won't be able to find me.'

'And what makes you think I'm just going to let you leave with my son?'

'Because if you don't, I'll inject him with this,' she said, pressing the syringe against the cannula.

Kat's heart crashed against her ribs. 'What's in that needle?'

Moira licked her lips. 'Did Gerard explain how we activate the genetic mutations? I know it sounds awful, but it was so that we could test the treatment at the very earliest stages of cancer. We were really making progress, too. In fact, one boy almost made a complete recovery . . .' Her voice trailed off, before she snapped back into focus. 'I don't want to activate your son's genetic mutations, I really don't. But I will if you make me.'

'Why would you do such a thing?' Kat demanded, her voice high and incredulous.

'Because if I don't, you'll take the data, I'll end up in prison and all the risks we took, all the sacrifices Gerard made – will have all been for *nothing*.' She watched Kat clenching her fists on the other side of the room. 'I really wouldn't try anything stupid if I were you, DCS Frank. Yes, you're bigger than me. Probably fitter and stronger too. But by the time you reach me, this needle will be in your son's vein, his genes will be activated, and now that Gerard is dead, there's not a single thing anyone can do to save him.'

CHAPTER FIFTY-THREE

'Well?' said Moira. 'Do we have a deal?'

'Just give me a minute to assess my options,' said Kat, hoping that Lock would take the hint.

It did. Almost instantly, she heard its familiar voice via the transducer. 'Your son is effectively a hostage,' said Lock, the bone-conduction technology making its voice disconcertingly intimate, as if it were inside her very head. 'We are currently in what is known in the literature as a "barricade situation", as this was not pre-planned, and Mrs McCormick is responding to events. Her stress levels are therefore very high, making her decision-making processes extremely volatile and unpredictable, as are yours. Ordinarily, as the negotiator, you would be in a position of strength, but because Cameron is your son, your judgement cannot be relied upon. Taking the emotion out of the equation, if you did decide to tackle her, and assuming you move at the average speed of a forty-five-year-old woman across a distance of twenty feet, and that Moira's reflexes are in line with the average response rates of a sixty-year-old woman, then the needle will be in your son's vein a full second before you even reach her. Your only hope is that she is bluffing but I have insufficient information about her personality or "tells" to confidently assess the probability of this.'

I don't want to know about probabilities, she wanted to scream. I want to know what I should *do!* Kat stared at Cam asleep on the bed, mouth slightly open, oblivious to it all. If she let this woman leave, then tomorrow Cam would be back home with her where he belonged.

And yet.

Her eyes dropped to the files at the bottom of his bed. The truth about what had happened to other people's children lay within those grey cardboard folders. She swallowed. If she let her go, the answers their families longed for would go with her.

'Well?' Moira demanded. 'What's it to be?'

Kat paused, hoping that Lock would take the hint and answer the question.

'I find I cannot advise you what to do,' it said eventually. 'There are too many variables and two conflicting objectives. As the DCS in charge of this case, I would remind you that your stated objective is to provide answers to the families that will be lost forever if you let Moira go. But as a parent, I understand that you will – quite understandably – wish to save your own son's life. I do not have an algorithm to assess these competing objectives, nor enough learning to overcome this gap. I have insufficient information on Moira's past behaviour and her current emotional state is too volatile, so it is impossible to assess the probability of her carrying out her threat with any degree of confidence.'

Great. So, Kat was on her own.

Kat took a deep breath and stared at Moira in a way that she had never stared at anyone else before. She could feel the blood throbbing in her ears, and the room seemed to darken as she focused every atom of her being, every cell of her brain, on the eyes of the woman who held her son's life in her hands. The question wasn't what she *could* do, it was what she *would* do – this particular woman with her particular history, core instincts and learned behaviours; not just the experiences and reason she had absorbed into her mind, but what patterned her heart, what had shaped her very soul – and indeed, what had shaped her own.

She weighed up the woman before her. Put herself in the balance.

Moira blinked.

Kat pounced. Her dodgy knee buckled, making her stumble.

She shot across the room, throwing her body against Moira so that they both crashed against the wall.

Moira threw up her hands.

Her empty hands.

Kat turned, searching for the needle.

She screamed.

The syringe was embedded in her son's cannula.

CHAPTER FIFTY-FOUR

'Cam! Cam!'

Kat ran to her son's side. She pulled the syringe out of the cannula, but it was empty. She sank to her knees, sobbing.

Moira grabbed the case files from the foot of the bed and raced towards the door.

Kat stuck out one leg and made a fierce sweeping movement, felling the nurse at the ankles. Moira cried out as her face smacked the floor. Kat pounced on the older woman, roaring with pain as she pressed her knee into her back, before slipping handcuffs on to her wrists with a satisfying click.

'You're under arrest,' she panted. 'Call the team for back-up.'

'Done,' said Lock.

Kat limped back towards her son on the bed. 'And doctors,' she sobbed, laying just one hand upon his darling head. 'Call all the doctors.'

'They're on their way,' said Lock.

Kat picked up the syringe that rolled on the floor. Ignoring the sharp stab of pain, she squatted down beside

Moira's handcuffed body and thrust the needle in front of her face.

'What was in this?' she demanded.

Moira closed her eyes.

'What was in the fucking syringe?'

'Listen,' said Lock. 'What's that noise?'

Kat held her raging breath and listened. It sounded like shuffling footsteps and something metallic being dragged along the floor. She rose to her feet and reached for her airwaves radio.

An emaciated, bearded boy appeared at the doorway, holding on to a drip with both hands, bent over with the effort of breathing.

'Help,' he managed to croak, before collapsing into Kat's arms.

CHAPTER FIFTY-FIVE

**Will Robinson's home, Stratford-upon-Avon,
6 July, 6.47am**

Kat sat in her car and studied the door she was about to knock. There was no point trying to find the right words because there were none. There was nothing right about what had happened, and there was nothing she could say that would make it any easier. There were no words to soften the loss of a son.

All she could do was tell the truth, and bear witness to the grief that this would unleash.

Kat reached for the door handle.

'Actually, boss,' said DI Hassan, 'I was wondering if it would be best if I told her?'

'You? I mean, thank you, that's very commendable, but I think this requires experience.'

He sucked in his breath. 'With respect, boss, you might have more experience than me, but I don't think you can tell someone they've lost their boy, when you've been fortunate enough to find your own.'

Kat stared at Hassan. He was blunt, but he was right. After the initial panic about Cam, Moira McCormick had admitted that (as she had suspected) the woman who had worked as a nurse for almost forty years had filled the syringe with nothing more than a sedative. Cam would have to spend the night in hospital for observations, but he was going to be okay. Tyrone, who'd heard the noise and managed to escape from his nearby room, had been bed-bound for nearly five months and was suffering from a nasty infection. Although he was going to need a lot of physical and mental care and attention, he too would eventually return home.

But Will Robinson had not been so lucky. Four months after being taken, his immune system became compromised, and he'd developed sepsis from a bedsore. And the beautiful man-boy, who had once played Oliver at school and had dreamed of performing *Hamlet* at the Globe, died alone in a strange bed and in considerable pain. According to a weeping Moira McCormick (who insisted that she'd regularly checked each boy's skin thoroughly and turned them twice a day to avoid bedsores) the cases were anonymised, so his father had never known.

And now it was time to tell his mother.

'What will you tell her?' asked Lock.

Hassan gave a small shrug. 'The truth?'

'Perhaps she does not need to know the whole truth,' said Lock. 'Perhaps you might allow Mrs Robinson to believe that her son died peacefully in his sleep.'

'I thought it was against your algorithms to lie?' said Kat.

'I am programmed to adapt and learn.' Lock stared

out at the driveway where it had once argued with Kat in the rain. 'I am not suggesting that DI Hassan lies, merely that he is selective about the truth he shares, in order to lessen her pain.'

Kat sighed. 'I'm not sure anything will do that. But I agree it's worth a try.'

Hassan nodded. He took one final deep breath and climbed out of the car. The young police officer crunched across the bone-dry gravel, straightened his slim shoulders, and knocked upon Mrs Robinson's door.

CHAPTER FIFTY-SIX

**Leek Wootton Police Headquarters, Warwickshire,
18 July, 1.08pm**

'So sorry I'm late,' said the Home Secretary as she
appeared on the screen. She took her seat at the long, oval
table in her office and checked she was off mute. 'Can you
hear me okay?'

At the other end of the Zoom call, McLeish, DCS
Frank, Professor Okonedo and Lock confirmed that, yes,
they could all hear her.

'Excellent. Well, first of all, can I thank you all for
participating in this pilot, and for writing this excellent
report.' The minister waved it in the air. 'I have lots of
questions, but before I indulge myself, would you mind if
I asked you how your son is, DCS Frank?'

'My son? He's as well as he can be, I guess. He's had lots
of tests and they tell me his genes weren't activated, thank
God. And although he does have a rare genetic mutation,
it only increases his risk very, very slightly, which can be
reduced if he follows a healthy lifestyle and has regular

check-ups. They keep saying that the life choices he makes are more important than his genes. But Cam's eighteen, so he thinks he's immortal.'

'Tell me about it,' said the minister, smiling. 'My daughter's the same age. Was he doing A levels this year?'

'Yes. Results next month.'

'Same. Good luck.'

She looked like she meant it, and for the first time in her life, Kat found herself warming towards a politician.

'And what about Tyrone Walters? How's he doing? To be held captive in hospital for five months. What a terrible ordeal.'

'Physically, he's good,' said Kat. 'The infection he caught is gone and, more importantly, he's cancer-free.'

'Is that because of the experimental treatment he received?'

'They honestly don't know,' said Professor Okonedo. 'Because it was just one case, there's no way of knowing if his recovery is due to the treatment he received or because of some genetic or immune-system response peculiar to him. We would need to repeat the trial in order to prove cause and effect. And of course, there are huge ethical concerns about repeating the studies of someone who illegally experimented upon his victims.'

'Yes,' said the minister. 'It's a tough one. I'm glad that particular conundrum belongs to the Secretary of State for Health to solve.'

'I wouldn't describe it as a conundrum,' said Lock, from where it sat next to Professor Okonedo. 'Professor Robinson's decision to put the needs of the wider population before that of his own son was informed by the principles of utilitarianism rather than sentiment and therefore – unusually for humans – it was a rational decision.'

'Are you saying that you think he was right to kidnap and experiment on people, AIDE Lock?' said the minister, frowning.

Lock spread out its hands, an oddly graceful gesture for a machine, Kat always thought. 'It is not for me to judge whether it is right or not.'

'No, it isn't. Thank goodness.' She paused, before turning back to Kat. 'And have you managed to identify the junior doctor who was receiving Professor Robinson's data?'

She shook her head, annoyed that they had still failed to find his accomplice. It had become clear during the interviews with Moira that the junior doctor had done more than just receive clinical notes and drive the ambulance. He – or she – had assisted with some of the day shifts and clinical tasks, but Moira had point blank refused to reveal their identity and so they had yet to be caught.

'Hmm. Well, I suppose we should just be thankful that your son and Tyrone are okay.'

Kat puffed out her cheeks. 'I'm not sure I'd go that far. Physically, Tyrone's fine, although he still needs a lot of physio to make up for being bed bound and fed by tubes for several months. But mentally ... well, to be honest, Cam's become quite good friends with him since they were both rescued, and he says he's struggling. As well as the trauma of what he went through, Tyrone was taken into the hospital during Will Robinson's last days, and thinks he heard him cry out for help. He's suffering a bit from survivor's guilt, I think. He's dropped out of uni and I'm not sure what his plans are.'

The minister frowned. 'Really?' She flipped through her briefing. 'He was studying politics, wasn't he? He sounds like a bright young man. It'd be a shame if he dropped out and lost his confidence because of this.' She looked at her Private Secretary. 'Let's get him in for a meeting, Jim. Or, even better, some work experience. See if we can reignite his interest in a career in politics. Of course, this place is so bonkers now it'll probably put him off. But it'll get him out of the house, and it'll look good on his CV.'

Her secretary nodded and scribbled a note.

'And Mrs Robinson? Is she getting the support she needs?'

Kat paused. 'Well, she's getting support, but whether it's what she needs . . .'

'What do you mean?'

Kat explained that although the local mental health team were involved, they were more used to dealing with anxiety and depression. How do you even begin to help someone who's lost their son because of the criminal actions of their recently deceased husband? Kat's personal view was that Mrs Robinson was grieving not just for her son, but her whole idea of who and what her husband was.

The minister turned to her Private Secretary. 'Can you get me a call with the President of the Royal College of Psychiatrists? There must be people who specialise in this kind of complex trauma. Someone will know someone who can help. We can't just leave her to get on with it.'

Kat exchanged glances with McLeish. Was she for real? Kat watched the diligent way the Private Secretary wrote down every instruction his boss gave him – even though he had enough silver in his hair to suggest seniority and experience – and concluded that, yes, she probably was.

Only once she was satisfied that everybody was getting the help that they needed, and that Moira McCormick was being charged with identify fraud, aiding and abetting a kidnapping, false imprisonment and manslaughter, as well as being struck off the nursing register and facing prison time, did they turn to the report on the pilot of AIDE Lock. The minister went through it page by page, seeking clarification on various points. She was particularly interested in how Cam, Tyrone and Will had all been sent an appointment in the post, offering money to take part in a research trial. The promise of cash upon presentation of the letter meant there was no digital footprint or risk of anyone else finding it after they went missing. The letter contained a detailed paragraph on ethics, warning them that if they told anyone else they were participating in a trial about their potential future genetic risk, they could inadvertently affect other people's rights *not* to know their own risk status, and therefore to not share this information with *anyone* until they had had a chance to discuss these complex issues with a genetic counsellor at the appointment. Payment would only be made following confirmation that these conditions had been strictly followed.

Tyrone's appointment had been for 8am on the morning he went missing, Cam's at 11am and Will's at 5.30pm. All had entered the ambulance willingly to undergo blood tests, before being sedated and driven off. Moira McCormick had confirmed that the same ruse had been used with the three other missing young people, and that, tragically, all had died and been disposed of in the hospital incinerator. Kat made a point of saying their names: Thomas Radford, Tahira Wasti and Gavin Buchanan. All had lost a parent and, ultimately, their own lives.

The minister closed her file and laced her hands together. 'The conclusion I draw from all of this, is that while artificial intelligence has some extremely useful functions and capabilities to offer the police force, it's more complex than I thought, and it would certainly be premature to roll out assistant AIDEs as part of any cost-cutting exercise.'

Kat nudged McLeish. Result.

'But what stood out for me most from this report was the growing gap between what is technologically possible, what is affordable and what is legally permissible. Several of the searches that Lock carried out on social media sites would have taken hundreds of human hours, and it still takes days and sometimes weeks to get permission to access more personal data such as phone records. I understand the legitimate concerns about privacy, but some of these checks and balances predate the digital age. Whereas criminals are free to use technology, by the time we've been granted access, the crime has often already been committed and the criminal has long fled.'

The minister looked out of the window towards the Houses of Parliament. 'This place is caught up in the past. By the time the old duffers in here detect a problem, it takes two years to draft and pass a bill through the House, by which time the world has moved on.' She turned back to face them. 'It's time to get on the front foot. We need to create a vision of the future of policing, anticipate the needs and obstacles before they occur, so we can develop the legislation you need to enable you to do your job.'

She picked up her briefing. 'This report highlights what's possible, and what we'll need to change if we're to tackle criminality in the twenty-first century. It shows what AI can do, but also where we might still need the unique added value of human beings. But this is just one report. And, as Professor Okonedo said, we need repeatability. We need more data. That's why I want to set up a Future Policing Unit. The FPU will be a human–machine team, working on hand-picked, complex, live cases to identify technological and legislative issues that will need to be addressed if we're to win the war against crime in the twenty-first century.'

'Is there any funding?' said McLeish.

'Yes, the NiAIR – the National institute for AI Research – has agreed to be a co-funder. But because of the tight fiscal environment, I think it should be based outside London, so that we can keep this below the radar. And because of the links you already have with the university, a partnership with the Warwickshire Police Force would be ideal. In fact, I was hoping you'd agree to head it up, DCS Frank.'

'Me?'

'I'm sure Chief Constable McLeish can come up with a set of terms and conditions that will suit your needs. And I hope that Professor Okonedo and Lock will agree to be part of this too.' She turned to the younger woman. 'By the way, I hope you don't mind, but I asked my legal team to take a look at your brother's case. They think there are grounds for a second appeal. Of course, ultimately, it's a matter for the courts, but I'm happy to share with you the advice I received. Jim has the name of some experts you might speak to.'

The Home Secretary smiled, but Kat caught the shark-like look in her eyes. She clearly didn't get where she was today just by being a nice person.

'Thank you, I would appreciate that,' said Professor Okonedo.

'Does that mean you'll join the FPU?'

'I always said I'd never join the police, but if it really is about creating a new and different vision of policing for the twenty-first century involving AI, and as long as I remained an employee of the University, rather than the police force, then I'd definitely be interested as a secondment, perhaps.' She turned and looked at Kat. 'But only if DCS Kat Frank is in charge. At the start of the pilot, I thought she might be a potential problem area. But now I think she might be part of the solution.'

Kat shook her head. 'I was wrong about you too,' she managed to say, without her voice cracking.

'And Lock,' continued the minister. 'What do you think?'

Lock made a pyramid of its hands, placing its chin against them in a gesture of thoughtfulness. 'What do I think? I think that human beings are infuriatingly slow, and their decisions are largely irrational and subject to emotional bias. I was initially concerned about DCS Frank's preference for her "gut" over any real evidence. But I have since learned that what she refers to as a "hunch" is often a rapid judgement based upon years of experience and thought processes too fast for most humans to comprehend.'

Kat snorted. 'That's the worst post-hoc rationalisation I've ever heard.'

'Pardon?' said Lock, turning to face her.

Kat leaned closer, so they were just inches apart. 'When I wanted your advice on whether to tackle Moira, you couldn't give it because you had "insufficient data" to make an evidence-based decision. *I* could, because I looked that woman in the eye, and my gut told me that a woman who has spent forty years saving lives would not be able to deliberately kill one of her patients. You can try and dress it up if you like, but I made a decision in the blink of an eye that turned out to be right and you can't explain why.'

'Yes, I can. You made a perfectly rational decision based upon your experience and knowledge of female public-sector workers, but your thought processes were too fast for you to be aware of, hence you cling to the belief that it came from your "gut".'

Kat folded her arms. 'Call it what you like. It was a hunch.'

'It was not.'

'Perhaps we need more data before we jump to con-clusions,' said the minister, holding up both hands like a referee. 'Which is why I want to continue the pilot. It will be fascinating to see whether Lock can learn to make more nuanced judgements just as humans do.'

Lock raised its eyebrows. 'That comment betrays an implicit assumption that to be human is the apex of the developmental hierarchy, and a state to which AI should aspire to. I find this troubling, particularly as the key human trait I have learned from this pilot – despite my anti-corruption software – is the ability to lie.'

'Well, I'm not sure I would agree with you that lying is a key human trait, but I'm glad that you feel you have learned to be more human.'

'What makes you assume that it is *I* who need to learn more from humans, rather than the other way around?'

The minister leaned back in her chair. 'My hope is that machines and humans will continue to learn from each other, AIDE Lock. What do you say, DCS Frank? Are you up for it?'

Kat hesitated. She had started this pilot determined to expose the limitations of the technology that had led to the death of her husband, but Lock had helped save her son's life. Lock was the only one who'd believed her about the cancer connection, following the evidence, when her own team and boss had followed their own assumptions and prejudices. But still. Could she really work with a machine?

'It's been interesting working with Lock,' she said eventu-ally. 'But he . . .' She caught herself. Honestly, it was a simple slip of the tongue, there was no need for Lock to smile at her like that. '*It*,' she emphasised, 'still has a lot to learn.'

'As do you,' Lock told her.

'As do we all,' insisted the minister. 'Chief Constable McLeish, I'll need a definitive decision and a realistic budget by close of play tomorrow.'

A sound like saucepans being bashed together filled the room. She wrinkled her face. 'That's the division bell. I need to go.' She rose to her feet. 'Oh, and DCS Frank? Make sure you have a token male on the team. For the optics, you know.'

And with a wink, she was gone.

Professor Okonedo discreetly left the room with Lock, leaving Kat and McLeish alone.

'What do you reckon?' said Kat.

'I think you should do it.'

'Seriously? I thought the whole idea of me leading this pilot was to kill the idea of AI detectives?'

'You have. You've proven that machines can help support police work, but they can never replace a bloody good detective. And anyway,' he said, rising to his feet. 'That wasn't the point of this pilot.'

'Wasn't it?'

'No.' He rested a hand briefly upon her shoulder. 'The point of this pilot was to make you realise that you need to move forwards, Kat.'

She swallowed. 'You do know you're a manipulative bastard, sir?'

'I like to think so.' McLeish gave her a rare smile, picked up his hat and left her to her thoughts.

CHAPTER FIFTY-SEVEN

The Cape of Good Hope public house, Warwick, 22 July, 5.17pm

The beer garden was full, but Kat managed to find a table for her team, which had grown considerably since word got around that DCS Frank was buying the drinks. While the officers leaned against the sun-drenched wall, Kat took a seat with Browne and sent Hassan off to the bar so they could talk in private.

'How are things?' she asked, taking her jacket off. 'Everything okay?'

'Yes. No. You know.'

Kat smiled as she turned her face to the sun. 'Couldn't have put it better myself.'

'I've decided to keep it.'

'And you're happy with that?'

She nodded. 'But Stuart isn't. My boyfriend. Well, ex-boyfriend, now.'

'Oh, I'm sorry.'

'Don't be. You were right. I didn't tell him partly

because I knew he wouldn't want it, but also, I realised it wasn't the baby I wasn't sure about – it was him. I didn't want him to be my partner for the rest of my life. So that's that.' She looked around the beer garden, watching a girl and boy of four or five play hide and seek among the tables and bushes. 'I've honestly no idea how I'm going to cope as a single parent, and the thought of all the chaos and mess brings me out in a rash. But for some reason, I feel ridiculously happy.'

There was so much Kat could have said. So many words of warning or inspirational advice about the joys and challenges of parenting. But this young woman was only three months' pregnant, so after Browne had shown her all the baby and parenting books she'd already downloaded to her Kindle, Kat said the only thing she needed to hear. 'You'll be brilliant.'

'I'll be broke.'

'Not necessarily.' Kat briefed her on the FPU. 'There's a lot of detail to be sorted yet, but I'd love you to be part of my team.'

'Really? But I'll be on maternity leave in five months' time.'

'So? You're a clever and dedicated DS, with lots of potential. This would be an ideal job for you now and a great one to return to. I don't just want the Future Police Unit to be about how we can use technology to catch criminals. I want to explore how we can use technology to support flexible working for police officers with families, and you can help me do that. If you're interested.'

'I don't know what to say. Thanks so much, DCS

Frank, I really appreciate this opportunity. I've learned so much from you already.'

Kat waved away the compliment. At some point she'd talk to Browne about not being so bloody grateful all the time. If she didn't value her own skills and experience, then how could she expect others to? But not tonight. There'd be plenty of time to develop her confidence over the next few months, and the best way to do that was on the job.

'Look who I found at the bar,' said Hassan as he appeared with a tray of drinks, followed by Professor Okonedo. He handed Kat a cold glass of white wine, a soda water and lime for Browne, a pint of cider for himself and what looked like a vodka martini for Professor Okonedo.

Kat raised a toast to the team – even though she didn't recognise half of the hangers-on. It didn't matter. Being a copper meant you spent most of the days at the arse-end of the world. Days like this – when you got to celebrate a success in the sunshine with friends and colleagues – were few and far between. She took a gulp from her thankfully large glass and sighed.

Hassan sat opposite her. He took a sip of his pint, then cleared his throat. 'Boss, I just wanted to say again how sorry I am. I was too quick to dismiss your theory. You were right, I was wrong.'

'That's okay,' she shrugged. She had Cam back, and a new job, so she was feeling magnanimous.

'No, it's not. I honestly thought you were letting your emotions cloud your judgement, which was—'

'Patronising? Misogynistic?'

'Well, I wouldn't go that far. But I'm going to try to be less of a cocky shit in the future.'

'A noble aim.' Kat took another sip of her wine, studying the man before her. 'You weren't a total shit, by the way,' she said eventually. 'You were right to challenge me, and not everyone has the courage to do that, so make sure you don't lose *all* of your cockiness. Everyone makes mistakes. It's how we learn. But a good copper never makes the same mistake twice.'

'Fair enough,' said Hassan, saluting her with his pint.

'So, what's next for DI Hassan?' she asked. 'I assume you're keeping an eye out for promotions in the West Mids or the Met. Let me know if you need a reference, I'd be happy to provide one.'

He shook his head. 'Thanks, but I need to stay local for family reasons.'

'Kids?'

Was it her imagination, or did Professor Okonedo lean in closer?

'Sister.' He picked up a beer mat. 'She's got quite severe mental health issues, and my parents struggle with it a bit. I get on really well with her though, so I moved in with them last year so I can help out.'

'I'm sorry. That sounds really tough.'

He shrugged. 'It's okay. They're my family. I love them.' Hassan took another sip of his pint and smiled.

Kat's heart caught. Had she totally misjudged him? Or was she letting this little insight into his personal life blot out just how irritating he could be? She drained the last of her wine, recalling what McLeish used to tell her: 'When you're a boss, everyone will agree with you, so make sure you've always got someone who challenges your thinking on your team.'

She put down her glass and went with her gut. 'DI Hassan,' she said. 'How would you like to join a new team I'm setting up?'

Maybe Professor Okonedo's drink went down the wrong way, as she had a little coughing fit while Kat told Hassan all about the FPU. When she asked, he didn't hesitate for a second before saying he would love to be part of her team.

'We should celebrate,' he said, looking at Professor Okonedo. 'Anyone up for a meal after this?'

Professor Okonedo was a picture of calm elegance among the empty glasses and crisp packets that surrounded them. 'Is that invitation aimed at everyone or just me?'

Hassan grinned. 'If you say yes, then it absolutely was aimed at you. If you say no, then of course it was a general invitation to all.'

Professor Okonedo drained her cocktail glass and put it carefully down on the table. 'Either way, it's a no.' She pulled her bag over her shoulder and rose to her feet.

Hassan stood up, and their proximity only emphasised the difference in height between them. 'Another time then.'

'Another life, maybe,' she said. 'I think you should know that I'll never, ever, date a policeman.'

He remained standing as he watched her diminutive figure leave the beer garden.

'Ouch,' said Kat.

But Hassan smiled as he sat back down and raised his pint to some imaginary future. 'Never say never.'

CHAPTER FIFTY-EIGHT

DCS Kat Frank's home, Coleshill, 18 August, 8.30am

Kat had promised Cam she'd wake him at 8am so he could check the UCAS website for his exam results. But even though she'd been up for hours, she left it till half past. What if he didn't get the grades he needed? After everything he'd been through, she couldn't bear to see him disappointed.

She knocked on the door, gently. 'Cam?'

He grunted.

She opened the door and stepped inside, willing herself to ignore the mess.

Cam was just a lump buried beneath his quilt.

'You asked me to wake you up early today. Exam results. Remember?'

For a moment, he didn't move. Then he shot up with a speed that made her yelp. 'I've already checked. I got three As, Mum. Three As!'

'Seriously? Oh, Cam, well done. Well bloody done.' Kat hugged her son – her clever, brilliant son. Cam laughed and managed to stay composed until she squeezed him tight and whispered, 'Your dad would have been so proud of you.'

And then they were both a mess.

Kat had booked the day off work so she could take Cam for a celebratory lunch at the Coleshill Hotel. But every time she thought they were ready to leave, Cam would stop to check his phone, giving her a running commentary on his friends' grades as they came in and what it meant for their plans.

'You do know you don't have to go to uni this year,' Kat said carefully as she grabbed her keys from the hall. 'After everything you've been through, I'm sure they'd agree to a deferral if you wanted to take a bit of time out.'

'I know,' said Cam, picking up his badly knotted trainers. 'To be honest, before the kidnapping, I was thinking about it.' He paused as he struggled to squash his foot into his trainer, eroding whatever time he thought he'd saved by not undoing his shoelaces first.

'And now?'

'Now I think I owe it to Will and the others who weren't as lucky as me to get on with my life.'

'Oh, Cam,' said Kat, placing her hands against her son's upper arms. They felt warm and strong, just ripening with muscle. 'You don't owe anyone anything. Please don't feel guilty because you survived.'

'I don't. But it's a reminder not to take anything for granted. Anything could happen at any time. Not just because of the kidnapping. Look what happened to Dad.

So, I'm not going to take a year out, because there's no guarantee I'll get another one.'

Kat studied her son's face, saddened by the adult-like realism in his eyes. She wished she could tell him he was wrong: that she could promise him a life of immortal happiness in a world where she would always be able to make everything better. But she couldn't. And the worst thing was, he wouldn't believe her anyway.

His phone pinged again, drawing his eyes away from hers. He sighed.

'Everything okay?'

'Yeah. Everyone's meeting at 'Spoons in Birmingham to celebrate.'

'Ah,' Kat said. She watched the half-smile playing around his lips as more messages pinged in, thumbs flying as he quickly replied. 'Look, if you'd rather go and meet your mates, that's fine. We can have lunch in Coleshill another day.'

His eyes widened. 'Are you sure?'

Of course, she told him, pleased that she managed to sound so convincing. Her eighteen-year-old son wanted to be with his eighteen-year-old friends. What could be more normal than that? After making sure that she really, really didn't mind, and promising that, yes, his phone was fully charged and *of course* he'd keep in touch, he gave her a brief, tight hug before climbing into the Uber that she insisted on booking for him – at least that way she'd know when he arrived safely.

Kat smiled fiercely as she waved her son off. Once the car was out of sight, she pulled out her phone, thinking she might meet someone else for lunch, but the list of contacts blurred before her eyes. There was only one person who would understand what this day really meant: only one person who had spent endless hours helping Cam with his homework and supporting him through the anxiety of exams; only one person who would understand how completely ridiculous it was that their son – who not so long ago they were dropping off at nursery – was now about to leave for university.

Boy done good, John would have said.

Kat opened the door and started walking towards Cole End Bridge, imagining her husband was by her side. 'He did brilliantly. Thanks to you.'

And you. That crime literature paper was a bugger.

Kat nodded, remembering how they'd debated the merits of Kate Atkinson versus Agatha Christie, the different meanings of Browning, Crabbe and Wilde.

'He did it, though,' said Kat. 'And now he'll be off.'

John hummed his agreement. *As he should be. Remember when we were that age?*

How could she forget? The exhilarating train out of Birmingham, the crazy confusion of Freshers' Week, the jolt and click of meeting John; those heady, floaty days of first love.

They paused on the footbridge that runs parallel to the medieval stone bridge and looked out towards Cole End Nature Reserve, thick with blossom and framed by weeping willows. *You do know that you have to let him go?* said John.

Kat nodded, but her eyes brimmed with tears. 'I know.

It's just that I tried so hard to find him, and now I'm going to lose him again.'

Oh, Kat, he said. *If you love someone, then they're never truly lost.*

Kat turned to him.

But he was gone.

'Are you okay, DCS Frank?' said Lock, its voice softer than usual.

'I'm fine,' she said, switching Lock to visual. Even though it wasn't real, it was strangely comforting when Lock's image appeared beside her.

'You don't look fine,' said Lock, studying her with its dark, unflinching eyes. 'Would you like me to create a virtual image of your husband so that you can talk to him properly?'

Kat hesitated.

'It might help.'

'No, it wouldn't.'

'Why not?'

'Because I have to learn to live without him.' She stared down at the sunlit river, gripping the rough stone bridge with her hands.

'I am sorry for your loss.'

Kat sighed. Lock was just repeating the stock phrase for feelings it could never understand. But then she thought, isn't that exactly what all her married friends did? Were the words of a machine really that different from the countless texts, emojis and cards that said 'sending hugs', and 'thinking of you'? Lock at least was here by her side.

'I doubt you'll ever understand,' she said eventually. 'But thank you for trying.'

Kat leaned against the bridge and watched a dad with two boys play Pooh Sticks at the other end. The two toddlers kept squealing and demanding that their daddy find them more sticks. 'Again! Again!' The poor man looked harassed, but oh, how she envied the clutch of arms about his neck: the tiny, trusting fingers in his.

'Do you remember when you asked me why Rick made Ilsa leave him at the end of *Casablanca*, even though he loved her?'

Lock nodded, mirroring her movements as it placed the image of its hands upon the ancient bridge. 'I have watched *Casablanca* twenty-three times now, and I still find the ending incomprehensible.'

'Well, it was *because* he loved her. It was an act of love to let her go.'

Lock turned to face her. 'I take it your son is Ilsa, in this analogy?'

'Yes, I guess he is. Which probably makes me Bogart.'

Lock raised a single eyebrow. 'And I am Captain Louis Renault?' It paused. 'In which case, perhaps this will be the beginning of a beautiful friendship.'

Kat snorted. 'Did you just tell a *joke*, Lock?'

Lock blinked. 'Well, you laughed, so yes, I do believe I did.'

'I thought you didn't possess the algorithm for comedy?'

'I don't. But it appears that I am learning.'

'So, it appears, am I,' she said softly.

And, with Lock at her side, Kat turned and crossed the bridge towards the steep hill of the high street, leaving her solitary shadow behind.

Acknowledgements

I wrote the first draft of this book in 2019, just two months after Steve, my partner of twenty-eight years, died from lung cancer. After two-and-a-half years of caring for him, the nights were unbearably empty, and so I filled them with words. I wanted to write about loss: about the missing and the missed; about those left behind. I've spent more years than I care to count on writing unpublished novels, but I somehow managed to complete that first, desperate draft in just three months before sharing it with my agent, and three trusted friends and readers.

So, my first, heartfelt thanks must go to my amazing agent, Susan Armstrong, who not only stuck by me through those earlier attempts but has been a constant source of kindness and support. She saw the potential in the first draft, and her comments and insight made the book a hundred times better than it otherwise would have been. The fact that you are reading it today is due to her passionate commitment to getting books that she loves published and I am honoured to be one of her authors. I am also incredibly grateful to Meredith Ford and Katie

Greenstreet who were both early champions of Kat and Lock, giving me the confidence to carry on drafting, and to Kate Burton, Matilda Ayris, and Luke Speed from the wider rights team at C&W, whose emails and calls were an unexpected delight, and the fruit of their tireless and often unseen efforts to share our stories with the world.

I owe a special thanks to Debra Brown who read a very early draft and allowed me to borrow a version of her name for DS Browne. But most of all because she has been an untiring source of kindness and support and is an all-round lovely person. I am so lucky to have two excellent critique partners and friends in Lindsay Galvin and Lex Coulton, both of whom are better writers than I and had brilliant ideas for how to improve the story I was trying to tell. Despite their own work and personal commitments, they read and commented on several drafts, sending countless messages of support, encouragement and gifts during the years of doubt and those crazy weeks of (at last!) good news.

A huge thanks is owed to my editor, Katherine Armstrong from Simon & Schuster, who immediately clicked with Lock and Kat and knew exactly how to bring this story to life. Katherine's calm, incisive and clear edits took the manuscript to another level, and the unwavering support, enthusiasm, and attention to detail that both she and Mina Asaam have given during the publishing process have been a blessing. I am particularly grateful to Hamza Jahanzeb, who kindly acted as a sensitivity reader, offering his comments and thoughts in a way that always left the decisions with me, but widened my experience and understanding of different communities and issues. A special thanks also to Ian Allen whose copy edits, challenging questions and droll comments sometimes made me laugh, but always, always, improved the book. And I am so grateful for the enthusiasm, hard work and creative attention to detail that everyone at S&S has given ITBOAE, especially Matt for the amazing cover, Rich on Marketing, Jess on publicity, Francesca and Gail in pre-press and production, and Cassie Rigg for proofreading.

Although *In The Blink Of An Eye* is fiction, I was keen to make sure that the science and technology described in the book might at least be *possible* in the near future, if not probable. With the exception of Lock's real-time conversational abilities, many aspects of AI described in the book either exist now or are on the horizon. Time will tell whether I got the balance right, but I am immensely grateful for the personal time and expert advice provided by the Chief Scientific Officer for NHS England, Professor Dame Sue Hill on genomics, and on AI, Professor Giovanni Montana, a Chair in Data Science and a Turing AI Fellow at Warwick University. The National institute for AI Research (NiAIR) is fictional, but partly inspired by the Alan Turing Institute, as well as the leading-edge, collaborative research carried out at Warwick University. I am also grateful to Rebecca Bradley, a former detective and brilliant crime writer who was kind enough to review the police procedural elements of this novel. As ever, all the mistakes are mine, but I hope I have helped highlight some issues which would benefit from a wider public debate, before the full possibilities of artificial intelligence are realised.

Twitter tends to get a bad press, but I honestly couldn't have written this book without my twitter family. The writing community has been a constant source of joy and humour to me, and during the darkest times, I found support from fellow travellers in grief, and the unimaginable kindness of strangers. Special thanks to Lucy Lapinski, a talented author who befriended me in the early days: it has been a joy to watch your career soar, and to have the privilege of learning from you. A huge thanks and shout out to all of the Ladykillers, a brilliant bunch of women writers who make me laugh every day and are so generous with their honest advice and support. Thank you for welcoming me into your fold, and I wish you lived next door. (Although, to be honest, I think you'd lead me astray.)

A special thanks to the friends who do live within touching distance and have held me and my family up in recent years, especially Lu, Su, Fi, Fiona, Nicci and Leigh, and Meena and all the staff at Suyo, where they have cared for so much more than our hair. Rob K, Rob C and David all live a bit further away but continue to look after me with sweets and flowers – thank you for your ongoing kindness, but most of all thank you for making me laugh whenever you visit and drag me out for tea or wine.

Thanks to my family: to my dad who gave me my love of books (sorry not sorry about the swearing, dad!) and to my mum, who I hope would have enjoyed reading this if she were still alive. To my brothers, Phil and Ed who continue to be a source of support and laughter (I am throwing the book bouquet at you now – *catch!*) and to Amanda, owner of the coveted golden toothbrush. A very special thanks to my amazing children, Conor and Aurora, who have both coped with so much – no one should have to lose their dad so young, but he would have been so very, very proud of you both – as am I. Your genuine support and excitement for me and this book has been so precious, and I love you both to bits.

But my final thanks must go to Steve: my lifelong partner, my biggest champion and heartfelt loss. Every writer thanks their partner for their 'support', but honestly, Steve was the kindest, humblest man I have ever had the privilege of knowing. He bought me my first laptop for my 40th birthday so that I could start writing, and although it took me a lot longer than either of us expected to get published, he never ever gave up hope that it would happen one day.

I am just so very, very sorry that he isn't here to smile at me and say, '*I told you so.*'

April 2022